RAVEN FALLS

A CANNON FALLS MYSTERY

JILL SANDERS

GRAYTON

Printed in the United States of America

DIGITAL ISBN: 978-1-945100-24-6

PRINT ISBN: 9798672036182

PRINT ISBN V2: 9798731795067

Print ISBN: 9781666262544

Copyeditor: Erica Ellis – inkdeepediting.com

SUMMARY

Ten years ago, everything was taken away from Raven. When the fire swept through her small hometown, it killed everyone that she cared about. Not only did she lose her mother and father, but she also lost the one chance she had at true love. Coming home meant dealing with her demons, and the worst one was the sexy fire marshal who was hell-bent on getting answers about that night long ago. Answers that only she can give.

Cade was one of the few to stick around Cannon Falls after ninety percent of the town went up in smoke. The fire hadn't just taken most of the buildings in town. Over thirty of the one thousand residents had perished as well, including his younger brother, Reggie. Cade didn't know why his brother's school sweetheart was back in town, but he knew one thing for sure. He was having a hell of a time separating his desires from his determination to finally get some answers.

Some say the world will end in fire,
Some say in ice.
From what I've tasted of desire
I hold with those who favor fire.
But if it had to perish twice,
I think I know enough of hate.
To say that for destruction ice
Is also great.
And would suffice.
– BY ROBERT FROST

PROLOGUE

Raven ran as fast as she could. When she turned and looked back, the flames were right on her heels, as if they were following her. She opened her mouth to scream but choked on the smoke that had surrounded her. She scanned the darkness for any way out and intuitively knew that there wasn't a safe place anywhere around. All she could see was smoke and fire. She was surrounded. This was it. There was no hope.

She lost track of everything as she turned in circles. She didn't even know which way was which anymore. Her mind screamed at her to run. Every instinct in her body yelled at her to get away. But where? There was no safety, no shelter from what was about to happen.

Her throat stung, and her lungs burned. Her eyes were so filled with smoke that they watered, blurring her vision even further as tears rolled down her face.

There was no way she was going to survive this. No way anyone could survive this inferno.

She sunk down into the dry dirt, curled into a tight ball,

and waited for death to come. Welcomed it, since the weight of what she'd done was too great to bear.

CHAPTER ONE

Raven Brooks had been born on a Tuesday, just any other ordinary day in a busy world. But the date of that incredibly special day would come to be an incredible burden to not only the girl but everyone around her.

Seventeen years later, on that same day, she'd lost everything, including the first boy she'd fallen in love with, her childhood home, all her favorite possessions, and most importantly, her parents.

She'd been broken on that fateful early-summer day, broken beyond repair. Her only saving grace had been a distant grandmother, who had welcomed her in with open arms, helped her get counseling, and sheltered her from all those vengeful souls that surrounded her like flames. People who laid the blame on her for all the destruction and the loss of their own loved ones.

Her father, Patrick Ryan Brooks, and his brother, Colin Finn Brooks, had been best friends for as long as Raven could remember. She'd grown up under the watchful yet scrutinizing eyes of her uncle Colin, his wife, her aunt Roslyn, and her father's business manager, Liam Montford.

She knew every single one of the people who had helped keep Cannon Falls Ski Resort a successful venture, keeping Raven in designer clothes and a massive five-thousand-square-foot mansion for her entire young life.

The business had provided income for her family and her uncle's as well. Colin had married Roslyn, who was reportedly from one of California's wealthiest families, and they'd had two children. Their oldest was their son Cal. Their daughter Liza was just a few weeks older than Raven.

The only difference between the brothers was that her father owned the resort, while her uncle had only worked there. Raven's father had, at the tender age of twenty-three, purchased the property from an old couple, using his inheritance from their father as the investment.

Patrick, along with his new bride, twenty-one-year-old Rosemary, had spent the next ten years and every cent of their money building and molding the massive venture. Cannon Falls Ski Resort was tucked in the high hills near Mt. Shasta in Northern California. The closest town, Cannon Falls, had, at its peak, more than one thousand permanent residents.

Raven's parents had given up everything in order to turn the business into a highly successful ski resort.

Raven had spent most of her childhood days basking in what she would now describe as extreme wealth. She'd been immensely naive, decidedly spoiled, and exceedingly selfish.

All that had changed on her seventeenth birthday.

So, where had things gone wrong?

Reggie Stone.

Reggie had ruined everything.

Okay, so maybe her naivety and a broken heart had had something to do with it as well.

Still, if Raven hadn't fallen for the boy, one of the most popular in his senior class, she never would have lost so much. The town of Cannon Falls would have been spared its fiery fate.

She'd read once that death by fire was one of the most painful ways to go. But since the author of the statement had still been alive, she'd doubted its validity.

Still, all her nightmares for the past ten years, and the thousands of hours spent in counseling, confirmed her fears. The thirty people she'd killed haunted her every moment.

Why then was she now standing in the parking lot of Cannon Falls Ski Resort? After having just celebrated her twenty-seventh birthday, alone, something had called to her to return.

Looking up at the massive wood-shingled buildings gave her chills. Nothing had changed. Not really.

The three five-story buildings sat in a U shape. The courtyard, in the winter, had housed a massive skating rink when her father had run the resort. Now, there was early summer grass that needed a trim and some fertilizer.

Actually, the more she looked, the more work she could see the place needed. The bushes and flowers that had once been neatly trimmed and maintained now grew completely out of control and stuck up in odd shapes taller than a person.

Even the dark green shutters that sat on either side of the large windows needed a fresh coat of paint. The parking lot had massive potholes that she'd had to avoid when finding a parking spot.

Her eyes scanned up to the main building, tucked behind the other two. This was the building that filled most of her memories. There, she'd spent countless hours doing homework in her father's office on the main floor, tucked behind the reception desk. Or sitting in the massive dining room, eating meals alone, since her parents were too busy working. She'd spent countless hours alone during her childhood.

She'd had a few close friends over the years, particularly Carrie Edwards and Darby Nabers, in addition to her cousin Liza, who had been there for Raven all her life until they'd hit junior high. Then even Liza had abandoned her for a more popular crowd.

That had changed again when she'd caught the eye of Reggie Stone the month before her sixteenth birthday.

To be honest, she hadn't really liked Reggie at first. He'd been rude to her most of their childhood. Then, when he'd become the star of football, basketball, and baseball in junior high, he'd quickly grown to most-popular-boy stardom, and she hadn't been able to stop dreaming about him.

But as the only naturally ginger-haired kid in her class—Liza and Cal had inherited their mother's blond locks—she'd been the most-teased girl in school.

It was true that most people in her classes were friendly with her. After all, she was easily the wealthiest girl in school. But not a single one of them had taken the time to be actual friends with her.

And oh, how they had all turned on her, even her own remaining family members. Yet another reason she'd spent so much time in therapy.

She'd been standing next to her used Lexus in the parking lot, staring up at the buildings for a while now and surmised that she was drawing attention. She walked over to the trunk of her car, pulled out her overnight bags, and carted them through the courtyard, noticing the cracked sidewalks and overgrown grass and weeds as she went.

The moment that she stepped inside, memories hit her like a brick over the head, almost causing her to double over.

"Breathe," she heard in her head, the voice of Becca Morgan, LPC. "In for three, out for three."

Raven did what she'd done for the past ten years and took several deep breaths until the panic attack subsided.

When she felt under control again, she glanced towards the indoor fountain and, for a split second, an image flashed in her memory of a young woman with long auburn hair pulled back into a long braid sitting peacefully on the stone edge of the water. Her long flowing floral dress pooled around her crossed ankles. She was a vision of patience and love.

Raven broke free of the memory, blinked, and turned towards the front desk. She couldn't afford a walk down memory lane. Not yet. She had to secure her position before allowing herself to lose it.

"May I help you?" a young woman with a very thick Middle-Eastern accent asked her with a friendly smile.

"Yes." Raven straightened her shoulders and tried for a friendly smile. "I'd like to see Colin Brooks."

The woman instantly looked worried and a little somber.

"I'm sorry, Mr. Brooks isn't available at the moment." She glanced down at Raven's bags. "Are you wanting to check in?" she asked.

"I'm Raven Brooks," she said plainly.

The woman continued to look at her, waiting for the punch line, Raven imagined.

"Mr. Brooks is my uncle," she clarified. "I'm the owner of..." She motioned around the lobby of the resort with her hand.

The woman shook her head and blinked a few times.

"I... I'm sorry." She shrugged slightly, and Raven began to wonder what the cause of their miscommunication was.

"I'd like to speak with my uncle about a place to stay," she added.

"Was he expecting you?" the woman asked, clicking on the computer in front of her.

"No." She bit her tongue to stop herself from giving this stranger any further explanation.

"If you'll have a seat"—she motioned to the leather sofas in the middle of the waiting area— "I'll see if he's available."

"Thank you," she said, dragging her luggage, three bags that held every stitch of clothing she owned, along with her other worldly possessions.

When she sat down, she held in a little squeal as she sank deep into the old furniture. Her gaze ran over the worn sofa and outdated coffee table.

Her eyes stung at the state of everything. What had happened to the once-glamorous resort? If her father were alive, she imagined that there wouldn't be so much as a scratch on any of the furniture. Yet here she sat in a worn-out sofa, in the outdated resort, which was quickly and quietly dying and taking her and the rest of her family down with it.

Her eyes scanned over every detail of the lobby. She itched to explore other areas of the massive resort but knew that she'd have time to evaluate every detail in the coming days. After she'd had time to recover from the long drive.

Just here in the lobby, she mentally noted the dated wallpaper, the unpolished floors, the drapes that should have been thrown out ten years ago. As she continued to wait, she realized that the old broken furniture was probably the best part of the waiting area.

Her temper grew the longer she waited. What had her

uncle been doing with all the money coming into the resort? Some of it had been coming to her, she knew. Each month she'd received a deposit into her account, as per the arrangement between her and her uncle's lawyer. The funds had helped pay for her schooling as well as the hours and hours of counseling she'd needed over the years.

It was a little over half an hour before her aunt Roslyn walked towards her. Her aunt's low heels were the only sound she'd heard in all that time waiting, with the exception of the running water of the fountain.

Not once had the phone rang or any other customers or guests come into the facility. As each minute had ticked by, her heart had died a little more and her nerves had grown worse.

The moment she spotted Roslyn, she pasted on a smile and stood up. She stopped herself from rushing across and hugging the woman. The memory of the last time she'd seen her aunt played over in her mind, causing her spine to straighten and her smile to strain.

She was seventeen, standing alone over her parents' fresh graves, when Roslyn stopped next to her. She hoped for a few words of encouragement. What she got was far from it.

"You know, they're in there because of you," Roslyn said as she stood rail straight next to her.

Raven glanced through tear-filled eyes at her aunt. Over the years, Roslyn had always been distant—kind, but distant.

"I didn't do this," she said softly.

Roslyn leaned closer to her and lowered her voice. "Didn't you?" Her eyes narrowed slightly, then she straightened suddenly. "I don't want you anywhere near my children. It's very obvious you're a bad influence. I've talked to Colin's mother. She's willing to take you in."

"Take me in?"

"She'll be here in a few hours." Roslyn started to turn away. *"For the time being, your uncle and I will run the resort per your parents' wishes."* She walked away without another word.

"Aunt Roslyn." She nodded briskly.

"So, you've returned?" Her aunt's once-beautiful blonde hair had been cut shorter and had streaks of grey and dark brown in it, giving it an unwashed and messy look.

There were far more wrinkles and age lines than there had been and at least twenty extra pounds on the woman's normally fit frame.

Roslyn Brooks assessed Raven with dark, unemotional eyes.

"I suppose you want a place to stay?" she asked as she motioned to Raven's luggage, sounding as if Raven were asking for a handout. Raven nodded quickly and raised her eyebrows slightly, a move that she knew her aunt would take as a play for power. After all, this was her place. Willed solely to her by her mother and father. Her uncle and aunt had only been running the business while she'd been away.

Her aunt turned quickly and walked back over to the receptionist. Raven followed, leaving her luggage where it was.

"My niece will need a room," Roslyn started.

"A suite," Raven corrected quickly. "One in the west building." She remembered that it was the last building her father had added during his ownership of the resort and so the newest. "Top floor," she added at the last minute.

Roslyn sighed and looked even more annoyed, but she nodded to the woman. Then she turned back to Raven. "How long can we expect your visit to last?"

Raven smiled. "Oh, I'm not here on a visit," she said smoothly. "I'm back. I intend to take my place and run the resort." She leaned slightly on the countertop, making sure that her voice was raised just enough that the receptionist would hear.

When the woman's fingers stopped working on the keyboard, Raven knew that the employee had gotten the message, loud and clear.

Her aunt's eyes narrowed as her lips thinned. "Indeed?" she said between clenched teeth. "Does Colin know your plans?"

"No." She sighed and acted bored. "I had hoped to surprise him with the news. It's too bad he's out." She shrugged slightly. "You will have to let me know the moment he's back"—she glanced around and frowned— "at work. Until then, I'll take a day to get settled, some time to get caught up on where things stand before..."

"Before?" Her aunt watched her closely.

Raven smiled. "I'm sure we can work something out," she said with a shrug and turned away from her aunt to take the key card that the receptionist was handing to her.

"I've put you in the west executive suites," the woman said with a friendlier smile.

"Thank you..." She glanced towards the woman and noted that there was no name badge, no set uniform, or anything that could count as a dress code. Actually, the woman's attire was seriously lacking, messy, and just plain... unattractive. As the first impression of the resort, it was in dire need of correcting.

"Christina," the girl answered.

Raven frowned. "Is that really your name?"

The woman glanced over at Roslyn and then back at Raven before shaking her head slightly.

"What is your name, your real name?" Raven asked.

"Cemal," she answered in a low tone.

Raven smiled. "A much more beautiful name." She nodded. "Thank you, Cemal. Is there someone who can help me take my things up?"

"Yes, I'll ring for Tommy, umm, Tom, to help you with your things." The woman's smile turned more sincere as she turned to pick up the phone and call for help.

When she turned back to her aunt, Raven noticed Roslyn glaring at Cemal.

"Guests don't like names they can't pronounce," her aunt started. There was so much that Raven wanted to say to her aunt, but she settled for a quick jab instead.

"Guests?" Raven chuckled and looked around. "What guests?"

"It's off-season," her aunt threw back at her.

"It's early summer. In the mountains." Raven walked over to the large windows and looked out at the side of the mountain. There was still enough snow at the top of the ski runs that she could remember just how wonderful it felt to rush down the hills. "I would think there would be people in the city who need a weekend getaway and this view." She turned back to her aunt. "One must only give them what they want with the rest." She glanced around the rundown lobby and made a tsking noise. "Such a shame."

"Colin and I have done everything we could to keep this place afloat." Her aunt grabbed her arm, and her long well-manicured nails dug into her skin.

Raven jerked free, then walked over when a young, skinny high school boy came rushing out of the dining room. As with Cemal, the boy's attire was disheveled, and she realized that here, too, there was no set uniform or required attire.

"Miss." The boy saw Roslyn and turned almost sheet

white. "I..." Then the boy's eyes turned to her and went wide.

"Holy shit. You're her." He practically pointed at Raven. "You're the Firestarter," the boy said, still staring at her.

"That's quite enough, Tommy. Please help take my niece's things up to her suite," Roslyn said before turning away. "I'll contact you when your uncle has returned," Roslyn threw over her shoulder before disappearing down the hallway leading to Raven's father's old office.

Well, that went just as planned, Raven thought as she rode the elevator up to her rooms in the west building. She'd requested to stay in that building not only because it was the newest. It also had the best views, especially from the fifth floor.

Tommy, or Tom, remained quiet as they rode up together. She could tell that the boy was nervous and, at this point, she no longer cared. She wanted a shower and a few hours to shut down before she tried to find something to eat. Spending the past ten hours in the car, thinking about what she was going to say to her uncle and aunt, had drained her emotionally and physically. Worries about how they would react and fears of them tossing her out had played over in her mind the closer she had gotten to home.

Then again, it wasn't just her family's response to her return that would be a problem. No, she had the entire town of Cannon Falls to worry about.

Every single person she'd wronged. Every surviving family member of a loved one she'd killed.

When she opened the door to her suite, she genuinely smiled for the first time. Here, at least, she knew that she would be welcomed. The view of the still snow-covered peak warmed her.

Waiting for Tommy to set her bags down, she turned to the boy.

"Do you have a uniform?" she asked him as he waited for a tip. Raven doubted that the kid was popular in school. He was far too thin, wore thick glasses, and had a serious acne problem. She just bet there was a stack of books somewhere he'd been engrossed in when Cemal had called him.

The boy's eyebrows shot up.

"Yes," he answered quickly.

"Yes, ma'am," she corrected.

The boy looked irritated.

"Yes, ma'am," he said between clenched teeth.

"Tommy." She walked around him and tilted her head. "If I'm going to take my resort back, I'm going to need to make sure that each of my employees is on my side," she said clearly.

The boy seemed to take in her words, and his slight frown turned into a pout.

"Your...?" He cleared his throat. "Gosh, this is your place?"

"It is," she said easily with a smile. "My aunt and uncle have been running it while I was away at college."

"Well, shit," he said, straightening up. "I'm so sorry, Mrs. Brooks,"

She smiled. "Miss," she corrected. "You can call me Raven."

"I didn't know," he said quickly.

"No, I take it a lot of employees don't." Her aunt and uncle had probably hidden that detail from everyone over the past ten years. "But I bet you could enlighten them."

Tommy smiled and nodded, then turned towards the door, the prospect of a tip totally forgotten.

"Tom?" she said, getting his attention. "I'll expect to see you in the uniform next time."

He groaned slightly. "Miss..." He stopped when she arched her eyebrows. "Raven, it doesn't fit."

"It doesn't?" She frowned. "Well, we'll have to fix that. Until I have a chance to correct the issue, your best slacks and dress shirt should do nicely." She motioned to his worn jeans, T-shirt, and sneakers. "And some dress shoes. If you need an allowance to purchase some, see me tomorrow."

"Yes, ma'am," he said with a big smile. "Thanks," he said and left quickly.

She walked over and opened the doors to the bedroom suite and assessed the large space that would be her new home until she could secure her own place. The bedroom could use some freshening up, as could the bathroom, but she was thankful that the room wasn't as rundown as the lobby had been.

She headed back into the larger sitting room, pulled open the sliding glass doors, and stepped out onto the balcony. Leaning her hands on the railing, she took in a deep breath and enjoyed the fresh smell of the country air.

There was a hint of the crisp cold snow that floated down from the top of the mountain in front of her, and she took several moments to appreciate it all. Then she turned her gaze to the left and held her breath.

She'd avoided driving through the small town of Cannon Falls when she'd headed to the resort. Normally, tourists or guests would take the business loop directly through town to get there. However, locals knew the old highway that wound around the hills and avoided the heart of the town.

The fear of what she'd see had caused her to take the old route.

Now, she turned her eyes towards the small town of Cannon Falls, the place that had been so close to her heart. The place she'd destroyed.

She didn't know what to expect. Ten years ago, hardly a single building remained standing. Had they rebuilt it? What did it look like now?

Seeing the outline of the newer trees against the larger ones that hadn't been destroyed, she felt her heart swell. Where once had stood the charred remains of the forest that had burned down, it was now green for as far as the eye could see. The lines of everything she'd destroyed were blurred.

Her knees buckled and she folded down to sit on the floor of the balcony as her eyes watered.

What had made her think she could do this? Why on earth would she ever return to this place? It had been two months since she'd received the call that her grandmother had passed away peacefully in her sleep. Her father's mother had been the only family who had welcomed her after the fire. The only person in the world who had cared, really cared for her.

Now, that person was gone, just like everyone else who had cared in her life. She was once again, all alone.

The darkness was back, awakened once again after so long of a reprieve. Its gloriously dark tentacles reached out, consuming, overwhelming once again. Changing, twisting the mind. Splitting it in two as it had once before, long ago.

The smell of smoke hinted at its return. The sight of flames tickled and teased it from its hiding. Over the past ten years, nothing had allowed it its freedom, until it had seen the bright red of Raven Brooks' red locks once more.

Now, thanks to her return, the monster was finally free, and it was only a matter of time before someone paid the price.

CHAPTER TWO

"What in the hell do you think you're doing?" Cade Stone stormed across the yard and stomped on the pile of papers and dead plants, extinguishing the small flames his neighbor, Bobby Robert—yes, that was really the man's name—had started.

"Hey!" The middle-aged man pushed him. "What the hell." Bobby shoved him again. "Why'd you go and do that?"

"Bobby, I know you're smarter than to light a fire when we're under restrictions." Cade stomped on the pile again to make his point.

"Well, shit." Bobby sighed and wiped a dirty handkerchief over his face. "I was going to stand right here. Got my water hose and all." The man motioned to the hose, which wasn't even hooked up to the water spigot.

"Don't test my patience," he warned the man. "Now clean this mess up. Trash day is tomorrow." He motioned to the garbage can sitting at the end of Bobby's drive.

Jumping into his truck, he whistled for his dog, Blue, to follow him.

The old bloodhound took his time getting up and stretching before he hobbled from his spot on the front porch and climbed into the truck with him.

"Thanks for joining me today," he told the dog, who rolled his eyes at him. "Don't give me that look." He started the truck and headed into town. "Listen, if you don't give me attitude, you might get some cookies." The dog's ears perked up, as much as the droopy things could. "You'd think you'd be more enthusiastic to come to work with me. Man's best friend and all." Blue laid his head down in his lap and looked up at him with big begging eyes. "Yeah, yeah, we'll stop off and get you some cookies," he agreed, causing Blue's tail to wag frantically.

He parked in front of Upper Crust Bakery and let Blue follow him inside. Even though the building was newer, built after the fire, the bakery had been a staple in the town his entire life. This was the case with most of the other businesses in Cannon Falls. The ones that had stuck around and rebuilt, that was.

The old Cannon Falls Diner was the only building downtown that hadn't burned to the ground. That business, along with a little over a hundred homes, was all that had remained after that summer day. The day the town had lost thirty residents, including his younger brother.

"Morning, Cade," Dawn Highett, owner of the bakery, greeted him when he walked in. "How's Blue this morning?" The blonde woman, who was a few years younger than him, bent down and scratched his dog on the head. Blue, who wasn't a fool and knew who had the cookies, laid his head on Dawn's knee.

"Morning, Dawn." Cade walked over and helped himself to the self-serve coffee.

"Will you be bringing in donuts for the crew this morning?" Dawn asked, giving Blue a few cookies from her apron.

"You know it," he said, adding creamer to his coffee. "I've already extinguished one fire this morning," he said. He walked over to the counter and waited until Dawn finished washing her hands before helping him pick out two dozen donuts for his men.

He'd been tempted to ask Dawn out at one point. The pretty blonde had always been friendly to him, and he liked how nice she was to Blue. But then he'd found out that she had a live-in girlfriend.

It wasn't as if he'd been desperate for dates over the years since he'd returned to his hometown. And since he'd become fire marshal, he'd decided to keep his focus on his career. Blue took up a lot of his time as well.

"Oh?" she asked, glancing over her shoulder. "What happened?"

"Bobby." He said the man's name, as if that explained everything.

Dawn rolled her eyes. "Seriously?" She chuckled. "I swear, some people should be banned from buying matches."

He chuckled and started pointing at the donuts he wanted for his team.

"So, you heard the latest rumors?" she asked as she carefully placed donuts in the pink bakery boxes.

"Rumors?" he asked, pointing to the green-clover-covered sugar cakes. "About?"

"Raven Brooks is back in town," Dawn said as she filled the box. He froze in place. "Or so Tommy Andrews has been saying all over town."

"Raven?" He felt his blood start to boil. "Where is she staying?"

Dawn glanced up at him, no doubt because of his stern tone.

"As far as I know, she's staying at the resort." She gave a little shrug and walked over to ring him up. "Her family still owns the place, after all."

"Right." He paid Dawn and mentally rearranged his day to add a visit to the resort. He'd been waiting ten long years to talk to Raven Brooks. Ten long years that he'd spent without his brother, Reggie.

Now the day had finally come to question the person responsible for his loss and the losses of so many others.

After dropping the sugary breakfast off at the firehouse, he and Blue headed up to the massive resort that hung along the hillside overlooking Cannon Falls. He'd been to the place so many times over the years, as he was responsible for certifying and enforcing the fire code for the entire town, including the resort.

However, this time when he parked and stepped outside, he had only one goal in mind. Finding and questioning Raven Brooks.

He could vaguely remember his younger brother's high school girlfriend. He had at one point received a photo of the two of them at a school dance. Since Cade had been away at college most of his brother's senior year of school, he hadn't been around when his brother had been dating the girl.

He did, however, remember seeing the young redhead around long before then. After all, Cannon Falls had always been a small town, even before the fire that ravaged the place, destroying so many lives.

Snapping his fingers, he had Blue lying down just outside the doors. He knew the dog would remain there until he returned.

Stepping into the lobby, he glanced around. Over the years, he'd watched the decay of the once-elite resort that had housed thousands and thousands of wealthy families.

But he knew that it wasn't the fire ten years ago that had caused the resort's decline. No, he knew all too well the problems behind its demise.

"Morning." He smiled at Christina.

"Marshal." The young woman beamed up at him. "I didn't know we were having another inspection today."

He leaned on the counter and tried for charm. After all, he didn't quite know how to go about demanding to see Raven Brooks. Technically, he had no jurisdiction over a case that had been closed more than a decade ago.

"Oh, I'm not here for an inspection."

The young woman's cheeks flushed as she reached up and nervously wiped at her short bangs.

He knew the feminine equivalent of flirting and, for the next few minutes, he allowed the girl to drone on about how boring her job was.

Indeed, the phone didn't ring the entire time he stood there, nor did he see a single soul around the massive lobby area.

"Oh." She glanced around and leaned a little closer to him. "Did you hear the news?"

"No." He mirrored her move and leaned closer. "What news?"

"Raven Brooks is back. I, of course, had no clue who she was until yesterday." She shook her head and sighed. "I had no clue that she owned the resort."

"She does?" This wasn't surprising news to him. After all, it had been her parents that had started and owned the resort years ago. He understood that her uncle and aunt had been running the business for her over the past ten years.

"Yes, she checked in late yesterday afternoon." Christina leaned back, then smiled a little. "She seems nice, even asked me for my..." She dropped off and looked around.

"Your...?" he asked, curious why the girl suddenly looked nervous.

"My real name," she whispered.

His eyebrows jumped up in question. "Christina isn't your real name?"

"No." She shook her head. "It's the name Mrs. Brooks, Roslyn," she added quickly to clarify, "demanded I use. She claimed that no one was going to be able to pronounce my real name."

"What is your real name?" he asked, curious.

"Cemal Rahim." She glanced around again.

"It's a beautiful name, Cemal. And suits you much more than Christina," he added with a smile.

Her smile grew. "Thank you."

It was then that he noticed that her normal dull attire had been replaced by a crisp pressed red button-up shirt and black slacks. He could tell that she'd put a lot more effort into her attire than she had the past few times he'd seen her.

He wondered if that was Raven's doing as well. Was she intimidating enough to scare the girl into wearing different clothes?

"Is she around?" he asked. "Raven Brooks, I mean." He glanced around the empty lobby.

"Oh, she's inspecting the property today." Cemal

motioned to the long hallway that led to several offices and conference rooms.

"She is?" he asked. "Hm, I probably should go check and see if she has any concerns as far as the fire safety around here." He stood up straight. "Happen to know which room she's in?"

"I think she's in Mr. Brooks's office," Cemal said.

He turned his attention back to her. "Thank you, Cemal," he said, earning a bright smile in return.

As he made his way down the hallway, he could hear yelling from the office when he was still fifteen feet away, even though it was shut.

When he stood right outside, he eavesdropped and heard Colin Brooks' raised voice.

"I don't give a damn what you think," Colin practically screamed. "You are not coming in here after I have given this place everything in the past decade. This was my brother's place. He may have left it to you, but I've run it. I've worked hard to make it what it is now."

Cade glanced around at the worn-down furnishings. He knew who Colin and Roslyn Brooks were, knew their problems, as did most people in town. Colin's many affairs and gambling debts were well known, as were Roslyn's drinking issues. She got kicked out of the town bar on a weekly basis. Rumors were that she had a few DUIs that kept her from driving. Her husband's money and power had apparently kept her out of jail so far.

"I'm not going to let some young girl come in here with zero experience and destroy everything I've worked hard on. Your father may have wanted you to own this resort, but he had no intentions of having you run it." Colin continued to yell. "Besides, everyone in town knows you are the reason he's dead." Cade leaned a little closer to see if he could hear

Raven's response. Her voice was too low and soft to hear her response.

"I don't give a shit," Colin yelled in response to whatever she'd said. "I won't hand over this business. You can go to hell."

At this point, Colin heard something that had him moving quickly—a loud bang just before a woman's yelp. Cade recognized those sounds. He knew what they meant.

He never spoke ill of his father. After all, he'd been a colonel in the military and had died for his country. But whenever the man had returned home from duty, his mother had paid the price.

Moving quickly, Cade yanked open the door and charged into the office.

Colin Brooks was standing alone on one side of the desk, face red and full of anger, his hands lying down by his sides, balled into fists.

Cade's eyes skimmed over to where a red-haired beauty sat behind the desk, concern and confusion flooding her eyes. Raven Brooks looked nothing like what he remembered.

The woman had pale almost flawless skin, except for some soft freckles that dotted her nose. Her long red hair lay in soft curls over her shoulders, perfectly in place. She was wearing a soft white sweater that somehow made her look almost untouchable.

Her crystal blue eyes were watching him with interest and a hint of concern.

"I, uh." He cleared his throat, unsure of what to say now that he'd just barged in, having obviously misunderstood what had transpired in the office. "Heard a bang?" he said, feeling slightly stupid.

Raven stood up and motioned to the chair. "The chair," she said before turning to her uncle, "is broken."

Colin Brooks sighed deeply. "We'll finish this discussion later," he said, then he turned and stormed out, but not before nodding to him. "Cade."

"Brooks," he replied. It wasn't as if he hated the man. Cade just knew his type.

When Colin left, he slammed the door behind him, leaving Cade in the room alone with the person responsible for his brother's death.

Cade didn't know what to expect. If he'd had a moment to think about it, he would have said one of the millions of things he'd come up with over the years. Instead, he stood there in silence as they assessed one another.

He watched several emotions flash behind those crystal eyes of hers and knew that he was feeling much of the same. But he could easily add anger to his list, where she had none.

"Can I help you?" she finally broke the silence.

"I'm Cade..." he started.

"I know who you are," she broke in. "What can I do for you?"

He took a step forward. "I have some questions."

Her eyebrows arched up.

"About?" She wheeled the chair away from the desk and motioned for him to sit in one of the chairs before pushing a different chair behind the desk and sitting down.

"Ten years ago," he finally said after she sat down in the new office chair.

She tensed, her lips going very thin and her eyes growing blank. She stood again quickly.

"I have no answers for you. I think, Mr. Stone, you'd be better off..." She motioned towards the door.

"Fire Marshal Stone," he corrected. He may not be able to get her to answer him just because he was Reggie's brother, but with his job title and power, he could sometimes get what he wanted.

She tilted her head and ran her eyes over him. He wished he'd chosen to wear his uniform that day. Instead, he had on his plain clothes.

"Need to see my badge?" he asked, a little clipped.

"No, I'm sure you make a wonderful fire marshal." She sighed and moved to lean on the edge of the desk. "As I just informed my uncle, I intend to take over every aspect of the running of the resort. Today is my first official day back home, and I have a lot of work ahead of me, assessing what needs to be done around here to bring it... up to code." She glanced towards the desk filled with stacks of paperwork. "I'd suggest we set a time to meet next week to go over any issues you may have found at the resort." She ran her eyes over him again. "If you have any issues with the resort, we can discuss them then. But let me be clear. Personally"—she stood straight again and looked down into his eyes— "I owe you nothing."

He stood suddenly and noticed that she didn't move back. Normally, he towered over women, but Raven was tall enough that they were almost eye to eye.

He couldn't deny the instant pull of attraction that he'd felt the moment he'd laid eyes on her and felt disgusted at himself for the moment of weakness. Even now, he felt it and tried to focus on the challenge she'd just issued him.

"That is left to be seen," he said finally. "I'll have my office call and schedule a full inspection. I take it you're planning on making some changes around here?" he asked, knowing that he could wait a little longer and maybe approach her differently to get the answers he needed.

"Yes." She relaxed slightly. "From the looks of it, there's a lot that needs changing." She took a step back.

"I take it your aunt and uncle aren't happy with the changes?"

She tilted her head slightly. "You could say that." Then her eyes narrowed. "Are we going to have a problem?" she asked suddenly.

He thought about it. About what, legally, he could and couldn't do. He knew that the resort had just scraped by at the last inspection almost six months ago. He expected that their business licenses were up to speed but planned on making a stop off at the city building after he left here, just to confirm it himself.

As far as his personal feelings for the woman, he knew that the entire town held Raven Brooks responsible for the fire, even though the fire marshal from back then had deemed the fire an accident.

Since taking over the job, he'd scoured over every word in the file from that fateful day and had an extensive list of questions that Jon Jacob, the fire marshal Cade had taken over for, hadn't asked back then.

"That depends," he answered finally.

She exhaled and then shrugged. "If you're done trying to intimidate me"—she turned and moved to sit behind the desk again— "I have a business to run and save." She glanced towards the door. "I think you know your way out." She turned to the paperwork on the desk and dismissed him.

Whatever he'd believed he'd find in her, she had completely defied his expectations. The last time he'd seen her, she was an insecure teenager with extremely long thin legs and out-of-control-bright red hair. The woman who'd just dismissed him was a far cry from that girl.

There was no way her uncle was going to survive an attack and takeover from the strong-willed, powerfully intelligent woman he'd just left. He didn't know where Raven Brooks had spent the last ten years of her life, but he was determined to find out everything he could about the beauty. And he knew just the place to start.

CHAPTER THREE

EVERY REVOLUTION BEGINS WITH A SPARK

Raven relaxed back in the chair and allowed herself to finally breath. What the hell was that? Why the hell had her heart pounded out of her chest the moment Cade Stone had stepped foot in the office?

Of course, she remembered Reggie's older brother. What young girl growing up in Cannon Falls ten years ago wouldn't? If she'd believed Reggie to be the boy of her dreams, then Cade, his older brother had always been the man of them.

Even back when she'd been nothing but a pre-teen watching him play sports, she'd dreamed of him. Oh sure, as far as looks went, Reggie and Cade had been comparable. They both had thick dark hair, a strong firm jawline, and were well over six foot tall. That counted for a lot in Raven's book since she was taller than most girls and towered over many men at five foot nine inches. But where they really differed was their eyes. Cade had those smoldering eyes that hinted at what lay beneath—pure, unadulterated sex appeal.

There was no woman alive that could fight against it. Even someone who had sworn off the possibility years ago.

Shaking off the sudden urge to rip the man's clothes off and see what was underneath, she went back to work.

Her uncle had been less than enthusiastic about giving her access to the accounts. Even now, she had to hunt through his desk to find the business card for the accountant that ran the resort's books, Joseph Ramsey. She vaguely remembered the man being always around when her father ran the resort.

When he answered the phone, she quickly jumped in.

"Mr. Ramsey, this is Raven Brooks." She waited a beat.

"Raven?" The man sounded excited. "My little bird?"

She smiled at the man's nickname for her. "Yes."

"Well, how have you been? What are you up to?" he asked quickly.

"I'm back at the resort and hoping you can shed some light on where things stand."

He was silent for a beat. "I'd love to help you out, little bird, but I haven't looked at those books since your father passed."

"You haven't?" She sat forward and frowned down at his business card in her hand.

"Not since your uncle took over and hired the new company to oversee everything."

"Do you happen to know what company that is?" she asked.

"Sure do." His voice changed slightly as if he had a secret. "Um, it's Roche Accounting Firm."

She frowned. "I haven't heard of it."

"It was fairly new when they took over the books. Um, I can get you their number." She waited and wrote the name and number he supplied her on the back of his business card.

"So, you're back? Is it for good?" Joseph asked.

"Yes, I've taken over from my uncle."

"You have?" He sounded surprised. "How's Colin taking the news?"

"As you'd expect," she said with a sigh. "Listen, Joe, I don't know what my uncle's agreement with the new firm is, but I'd sure like someone I trust, someone my father trusted, to take a look at the numbers. Think you can spare some time?"

"Sure thing, anything for my little bird. Besides, I owe your dad. He's the only reason I was able to survive all those years and start my own business. He and I were best friends back in the day."

"It's why you were the first call I made," she said with a smile.

"Well now you went and did it." The man sniffled. "How does tomorrow sound?"

"Sounds wonderful. I'll see what I can get from Roche." She said goodbye and hung up.

She didn't get as far with the next call, which went directly to an answering service. Still, she left her name and cell number in hopes that Morgan Roche, owner of Roche Accounting Firm, would give her a call back.

Next, she'd called the maintenance company that worked on the ski lifts. They claimed that the last time they'd inspected or maintained the five lifts on the property was almost four years ago.

Raven was completely shocked that her uncle would let the resort fall into such disrepair. After all, if any of the lifts broke during ski season, god forbid, someone could be seriously injured or killed. After scheduling a full maintenance overhaul on all the equipment, she moved on to her next call.

She'd taken her time talking with the owner of the landscape company, All Things Green, and giving him an idea of what she wanted. Jake Green had immediately jumped at the chance of such a big job. They were scheduled to come first thing in the morning to mow, weed, and edge, with basic maintenance scheduled to begin up again the following day. She'd also arranged to meet Jake and his crew first thing in the morning to discuss improvements they could make to the grounds.

After the calls, she logged onto her laptop and scoured a couple of business outfit sites for new uniforms for the bellboys and front office staff. Moments later, her cousin barged into the room.

"So, it's true." Liza Brooks hadn't changed much. Her cousin was still petite, blonde, and perfect, right down to her heeled Gucci leather boots.

"Hi, Liza." Raven stood up and moved over to air kiss her cousin. She jerked away slightly.

"Daddy tells me you're kicking us out?" Liza said, crossing her hands over her chest, which sent the massive collection of silver bracelets on both of her arms jingling.

"What?" Raven frowned. "Kicking you out?" She shook her head.

"Oh, don't tell me you don't know that we're all housed on the top floor of the east wing."

This was news to her. The last she'd heard, the house her aunt and uncle had owned at the time of the fire was still standing.

"Liza, I just got into town last night." She sat on the edge of her father's old desk. "I haven't had time to learn anything, let alone decide what I'm going to do."

"You aren't kicking us out?" Liza asked with a slight pout.

Raven realized that she shouldn't make promises, not when it could be true that her family was taking up an entire floor of the resort. A floor which, if everything went as she planned, she would need the income from.

"Why don't you sit down, fill me in on what you've been doing?" Raven moved to sit behind the desk again and motioned to the chair. "Did you finish school?"

Liza glanced at the door and then shrugged before plopping down in the chair, much like a young child would have.

"No, I went to acting school in Hollywood for a year, but..." She shook her head, sending her blonde locks flying. "It wasn't for me. They couldn't teach me anything I didn't already have the natural talent for or the knowledge."

Of course, Raven thought to herself. Her cousin always did have a talent for being dramatic, overly so.

"What about Cal?" she asked.

"Oh, he's around somewhere." Liza shrugged.

Cal Brooks was a lot like his sister. Completely in love with himself.

"Is he back from school then?" she asked.

Liza waved her hand. "He never went. Not after he got all of those modeling gigs."

"Oh?" Raven tried to maintain her patience. "Modeling?"

"Sure." Liza sat forward slightly. "A few local shops, then that gig in LA." She shrugged. "There's no doubt that soon he'll have agents knocking down his door."

"Right," Raven nodded, fully understanding now.

Her cousins were totally living off the resort's money, along with their parents. No wonder they were upset at her.

She'd just moved back with the promise to take all of their security away.

Just one look at the place and anyone, including Cade Stone, could see that someone was siphoning the money, if there was any actually coming in, from the business.

"So, are you working?" she asked Liza.

"Working?" Liza balked. "As in"—she motioned with her many ringed fingers— "here?" She laughed.

"Then, what are you doing for money?" Raven asked.

Liza blinked at her, a blank look in her eyes.

"Oh, I have some money saved up," Liza added dryly.

"Right." Raven sighed. "And your brother?"

Liza's eyes grew colder, and Raven realized she'd gotten her answers.

"Well." Raven stood suddenly, knowing that if she was going to make the rounds to determine what needed to be done, she needed to get at it. Besides, she doubted she would gain any other knowledge from her cousin. "I need to start making my rounds."

"Rounds?" Liza stood up. "What is it, exactly, that you think you're going to do around here that Daddy doesn't already do?"

Raven pasted on a smile. "For one, I'm going to schedule some remodeling. It's time we brought the resort into this century," she joked. "Second, I'm going to tighten the belt around here." She locked eyes with her cousin. "The flow of money seeping out of the accounts will stop."

"You know," Liza jumped in, "everyone in town blames you for the fire. You know that, right?"

She'd witness her cousin's changing moods before and had prepared for them over the past ten years.

"What they or anyone else thinks about me no longer matters." She felt her gut twist but held her ground.

Walking out of the office with her iPad in hand, she decided to start at the bottom and work her way to the top. She hadn't expected Liza to follow her around for half of it, complaining and trying to convince her to leave. Two hours later, her cousin Cal found her making notes about purchasing some new equipment in the kitchen.

"So, it's true." Her cousin walked over and, to Raven's surprise, hugged her. "You're back."

Smiling, she nodded. Her cousin was even more handsome than she remembered. She knew that he had been hiding the secret of his sexuality from his family, but Raven knew the truth. Still, she kept his secret. It wasn't hers to give away.

"How are you?" she asked, setting down her iPad and getting a better look at him. "Liza says you're modeling?"

He shrugged. "A few gigs here and there."

"That's great," she said automatically.

"Liza says you're taking over this..."—he rolled his eyes—"hot mess."

"Trying to." She leaned against the counter. So far, she hadn't seen a single employee. Anywhere.

"Good. It needs some serious help. Dad's been absent lately." He leaned closer and lowered his voice. "Rumors have him and his mistress spending a lot of time together. Which is why Mom drinks." He sighed and shook his head. "You can find her in the bar upstairs or the one downtown most nights."

"I'm sorry," she said.

"Don't be. She made her own bed. Both of them did." His eyes ran over her slowly. "You've grown up. I like what you've done to yourself."

She laughed. "Ten years," she reminded him. "You've

gotten some new muscles and grown a few inches taller yourself."

He nodded. "You won't hear a word of discouragement from me. I can't say the same from my parents or sister. They'll fight you right up to the end. I wouldn't put it past them to sue you for control of this place." He shook his head. "Don't let them take it from you. Fight. I know you've got it in you. And Liza, well, she'll come around, after she comes to grips with the fact that her access to unlimited income has to end." He shrugged.

"Yeah." Raven sighed. "So, about that. I'm having my dad's old accountant take over. I don't want to put your family out, but unless they start working, actually working around here, things are going to have to change."

"Then change them," he said with a smile.

"What about you?" she asked, worried to make yet another enemy.

"Girl, I've got a place to stay. I've been... seeing some-one," he said.

She raised her eyebrows slightly.

Cal's eyes quickly ran over to the kitchen. "You'll meet him soon enough, when the dinner shift starts. His name is Tim. He works here in the kitchen and wants to be a chef." He shook his head. "During the season he's a ski instructor."

"That's wonderful. So, your family knows then?" she asked.

He shook his head quickly. "No, they think I'm seeing... someone else. I know you've known for ever and, well, I think my secret is safe with you."

"It always has been." She touched his arm. "It's good to be back," she said suddenly.

"I'm glad your back." He hugged her again. "Now, I'm

off. My family doesn't know it, but I have a part-time job down at an art studio in town."

"Good for you." She nodded. "Before you go, is there anything else I need to know?"

He thought for a moment. "My father's mistress... happens to run the books for the resort."

"Morgan Roche?" she asked quickly.

He nodded and walked away, waving over his shoulders. "See you later, cousin."

By noon, she'd run into a handful of employees around the facility.

Liam Montford reintroduced himself as her uncle's business manager. The middle-aged man reminded her of a retired lawyer. He was very careful in everything that he said to her and even wore a suit and tie. She scheduled a meeting with the man for the following afternoon, as he claimed his schedule was full for the rest of the day.

She met Eddie Mimms, a younger version of Montford, who claimed to be the manager of the resort. She didn't know what the difference was, between Liam Montford and Eddie but figured she would find out the following day, since both men seemed to be too busy for her.

She ran into Rachelle Braun in the hallway. The woman had been running around, yelling at a few of the cleaning staff for smoking in the hallways.

So far, Rachelle was the only employee Raven had met that was actually doing any work.

"If you find some time later today, I'll be in my uncle's office. I'd like to sit down and have a quick chat," Raven had requested.

The woman had smiled and nodded. "Will after lunch work out?"

"Perfectly. Thank you."

The woman practically sprinted down the hallway to finish talking to the cleaning crew.

Deciding she needed a break and that it was time to face the rest of the music, she headed into town for lunch.

Parking in front of the Cannon Falls Diner brought back so many memories. Her hands gripped the wheel tightly, and she had to breathe through another panic attack.

The diner hadn't changed a bit. The same neon sign hung over the old wood-sided building that sat just on the edge of town. Its outlying location had saved it from the fate the rest of the buildings in town had paid.

It took her almost ten minutes to build up the guts to walk into the diner. Just watching townspeople come and go added to her nerves, people she vaguely remembered or wondered if she should remember.

Finally, she took a deep breath, climbed out of her car, and walked inside.

Instantly, her eyes scanned the familiar surroundings.

"I thought you were going to sit in there forever," a deep voice said directly behind her as she stepped inside.

Turning, she saw Cade sitting on a barstool by the front door.

She'd been so nervous, she hadn't even seen him. From his position, he must have been able to clearly see her sitting in the car. She kicked herself for not parking further away.

When he motioned to the stool next to his, she tried to think of a reason not to join him.

Then a loud piercing squeal filled the diner. She jumped and spun around.

"Raven!" Darby Nabers, one of Raven's best friends, rushed towards her and engulfed her in a tight hug.

Darby, or Darb, had been a steady friend most of

Raven's life. The bubbly, energetic blonde had been like Phoebe from *Friends* in their group. Carrie Edwards had been their Monica. Which left Raven as the Rachel in the group. Well, they'd been a lot younger back then.

She'd kept in contact with Darby and Carrie over the years, though not by her doing. Darby was the kind of person that just wouldn't let go. Like cling wrap, she tended to stick to you.

After Raven had moved in with her grandmother, Darby had hunted her down and, ever since then, they'd texted one another on an almost weekly basis.

She knew everything about her friends' lives. Darby still ran her family's diner with her dad, Steve. Her mother, Barb, had died in the fire ten years ago, which was one of the reasons Raven found it hard to stay in contact with her friend. But Darby had made it perfectly clear that she didn't blame Raven for her mother's death. And, after ten years, Raven believed her.

Carrie had started her very own travel guide newspaper a few years ago. Her online version was more popular than the paper one that went out once a week. She mainly talked about current world affairs or places she'd traveled to. Both Darby and Raven believed the small town was holding their friend back from greatness. But Carrie loved the lifestyle in Cannon Falls and took several long trips each year to exotic places.

"You're here. You're really here," Darby said, spinning her around.

Laughing, Raven stopped her from knocking a few customers over.

"I am," she agreed.

Then Darby dropped her hands and narrowed her eyes.

"I'm mad at you." She pointed a finger into Raven's face. "You didn't tell me you were coming."

"Sure I did."

"You said you were thinking about it. Thinking. You didn't say, 'I'm coming.'" She shook her head. "Oh!" She pulled out her phone. "I have to tell Carrie you're here." She shot off a text. "The three musketeers are back together." She held up her hand, and Raven lifted hers as well in the friends' salute as she laughed. "Sit." She pushed Raven into the stool next to Cade, taking the decision to sit somewhere else away from her. "I'll get you your favorite." She quickly disappeared.

"I take it the two of you know each other?" Cade said dryly.

Raven chuckled and sighed. "Best friends in school," she explained.

"Right." He nodded.

"Darby's friendly with everyone," she admitted with a smile as she watched her friend disappear into the back.

"She doesn't seem to like your cousin or aunt and uncle much," he pointed out.

Raven's back tensed. "They're an... acquired taste." She wished more than anything she could scoot over or, better yet, sit somewhere else.

"How goes your assessment of the place?" he asked, taking a sip of his drink.

"Fine," she answered, unwilling to give him anything further.

It was then that she noticed the old dog lying by his feet. She hadn't even spotted him when she'd walked in.

Nodding, she asked. "Is he yours?"

Cade glanced down at the snoring dog and smiled. Up until then, she hadn't seen him smile. The movement transformed his entire being. Somehow, he went from a sexy broody alpha male to a too-hot-to-handle sex god with the slight curve of his lips.

Damn. She was in deep trouble. How the hell was she going to keep her secrets from a man who looked at her with eyes that seemed to bore into her soul?

She knew he wanted answers about that night ten years ago. So did most of the people who had survived. But she just couldn't give them to anyone. There was no way she could live with herself if her secrets were exposed. No amount of counseling could save her from the fate of saying the words out loud. Even alone.

She'd resolved herself to taking what had happened on her seventeenth birthday to her grave and no amount of sexy, sulky looks from Cade Stone could ever make her reveal her darkest secrets.

CHAPTER FOUR

THERE WERE NEVER BUTTERFLIES, JUST FIRE

Cade sat on the stool next to Raven and observed the interaction of the three friends with a watchful eye.

It was extremely hard to not get drawn into the laughter and fun. Especially when Darby and Carrie were involved. Over the years, he'd come to like both women. Darby for her quirkiness and ability to make anyone laugh, no matter how bad their day was going. Carrie for her seriousness and her ability to ask all the wrong questions at the wrong times.

Both ladies had survived the fire and had remained friends with Raven Brooks, the proof of which was displayed directly in front of him.

While he watched the trio, he realized that Raven was still so reserved. Guarded.

He surmised it had something to do with him sitting directly next to her. Then again, it could be that every single eye in the diner was on her.

No one in the place was watching the trio as if enjoying the friend's reunion. Instead, they watched Raven with spiteful gazes.

Some of those looks were downright scary, and he

wondered if anyone would have confronted her if he hadn't been sitting next to her. He didn't want to find out, not this early in the game, at any rate.

He needed to get information and answers out of her. Which meant he couldn't afford for her to get spooked out of town. Not just yet.

So he stretched his lunch out a little longer and waited for the friends to wrap up their reunion.

When Raven and Carrie walked out of the diner, he was right behind them.

Carrie gave Raven a hug, glanced at him, gave him a quick nod, then disappeared down the street, no doubt to the little building she rented for the newspaper she wrote.

"Why are you still here?" Raven turned on him.

"I live here," he answered easily.

Raven's eyes narrowed at him, then Blue walked over and nudged her leg with his nose.

Seeing the smile brighten her face as she bent down and gave his dog a pet, he felt his heart skip slightly at how utterly beautiful she was.

He'd always believed her to be plain looking when she'd been younger. So much had changed.

"What's his name?" she asked, smiling up at him.

"Blue," he answered. His dog's ears perked up slightly.

"Blue?" Raven questioned. "What a... unique name." She chuckled when the dog nudged her for more attention.

"He came with it," he said. When she looked up at him in question, he added, "He flunked out of the police force. It was his lifelong dream, when he was a young pup, to be a search-and-rescue-dog, but alas, his training interrupted his nap time too much." He shrugged slightly and enjoyed the sound of her laughter.

This time when she stood up, he saw kindness in her eyes rather than concern.

"They say you can tell the kind of person by the company they keep." She tilted her head slightly and assessed him. "Blue, here, proves that you can be a kind person."

His eyebrows rose slightly. "Did Blue tell you that?"

"No, but my gran always says that she never trusted a person who didn't like dogs."

Since she'd given him the opening, he figured he'd take it.

"Your gran and mine were best friends," he said.

She looked slightly surprised, before nodding. "Yes, I seem to remember that. How is your grandmother?"

"She's doing well."

"Is she still living in the big place?" Her voice dropped off slightly, and he saw worry fill her eyes.

"Yes," he added quickly. "She was lucky that it was spared since it was made of stone and set aside from the rest of the homes due to the yard being much larger."

"That's good." She seemed to shrink back as if disappearing into her thoughts. Her eyes moved to the diner and then down at her watch. "I have... a meeting." She started to move away.

He wanted to say something more, to get her to feel more relaxed around him. It was the only way to get her to trust him and open up. But instead, he snapped his fingers and helped Blue into his truck and then watched her drive away in an older sedan.

As he was making his afternoon inspection rounds, he ran into Jake Green, who owned and ran a local landscaping business, All Things Green.

"Hey, man." Jake bent to give Blue some attention.

"You're just in time. We're celebrating getting the new gig up at the resort."

"Oh?" Cade asked, a little curious.

"Yeah, I guess Raven Brooks is back in town. Seems like she wants to do an entire overhaul on the grounds," Jake said.

"Really?" He figured on letting Jake tell him everything, since he knew the man was a talker.

"Yeah. We sure needed the job. You know how it's been lately. Not a lot of people can afford to have someone do their yard work. But getting the job to do the entire grounds up on the resort..." He whistled. "Not just maintenance, but an entire restoration. She wants plants, new pathways, the whole nine yards."

"That's good." Cade wondered where the money was coming from. His grandmother had mentioned that Raven had attended business school in San Diego shortly after graduating high school, when she'd moved in with her grandmother.

Since his grandmother had lost contact with Raven's grandmother two years ago, she didn't know much more.

Rumors around town were that the resort was in the red. Deeply so.

Everyone knew that it was just a matter of time before it went under. The people and businesses in town that had depended on the resort for their income had been suffering for a while. Many had decided to leave Cannon Falls for the city.

After the fire, some had rebuilt, but of the survivors, more than half had picked up and left everything behind, leaving plenty of vacant lots with charred foundations where their lives had once flourished.

For those that stayed, new homes were built. Some took

longer than others and for the first years most families were crammed into modular government trailers.

When homes did start to sprout up, he'd been there, helping his neighbors rebuild.

Leaving the city and his own dream of medical school behind, he'd returned to the charred remains of the home he'd known. His family had been broken after the loss of his brother, but they'd pulled together. With their family home burned to the ground, his mother had moved in with his grandmother.

It had taken them close to a year to rebuild his childhood home, which his mother still lived in. His father had died shortly after his tenth birthday while he was stationed overseas. The day they had received word that his team had been caught in a road bombing had been the worst and yet the best day of Cade's life.

Reggie hadn't really remembered their father, but Cade had held some memories that he couldn't shake.

Shortly after returning home, Cade had started working for the fire house and soon after had taken over as fire marshal, thanks to his uncle, Sean, having some pull down at the station. Sean Stone had worked for the Cannon Falls police department for as long as Cade could remember. His father's younger brother had been the perfect male role model most of Cade's and Reggie's lives, the one their father should have been when he'd been alive.

Sean had helped Cade purchase land from a family that had wanted to move on and then helped as Cade spent the next year building his own home.

He'd been thankful he'd had the opportunity to do so, thanks to the position. He'd seen others struggling to recover after losing everything. He'd helped others rebuild, recover, and move on while the person who had been responsible for the destruction had run and hid.

He wasn't going to lose the opportunity to get answers from Raven one way or another, even if he had to play dirty. He wasn't going to let her get away, not this time.

Cannon Falls deserved answers. He deserved answers.

For the remainder of his workweek, he tried to formulate a plan to get Raven to open up to him. His first plan of strong-arming answers out of her just wasn't going to work. He'd witnessed what kind of person she was and, as much as he'd like to demonize her for her past transgressions, he just couldn't now. Whoever she'd been ten years ago, that girl was long gone.

Each day Raven was in charge of the resort, the entire town buzzed with news of her hiring more and more workers, utilizing local businesses and suppliers.

He couldn't deny that Raven's return was a good thing for the town. Which meant that he had to change his tactics to get information from her.

He hadn't even seen Raven back in town again. He'd overheard that she'd been extremely busy at the resort making changes. She even called his office and scheduled a full fire inspection for the following day. He was going to oversee it personally.

He'd been so preoccupied with his plans to get closer to Raven so he could get answers that he hadn't been paying attention and had bumped into Heather Craft in the grocery store aisle.

Heather had been in the same class as Raven, Darby, and Carrie. For the life of him, he couldn't remember ever having seen the girl before he'd moved back to town after the fire. He did, however, remember her family.

He remembered the name of every single person who

had died ten years ago, including both of Raven's and Heather's parents. Since Raven didn't have any family left in town, she'd been shipped off to her grandmother in southern California, while Heather had an aunt whose home had survived just on the outskirts of town. The girl had quickly gained a reputation shortly after the fire as the town's biggest partier. Maybe that was why he couldn't remember her. He'd never really been in the party scene. Both Reggie and he had been into sports, any and all sports.

It had gotten him a scholarship to the University of California. Two years after heading to San Francisco, he'd watched the news in his dorm room about the fire ravaging his hometown. Moments later, he'd gotten the call from his mother that she and his grandmother were okay, but they were searching for Reggie in the midst of the evacuation.

He'd spent the next hours calling and recalling his brother's cell phone as he headed north to help.

They'd been together when they'd gotten the news, days later, that Reggie had been found. It had been the worst day of his life, one that had sparked so many questions. Over the years, his list had just grown.

"Evening, Heather," he said as he tried to avoid tipping her over. He wished he had been on the lookout better. The woman had several bottles of wine in her cart and nothing else.

"Cade Stone." Her eyes ran up and down him. "Fancy running into you here," she practically purred.

Heather was easily one of the better-looking single women in town. She was tall, slender and fit, had long dark caramel-colored hair, and always wore very stylish clothes. Still, there was something about Heather that had made him keep his distance over the years. Especially after she'd made it clear that she was extremely interested in him a few months ago.

Heather was very persistent and often showed up at his work with homemade meals for his crew, a nice gesture that had gained her a lot of attention from the other single men on his squad.

He tried to steer clear of her anytime she showed up or if he bumped into her in town. Now, however, he was stuck and figured he would stop and chat with her. Maybe he could see if Heather knew anything about Raven that might be useful.

"I heard you've been hired on at the resort." He shifted his basket slightly so he could move a little closer to her. Instantly, he saw desire flash in the woman's eyes.

"Yes." She smiled. "I'll be bartending there on the weekends." She leaned into his chest slightly, lifting her hand to his shoulder. "You should swing by sometime and..."—her eyes ran up his chest to his mouth— "come check me out."

"I might just do that. So, you must have been close to Raven?" he asked.

Heather's eyes narrowed slightly, betraying her true feelings. He wondered if Heather blamed Raven for her parents' deaths just like so many others in town.

"Not really. We were in the same class, but..." She shrugged. "That's about it. I don't think Raven knew that I existed back in school."

"Oh?" He frowned slightly. "I thought you, Reggie, and Raven hung around in the same circles?"

Heather laughed, the sound almost a cackle. "No, hardly. Reggie was... untouchable, and Raven, well, she was..." She shook her head. "No, we didn't run in the same circles."

"Yet she hired you," he pointed out.

"She didn't, personally. One of the resort's two managers, Rachelle Braun, hired me. Rachelle was a friend of my mother's," she added with a slight sigh.

"Well, at least it's nice that Raven is hiring so many locals." He changed tactics.

"Hardly. Who else is she supposed to hire?" Heather giggled again. "I mean"—she motioned to the town—"there's barely anyone left, and it's been ten years." He saw something close to anger cross her eyes.

It was obvious how Heather felt towards Raven. But since the girl had been bouncing between jobs all over town, he figured she needed the work just like everyone else in town.

"You know, rumors have it that Raven's come into a great deal of money," Heather added.

"Oh?" He tried not to recoil when her hand moved to his chest. The last thing he wanted to do was lead the girl on.

"Yes." She pretended to straighten his collar as she shifted her hips closer to his. "It would be a shame if she spent it all on the resort only to have it fail."

He opened his mouth to respond, but then Heather's eyes moved past him, and such a look of pleasure crossed her face that he glanced over to see who had caused it.

He felt his entire body go on guard when he noticed Raven standing a few feet away, assessing the pair of them. Each time he saw her, his body reacted the same way, telling him it was past time to find someone to help him release his pent-up sexual frustration.

It was then that he realized that Heather had practically wrapped herself around him. And they were standing in the middle of an aisle in a very public place.

Reaching up, he dislodged Heather and took a step

back. "I'd better get back to shopping," he said, stepping away.

"Don't forget to come see me later," Heather called after him as he continued down the aisle.

He noticed Heather making her way to the checkout counter as he headed towards the freezer section in the back.

He hadn't planned on talking with Raven, since he figured he'd see her in the morning, but when he was reaching for some chicken, he heard her directly behind him.

"You don't want that kind," she said easily.

He glanced over at her in question. "Oh? Why not?"

"There was a report on the news about a possible *E. coli* outbreak. It shouldn't be on the shelves." She glanced around as if looking for someone who worked there.

"Thanks." He set the container back and put a different brand in his basket. "I wouldn't think someone as busy as you would have time to watch much news." He watched her grab a container of some cold cuts.

He didn't normally spy on what women bought at the store, but the difference between Heather's and Raven's carts was striking. Raven had some feminine products, shampoo bottles, a loaf of healthy grain bread, some sliced cheese, fruit, and spicy mustard.

"Not a big cook?" he asked, motioning to her cart.

She glanced at his basket, and he looked down at the items he'd already gotten. Besides the chicken, he had a few steaks, some raw veggies he planned to grill up, a couple bags of potato chips, a large bag of dog food, and toilet paper, since Blue had decided to chew on his last roll that morning.

"I don't have a kitchen in my rooms," she said easily. "Having a dinner party?"

"My gran is coming over," he answered. "She likes red meat."

Raven nodded slightly. "Oh? I would have thought that you and Heather..." She glanced to where the woman had left out the front door.

His eyebrows shot up and then he laughed. Just the thought of him and Heather together, in that capacity... it was beyond humorous.

CHAPTER FIVE

FIRE IN THE HEART SENDS SMOKE INTO THE
HEAD.

Raven didn't know what had caused her to say what she'd just said to Cade.

When she'd turned the aisle in the grocery store and had seen Heather wrapped around Cade, she'd been... jealous.

Maybe it was her and Heather's past rearing its evil head. Maybe it was the fact that she still, after all these years, couldn't stand the other woman.

Whatever the reason, she'd tried not to think about it, until she'd bumped into Cade and then the words had just flown out. She regretted them the instant they left her lips, and she felt her face heat. Then he started laughing at her, and her temper reared its head.

After all, she'd been gone for ten years. She had no idea about any of the dynamics in the town. After what she'd witnessed earlier, it seemed clear that he and Heather were... involved.

"After the little display earlier, I assumed." She narrowed her eyes.

He sobered and shrugged. "Heather has had a thing."

He rolled his eyes slightly. "She's been..." He shook his head. "I've been avoiding her for a while now."

"Oh?" She felt herself settle down again. "I guess not much has changed in that arena." She stepped past him to continue her shopping. She hadn't expected him to fall in step with her.

"How about you?" he asked. She stopped and glanced at him.

"Me?"

"I haven't heard about anyone following you into Cannon Falls. Did you leave a trail of broken hearts in San Diego?" he asked casually.

How had they gotten on this topic? Oh, right, she'd started it.

"No," she answered. "No trail of broken hearts that I'm aware of." She put a bag of her favorite chocolates in her cart. Even though her rooms didn't have a kitchen, she figured she could keep some of the basics so she wouldn't have to run down to the kitchens all the time.

The small fridge was plenty large enough to hold a couple days' worth of meals, and she was tired of using the tiny bottles of shampoo and conditioner each day.

"My gran was excited to hear that you were back in town. She wouldn't mind a visit from you." He stopped her by putting a hand on her arm. "You should come over tonight. She'd love to catch up with you."

Raven's first instinct was to decline. But Janice Williams had been one of Raven's favorite teachers. The woman had been a close friend to not only her grandmother, but her mother as well.

She hadn't had a chance to talk to the woman since coming back in town. It had been on her to-do list. She had something special that she was supposed to give her from her own grandmother.

Thinking about it, she figured that having Cade there as a buffer might make the difficult situation a whole lot easier.

"I'd like that," she finally said.

"Great." He pulled out his phone and held it up. "Put in your number. I'll text you the details."

Here, she hesitated. She hadn't given anyone in town her private number except for Carrie and Darby.

Shortly after the fire, someone in town had leaked her number, and she'd spent the next year getting hate calls at all hours of the day. She understood that there were still a lot of people in town that blamed her and wanted her gone.

"I won't share your number with anyone," Cade finally said softly, "if that is what you're worried about."

Straightening her shoulders, she took his phone and added in her contact information.

"Great," he said, tucking his phone back in his pocket. "I'll text you the details later."

"Should I bring anything?" she asked.

"My grandmother loves red wine," he answered easily as he turned to head the other direction. "Any red wine," he called over his shoulder.

As she finished up her shopping, she added a bottle of her favorite red wine to the mix. She saw Cade leave a few minutes before she made her way up to the checkout.

There were two clerks working the front. She waited in line to be checked out, and just as she started unloading her items, the middle-aged woman took one look at her, narrowed her eyes and gave her a terrible look, then set a closed sign on the counter and walked away without a word.

Raven held in her anger and moved over to wait in the next line. When the other woman did the same thing,

Raven felt her temper boil. It was obvious they were doing this on purpose. She didn't know what she'd done to either of the women, but after the last week she'd had, she knew there were still some in town that didn't want her around. Since she was now the only person waiting to be checked out, she knew their actions were directly aimed at her.

"I'll just leave my money here then." She took some cash out of her purse and laid it on the counter.

"Can I help you?" a man said, getting her attention.

She glanced over to see a man walking towards her from the manager's office.

"Yes, I'd like to check out." She motioned to her items.

The man glanced around and frowned before heading over to start checking her out.

"I'm sorry about this," he said easily.

"Don't be." She sighed as she read his nametag. "Peter." Then she frowned. "Peter Eggert?" she asked, a little surprised.

"Yes." The man frowned at her. "And you are?"

"Raven, Raven Brooks. I used to babysit you when you were..." She held up her hand to her hip. "This high." She smiled.

"Raven?" He shook his head. "Of course. I'd heard you were back in town. How are you?" he asked as he continued to work to check her out.

She didn't want to mention the two women. Whatever their beef with her was, she wasn't going to be responsible for getting them fired. So, when Peter apologized that someone hadn't been there to help her, she shrugged and told him it was no problem.

The fact was, she'd received the cold shoulder from so many in town. It was one of the reasons she'd had Rachelle doing all the hiring. It was the woman's job anyway, and so far, it appeared that Rachelle was enthusiastic about the changes Raven was making around the resort.

She'd spent an entire day going over all of the employee's files and had to admit that Rachelle was the most qualified. There was no doubt that the woman had been the only one working hard in the past few years.

From what Raven could tell, her uncle hadn't really done much.

After her meeting with Joe Ramsey, she trusted that the man would give her full updates on how the finances looked for the resort.

She knew that the business had been basically cut in half as far as the books went.

The hotel ran year-round and, during ski season, the lifts, rentals, and classes picked up. A glance at the numbers in the outdated system showed a serious decline in the past five years.

She didn't know how her uncle was making it work—paying the bills, employees, and still maintaining his family's lives.

One thing that hadn't wavered in the last ten years had been the checks she'd received every single month. Checks she had placed in a savings account and thankfully had never touched.

Carrying her groceries inside, she passed Cemal in the lobby and waved to the girl. She'd noticed such a change in her. The day after Raven had arrived, Cemal had changed the way she'd dressed and had almost bloomed overnight. It was as if being seen for who she was had unlocked a door.

Raven was happy when Cemal had approached her and asked if it was okay for her to pick her own outfits, instead of wearing the drab uniform her uncle had requested.

Raven had agreed to it since it would be a few days

before the new uniforms could arrive. After seeing how stylish the woman was, Raven had let her know that, during off-season, she could continue wearing what she felt comfortable in, just as long as it maintained the quality of what she'd been wearing in the past few days.

She was really starting to like Cemal. The young girl, fresh from high school, seemed eager and excited about the changes as well.

Two employees, at least, on her side. She'd have to drag the rest of them along for the ride, it seemed. Most were courteous, but some were downright rude to her.

She wondered if her aunt and uncle had something to do with the backlash she was getting every time she tried to make a change.

Thankfully, she'd hired a few of the companies in town, which all seemed eager for the work.

She'd been informed that the entire sprinkler system had been disabled years back. It had taken a few thousand dollars to repair the pump and all the underground lines.

Now that it was back up and running, the grass and flowers around the courtyard were springing back to life.

The ski lift maintenance company was having to over-haul two of the lifts completely. The other three just needed the basics. She was assured that, by the first snowfall, all five lifts would be fully operational.

Once the grounds around the resort were done, the crew would hit the slopes to clear downed trees, fallen rocks, and any other obstacles from the runs.

The biggest snafus so far had involved her family. Well, everyone except for Cal, who had made himself scarce after he'd found her in the kitchen that first day.

Every night since her return, she'd found her aunt at the bar that sat off to the side of the lobby. Since the local bar in town was extremely limited and didn't cater to... a certain class, most couples or people on dates drove up to the resort and enjoyed dining and drinks in the formal dining room and bar area.

It was somewhat of a surprise to see so many people there the first night she'd walked down to look for some dinner. She'd watched people come and go and knew she'd have to reevaluate her plans for the dining and bar.

She'd been expecting to just do a quick overhaul of both areas, but after seeing how things had gone over the past week, she was talking to the local contractor she'd hired about expanding the dining hall and bar.

Currently, the dining area was separate from the bar and lobby. She planned on keeping the formal part separate by adding a more casual dining area for breakfast and lunch between the two areas. The area would surround the fountain and have a more casual atmosphere.

The way she figured it, they could easily take half of the lobby and still have enough room, at least the space around the fountain. They could add tables and chairs for extra seating. With a few minor changes, and some planters with seasonal flowers in them to separate the two areas, guests could choose a more formal atmosphere or a casual one.

Expanding the bar would be a little more challenging.

David Green, the contractor, brother to her landscape contractor, Jake Green, had moved back into town after the fire ten years ago for the work. He had suggested tearing out the back wall behind the bar. He would reclaim the storage room behind the back mirrored wall, which only held a few extra chairs and tables, turning it into a smaller storage area. There were some narrow stairs that led down to another cold storage area where most of the wine and liquor was currently stored. Those areas would be updated in phase two or three.

David suggested getting rid of the mirrors and the dark wood paneling, modernizing the entire space and giving it a friendlier feeling.

The change would make the bar a large U shape and easily double the seating around it.

He was drawing up a few options for her and told her he would email some concepts to her by the following week. She was anxious and excited about the update.

She'd talked to him about replacing the flooring in the lobby area as well. If it was within her budget, she wanted to replace all the flooring in the rooms as well.

Determining what needed to be done in the rooms was going to take a lot longer than the rest had. She was planning on going room by room, as soon as she had everything else handled.

She had scheduled the fire inspection for the following day and had planned for updates in her budget. She wasn't working with an unlimited amount, but she had enough to do what was absolutely required. Some more elaborate changes might have to wait until after the grand reopening she was planning this fall. For now, she wanted to give the place a complete overhaul, which meant new mattresses, new comforters, new furniture, and new window coverings. On the outside, the old green was going to be replaced with a more natural color that would work with the wood siding. Some of the windows and doors needed replacing and had been ordered, and the indoor and outdoor pools, which she had found out had been shut down years ago, were being repaired and filled.

Her grandmother had always instructed that, whatever she chose to do in life, she do it to the fullest. And she was all in. She would spend every last dime she had to make the resort a success. Even if she had to trample the rest of her family to do so. This was hers. Her parents had given up so much to build a legacy for her, and she'd sat back and let her uncle and aunt ruin it in the past ten years. All because she'd been weak.

Well, she was no longer going to let anyone tell her what to do or, more importantly, what she couldn't or shouldn't do.

She was thankful for the friends and comrades she had. Carrie and Darby had come to visit her the weekend after she'd arrived for a much-needed girls' night in.

She couldn't remember the last time she'd laughed or enjoyed herself that much. It had been like it had been in the past. Her two friends seemed to not have changed at all.

She'd been a little shocked when Carrie had looked at her over an almost empty glass of wine and had shaken her head.

"You've changed so much," she'd said.

"How so?" she'd asked.

"Everything about you. I mean, you're still knock-out gorgeous. I mean, that hair." Carrie had sighed. "By the way, you're still the only natural redhead in town."

Raven had laughed and sipped some more wine.

"And you're still the only black woman in town," Darby had pointed out to Carrie.

"True." She'd held up her glass. "This town isn't big enough to handle two gorgeous redheads and two strong black women."

"Or two Darbys," Raven had added with a chuckle.

"I'll drink to that," Darby had cheered.

She had hoped to find out more about what Carrie had meant, but then they had started talking about men. She'd tried to ask about Cade, to see if he was seeing anyone or just to find out how long he'd been back in town, but Carrie and Darby talked about a guy named Andre Walker all night. Apparently, he was the town's hottest catch.

Now, after accepting Cade's dinner invitation, she hoped that she'd at least gotten a little more about Cade out of her friends. She felt like she was walking into dinner completely blind.

The only thing she had learned over the past week was that he had an ex-girlfriend, Julia, who worked at Darby's diner.

Raven couldn't remember if she'd seen the woman last week when she'd been there, but she made a point to look for her the next time she went in.

Shifting the bottle of wine under her arm, she reached up and knocked on Cade's door. The home, a newer place that sat on the outskirts of town, was a two-story contemporary wood-sided home with a massive wraparound deck.

The home was tucked deep into the property with a detached garage and what appeared to be a work shed off to the side.

When the door opened, she had to shuffle the wine as his grandmother, Jan, wrapped her arms around her.

"Oh my god, it's so good to see you again," Jan said, holding onto her.

Janice Williams hadn't changed much over the years. The woman still had her silver hair cut in a straight bobbed style. She was wearing a stylish rust-orange jacket with a grey shirt underneath paired with slim-legged jeans.

Raven instantly felt overdressed in a lacey white top with a dark purple skirt and matching half boots.

"Come on in," Janice said, pulling her inside.

Blue was there to greet her just inside the door.

Raven bent down and gave the old dog some attention before following Janice into the house.

The inside was just as glorious as the outside. The living room and kitchen were one massive room. A two-story stone fireplace sat within a wall of arched windows.

She took a quick moment to take in the warm colors, masculine furniture, and tidiness of the home and was impressed with the space.

"When Cade stopped by last week and told me you were back in town, I was so happy and tried to reach out to your gran," Janice said as she took the wine bottle from Raven.

She swallowed. "You didn't hear?" Raven's heart sank. "My gran passed away last month."

"Oh no." Jan sank down on a barstool and laid her hand over her heart. "I'm so sorry, child."

Just then, the sliding door on the back of the home opened, and Cade walked in holding a plate filled with grilled steaks.

He was wearing a tight black T-shirt and worn jeans, and she saw the anger wash over him when he took in the scene of his grandmother crying and Raven standing over her. She felt her entire body go on high alert.

"What's happened?" He set the plate down and rushed over to his grandmother.

"Ellen." Jan shook her head and wiped at her eyes. "Raven, I'm so sorry for your loss." She pushed up and wrapped her arms around her again.

Raven had believed she'd spent all of her tears for her grandmother. Yet now, with her grandmothers' best friend holding tight to her, her eyes stung, and she shut them before she lost full control.

"Let me open this bottle, then you can tell me how she

went and catch me up on everything you've been doing since I last saw you." Jan dropped her arms and walked behind the counter to open the wine.

"I'm so sorry," Cade said softly. He looked over at his grandmother. "We hadn't heard."

She shrugged. "As far as I know, only family knew," she replied quickly, feeling a little uncomfortable suddenly.

"Here, Gran." He walked over and finished opening the wine bottle for his grandmother. "I've got this. Why don't the two of you head outside on the deck and enjoy the warmth before the sun goes down? I'll bring the wine out for you."

His grandmother lifted her hand to his face and smiled up at him. "Thank you, dear."

Then she took Raven's hand and pulled her outside onto a massive deck that hung over a pristine backyard with a small brook running through it.

Raven couldn't imagine a more beautiful spot to live, or to tell her grandmother's best friend everything she'd lived through in the past ten years.

Even if Cade was tagging along for the ride.

CHAPTER SIX

He knew better than to jump to conclusions. But when he'd stepped inside and had seen his grandmother crying with Raven standing over her, looking guilty, he'd done just that.

Now, after hearing that she'd just informed his grandmother of her grandmother's passing, he wanted to give the two of them some time to catch up before starting the night.

After opening the wine and dropping it and two glasses off outside, he returned inside to finish dinner prep.

He wasn't the best chef, but he did know how to make the basics. Especially anything that went along with steak.

He'd baked some potatoes and loaded them on a platter along with fixings, including bacon strips, sour cheese, cheese, and onions. Then he pulled the grilled veggies off the grill. Since the sun had gone down and the summer night had turned a little chilly, he set up the table inside. He stepped outside and let Raven and his gran know that dinner was ready.

Both of them looked more relaxed and happier than they had before, which put him more at ease as well.

"Did you two have a good time catching up?" he asked as he pulled out the chair for his grandmother.

"Yes." She touched his arm as she sat. "Thank you for inviting Raven tonight. It's just what I needed," his gran said. "I think it's what we both needed." She glanced over at Raven. The smile Raven gave her in response had him tensing again.

Damn, why did she have to look so incredibly hot tonight? And what was with that skintight skirt? Those legs. Had he ever seen sexier legs before? Not in years, he determined as he ate while half listening to the conversation.

She'd straightened her red locks and had on a lot more eye makeup than when he'd seen her in the store. The darkness around them somehow made her crystal eyes more haunting.

He couldn't figure out why he was being pulled closer to her the entire evening. He started relaxing and forgetting his original mission. At one point, he even started daydreaming about what she would taste like. What her body would feel like up against his.

"Well." His grandmother stood up suddenly, pulling him out of the fantasy. "I think it's about time I head home." She touched his shoulder. "I'll leave you two young kids to enjoy the pie I made. You should take it out on the deck and light a fire in that new firepit you got last week," his grandmother suggested.

He stood up suddenly, "Gran, I'll—"

She nudged him. "Do as your told." She narrowed her eyes at him. She walked over and hugged Raven. "Enjoy the rest of your evening. Thank you for letting me in," she said softly.

Raven kissed his grandmother's cheek. "Thank you for listening."

"Night," his gran said. She walked to the door, pulled on her coat, and left.

"You don't have to stay," he said, turning to Raven. Her eyebrows shot up and an almost offended look crossed her eyes. "I mean, if you don't want to," he added quickly.

"I could eat pie," she said after a moment.

"Pie it is." He nodded, then started taking the plates from the table.

She helped him by grabbing the silverware and glasses.

"Want more wine with the pie?" he asked her.

"Do you have coffee?" she asked, setting down the wine glasses by the sink.

"I do. I'll deal with the dishes later." The pie was warming in his oven, where his gran had placed it after she'd arrived earlier. He opened the cabinet that held his dishes and pulled out two small plates and mugs.

"Pick your poison." He motioned to his single serve coffee maker and the tray of coffee selections right next to it.

"Organized, aren't you?" She glanced at him and then scanned through the coffee selection.

He thought about it and realized that over the past eight years he'd lived there, he *had* become organized. He had never really been a tidy sort of person. But after a while, he'd just fallen into that pattern.

"It helps, especially when you get the wrath of your grandmother and mother if you aren't," he joked.

"What kind of pie is it?" she asked him, glancing over her shoulder.

He walked over to the stove and glanced inside. "Blackberry," he answered with a smile. It was his favorite flavor of pie, and his gran made it for him all of the time.

She made some French vanilla coffee, and he decided to

have some of the same. She stood by while he made his own cup.

"Cream?" he asked, walking to the fridge.

"If you have it." She waited and poured some cream into her mug.

When he started to pull the pie out of the oven and cut slices, she jumped in.

"Why don't you head out, start that fire? I can cut us some slices and bring them out." She motioned towards the back door.

"There's a tray there." He nodded to the cabinet, then pulled on a jacket that hung by the back door and disappeared with Blue right on his heels.

He didn't feel weird leaving her in his house alone. He would think about it later, since the last time he'd had a woman in his home was Julia almost a year ago.

Even then, he and Julia had only dated for a few short months. When she'd grown too clingy, he'd backed off. Completely.

The more he'd gotten to know Julia, the more he'd realized they had nothing in common. She'd been a nice package, but after a few weeks, he'd started to see bits of her real self. The woman was as ugly as it came. She was not only privileged, but she was also spoiled.

On their one-month anniversary, she'd gotten upset that he hadn't remembered and bought her something to mark the date.

He normally would have, but he'd been busy that week dealing with the controlled burns. He'd been tired and overworked and it had been the last thing on his mind. She hadn't let him forget it and for the following anniversary, he'd taken her out for a nice dinner and had brought her flowers.

Apparently, it hadn't been good enough and she'd caused such a stink that they had parted. Shortly after that, she'd hinted that she'd like to get back together with him, but after seeing her true self, he'd stepped away for good.

"Oh, it's still nice out," Raven said, stepping outside with the tray in hand.

He stood up and took it from her, then set it down on the small end table.

"Yeah, we didn't really need the fire, but it's nice still." He motioned for her to sit, then handed her a plate and her coffee before sitting beside her with his own plate.

"You have a very nice place," she said. She took a bite of the pie. "Oh my god. This is amazing." She waved her fork.

"Yes, on both counts. I purchased the lot and built the home after finishing the rebuild on my mother's home," he said easily. When she remained silent, he glanced over at her. It hadn't even occurred to him that she would feel uncomfortable talking about rebuilding after the fire. "Does it bother you?" he asked, turning slightly towards her.

"What?" She shook her head and took another bite of the pie.

"Talking about the fire?" he asked, deciding to be open with her. After all, if he wanted to get answers from her, he couldn't continue to hide the subject.

"No." She shook her head. "Not really. It's just... I've been gone for so long and everything is grown up around here again." She gazed past the fire into the darkness of his yard.

"It's taken ten years. When I first purchased this place, there wasn't a tree in sight. The brook"—he motioned to where the stream ran through his yard— "was nothing but ash and sludge. Whenever it rained, it flooded the backyard. I replanted everything."

"You did a great job. Earlier, in the sunlight, it looked wonderful." She set her empty plate aside. He finished his and did the same.

"Why come back to Cannon Falls?" he asked suddenly.

She looked at him and sighed. "I thought I could make a difference. Build up the business to its former glory. To what it had been when my parents had started it."

"Is that all?" he asked.

She tilted her head and thought about it. "I found out that my grandmother had been sending money to my uncle the past few years." She set her coffee mug down and folded her hands together. "My father had left him in charge until I decided to take over. If he was borrowing money from my grandmother, that meant the resort was in trouble."

"You didn't know?" he asked.

She shook her head. "I didn't know anything that had gone on in town after..." She took another deep breath. "My grandmother decided to keep me in the dark. She thought it would be best for me."

He wanted to ask more about why her grandmother would want to protect her but decided it was far too soon. He didn't want to spook her away just yet.

"What about you?" She turned slightly. "You left college to become fire marshal?"

"I did." He nodded. "After seeing what the fire had done to the families around here, to the livelihoods of everyone, I couldn't go back to school and hide. Besides, I had to help my mother rebuild. To be here when Reggie couldn't be."

"She decided to stay." It wasn't a question really.

"This is the only place she's ever lived. She loves it here. Her house is in the same spot, almost the same floorplan, with a few upgrades." He smiled. "My mother had always wanted more storage and a fireplace." He shook his head.

"Still, I know what it's like to lose everything," she said softly. He glanced over at her and nodded.

"It was hard on her, but things were easily replaced."

"Reggie," she said under her breath. "My parents." She shook her head and her eyes scanned the darkness beyond the fire.

"Family can never be replaced," he agreed.

"My counselor would agree," she said with a sigh.

He leaned forward a little. "Counselor?"

Her eyes snapped to him and then she stood up and walked to stand by the fire. She reached her hands out for the warmth.

"Yes, my gran thought it would help me cope with the loss."

Standing, he moved next to her. There hadn't been any time for him or his mother to seek counseling after Reggie's loss. There'd been too much work to do. Sean and his grandmother had been there. They'd had love and family, which had helped heal them.

Also, in the months after his family had lost everything, he'd worked through his own anger and pain by rebuilding and helping others to rebuild. There had been days he'd gone without eating, with little sleep, just to keep his mind focused away from the fact that Reggie wouldn't be there to help out. Wouldn't be there to celebrate the birthdays, the holidays.

He'd played over just how he would deal with Raven Brooks once he finally got a moment alone with her. He'd never, in all the past years, thought about what Raven had gone through or the pain that she'd dealt with herself. The bitterness he'd felt for her had bubbled and boiled until it had built up to almost a full hate. But when he'd overheard her and her uncle fighting and had believed the man had hurt her, the first thing through his mind had been to defend her.

He wasn't so arrogant of a man to think that he couldn't change his mind.

She threw him completely off balance and that only made him more curious about her. Not only had he instantly been attracted to her, but he'd also actually felt guilty for believing the rumors that she could have purposely cause so much pain to others.

Even though she'd only been back in Cannon Falls for a week, he felt like he could see through her protective walls enough to tell what kind of person she was.

From the sounds of things, she wasn't planning on leaving town. So he guessed that he had plenty of time to get the answers he wanted.

Her eyes turned to the fire and her shoulders sagged slightly.

"Your grandmother told me how difficult it was on the people around here to recover. How many just packed up, took their insurance money, and left, while others like you and your family rebuilt. I wish I could have stuck around to help, but..." She shook her head slightly.

"Everyone blamed you," he jumped in, not sure why he wanted to see her reaction. What would she do? Get angry? Cry? Whatever her response, he figured it would give him a little more insight into who Raven Brooks was.

As he watched, she transformed herself. Her shoulders straightened and she stood up a little taller.

"Yes, I supposed some still do," she said quietly. "A lot of people in town have shown me just how they feel since I've returned. Some would rather let their families and businesses go bankrupt than to associate with me. I'm having to ship materials from Redding since Phil down at the hardware store won't supply my contractor with anything now that he's found out who he is working for." She closed her eyes and wrapped her arms around herself. "I've had to pay David Green extra for the trouble just so I wouldn't lose him."

"I could have a talk..." he started, but when her eyes flew open and she gave him a hard look, he sighed. "If you need any help there..."

"Thanks," she said after a moment. "But I've handled it."

"Independent, aren't you," he said with a smile, earning one in return from her. "People will get used to you being around. Once they see the good that you're doing. How what you're doing will benefit them and theirs. Something tells me that this next season, we're going to see a huge influx of visitors spending their money in Cannon Creek. The blame game can grow old." He knew that himself. After the first few years, the red-hazed anger he'd felt had dulled.

"My counselor claims that in order to see other's pain, you have to work through your own first. And you have to realize that the loss was out of your control," she said with a sigh.

"Was it?" he asked, watching her carefully, waiting for the anger.

Instead, she turned to him, and gave him a weak smile. "Thank you for dinner," she said suddenly and moved to walk past him.

"Hang on." He took her by the shoulders. Seeing the sorrow in her eyes almost undid him. Whatever he'd believed of her in the past, the woman standing in front of him could have no more caused so much pain as he could have. At least not on purpose. So, either she was an amazing actress, or he was totally off base about her. "I didn't mean to..." He shook his head. "There are so many questions I have. Not just about what happened, but about the time before. About Reggie. I'd left two years before... I wasn't around..."

She nodded. "I'm not prepared to answer them tonight. I'm tired. It's been a long week."

He nodded, seeing the weariness behind her eyes.

"I'll walk you out." He stopped her from turning around. "I hope that you understand that I'm not one of the people who will block you from your goals. The inspection tomorrow will be fair and just. I'm good at my job."

She smiled up at him. "After you rushed into my office, thinking you were rescuing me from my uncle, I never doubted it."

"I'll see you in the morning then," he said after they walked out front and stood by her car.

"Yes," she said then bent down and gave Blue some attention. "Does he always go to work with you?"

"He does when he's welcomed. Tomorrow he'll stay home or with the guys at the firehouse since your aunt has requested he stay outside," he answered.

"My aunt is no longer in charge." She looked up at him. Then she turned back to Blue. "You're welcome anytime you want." She leaned in and placed a kiss on his dog's nose. For a moment, a wave of jealousy for the attention flooded him. Then she was standing and reaching for her door handle. "Thanks again for the dinner."

"Any time," he said, holding her car door open for her. "I'm sure my gran will be stopping by your place soon to see all the changes you've made up there."

She smiled as she climbed behind the wheel. "She mentioned stopping by later this week."

He chuckled. "Night."

"Good night," she said before he shut the door.

He watched her taillights disappear down his drive, then looked down at Blue.

"Well? What do you think?" he asked.

Blue sat down and glanced towards the dark driveway and let out a happy bark.

"Yeah," he responded with a sigh. "She's not what I thought she would be either." His dog barked again and then groaned. "I like her too," he said, then he turned back to head inside.

As the taillights disappeared and the man and dog disappeared into the house, the red ambers of a cigarette were flung into the lush green grass. The monster screamed when the ambers were snubbed out easily, the moisture giving life to the surrounding foliage.

Soon. It could feel the power building. The demand for blood. The desire for it. Soon.

CHAPTER SEVEN

FIRE TAKES NO HOLIDAY

There were a few things that Raven was growing to hate. Her aunt and uncle were the top two items on that list.

Every turn she took, every decision she made, they were there undoing it or criticizing her. She was pretty sure they both had spies sneaking around the resort, watching and waiting to tattle on her.

She'd had more arguments with her uncle in the last week than she could ever remember having with her own parents.

It had continued even after she'd assured them that she wasn't going to turn them completely out, just as long as they continued to work around the resort. After all, she wasn't a complete villain.

She had, however, arranged for them to move into some of the lower rooms, but she hadn't worked up the courage to tell them about it yet.

She figured that after the lower rooms were updated, she'd convince them to move down a few floors since their rooms would need to be updated as well.

In the last week, she'd only had time to inspect about a tenth of the property herself. After walking through several rooms, she was convinced David Green understood what she wanted and was planning on leaving it up to him and his men to maintain the quality of the vision she had for each room.

When she got off the elevator and walked into the lobby the next morning, it was to the sounds of construction work. Saws buzzed and nail gun shots echoed in the three-story rotunda. To her, it was a wonderful sound that signaled progress.

She was excited to see the new wood slat ceiling for the bar area being installed. The workers had torn out the back wall the first day on the job. She'd been surprised at how quickly they'd gotten to work.

Here it was, four days later and so much had already been done. David had assured her that by the end of the following month, the bar, dining, and lobby areas would be completed, as long as all the new furniture she'd ordered arrived on time.

Then part of David's crew could move over to the larger ski resort area, where resort guests gathered their gear and rentals for the slopes, as well as the other public seasonal areas, such as the gift shops, a cafeteria, and the changing rooms. David assured her that the carpet replacement and painting in those areas could easily be done within days.

She hadn't wanted to go with square tile carpeting, but David had shown her a few images that she'd been impressed with, so she'd ordered the same style and hoped for the best. She figured if she didn't like it, she could replace it in a few years. After all, the high traffic areas required constant maintenance. The current carpet had been there when she'd last seen the place and there were holes and rough spots everywhere.

Once they finished on the main public areas, David and his crew would start the more extensive job of upgrading the private rooms.

The moment she stepped into her office, she held in a groan upon seeing her uncle sitting behind the desk.

"Morning." She made a point to set her things down and hint that her uncle was in her way.

Thankfully, she'd transferred all of the financial data from the desktop computer to her laptop. Joseph had set up some online accounting software and was in the process of converting all the old data to the new system, a system her aunt and uncle did not have access to. Neither did the old accountant, Morgan Roche.

Raven had yet to meet the woman, since apparently, she'd been in Paris all last week.

"Is there something I can help you with?" she finally asked when her uncle didn't move.

"I'm just going over the figures." He motioned to the screen. "I can't seem to find—"

"They aren't there. I'm no longer using that software."

"What?" He jerked around and looked up at her. "Morgan's going to be here any moment to go over everything."

She locked her purse in the bottom drawer of the desk and thought about having David change the lock on the office as well. After all, she'd informed both her uncle and her aunt that this was now her space. She'd given them smaller joint offices down the hallway next to Rachelle's and Eddie's offices. The larger office that had been her father's belonged to the owner. Not only because she wanted it, but because it had been her father's, and she had so many memories of spending time in there with her parents.

"I have left many messages for Morgan Roche informing her that her services are no longer needed. I've hired Joseph Ramsey back. He's taking care of everything now. You no longer need to worry about that part of the business anyway."

"What?" Her uncle stood up, and she realized just how much he towered over her.

Her father had been a tall man, and she had always enjoyed being close to him. Colin, however, used his height as a tool to intimidate her. Raven wasn't going to back down. If she did, he would continue to push her even further and further.

"You can't do that," her uncle said. "I've been running the finances of this place for ten years now. Morgan expects—"

"I don't care what Morgan expects," she interrupted. "She is no longer employed by this company. Now, if you don't mind, I have some work—"

Her uncle reached out and wrapped his hands around her arm, squeezing her tightly as his face grew red.

"I won't be strong-armed into anything," she warned. Her uncle shoved her a little.

"You bitch. You think you can come in here and ruin me?" he growled out, inches from her face. When he spoke, spit splattered over her face, and she tried to recoil.

"Let go of me." She tried to jerk her arm free.

Suddenly, the office door flew open, and she fell backwards as her uncle was shoved away from her. Her hip hit the side of her desk, and she instantly reached up and wiped the moisture from her face, wishing instantly for another shower.

Then she noticed Cade standing over her uncle and rushed forward. He must have pushed Colin away from her, since he was now sitting on the ground between her desk and the two worn leather chairs that faced it.

"Cade," she said, grabbing his arm.

"Get up, old man," Cade was saying. "Pick on someone your own size."

"I'm okay," she said to him, trying to pull him away.

"I'll sue you," her uncle spat out, his eyes wide and focused on her, and his face even more red than before.

"For?" She turned on him.

"Everything you have," he answered as he shifted to get up.

"You've had control of everything of mine for the past ten years, and you've let it rot away," she countered and stepped between Cade and her uncle, who was slowly getting off the ground.

"I believe your services are no longer needed here," she said. She had to stand her ground. She didn't even want to think of what her uncle might have done if Cade hadn't come along.

Colin's eyes narrowed at her. "The hell they aren't," he spat back. "You can't fire me."

"The hell I can't," she responded firmly. "You can either leave now without another word and with your severance package, or I can have you hauled off my property by the police with nothing." She crossed her arms over her chest, thankful for the feeling of Cade directly behind her.

Just then there was a knock on the office door. A petite woman with jet-black hair walked in. She was dressed in a cream-colored designer suit and expensive heels, and she carried a red Gucci bag the same shade as her lipstick. The woman's long fingernails were painted the same shade, making Raven realize that it had been too long since she'd even thought about painting her toes or heading in for a manicure.

"Am I early?" the woman asked with a slight French accent as she smiled brightly. The smile slipped slightly upon seeing Colin's face.

Raven guessed that this was Morgan Roche, the woman his uncle had been rumored to be having an affair with for the past few years.

Before her uncle could speak, Raven stepped forward.

"Miss Roche, I've left you several messages over the past week. I'm Raven Brooks." She made a point not to hold out her hand.

"Yes, I was in Paris." She waved her hand in the air as if excusing Raven and started to step past her.

"As I mentioned in my messages," Raven said, blocking the path to her office, "Cannon Falls Resort is no longer in need of your services."

"Who are you?" The woman's eyes narrowed, then she glanced over to Colin.

"I am the owner of this establishment," Raven clarified. "My uncle has been running the business in my absence."

"Oh?" Morgan's eyes moved to Colin. "I was unaware of this."

"I assumed, which is why I left several messages," Raven said again.

"As I said, I was in Paris." Morgan waved her hand again.

"The last I knew, cell service works in Paris," Raven countered. "Thank you for coming out today, but as I mentioned, your services are no longer required. Actually" —she turned back to her uncle— "you are both welcome to leave." She walked over and held the office door open for them. "We're done here."

As Morgan walked out, she had a few choice works in French, which Raven fully understood thanks to three years of French classes. Still, she was just thankful the woman was leaving.

Then she turned to her uncle and waited.

"I think the lady has asked you to leave," Cade said firmly.

Her uncle glared at him. "Stay out of this, Stone."

"I'm here on business," Cade shrugged. "The last I heard, you've been asked to leave by the owner of this establishment."

"I live here," Colin spat out.

"I'm willing to give you a week to find someplace else," Raven answered.

"You said we were welcomed here," Colin said.

"You were, until today. Roslyn, Cal, and Liza are still welcome. You wore out your welcome just now." She nodded back towards her desk, where he'd grabbed her.

"You haven't heard the last of me," Colin said, moving towards the door.

She stopped herself from flinching as he passed by her and, after he stepped out, she shut the door and leaned against it after flipping the lock.

"You okay?" Colin asked, directly behind her.

Straightening up, she put up her protective shields once more as she turned to him.

"I'm fine. Thank you."

"You don't have to do that," he said softly, his eyes scanning her.

"What?" She tried to hold it together, but her arm throbbed where her uncle had grabbed, which was making everything inside her throb with anger. Not all of it was aimed at Colin, since she'd allowed him to manipulate her.

"Put up the walls," Cade answered, moving a little closer to her. His eyes went to her exposed arm. "He bruised you." He moved closer to her, then surprised her by running the back of his finger over the spot gently. "Your skin is so pale, so..." His eyes moved up to hers. "Flawless."

The breath in her lungs practically burst from her in short bursts as she felt her heart kick. Going from anger and hurt to lust so quickly had her head spinning. Even the room seemed to spin around them as she looked into Cade's eyes.

Her mind wandered to what it would feel like to have him lean in and place those sexy lips of his over hers. How would it feel having strong arms wrap around her? Hold her? How long had it been since she'd allowed herself a moment of pleasure?

Reggie. She closed her eyes on the pain.

"Does he do that often?" Cade asked, his voice low and soothing.

"No," she answered truthfully, not opening her eyes. "Normally he just yells at me."

She felt his entire body tense next to hers. The air almost crackled with his anger. Opening her eyes, she could instantly tell that he was trying to get his temper under control.

Seeing it had an awakening effect on her. Blinking a few times, she shook the lustful thoughts she'd just had about him away and refocused.

Then she noticed for the first time that he was in a dark blue official-looking fire marshal outfit. Her heart skipped another beat seeing just how sexy the man was in uniform.

"I think we'd better get started on our work," she said,

taking a step away from him. Instantly, she felt more leveled. More in control.

She noticed that it took him a moment, but after a few deep breaths, he nodded.

"We'll start in the kitchens," he said.

As they made their way to the back of the building towards the kitchen, she glanced behind him.

"No Blue today?" she asked.

"No, he's keeping Gran company. She's working in her garden today, and he likes hanging out and helping her dig." He smiled. "Course, I think he just ends up digging holes everywhere and chasing gophers before sleeping the rest of the day away."

She chuckled as she imagined the old dog enjoying himself.

They stepped into the kitchen. Normally, during season, there'd be a large crew of employees there, handling the morning rush. Now, there was only one cook and two other staff slowly moving around the space. "So, what exactly are you inspecting?"

"The older buildings have an outdated system that needs to be checked more often. I've been coming by every six months to make sure it's still working. The main system room is back here." He headed towards a closet near the back of the kitchen and she followed.

For the next hour or so, she followed him around to various places and rooms that she hadn't known existed. When she was a child, she'd only been allowed in several areas. Then, when she was a teen, she'd been too consumed with her own problems to care.

It was one of the reasons she hadn't really known how much her parents had done to keep the resort functioning. The first years of college, she'd avoided business classes and had stuck with the basics. Then her counselor had suggested she take at least one to see if she might be interested in someday returning to Cannon Falls and taking over her parents' business.

At first, she'd shied away from the idea, but then she'd started the class and had enjoyed it. After a few more classes, she realized she had an aptitude for business. She enjoyed the classes more than anything else she'd tried.

They made their way back to her office, and when she opened the door, she noticed Liza standing by her desk. When Liza noticed her, she stormed over to her.

"Is it true that you've kicked us out?" Liza asked, just before Cade stepped into the office behind Raven.

Her cousin's entire demeanor changed in a heartbeat.

"Cade?" Liza blinked a few times, then she smiled brightly. "What are you doing here?"

Raven watched as Liza arched slightly so that the impressive boobs that she'd bought shortly after her eighteenth birthday stuck out further.

Cade's smile looked a little strained, but he seemed to pour on the charm just to be friendly.

"Fire inspection," he responded quickly as Raven moved to sit behind her desk.

Since she'd known Cade had been coming that day, she'd decided on upping her game with her outfit for the day. The dress slacks and blouse were comfortable enough, but the low heels were fairly new and not yet broken in all the way.

Sitting down, she motioned for her cousin to sit down.

Cade nodded towards the door. "I'll go check the last closet we talked about and then stop by before I head out."

"Thanks," she said and waited until he shut the door behind him before asking Liza once again to sit down.

"No, I'm not going to calmly sit down. Not when you've just taken everything away from us." Her cousin crossed her arms and glared at her.

"Liza, I'm not forcing you, your mother, or Cal out. Just your father," she clarified.

"Why?" Liza shook her head, confusion crossing her face. Even though it felt wonderful to be off her feet, she stood up, walked over to her cousin and held out her arm. The slight red marks had turned into full-on purple and blue bruises by now.

Liza's eyes narrowed. "He did that to you?" she asked, softly.

"If Cade hadn't stepped in..." She took a deep breath. "Has your father ever hurt you before?" she asked her cousin, worried.

"No." Liza took a step back as she shook her head vigorously. "Never."

"Has he ever hurt your mother?"

"No!" Liza gripped her face as her eyes filled. "My god. Raven, what's come over him? He's upstairs right now, forcing us all to pack up." Her eyes moved to the ceiling, as if she could see up to her rooms.

Raven laid a hand on her cousin's arm. "As I said, the rest of you are welcome to stay."

"Are you going to press charges?" Liza asked suddenly.

Raven had thought about it and, after talking with Cade, had decided that if her uncle steered clear of her, she would allow him to leave with just the warning.

"No, just as long as he leaves. He's not welcome back here. I can tolerate a lot of things, but physical violence isn't one of them."

"Agreed," Liza said softly. "I'll—" She took a step towards the door. "I'll go tell the rest of the family."

"They're welcome to stay, however." She moved closer to Liza. "In a few weeks, I'll need to move the three of you to lower rooms when the crew begins updating all the suites."

Liza's eyes narrowed. "Lower rooms?"

Here it was, Raven thought, here is where her cousin would fight her.

"I'm having all of the upper suites remodeled last. Once the construction crews need to get into the upper rooms, you'll need to move. We can't afford not to have those bigger rooms for some of our more high-dollar guests."

Her cousin gave her a look that hinted at what she thought of her after this news before turning around and storming out of the room without another word.

Raven sank back into her new office chair. She closed her eyes and leaned her head against the cool wood desk.

"Why must I have to keep disappointing people?" she asked the empty room.

Shaking off the dark mood, she jumped back into work, knowing she had to make a few phone calls before Cade returned after finishing with his inspection.

It hadn't been a hardship watching the man work. The inspection wasn't a particularly physically challenging job, but there were aspects of it that had her enjoying the view all the same. Especially when he'd had to remove his jacket and stand up on a ladder to inspect a few of the sprinklers. Just seeing his long, lean frame extend fully had her realizing the differences between Cade and what she remembered of Reggie. She had no other comparisons in her repertoire.

It hadn't been possible for her to start another relationship after what had happened with Reggie. She didn't trust herself or others with her heart. Other than her grand-mother, of course.

When a knock sounded at her door, she glanced up to see Cade leaning against the doorjamb.

"Busy?" he asked easily.

Removing the computer glasses she wore to ward off eye strain at the end of the day, she motioned for him to come in.

He stepped inside, shutting the door behind him.

"Bad news?" she asked, feeling her heart jump in her chest. She didn't know if it was from the prospect of his inspection highlighting more problems that would cost her a lot of money or just the way he moved that had her body reacting so.

"Some. I'm afraid the west building will need a completely new fire system. Just the mechanics of it. Until I have a chance to check the individual sprinklers and alarms in each of the guest rooms, we can start there. The old computer system has finally died." He sat down across from her and leaned back as if expecting to stay for a while.

"I'll arrange for a new system." She turned back to her laptop and added a reminder to talk to David about pricing one out. "Anything else?" She looked up at him.

He was smiling at her. "Anyone ever tell you that the glasses are sexy?"

Her entire system jumped into overdrive at the look he was giving her.

She didn't know how to respond. She'd never been any good at flirting. One more reason why it had been ten years since she'd dated.

Swallowing, she shifted in her chair uncomfortably and was thankful when another knock on the door saved her from having to answer.

CHAPTER EIGHT

Cade hadn't expected Raven to react to his compliment the way she had. Seeing the blood drain from her face and her eyes searching the room for an escape route had at first confused him.

Had he misread how she'd been reacting to him or the sexual tension he'd felt building up between them?

Either way, he'd realized that the only way to get what he needed from her was to get her to be completely relaxed and trusting around him. Which meant letting loose about his own desires around her.

When Rachelle Braun knocked on Raven's door and entered, he could tell Raven was relieved.

"Raven, I need your..." Rachelle stopped just inside the doorway. "Oh, Cade, I didn't know you were here." The woman smiled at him. Rachelle was a close friend of his mother. The two women often met for drinks or shopping trips.

"Hi, Rach." He stood up. "I was just leaving." He turned back to Raven. "I'll let you know when I can start inspecting each of the suites. Until then..." He flipped open his notebook and took out the duplicate of his inspection report. "Here is my preliminary report. Until these items are met, I'm afraid that the west building is off limits to guests."

Raven sighed as she took the report from him. "I'll see to it." She set the report down on her desk. "Thank you."

He nodded to Rachelle as he left Raven's office. Heading back down the hall towards the lobby, he held in a groan when he noticed Liza standing around trying to act like she wasn't waiting for him.

"Oh." She turned slightly as if just noticing him. "Cade." Her smile grew. It wasn't that Liza Brooks wasn't pretty. She was easily as good-looking as Raven, just... different.

Where Raven had natural beauty in her long red hair, porcelain skin, and subtle elegant style, Liza had shorter blonde hair with tons of product in it and her style was... well, louder and more expensive.

Not to mention that Raven had an inner beauty that showed each time she talked to someone around her with respect. Liza talked down to everyone as if they were there to serve her.

"Are you still hanging around here?" she asked when he stopped directly beside her.

"I was just leaving," he told her, hoping this would discourage her from a lengthy conversation.

"Oh, well"—she wrapped her arm through his and started pulling him towards the bar area— "I was hoping you'd join me for lunch."

He quickly glanced down at his watch and realized it was a quarter past one in the afternoon. He'd lost track of time working and when he'd been with Raven.

"I..." He tried to think of an excuse, but then Liza

broke in.

"Don't say no. I simply can't stand that we haven't had time to chat lately." Liza stuck out her bottom lip in a pout that looked a little overacted.

"I suppose a sandwich—" He didn't get anything else out, as she pulled him through the construction and into the seating area.

"There," she said, sitting next to him at a table in the rotunda. "Isn't this nice? I suppose some of the changes my cousin is making around here are... tolerable." Liza waved her hand as if motioning to the area.

He had to admit, he'd admired every change Raven had made so far. Even though there were large sheets of plastic hanging up everywhere in the lobby to keep the construction dust to a minimum, he could see that when all the work was done, it would be a vast improvement from what it was before.

"It is starting to shape up around here," he agreed, setting his binder down in the chair next to him.

Liza waved a waiter over and quickly rattled off her order. Since he'd been down in the kitchens earlier, he knew they were short-staffed at the moment and ordered the same thing Liza had. After they received their drinks, Liza narrowed her eyes at him and asked.

"Why is it you and I have never..."

He almost choked on the sip of water he'd taken.

"Excuse me?" he asked, trying to sound relaxed.

Liza leaned forward, placing her impressive breasts slightly on the table. No doubt after seeing him in Raven's office earlier, she'd rushed up to her rooms to change out of the slacks and blouse she'd been wearing earlier to the outfit she now wore. The low-cut top and skintight pants were more fit for a club than an empty hotel dining room.

"You know what I mean. Why haven't we gone out? Partied?" Her smile grew as her breath lowered. "Surely we could have had some fun times together."

He shook his head. "I suppose it's because I've been busy working," he said, thinking a completely different thing. After all, in the past ten years since his return, he'd been hard at work helping rebuild Cannon Falls, helping others in their time of need, while Liza had been sulking and selfishly partying her time away.

"Oh." She frowned slightly at him, then playfully slapped his shoulder. "We'll just have to change that."

He held in a groan. "My job..." he started, only to have her roll her eyes at him.

"How hard could your job be? There hasn't been a fire in Cannon Falls for ten years." She giggled.

He felt his entire body stiffen. "That's a good thing," he reminded her. "And part of my job. A fire marshals' main job is fire prevention."

"Oh, don't get me wrong," she continued, as if she wasn't aware that she was being offensive. "It's a sexy career, being a fireman, but I would think that you have a lot of downtime. Time to fill." She leaned closer to him and wrapped her finger around his arm. "With other things," she finished with a purr.

"Sister, can't you see that you're scaring Cade." Cal Brooks walked over and sat down in the chair directly across from him.

Cade had gone to school with Cal. He'd always liked the guy, since Cal had stuck up for the underdog in school. Maybe it was because Cal was one of them himself, being gay. Whatever the reason, he thought that the two siblings couldn't have been more different from one another.

"Afternoon," he said to Cal.

"I'd heard you were roaming the halls," Cal said with a smile. "I hope Raven hasn't worked you too hard."

He smiled and shook his head. "No, just checking a few systems out before I have to go room by room. How are—" He saw Cal's eyes grow large and move over to his sister. "Things?" he finished, remembering that Cal was keeping his job from his family.

It was strange. He was pretty sure everyone in town but his family knew the man worked part time down at the art studio.

"Things are going good," Cal answered, relaxing a little. "Put out any fires lately?"

Cade smiled easily. "Nope."

"Cal, can't you see Cade and I are having a private..." Liza started but just then Raven came in and, seeing the three of them, walked towards them.

"Is this seat taken?" she asked, motioning to the chair Cade had set his binder in.

Quickly moving his binder to the floor, he motioned. "Please, be my guest."

Raven smiled as she sat down. For the next few moments, more drinks and food orders were delivered while the chatter turned towards what had happened in Raven's office earlier that morning.

Cal mentioned that his father was upstairs, packing his things and demanding that his family move with him.

"Of course, we won't." Liza chuckled. "Mom's told him he just needs to move in with that slut that he's been seeing for years."

"Liza!" Cal scolded.

"What?" Liza rolled her eyes. "Everyone in town knows about their affair. Why Mom didn't divorce Dad years ago is beyond me."

"Because if she did, she wouldn't have this place," Cal answered and turned towards Raven. "Mom's the one who has been trying to keep this place afloat over the years while Dad was busy..." He waved his hand. "Elsewhere."

Cade watched Raven take in this news. He could see her thinking and found it even more sexy than the black-rimmed glasses she'd been wearing earlier when he'd walked into her office.

"Maybe it's the reason this place has gone downhill," Liza said, sounding bored. "Mom was never any good at figures. Its why Dad had to hire the slut."

"She has a name," Cal pointed out.

"Morgan Roche no longer works on the resort's books," Raven supplied.

"Oh?" Liza smiled. "So, both Dad and his..."—Cal cleared his throat to get his sister to stop calling the woman a slut— "lady friend," she corrected as she narrowed her eyes at her brother, "are out of jobs. Plus, Dad has to move. This is rich."

"How so?" Cal asked.

"Oh please. Dad's finally getting what he deserves. He's not only been cheating on Mom for all these years but cheating this place as well."

"How so?" Raven asked.

Cal gave his sister a look that said *enough*. But Liza being Liza, she either didn't see it or didn't care.

"Oh please, you think that a small-town accountant like Morgan Roche has enough business that she can afford to have her offices in one of the swankiest buildings in town, drive a Mercedes, and take at least three trips a year to France?" She chuckled. "Especially in this small town. There's not enough business in Cannon Falls for anyone to afford to drive a new Mercedes."

"Maybe she gets her money from somewhere else?" Cade suggested, keeping his eyes on Raven. He hadn't heard any rumors about the woman, other than she and Raven's uncle were possibly having an affair.

"Did you know she was a washed-up soap opera actress before moving to Cannon Falls shortly after the fire?" Liza said as she finished her lunch.

"If you'll excuse me," Raven said, suddenly standing up.

As she walked away, Cade noticed that she'd barely touched her sandwich and soup.

"Excuse me," he said after a moment. Taking his binder, he followed Raven back down the hallway to her office.

When he stepped in, she was on the phone, but waved him in. As with before, he shut the door behind him and waited.

Instantly, he could tell she was leaving a message. When she hung up, she glanced up at him.

"Was there something else?" she asked him.

"I'm sure it's just Liza being... Liza." He shrugged.

"No, it's not." She sighed and leaned back in her chair. She motioned for him to sit. When he did, she continued. "Shortly after returning, I rehired my father's old accountant. Joe Ramsey is an old family friend. One that I trust. His initial findings show tens of thousands of dollars missing from the accounts this year alone."

"Your uncle?" he asked.

"Joe was thinking it was just poor oversight by Morgan Roche's company. Joe doesn't live in Cannon Falls anymore. After the fire, he moved to Redding, so most of our communications has been over the phone or virtual." She leaned back. "I have met with Joe on three occasions since my return, whenever he came to town. I hadn't heard the rumors about my uncle and Morgan stealing from the resort until now. But I have to say, it makes sense. More than just slight accounting oversight."

"I'm sure your guy will figure things out," he suggested.

"Either way, the money is most likely long gone." She shrugged. He could see the sorrow in her eyes and felt an overwhelming need to comfort her.

"Have dinner with me?" he blurted out.

Her eyebrows rose slightly. "Didn't we just have dinner last night?"

He smiled. "This time, we can eat out, and I won't bring my grandmother."

Her curious look turned to a slight frown.

"I don't think I have time—"

"It's just dinner." He stood up and walked behind the desk. Taking her arm, he pulled her up until they were eye to eye. "Are you afraid?" he asked, his eyes moving down to her lips.

He knew he was pushing it, pushing her, but part of him wanted to see how she would respond. What she would do.

She was stiff against him. Her hands moved to his shoulders, until he moved closer. Their bodies bumped together softly.

"I haven't asked a woman out in a while. I may be rusty, but I'd really enjoy having dinner with you tonight," he said a little more smoothly.

"Okay," she answered after a moment.

He smiled. "I'll pick you up at seven?"

She nodded and when her eyes moved to his lips, he knew that if he kissed her now, she wouldn't pull away.

When he stepped back, dropping his hold on her, he noticed a slight look of shock cross her face.

"Tonight then," he said, and he turned to leave.

He left the resort and headed towards his parents' place before picking up Blue at his gran's. He didn't know why, but he needed his mother's advice about what he was planning.

Fiona and Henry Stone had fallen in love when they'd been ten. Or so his mother had always claimed. Shortly after graduating from school, his father had entered the Marines. It had been rough on his childhood, always traveling and living different places. Not to mention having his father gone most of the time. When the man returned, they never knew which version they'd get—the loving, caring husband and father, or the soldier who jumped and lashed out at any little transgression. Then shortly after Cade's tenth birthday, he'd been killed, and his mother had returned to Cannon Falls with her two young boys.

His mother hadn't changed at all over the years, or so he felt. Her once-long dark hair was now cut in a shorter style. She still worked out twice a week at the local gym and did yoga with his gran three times a week in Gran's garden.

Where Reggie had taken after their mother in the looks department, Cade was all their father's side of the family.

Growing up, he'd never really thought about the fact that he looked like his dad and uncle. But since returning home, it was sort of strange to see just how he'd look in twenty years. All he had to do was look at his uncle, Sean.

Some people in town confused them for one another. Of course, Sean had more grey hair and was usually in his police cruiser and uniform.

"This is a surprise," his mother said, setting down a book she'd been reading when he stepped into the house.

Louie and Bentley, his mother's French bulldogs, rustled over to greet him.

"Sorry, guys, Blue's at Gran's place," he told the two

brothers as he petted them. "Sorry to drop in on you like this."

His mother waved him away and stood up to hug him. "It's no problem. How about some tea? I was just sitting down, trying to recover from my yoga class. I swear my mother is trying to kill me."

He chuckled. "You've been saying that for years and yet you still do yoga with her three times a week," he pointed out as he sat down on one of the barstools to watch her put together some tea and the cookies that he knew she always had after yoga.

"I've got a date tonight," he blurted out.

"Oh?" His mother stopped mid-stride. "With whom?"

"Raven Brooks," he answered, hoping to rip the bandage off quickly so it wouldn't sting his mother so much.

"That's nice," his mother surprised him by saying before returning to her task.

"That's all you have to say?" he asked after a moment.

"Mom mentioned that you'd invited her to dinner last night," his mother said over her shoulder. "I haven't seen her around town yet and was thinking I would stop by the resort to say hello."

"She kicked her uncle out today." He looked down at his hands as they fisted. "I walked in on the man grabbing and threatening her this morning."

"Was she okay?" His mother looked worried.

"Yeah," he sighed. "It appears that the man has spent the last ten years stealing from the resort. Him and Morgan Roche."

His mother moved over to stand directly across from him. "I never did like that woman. When she moved into town, I just knew there was something about her." She shook her head. "Has Raven talked to your uncle about this yet?"

"No." He shook his head. "I was hoping to talk to him about it myself. Raven claims that since most likely the money is all gone, it's not worth it."

"That's bull." His mother set the plate of cookies in front of him.

Since he was still hungry, he grabbed one and bit into it.

"It's not my decision," he added with a shrug.

"Does she have proof?" his mother asked, walking over and taking the kettle off the stove.

"I'm not sure. It sounds like her parents' old accountant found some discrepancies. I don't know if it's proof." He shrugged as she set a mug in front of him. Dipping another cookie into the tea, he finished, "She left a message for the man."

"And kicked her uncle out. What about Roslyn? Liza and Cal?"

"She's told them they can stay. For now," he answered.

His mother's eyes ran over him. "So, you asked her out?"

He nodded. "Does it bother you?"

"What?" His mother looked a little surprised. "Why would it?" When he shrugged and took another bite of cookie, she continued. "Do you think I pay any attention to the gossip that's been going around town all these years?"

He nodded. "If the rumors are true, Raven is the reason Reggie and so many others are gone. The reason you lost your home, the reason so many others lost everything."

"Son, if I paid attention to rumors, I would have never married your father." She smiled. "If all rumors going around Cannon Falls were true, Sean is your father, not Henry."

"What?" He set his teacup down a little hard and some of the amber liquid splashed out. "Who says that?"

His mother laughed. "See, we shouldn't put any stock in rumors." She motioned with her cookie. "Oh, and there's one that your gran is a lesbian." She laughed. "Gran loves that one. She claims that if she'd found anyone to put up with her after grandpa Burt died, she wouldn't have cared what gender they were."

He smiled. "I see what you mean." He sighed. "So, you don't think that Raven had anything to do with the fire?"

His mother grew silent and tilted her head slightly. "Whatever that girl and Reggie were doing out in the woods that night, I doubt it was their plan to start a fire that would wipe out Cannon Falls. Sometimes young people do stupid things. If I blame her, then I have to put some of that blame on Reggie. You have to ask yourself what kind of person Raven is now. Gran mentioned that Raven has spent the last ten years in counseling. That for the first five years after, she was on antidepressants. Now, I don't know much about her since she's returned, but I know that she's hired a lot of good people. Put them back to work again. Not to mention that when the resort opens back up this winter, she's going to bring a lot of tourists back into town. That's a good thing. It means that Cannon Falls finally has a chance to recover. Ten years later. And it's all because of her."

"Yeah," he agreed. He'd known all of that. Had thought the same thing. But somehow hearing it from his mother made it resonate. "I guess that's why I asked her out."

His mother smiled again and laid a hand over his. "You are an excellent judge of character. You deserve to be happy. Don't let rumors stop you from finding happiness. I didn't." She sighed. "Now, where are you going to take her for dinner?"

CHAPTER NINE

Why in the hell had she agreed to go to dinner with Cade again? She'd had dinner with him last night, and lunch earlier. Okay, technically, she'd had lunch with him and her cousins, but still. That counted. Right?

The only reason she was standing in front of the bathroom mirror, trying on yet another outfit, was because she'd had a moment of weakness looking into his sexy brown eyes.

Deciding on the deep yellow off-the-shoulder flowing dress, she wrapped her black belt around her waist, found her favorite black cardigan and purse, and decided not to second-guess herself.

She still had so many things to do on her list, including moving out of the west building and into the east building until the new fire system could be installed. She would have to make time for it soon.

When the elevator swung open, her cousin was standing there, as if waiting for her.

"Going somewhere?" Liza's eyes moved up and down her.

"Out," she said and started to pass her. Liza moved in front of her and blocked her completely.

"With?" Liza asked, her eyes locking with her own.

"Not that it's any of your business," Raven began just as Cade turned the corner.

"There you are," he said with a smile. "Ready?" His eyes moved to Liza and he gave her a quick nod before taking Raven's hand in his.

"Seriously?" Liza called after them.

"Just keep walking," Cade said between clenched teeth.

"Is there a problem between you and my cousin?" she asked once they'd stepped outside.

He turned to glance at her, then stopped. "You look beautiful," he said with a smile.

"Changing the subject?"

He took her hand and started walking towards a parked car.

"That I know of, there is nothing between me and your cousin. Either of them," he added with a wink. "Liza did, however, make me an offer before you and Cal stopped by the lunch table."

"Oh?" she asked as he opened the car door. "What kind of offer?"

He shrugged. "The usual kind, I suppose. She wondered why we hadn't... done it," he finished with a smile.

"Seriously?" Raven asked, a little appalled. He chuckled as an answer. "Why haven't you?"

He rolled his eyes and took a step closer to her, and she felt the air in her lungs back up.

"Because she is not my type," he said just under his breath.

"What is your type?" she asked before thinking about it.

His eyes moved to her lips quickly, then back to her eyes.

"I think you know that answer." His hand moved to her waist. Just feeling him touching her, holding her with just one hand, made her knees go weak.

Before she made a fool of herself, she climbed into the car and watched him move around to get behind the wheel.

"I thought you had a truck?" she asked as he started to drive.

"I do, a work truck. This is my personal car."

They rode in silence for a while. She was so nervous, and she suddenly realized she hadn't even thought of a few topics to talk with him about.

When she'd dated Reggie, there hadn't been a lot of talking. It was high school and, well, theirs was a more physical kind of thing.

She glanced sideways at him and hoped that he would start talking about something.

"Did you get everyone moved out of the west building?" he asked as he turned onto the highway.

"There isn't anyone in it at the moment. Except me."

He glanced over at her. "You're staying in the west building?"

"Yes, it's the newer building. I thought it would need the least amount of work." She sighed. "I was wrong."

"Oh?" he asked.

"My list says otherwise. It's as if my uncle didn't do any maintenance on the west side at all." She relaxed back. She could easily talk about work. After all, it consumed her every waking thought and some of her thoughts while sleeping. Well, when she wasn't dreaming of Cade or running from a fire.

"You grew quiet," he said, breaking the silence.

She hadn't realized she'd retreated into her thoughts.

"Sorry." She cleared her mind. "Where are we going?"

"There's an Italian restaurant just on the outskirts of Azalea. They have some really great meatballs, and their breadsticks are to die for." He grinned.

"So, you like Italian." She shifted slightly and held up her fingers. "Own a dog named Blue, work as the fire marshal, drive a used... Is this a Jeep?"

"Yes. I'm hoping to trade it in for a real Jeep, not a Cherokee. But she gets me around all year long, so I've held onto her." He patted the steering wheel.

She smiled. "Is there anything else I should know about you?"

"Nope, that's it. Oh, I like having tea and cookies with my mom or my gran." He shrugged. "Gran's mother came over from England and teatime sort of became a family tradition and stuck." He turned towards her. "What about you?"

"Me?" Her stomach dropped. "There's nothing really to tell." She instantly wished she hadn't asked him about himself.

"You moved in with your grandmother just before your senior year. You graduated from?" he let the question hang in the air.

"South San Diego High."

"College?"

"University of California in San Diego."

"For how long? What'd you major in?"

"Seven years. I kept switching majors," she admitted. "But my central focus was business."

"From what I've seen, you're pretty good at it." He glanced at her.

"That remains to be seen. I haven't even had time to think about my marketing plan for this fall." She shook her head.

"I think word of mouth has grown so much. I mean, everyone in town is talking about the changes that you're making up there. People are excited to see what you're doing."

"I plan on having an open house, once everything is ready. Of course, we'll be lucky if everything is done by the start of the season."

"David and his men will get it done. I can't tell you how much those men have been looking forward to working. Some of them have been scraping by since the big rebuild after the fire."

"I've noticed they are eager to work," she agreed. "The way things are going, I'll have enough work to keep them busy for over a year."

"Oh?" he glanced at her. "What else needs to be done?"

"Besides all the work I'm doing in the common areas like the bar, the dining room, and the pool house, I'm overhauling each of the guest rooms. Putting in new carpet everywhere, and in some cases, new tubs, toilets, and tile. When that's all done, I'm thinking the kitchen might need an upgrade." Her eyes grew unfocused as she thought about all of the changes she'd dreamed of. "I would like to add an outdoor dining area for the warmer months, to bring spring and summer clientele. Maybe add a few attractions for those months. Build up the outdoor pool area." She closed her eyes and tried to plan out. "Make a beautiful area to rent out for weddings or larger events."

"You know, back when I was in high school, a couple buddies and I took a weekend trip to Colorado. In the summer months, they host downhill bike races on the slopes," he said.

She turned to him. "Like, extreme sports kind of stuff?"

"Sure. We found out about it and went to see it ourselves. There were more than three thousand people there just to watch a bunch of grown men going downhill and falling off bikes." He chuckled.

She smiled. "Not into that sort of thing?"

"At the time, I was still thinking I wanted to go into the medical field. All I could think about was the cuts, bruises, and broken bones."

She chuckled. "I seem to remember you breaking a few bones and getting cuts and bruises on the field. Just how many sports did you and Reggie play in school?"

"That was different," he countered as he pulled off the highway.

"Oh?" She narrowed her eyes. "How so?"

"Because it was a team sport." He chuckled. "Okay, so maybe not that different. But still, I was a lot younger back then."

"Old man?"

He pulled into the parking lot. "No, but when we do drills, my body reminds me that it's not as young as it used to be." He smiled as he shut off the car.

She waited while he rushed around to open her door for her. He took her hand again, and she held back a giddy giggle as they walked into the restaurant together. She felt like a schoolgirl all over again, like when Reggie had taken her to the Cannon Fall's Grill for her very first date.

They were seated in a booth and told that someone would be over to take their order. A woman walked over to their table and at first Raven didn't recognize her. Then she spoke, and Raven went completely on guard. She wondered why she hadn't remembered the girl until now.

"Well, well, isn't this cozy. Imagine running into the two of you here. I've been meaning to stop by and... see you," Julia Garza said, her eyes never really leaving Cade except to jump over to run quickly over Raven.

Raven had never gotten along with Julia. The girl, and now woman, had been such a bully but also easily the most popular girl in school.

And from the looks she was giving Cade, she was a woman after a man.

"Julia, I didn't know you worked here," Cade said in a clipped voice. "I thought you worked at the diner in town?"

"I do," she answered quickly. "And here as well. So, are you two on a date then?"

"We were just..." Cade started.

"Getting drinks," Raven interjected quickly. "A quick stop." She motioned to the bar area. "The bar was full." Thankfully, it was at this time.

Julia tilted her head slightly as if annoyed that Raven had spoken to her.

"Do you want your usual?" she asked Cade.

He glanced at Raven.

"I'll have a glass of Merlot." She set down the drink menu.

"I'll have the same," Cade added and handed over the other menus.

After Julia assessed them again, she left.

"That was..." Cade started.

"Uncomfortable?" she said with a slight smile. "It usually is, bumping into your ex."

His eyebrows shot up slightly. "Oh? Have a lot of experience with that?"

"No, but I've seen enough movies to spot the situation." She leaned on the table. "So, you and Julia? How did that happen?"

He sighed, then scanned the room, no doubt making sure she wasn't within earshot.

"A moment of weakness. Needless to say, I hadn't known about her... personality flaws until after we'd dated for a few months."

"Months?" she asked, a little shocked. "It only took me two days to know who she was. And that was in second grade."

He chuckled. "You didn't have the hindrance of hormones." He leaned a little closer and lowered his voice. "And a two-year sexual dry spell beforehand."

"Two years." She shook her head and felt her heart flutter. What would he do if he knew she'd had a ten-year dry spell?

"I had been busy." He shrugged. "Rebuilding around town and building my place."

"So that was when? A few years back?" she asked. When he nodded, she continued. "Does Julia know? She's acting like you broke up with her yesterday."

"Yeah." He nodded behind her, signally that Julia was coming back. He waited until she set the two glasses in front of them and left before finishing. "She only started acting like that in the past few weeks." He sighed. "Which tells me that she's building up to something. I'm sorry about this. We can head out." He motioned to the wine.

She took another sip and then glanced around. Julia was leaning on the bar, watching them as customers waited for their orders. She agreed.

Cade tossed some bills on the table and helped her slide

out of the booth. He held her hand as they walked out together.

"There's a good burger place just down the street?" he suggested.

"A burger sounds great," she admitted as he held the car door open for her.

"I'm sorry about this," he said again after sliding into the driver seat.

"Don't be. No one but Julia should apologize for anything she does."

"True," he agreed. "Did you learn that in counseling?" he asked, glancing at her sideways.

She'd learned early on not to be ashamed of getting help. After all, talking to the doctor was the only reason she'd felt strong enough to get out of bed each day.

The guilt she'd felt had pretty much paralyzed her those first few months after the fire. After losing everyone who had ever mattered to her, she'd learned to let go of her teenage pride that made her care what other people thought of her.

"That, and a few other things," she said with a slight shrug as he parked in front of the burger diner. "Wow, this place is still around?" She glanced out the window. "My parents used to take me here when I was a kid." She smiled, remembering the memories.

He chuckled. "Paul, the original owner, still runs the place. I think."

Instead of waiting for him to come around and open her door, this time she climbed out herself.

"It's strange, seeing some things that haven't changed over the years," she said after stepping inside. "In town, everything is so... different. With a few exceptions."

"Yeah, a few people got really lucky," he agreed as they

walked in and sat themselves in a booth near the front door. "My grandmother being one of them. Actually, it was only because her house was still standing that we could tell where everything else in town had been."

"Part of the guilt I felt for years was because I'd had to leave town," she admitted.

His eyebrows rose, and she waited for more questions she knew were coming from him. But he surprised her by changing the subject to the progress on the resort.

She supposed he wanted to avoid going too deep into the conversation so as not to upset her or himself. Still, she reflected on it while she filled him in on the progress.

While they waited for their food, she told him how things were moving much faster than she'd expected with the construction in the lobby area.

"Most of the changes are superficial. I mean, it's not like they're tearing down walls or rebuilding the entire space. Well, they did tear down one wall," she pointed out with a smile as their burgers were delivered by an older woman. "Which took five men less than five minutes." She giggled. "Part of me wanted to be swinging the sledgehammer myself." She took a bite of her burger. "My god, these are just as good as I remember them being."

"I try to make it out here at least once a month," he admitted before taking his own bite. "Too much of the greasy foods and my uncle will whoop my ass in the gym."

Her eyes narrowed when she remembered his uncle. "Your uncle Sean, right?"

"Yeah." He nodded and took a sip of his soda.

"He was a police officer?" She felt her stomach roll. She didn't know why she'd forgotten that he was related to the man who had found her, tucked away, hiding from the fire in a cave. A cave she couldn't remember crawling into as the fire raged around her, taking everything that was dear to her away.

"Yeah, still is," he said easily, too engrossed in his food to notice her incertitude. "Became sheriff a few years back. That's how I walked into my job. The position became available, and he encouraged me to run." He shrugged and she forced herself to relax and to continue eating.

Normally, when she grew too upset, she'd go without food. Which was why for the first few years after the fire, she'd lost so much weight that they'd talked about putting her on feeding tubes.

"You like your job?" she asked, trying to sound cheerful.

His eyes met hers and, for a moment, she thought he could see through her façade.

"I do. I think it's a far better fit for me than the medical field I was aiming for. What about you? Did you work before returning here?"

"I had a few odd jobs here and there. My last job was working for a marketing firm."

"And you decided to return here after your grandmother passed?"

"Yes, it was one of her last wishes. She'd helped my parents when they'd purchased the property all those years ago. Something tells me that she knew my uncle was running it into the ground." She nibbled on a fry.

"Is it that bad?" he asked.

"I'm not sure yet. I'm meeting with Joe Ramsey tomorrow. Now that my uncle can't get into the accounts..." She felt a huge weight release when she remembered removing him from all the accounts and locking him and her aunt out of all the financials.

"I bet you're relieved knowing that part of the job is over. Having to deal with Colin," he said.

"I'm struggling with feeling sorry for him," she admitted. "I mean, if I find out that he really did steal from me, from the resort, then I won't struggle any longer, but until then..." She shrugged. "Part of me wants to believe he couldn't do something like that. The man I remember..." She pushed her half-empty plate away.

"And the other part?" he asked.

"The other part wants him to be guilty so I can never have to deal with him again." She closed her eyes. "Which makes me just as terrible of a person as he is."

She opened her eyes when Cade took her hand in his. "Why would that make you a terrible person?"

"Because I'd enjoy knowing he was locked up. Alone. Suffering. Away from his family." She looked at their joined hands, Cade's large tan hand next to her own smaller, pale, freckled one.

Just the simple kindness he showed her by the move almost had tears building up behind her eyes.

"One way or another, I guess I'll find out tomorrow," she added with a shrug. For some reason, she was growing tired. Maybe it was opening up to someone, other than her shrink, for the first time in years. Maybe it was the long day she'd had. Whatever the reason, she leaned back in the booth, breaking their connection, and looked out the window.

"It will get better," he said suddenly. She glanced back at him.

"Most of the town still believes I'm responsible for..."— she motioned with her hand— "everything."

She watched, waiting, guessing that he wanted to ask her if she was, but instead, he sighed and leaned back, mimicking her move.

"How do you feel?" he asked.

At least he hadn't blamed her. How did she feel?

For so long she'd hid her feelings. Denied them. Repressed them and tried to forget that she had feelings or emotions at all.

It was one of the reasons that she hadn't dated after Reggie. She'd been too afraid to unbottle that genie.

"Weary."

CHAPTER TEN

There was so much Cade wanted to ask Raven, but he could tell that she was beyond tired.

"I bet you haven't gotten a lot of sleep since you came back." He leaned in and ran his eyes over her.

There was no denying that she was beautiful. Her skin was pale and flawless, her crystal eyes, which also had a knack for drawing you in, were haunting. Her lips were full and, well... perfect.

Still, under all that, he could see slight dark circles under her eyes, as well as the lost look that crossed there on several occasions. Each time it did, he could see her consciously pushing the emotions away.

It somehow only made him want to expose them even more. What would Raven be like unhinged?

She'd barely eaten anything really. A quarter of her burger along with a few French fries. Since he'd wager that she was a few pounds underweight, he guessed she wasn't a stress eater.

"How about we get out of here?" He nodded towards the door.

She nodded as a response, and he moved to help her slide out of the booth.

Since he didn't feel like taking her back just yet, he took the long way back to the resort.

Even though it was now full dark, she looked out the window as if she could see everything.

"How long did it take for things to grow back?" she asked.

He glanced over at her. "In some parts, less than a year. Others"—he shrugged— "it's still growing back."

"A lot of people left." It was a statement, not a question.

"More than half the town. People took their insurance money and split. I guess some decided the country living wasn't for them. When your uncle stopped hiring locals..."

"He stopped..." She sat up a little and looked at him.

"During the season."

"Where did he hire them from?" she asked.

"Anywhere but Cannon Falls. I know that several regulars who used to work for your uncle were turned away the year after the fire. Some had to move on, out of the town, to find work."

"I'm sorry," she said softly.

"Like you said before, no one but your uncle should apologize for anything he has done." He reached over and took her hand in his again. He liked the way it felt. Liked the way she felt.

He'd gained enough information about her over the past few days to know that whatever had happened ten years ago, there was no way she'd caused the fire on purpose. If he'd learned one thing over the years, it was that accidents happened. Hell, he'd caused his mother and grandmother enough grief in his teenage years that they both swore that every grey hair they had was due to him.

Whatever had happened in the past, Raven had a good heart now. She'd suffered as much as anyone had, maybe even more so.

Still, that didn't stop him from wanting answers. Needing them. But he had time. For now, he wanted to explore what he was feeling between them. What had been building up since the moment he'd walked into her office.

She sighed heavily. "I know you're right. Still, one thing I've learned in the past few weeks is that everyone in town doesn't believe the same."

"They'll get over it. It may be after the first ski season, after you've proven that you're going to keep your word and keep hiring local," he suggested.

"At this point, I doubt there are enough people left in town to fill all the spots, or places for out-of-towners-to live."

"You could always block out some rooms for employees."

"I had already planned on it. My dad always did. I'll have to see when it gets closer to the season to how many out-of-town employees we'll need."

He parked in the empty parking lot, but when he moved to get out and open her door, she stopped him.

"I can make it from here." She held his arm. "Thank you for dinner."

He relaxed back. "Sorry about..." She arched her brow and gave him a look, and he remembered what she'd said about apologizing for Julia. "Right." He nodded. "At least the burgers were good."

"They were."

"We could always try this again. Have dinner at a place that doesn't employ a crazy ex of mine."

She smiled. "We'd probably have to head to Redding for that."

He chuckled "I don't have that many exes."

She narrowed her eyes at him. "Something tells me that isn't true."

"Maybe from when I was in college," he added with a low chuckle.

She turned slightly to run her eyes over him. "What about Heather Craft? Did you ever date her?"

He quickly shook his head. "No. Where Julia hid her crazy on the inside, Heather wears it proudly right out front."

She nodded. "Yeah, she was hired on as a bartender."

"I'd heard." The tone of voice hinted of his concern.

"Rachelle hired her. I only found out this morning. At this point we need all the locals we can get. I can't afford to be too picky."

"A few of the volunteers have been looking for jobs. I can send them your way," he suggested.

"Send them to either Rachelle or Eddie if they want to work the lifts or rentals for the season." She leaned back and ran her eyes over the trio of massive buildings in front of them. The cluster wouldn't look so out of place in the city, but tucked at the base of the mountains, in the middle of the wilderness, the wood, metal, and glass structures stuck out. Especially at night. Large lights shined on the grounds and lit up the first three floors of each building.

The rest of the floors remained dark for now. During the season, he knew they would switch on or off, depending on the guests. There would be lights shining on the multiple ski runs in the distance as well.

"It feels weird being back," she said after a moment. "I haven't really had a moment to appreciate just being back yet."

"Something tells me you'd better take that time now. Come season, you're going to be busy."

"I hope so." She closed her eyes then shook her head and opened them again. "I'd better head in. Joe and his new assistant are going to be here early."

"Are you sure I can't walk you up?" he offered.

She smiled. "No, thanks. I want to walk around and take a look at what the construction crew got done before leaving today. It's amazing how quickly they're working. Thanks again for tonight." She started to reach for the doorhandle, but he stopped her by gently laying a hand on her arm. Then he pulled her closer until they were a breath away.

"The date's not officially over just yet," he said, and when she smiled, he leaned in and brushed his lips over hers.

Since he'd returned to Cannon Falls, he'd handled his fair share of fires, but the moment his lips touched Raven's, he realized he'd never handled anything this... explosive before.

He felt her move slightly, which brought her body directly up against his. His arms tightened around her, pulling her even closer as he slanted his mouth over hers and took what he wanted. What he hadn't known he'd been needing.

When her fingers tangled in his hair, a low rumble vibrated from his chest, which caused her to release a soft moan.

God, he wanted to take her. Here. Now.

Then headlights washed over them, and she jerked out of his hold and glanced around.

"I'd better..." She was out of the car before he could respond.

Damn. He sat there for a few moments, trying to collect his thoughts before starting the car and heading home. Alone.

Blue was eagerly waiting for him at the door. He let him out to run around the yard to pee on every bush and tree, and then they headed up to bed.

It was strange. Over the past ten years, he'd never felt like the house was lonely. Until tonight. Lying in the massive bed with the mutt snoring next to him, he realized how empty it felt.

The next morning, he stopped by the firehouse to check on his appointments for the day. The majority of his job consisted of dealing with fire regulations around town. The next big chunk was slotted for training and, occasionally, he delt with an actual fire.

Since he was officially the only full-time paid position, there was a crew under him that constantly needed his guidance and training.

Today, he was taking a few of his trainees out on a new construction site on the outskirts of town, a much-needed storage unit going up next to the old one. It wasn't a big job, but walking both Kevin and Tony through the site and showing them what troubling items to look out for still filled up most of his morning.

The three of them grabbed lunch at the diner, and he sat back and watched Tony flirt with Darby the entire time.

"Why don't you ask her out?" Kevin asked Tony.

Kevin was fresh out of high school while Tony was a few years older. Still, Tony had to be two or three years younger than Darby. But the way Darby was smiling at the man made it clear to everyone around that she was into him.

"Naw, we're just friends," Tony responded as he finished off his milkshake.

"Darby is totally into you." Kevin bumped Tony's shoulder. "I'd hit that if I was a few years older."

"Older women rock," Tony responded.

He held in a chuckle, but apparently not well enough.

"What?" they both said, looking at him.

"What is she? Two years older than the both of you?" he asked with a shrug.

"Are you kidding? I just graduated last year and Tony here was the year before me," Kevin said.

"Try seven years," Tony added with a shrug.

"So?" Cade asked. "Age doesn't matter once you pass a point."

"So, you'd date an older woman?" The duo glanced around and smiled. "What about her?" They motioned towards the back of the diner.

He turned slightly to see Morgan Roche sitting in the back booth, having a heated discussion with a man with sandy-blonde hair, who was facing away from Cade.

"Morgan?" He shook his head. "Age would have nothing to do with why I wouldn't date her," he answered quickly.

"Rumors are that Morgan's the reason the resort has been under all these years," Tony added. "At least that's what Darby says."

He thought about Raven's meeting with her CPA that morning and what the man had discovered and whether there were charges coming against Morgan and maybe even Raven's uncle.

He figured a stop off at his own uncle's office after lunch might offer him a few answers. What was the use of having an uncle as sheriff if you couldn't exploit it once in a while?

After dropping Kevin and Tony off at the fire house, he drove the few blocks to the police station and walked past the front desk to his uncle's office. He knocked quickly and entered when he heard Sean Stone call out to come in.

It still was strange seeing so much of himself in his uncle. It was no wonder that rumors had been flying around town ever since he'd been born.

Cade Stone was the spitting image of his uncle Sean. Even more so now that he was an adult. The only difference between the two of them was the streak of silver that ran just above his uncle's ears. That and the uniforms they wore.

"Hey, buddy," Sean said, glancing up from his laptop.

"Hey," he said easily as he sat down in the chair across from his uncle. "I heard the Browns got in a fender bender this morning?"

His uncle nodded and leaned back in his chair. "Just finishing up with the paperwork now." His uncle's eyes narrowed. "What's on your mind?"

Cade shifted slightly. "I'm just curious to see if you'd heard anything about money laundering from the resort?"

His uncle's eyebrows jumped up. "Brooks?"

"Colin and possibly Morgan Roche," he answered with a slight nod.

"Roche?" His uncle leaned his elbows on the desk. "Legally? No. Nothing has come through my office. However, the gossip has been buzzing around town."

Cade frowned. "What are your thoughts on Raven Brooks returning to town?" he asked after a moment.

His uncle was silent for a while, then he stood up and shut the office door. He waited until he was sitting behind his desk to respond.

"My personal opinion? I think it's about time she came home. It can only be a good thing for the resort and for the town, if the rumors are true about her hiring locals again.

My professional opinion..." He glanced towards the door and sighed. "She's caused quite the stir. There are still a lot of people in this town that would like to see her pack up and leave again, never to return."

Cade's eyes narrowed slightly. "I've seen it for myself. She's hiring locals. She mentioned last night—"

His uncle's eyebrows shot up, and Cade winced slightly. He hadn't meant to let anyone know about their date. At least not yet. "She's going to hire as many locals as she can," he finished.

"Last night?" his uncle asked.

"Yeah, last night," he said dryly. "I stay out of your love life; you stay out of mine."

His uncle smiled and nodded. "Fair deal." Then his smile fell away. "I was the one who found Raven. That next morning."

Cade sat forward. "You were?" He frowned slight. "Why didn't I know this?"

Sean shrugged as his eyes grew darker. "I was out looking for your brother. I remembered the caves up on the old walking path. Some of the high school kids used to go up there and smoke weed." He smirked. "Okay, to be honest, I used to go up there with your dad a lot."

Cade sighed. "Yeah, Mom has told me some stories about you two."

Sean's eyes grew distant and sad again. "I thought that if Reggie remembered the cave, maybe he'd make his way there."

"You found Raven instead?"

Sean nodded. "Most of her clothes had been burned or had fallen off her. She was barely breathing but, oddly, there wasn't a scratch on her, except for her hands and knees. From what I saw, she'd crawled her way out of the fire."

"She crawled into the caves?" Cade asked. He'd known that Raven had been found up near there and that she hadn't been burned, but the rest of the details hadn't spread around.

"The official report confirms that she was nowhere near where the fire started." Sean nodded.

Again, this was the first he'd heard of this fact. For the past ten years, he'd tried to get as much information from his uncle and from the reports as he could. So far, none of them had given him as much as his uncle had just said.

"Then why are there rumors floating around that say otherwise?" Cade asked.

Sean shrugged. "People will spread the rumors they want. There were even rumors that she was some sort of a witch since she'd been untouched. Rumors are just that, like the one about me and your mother."

"Anyone who knows you two can tell that's a lie," he said quickly.

"When Henry was alive, I only thought of Fiona as a sister," Sean agreed.

Yet, there was something in his uncle's tone that had him asking, "And now?"

Sean sighed and shook his head. "You did say we'd stay out of each other's love lives."

Cade laughed. "Fine."

CHAPTER ELEVEN

FIRE IS NEVER A GENTLE MASTER

The meeting with Joe and his assistant Ruth Downing went better than Raven had expected. With the exception of the part where they informed her that in the past ten years, more than three million dollars had been misplaced from the resort's general funds account.

What could her uncle possibly do with that much money without anyone noticing? It wasn't as if he had a line of luxury cars in the garage. Or even a mansion filled with expensive jewelry.

That came down to over three hundred thousand dollars a year. More than her parents had made in combined salaries when they had worked there.

Ruth, a middle-aged woman who was dressed in the latest fashion and sporting a cropped haircut, explained how her uncle and aunt had also doubled their salaries each year. All while hiring fewer and fewer employees and maintenance crews. They'd even cancelled all of the services needed each year to run the massive resort.

"So, now we just need to find out who was responsible

for the embezzlement," Ruth had said. "If you want to file formal charges."

Raven's heart skipped at the thought of that. "How will we be able to find that out?" she asked, dreading the process already.

"We'll have to file a police report, so that we can legally look at your aunt and uncle's personal finances. We'll need to file a report against Roche Accounting Firm as well," Ruth added. "Her firm was reluctant to supply us with the resort's financial records."

"Morgan Roche and my uncle... Rumors are..." She couldn't even bring herself to say it.

"Right, we heard the rumors all the way in Redding," Joe added. "For now, I'm going to hand over everything so that Ruth can take care of you." Joe stood up and held out his hand for her.

"You won't be taking the lead?" she asked, standing up.

"I'm retired, remember?" Joe shook his head with a smile. "Ruth here runs my business for me. I only dabble in numbers every now and then when I'm bored."

"I'll take good care of you," Ruth said. "When I leave here, I'll get everything together for you for when you file the police reports."

"I..." She paused. "I'm not sure about filing..."

Ruth stood up suddenly and turned towards her.

"Miss Brooks, I understand that it's your uncle. I get why you might not want to turn him in. Remember this, it's not just you they stole from. Think of all the people that went without jobs. All the employees and guests they stole from. This place." She motioned around them. "Everything they took from here."

Raven swallowed and knew that Ruth was right. It hadn't been just her they'd stolen from. Even though her parents were gone, her uncle had stolen from them as well. They were the ones who had worked so hard to build this place, only to have him walk—no, slither—away with over three million dollars' worth of profits. All while letting the place slowly rot around him.

"All right." She nodded. "I'll call the police once you have the information together."

Ruth nodded. "I'll email you later today. I just had a few things to finish up so our case is rock solid."

"Thank you." She shook the woman's hand. "Both of you." She hugged Joe.

"It's good to have you back," he said as he hugged her.

Shortly after they left, her cousin Cal found her still sitting in her office, staring at the blank screen of her laptop.

"Hey, girl." Cal sat on the edge of her desk, looking at her with worry. "You okay?"

She had to blink a few times in order for her eyes to focus.

"Yeah." She took a couple deep breaths. "You?"

"Fabulous," he said easily. "I'm here with good news."

"Oh?" She shifted. "I could use some right about now."

Cal smiled. "I figured, which is why I came the moment I knew."

"Knew?"

"It's official. I'm moving in with Tim." Cal's smile grew.

"You..." She jumped up and hugged her cousin. "That's wonderful." She held onto him. "That *is* good news."

Cal laughed. "We figured that after my father... That it was time." He shook his head. "Besides, Tim thinks that he'll be able to keep his job if you don't see me as a burden like my father was."

"You are no burden," she countered. "And Tim will

keep his job as long as he continues to be the outstanding employee that he is."

"You know it. He loves his job. He wants to go to culinary school. He's taking a bunch of online classes now." Cal's eyes ran over her. "You know, out of the three of us, you could have absolutely made it in the big leagues as a model." He reached up and ran a finger down her braid. "Flawless skin, perfect hair, and those eyes." He shook his head. "Liza's always been jealous of those eyes."

"Thank you," she answered with a smile.

"Now, I'm off to pack." He stepped away. "Oh, and officially come out of the closet with my mother." He rolled his eyes.

"Good luck," she called after him.

"Thanks." He waved as he left.

Cal's visit put her in a better mood for the rest of the day. Paperwork didn't seem so dauting and, after looking over the initial budgets that Ruth had given her, she was happily surprised to find that she was underbudget with the repairs.

Which meant she could afford a few more items on her list of things that she wanted to get done before the season —new carpet in the elevators, new paintings in the lobby, and new computer systems in the guest computer lab. She'd had to use them the other day when she'd forgotten her laptop upstairs, and they were at least ten years outdated.

Not to mention they were still using dial-up. She'd already scheduled the internet services to be updated in the entire resort and planned on offering free Wi-Fi in all the guest rooms, something that should have been done a long time ago.

She worked through lunch and only stopped in the

afternoon when her stomach growled loudly, and she realized she was out of water as well.

Taking her refillable water bottle, she locked her computer and her office door and headed downstairs, hopefully to get some leftovers.

Seeing that everyone in the kitchen was busy, she logged into the nearest wait station and put in an order to be delivered up to her room. She filled up her water bottle and headed upstairs. She took the time to stop off in the lobby and once again check on the day's progress.

Since she'd worked late, she wasn't surprised to see that all the workers had gone for the day. They'd left behind them new floors, new ceiling tiles in the bar, and a freshly painted wall that she had plans to cover with local artwork that Cal had talked her into purchasing.

Everything was coming together nicely. Since they had been trying to finish the bar area first, the dining area was still cut off from the lobby by a wall of plastic sheeting. Since there weren't any guests, shutting down the main dining area hadn't been a big problem. Hotel employees enjoyed their meals in the makeshift dining area they'd set up in the front lobby area.

She doubted they'd been able to do anything in there but still wanted a look. The fountain had been drained in order to prepare it for a fresh coat of paint and some pipe updates.

Stepping through the plastic, she instantly noticed that nothing had changed in the area yet. The old flooring hadn't even been ripped up yet.

She'd been assured by David that the bar would be finished in a few days. Once done, the dining area in the lobby would be shut down and eating would be limited to the bar area.

Just as long as they finished the two dining areas before the season started, she figured it wouldn't disrupt guests too much.

Not that they had a lot of guests scheduled to come through their doors. Yet. She'd looked at the reservation log herself. But she had a few ideas about getting more guests once all the work was done. She knew that the season always brought a steady flow through the resort, but with her plans, she was determined to be just as busy in the off-season as well.

Standing facing the fountain, she glanced around and imagined how it would all look. How it would feel crowded with families, people enjoying themselves like they used to, back when her parents were in charge.

Her phone chimed, and she glanced down at it. She was walking by the elevators and had started reading the email from Ruth when she slipped on the wet floor. She reached out to catch herself before she fell completely and got a handful of the plastic as she went down hard.

She landed on her hip and winced as pain shot through her upper thigh and her hands, which she'd put out to stop her fall.

Taking a moment, she closed her eyes and tried to breathe through the pain. When she opened her eyes again, she glanced around for her cell phone, which she'd dropped.

It had slid across the floor back towards the fountain. From here, she could see that the screen was cracked and groaned at the thought of replacing it.

When she moved to stand up, she frowned down at her hands. They were covered in blood. Had she cut herself? She figured that she wouldn't walk away without any scrapes, since she'd gone down hard, but there was so much blood covering her fingers that she instantly worried she'd sliced herself deeper.

Frantically, she searched herself and only found a few cuts that were barely bleeding.

Then she noticed her pants were wet and looked around behind her, where she'd slipped. A puddle of dark red liquid pooled just inside the plastic that led towards the elevators.

She carefully stood up, avoiding the blood, and stood directly in front of the sixth elevator and held her breath. The elevator, one of the only original elevators left in the main building, had been shut down recently for repairs and, since it led directly to the closed dining area, it had been sealed off until all the renovations were done.

She looked down at the tile just outside the elevator doors and frowned at more dark liquid pooling there as she reached for the button. It shouldn't have worked. It should have had no power to it. Yet, she listened as the car moved closer to the main floor. When the doors slid open, she scrambled backwards and once again, landed on the floor in the sticky liquid as her scream echoed through the lobby.

Half an hour later, she sat in the bar area, a blanket wrapped around her and a cup of hot tea held between her hands.

"Are you sure you're okay?" Cemal asked again.

Raven nodded as she'd done a dozen or so times before. She didn't trust her voice. She'd screamed and screamed until Cemal had rushed through the plastic to find her and the... Raven closed her eyes at the memory. Of seeing all the blood around a man's shoulders where a head used to be.

She'd never seen a dead body before. Well, not like that. She'd been the one to find her grandmother that morning.

But her gran had looked like she was sleeping. She'd looked so... peaceful.

Whoever it was in the elevator, there was no way he'd gone peacefully. Then again, being decapitated in such a manner had to have happened quickly.

"Miss Brooks?"

Raven glanced up through her tear-filled eyes and, for a moment, she believed it was Cade standing in front of her. Then she blinked and saw it was his uncle, Sheriff Sean Stone. If she'd been in a different mental state, she would have taken a moment to appreciate how sexy the man was. How much Cade look like him, would look like him in a few years.

"Yes," she said, setting down the teacup.

"May I?" he asked, and Cemal jumped up to give the man her seat.

She was thankful that by the time Cemal had shown up beside her, the elevator doors had shut again, blocking the horrible view from the young girl.

"Please." Raven motioned towards the chair.

"I'll just..." Cemal motioned towards the front. "If you need me." She touched Raven's arm.

Raven had been allowed to go into the bathroom and clean up after the first officers had arrived and snapped a few pictures of her hands and arms with their cell phones.

"Think you can go over everything that happened with me?" Sean asked in a calm voice.

"I can try," she said in a shaky voice.

By the time she was done telling Cade's uncle what she'd gone through, she felt a little steadier. Her tea had been replaced by a shot of bourbon at Sean's request, and she was sipping it and feeling slightly more relaxed.

Since she hadn't had any dinner yet, she was now

feeling tipsy as well. Her food had been delivered to her there in the bar, after word had gotten out about what had happened, but so far, she hadn't opened the lid. If she did, she'd probably lose all the liquid in her stomach.

"My god. What the hell happened here?" They both turned to see Cade rush towards them. He didn't stop until he'd pulled her up out of the seat and into his arms. "Are you okay?" Cade asked her softly.

"I am." She closed her eyes and held onto him.

"You should have called me," Cade said over her shoulder to his uncle.

"I sent you a text the moment I knew about it," Sean answered.

He leaned back as his eyes scanning her face. "You're pale."

She nodded and swallowed.

"What happened here?" Cade asked Sean as he helped her sit down again.

Sean took Cade's shoulders and stepped away from her. She heard him whisper into his nephew's ear quickly, relaying what she'd gone through.

Cade's eyes moved to her as he listened.

Then he was back beside her. "You're done?" he asked Sean.

"For now," Sean agreed. "I'll be by in the morning with any other questions." Then he turned to her. "If you think of anything else, write it down, and we can go over it in the morning."

She nodded again in response. They watched his uncle disappear through the plastic sheet wall, heading towards the elevator.

Closing her eyes, she tried not to think about what was beyond the barrier.

"I'm taking you upstairs," Cade said. "Is this yours?" He motioned to the covered food and the glass of bourbon.

She nodded. He lifted the lid of the food and then smelled the drink. "Sean's idea?" he asked her. Again, she nodded.

She realized she'd used up all her energy talking to his uncle. She was completely drained.

What she wanted now more than anything was to get out of the soiled clothes, take a long hot shower, and go to sleep.

Cade helped her stand and then took the tray and led her towards the bank of elevators across the lobby area that led them to the west building.

"I assume you haven't had a chance to move rooms yet?" he asked her.

She shook her head and hit the button for the top floor.

"I did stress how dangerous it was having anyone stay in this building until it was updated, correct?" he asked once they were in the elevator.

She sighed and closed her eyes and the moment the doors shut, a full-on panic attack hit her at the thought of the body lying on the floor of an elevator just like this one.

"Hey." Cade's arms wrapped around her. "Breathe. I'm here," he said into her hair as her eyes closed tighter. "Just breathe." He nudged her chin up and started kissing her. His lips ran over her face softly, raining tender kisses over her cheeks, her eyes, down her chin and neck until she felt her breathing level.

When she heard the elevator door open, she pulled back and took a deep breath.

"Okay?" he asked.

She nodded once again and held the doors open while he retrieved the tray he'd set on the floor.

He followed her to her room and stood back while she unlocked the door.

She hadn't really thought about how she looked until she passed the large mirror over the desk. Wincing at the mess she was, she motioned to the table.

"You can set that down there. I'm going to go..." She looked down at her blood-stained clothes. "I'm okay, if you want to..."

"I'll stay," he said firmly. "Go, clean up. I'll order myself a sandwich as well." He motioned to the tray. "Want anything else?"

She shook her head and turned to head into her room.

Shutting the door behind her, she stripped off the soiled clothes and, instead of putting them with her clothes to be cleaned, she tossed them in the trash can, knowing the pants were beyond help.

She stepped under the hot spray, leaned against the tile, and slid onto the shower seat. She buried her face in her hands and cried until she felt too tired to continue.

After scrubbing her entire body raw, she turned off the water, ran a comb through her hair, and pulled on her favorite pair of plaid pajamas.

When she stepped out of the bedroom, Cade was sitting at the table, looking down at his phone.

"Any updates?" she asked, sitting across from him.

His eyes ran over her, no doubt assessing her. She was too tired to care that he was seeing her raw; no makeup with her hair dripping wet.

"Yes, they've identified who... you found." He leaned a little closer.

"Who was it?" she asked, bracing herself.

"Joseph Ramsey," he said quickly.

"What?" She jerked up a little. "No." She shook her

head and searched his eyes for the truth. "How? I... just met with him earlier today."

She'd been too shocked to recognize that the body had been wearing the same clothes Joseph had been wearing earlier.

"His car is still in the parking lot. His wallet was in his pocket." Cade sighed. "Sean has more questions for you. I've convinced him to wait until the morning."

She leaned back and closed her eyes. "He left my office. I... I thought he'd left the resort." She remembered him hugging her and his last kind words to her and tears slipped down her cheeks. "Why was he using that elevator?"

"Hey." Cade was there again, pulling her into his arms as she sat there and cried for her father's old friend.

"His assistant, Ruth," she said a few moments later, her voice laced with worry as her heart raced for fear of the woman's well-being. "Ruth Downing. She was with him. She wasn't harmed, was she?" she asked quickly.

Cade lifted her into his arms until she was sitting in his lap. He stroked her hair gently. "She's safe," he assured her. "Sean claims he's already talked to her. They had driven here separately. She claims Joseph mentioned something about another meeting in town after leaving your office. They parted ways in the lobby shortly after your meeting."

"It's all my fault," she said, resting her head against his chest. She was too tired to go on. She couldn't even open her eyes anymore.

"What is?" Cade asked, his voice vibrating against her ear, lulling her even further.

"His death," she said. She felt her entire body floating. "The elevator. I... I thought that I shut it down." She felt everything drift off as she fell into a deep slumber brought on by utter exhaustion.

That had gone down better than expected. A calm wave washed over them and there was pride and excitement at going undiscovered, which caused delight to surface. Joy which hadn't been felt in years mixed with desire for more.

The thrill of seeing the blood had only lit more fires. An exhilarating feeling swelled at how close to getting caught they'd come.

Giddiness rippled while hiding only steps away from Raven as she'd discovered Joseph's body in the elevator where it had been staged. It was almost too much to hold in the laughter as Raven slipped on the blood. The laughter had almost escaped and given them away.

Then hearing the bitch scream had inspired further. After all, the bitch had it coming, but not quite yet. There was more to do first.

Hopefully, now that Joseph was out of the way, the secret that had threatened to surface had died with him.

It wasn't the first time killing and thanks to the slut's return, it wouldn't be the last. Uncaged. They were finally free, and nothing was ever going to imprison them again.

CHAPTER TWELVE

Cade laid Raven down on the bed and watched her sleep for a few moments.

Her damp red hair fanned out like flames on the crisp white sheets. Her skin against the snow-white sheets showcased just how much paler she was than they were. He could see a few light freckles just under her eyes and on the tip of her nose. He must not have discovered them before because they were hidden under the makeup she wore. Now, however, her face was free of any cosmetics, giving him the chance to really assess her.

He'd thought she was beautiful before, but now, as she lay raw and exposed in vulnerable slumber, he realized just how beautiful she really was.

When she'd mentioned it had been her fault that her CPA was dead, he'd tensed for just a moment, remembering all those years he'd believed she'd been responsible for his brother's death. For so long, he'd believed the rumors and the lies that had spread around town.

Then his uncle's words from the phone call he'd

received while Raven had been showering played in his mind.

"Joseph Ramsey was murdered," Sean had blurted out when he'd answered the call.

"He what?" Cade had almost yelled. Since Sean had only mentioned earlier that Raven had found a man's decapitated body in an elevator, he'd assumed what everyone else had, that somehow it had been a freak elevator accident.

"He was murdered," his uncle said. "Are you still with Raven?"

"Yes." Cade's eyes had moved to the bedroom door. He could hear the shower running in the other room as worry flooded his mind for her.

"I have a few more questions," his uncle had started.

"Tomorrow," he broke in. "Trust me, I doubt she'll be able to keep her eyes open after she's done showering."

"Right." Sean had sighed. "Until then, will you do me a favor and keep an eye on her?"

Cade thought about it. "Can you swing by my place and keep Blue with you for the night?"

"Sure thing. I'll grab him once we're done down here, then I'll stop by first thing in the morning. What room is she staying in?"

"We'll meet you in the lobby," Cade said quickly.

"Nine?" Sean asked.

"See you then," he had said as a knock sounded at the door when his food had arrived.

Now, looking down at Raven, he wondered how she would take the news that someone had murdered a man in her resort. A man she'd had a meeting with earlier that day.

He left her sleeping and went back into the other room to eat his dinner, alone.

His mind played over a million questions. Why? Who? Did it have anything to do with Raven's meeting with the man earlier? Had Joseph Ramsey found out for a fact that Colin Brooks had embezzled money from the resort?

Shit.

Fumbling, he pulled out his cell phone and dialed his uncle.

"Colin Brooks," he said when Sean answered. He could hear Blue barking in the background.

"What?" Sean asked.

"You don't think this has anything to do with Colin Brooks and Morgan Roche, do you? Joseph Ramsey was looking into the possibility of them embezzling money from the resort."

Sean sighed. "I thought of that the moment I found out who it was. After our talk, it's more than crossed my mind. I'm having my guys look into where both Colin and Morgan were today."

Cade relaxed back. "Is Blue okay?" he asked after he heard his dog bark again.

Sean chuckled. "Yeah, he's got a squirrel trapped in the tree. I was just about to get him and take him back to my place."

"Thanks. You can bring him here in the morning. Raven claims she's okay with him visiting the lobby and, to be honest, I think she'd like seeing him after today."

"How is she?" Sean asked.

"She's sleeping. Dropped off quickly." He glanced towards the darkened bedroom. "Sean, if it wasn't Colin or Morgan..."

"We'll find out who it was," Sean assured him. "Get some sleep. We'll see you in the morning."

"Thanks," Cade said and hung up.

He removed his shoes and jacket. Then he grabbed an extra blanket, sat on the sofa, and turned the television on, making sure to mute the set. He watched the replays from a college football game.

He woke when he heard Raven scream. His body instantly went on full alert. He jumped up from the sofa and tripped when his legs got tangled in the blanket.

It took him longer to get to her than he liked. Seeing her asleep and fidgeting in the bed, he relaxed slightly. By the time he gently shook her awake from the nightmare, he'd settled his racing heart.

"Raven?" He pulled her up into his arms. "Shh," he said, stroking her now dry hair. "I'm here. You're safe."

"Blood and fire," she mumbled. "So much of it."

"I've got you," he murmured against her hair as he held onto her. He felt the moment she relaxed back into sleep.

Leaning his head back, he tried to get comfortable as he followed her into sleep.

The next time he woke, it was to the feeling of Raven tensing in his arms. He smiled slightly when she tried to pull away slowly, so as to not wake him up.

"Too late," he said, opening his eyes. "I'm awake." He looked down at her.

Her crystal eyes looked up at him, and he could tell she had a million questions.

Chuckling, he answered the unspoken first one.

"I only came in her a few hours ago when you were having a nightmare." He felt her instantly relax.

"I wasn't concerned," she said with a slight nod. "I was just trying to determine if last night really happened. But since you're here..." She sighed.

"Yeah," he sighed, "you really did find your murdered

CPA's body in an elevator," he said before really thinking it through.

The moment her body tensed and her eyes grew wide, he groaned.

"Shit, that wasn't how I was going to tell you." He took her shoulders and sat up a little. "I'm not really fully awake. It usually takes a long shower or two cups of coffee."

"Murdered? Joe was murdered?" She wrapped her arms around herself as she leaned against the headboard. "Why? How?"

"I don't know the details yet; we're supposed to meet my uncle in the lobby at nine." He glanced down at his phone. "We have some time, if you want to get ready. We can grab something to eat while we wait."

A look crossed her face, and he could tell she was going to turn the offer of food down.

"You skipped dinner last night and something tells me you missed lunch yesterday as well," he jumped in.

Her shoulders sagged, and then she nodded. "I'll get dressed." She rolled out of bed and disappeared into the bathroom.

Heading back into the other room, he realized the television was still on and paused when a picture of Joseph Ramsey flashed on the screen.

After finding the remote, he turned on the sound to hear the last part of the story from the local Redding news station. He switched it off quickly when they offered no more updates. Raven wasn't going to like the negative publicity of someone being murdered at her resort before she could reopen the doors.

It broke his heart a little seeing her step out with red eyes. She'd tried to cover her distress with makeup, but he could see right through it.

She'd dressed in a pair of dark dress pants, a dark grey button-up blouse, and matching low-heeled boots. She had slicked her hair back into a low ponytail. The outfit was meant to project confidence and power. Her eyes, however, gave her away. At least to him.

"Ready?" he asked, taking her hand in his.

She nodded. "Thank you for staying with me last night."

He opened his mouth to explain that his uncle had requested he stick around, then thought better of it. After all, he didn't want it to sound like she had been a burden. She hadn't been. He only wished that the circumstances of his overnight stay had been different.

"I'm glad I did," he said instead. He walked with her to the elevator.

"How about we take the stairs?" she asked, pulling him to a stop.

He turned and looked at her.

"It's not... it has nothing to do with last night. I normally take the stairs in the morning for exercise. Once I sit down, some days I don't get back up for hours."

He shrugged and nodded, then followed her to the staircase.

"Of course," she said as they headed down, "I should be climbing these at the end of the day. Going downstairs isn't as good of a workout as going up."

"Still, it's something. Don't you guys have a gym around here?" he asked once they reached the bottom floor.

"Not yet." She glanced over her shoulder. "I have plans to put one in, though. It's going to have state-of-the-art equipment. I plan on putting in a few walking paths outside as well, for summer guests." She turned to him, and he saw a slight smile on her lips. "And those bike paths you mentioned. I had a talk with Jake about it, and he sounded very excited about the possibility of using the paths himself."

Cade chuckled. "Jake's one of the guys I went to Colorado with that summer. Trust me, he'd be first in line to test the runs out."

She turned, and he noticed the moment she remembered yesterday. The slight spark in her eyes disappeared quickly, and her gaze darted to the large plastic sheeting hiding the view of the area where she'd found Joseph.

"Hey." He squeezed her hand. "I'm here." He nodded towards the bar area. "Let's order some breakfast, shall we?"

The moment after they ordered their food, his uncle strolled in with Blue by his side. The dog paused at the doors and looked up at Sean, as if to make sure it was okay to come inside. God, he had such a good dog.

"Oh!" Raven smiled. "Blue's here."

"Yeah, I had my uncle bring him. He watched him last night. I thought he could help you get through today."

"Thank you." She got out of her chair and gave his dog a warm greeting while he greeted his uncle.

"Morning," Sean said. He took the seat Cade offered.

"We just ordered food, if you want something," Raven said, sitting again.

"No, Blue and I stopped for baked goods in town before heading out here," Sean answered.

Cade snapped his fingers, and Blue sat beside him. He bent down to give his dog a little love while Sean talked with Raven.

"I'm not sure if Cade filled you in yet. We have confirmed that it was Joseph Ramsey you found yesterday," Sean said.

"Yes." Raven sighed and looked towards Cade. "He mentioned something about murder?"

"We found scratch marks on his hands and arms. His associate claims they weren't there before they parted ways in the lobby shortly after their meeting with you," Sean said. "I know you've been through a lot in the past twenty-four hours, but if you could answer a few more questions?"

"Of course." Raven nodded.

Sean continued, "Yesterday, I didn't get a chance to ask you why you hired Mr. Ramsey. His office is in Redding, not to mention he's retired."

"Joe was a good friend of my parents." Raven shifted and crossed her legs. Cade noticed instantly that she was trying to reclaim some form of control by being professional. "He used to live in Cannon Falls, before the fire." Raven's eyes changed slightly. "Then he moved his office to Redding and, a few years back, retired. When I returned, I noticed a few discrepancies on the books and called him to help out."

His uncle had been writing in his notebook and glanced up. "Discrepancies?" Sean's eyes moved to his quickly, then returned to Raven's.

"Joe and his assistant, Ruth, informed me yesterday that over the past ten years, more than three million dollars has gone missing out of the general fund." She paused and took a sip of her water.

Sean whistled. "Wow, that's a lot of change."

"Yes. Ruth was going to get me the details later so I could call you and file an official report," Raven added.

"Any idea who would have taken the money?" Sean asked.

"Yes," Raven answered, her chin rising slightly. "My uncle. I officially fired him the other day and requested he move off of the resort property after a..." She stopped suddenly and looked over at him.

"I walked in on Colin strong-arming Raven the other morning in her office," Cade supplied.

Sean's eyebrows rose. "Physically?"

Raven nodded and released a slow breath. "Yes. I wouldn't have had the courage to kick him to the curb if..." Her eyes moved to Cade's, and he nodded with encouragement. "If Cade hadn't interjected. As it was, I requested he move out immediately and insured that he no longer has access to any of the resort's accounts."

"What day and time was this?" Sean asked.

Raven answered him after looking down at the cracked screen on her phone.

"And he moved out?" Sean asked.

"Yes. My aunt and cousins are still on the premises." She frowned. "Well, Cal has since moved out."

"Do you know if he's been back?" Sean asked.

"Here?" She frowned. "No. I'm sure Cemal would know if he had. I've been tucked in my office most of the time."

Sean wrote more notes. "Have you met with Morgan Roche?"

"She showed up the other morning with my uncle. I turned her away," Raven answered.

"Time and date?" Sean asked. Again, Raven looked at her phone before answering.

"You seem very organized," Sean commented, motioning towards her phone.

"Business school one-oh-one. I've even marked down our meeting." She turned the phone and showed his uncle the screen.

Sure enough, there in a calendar app she had the meeting marked with date and time.

"I fully intend to turn the resort around. I can't do that if I don't follow the basic rules of business." Raven set her phone down.

He noticed her reaching down and stroking Blue's head, which was resting on her lap. His dog had a knack for comforting the unsteady.

Sean glanced around. "The construction crew? What time do they normally leave?"

Raven narrowed her eyes. "Normally?" She shrugged. "If you can get David Green and his men to work normal hours, let me know. I have no issues with their work ethics and have given them free rein just as long as the work gets done. They've done a wonderful job so far. I determined within the first few days not to babysit them. If you want to know what time the crew left yesterday, you'll have to ask them."

Sean wrote down more notes. "Cemal..." Sean started flipping through his notes.

"Rahim," Raven supplied.

"Yes." He nodded and looked back up. "She works the front desk alone?"

"She does for now. When we officially reopen, I'll hire a few more employees to help her out."

"Her hours?" Sean asked.

"Currently, seven days a week, six in the morning to six in the evening," Raven answered.

"Is that allowed?" Sean tilted his head.

Raven shook her head. "Normally, no. But since it's slow here and I'm allowing her to take her online classes while she sits behind the desk"—Raven leaned closer— "she's agreed to only clock eight hours a day officially.

Considering my uncle had her working those hours and refused to let her study, I'd say it's a step up."

Sean smiled and leaned back slightly. "I've heard good things about you since your return."

Raven glanced down at Blue, and Cade could see that she felt more relaxed than when his uncle had first arrived.

Just then their food was delivered by the kitchen staff.

"Thank you, Tim." Raven smiled up at the extremely good-looking man, who was roughly her age.

"Thank you." The man winked back at Raven before turning and leaving. Cade couldn't stop the wave of jealousy that washed over him as he watched the man walk away.

"Is there something wrong with your food?" Raven asked him, gaining his attention again.

"No." He turned back to the table and glanced down at his meal. "It's fine."

Raven turned back to his uncle and asked, "Do you have any other questions for me?"

"Currently, no. I'll let the two of you eat in peace." Sean stood up.

"Sheriff," Raven said quickly, getting his uncle's attention, "when possible, I'd like more details about Joe's death."

Sean nodded. "I'll get you what I can. For now, if I have any more questions, I'll be in contact."

"Thank you," Raven replied as his uncle walked away.

He saw her look at the plastic and then back to her food. When Blue whined, she glanced down at him.

"If you let him, he'll eat the entire meal himself," Cade joked, trying to get her mind off her dark mood.

Raven smiled and petted Blue. "He's probably hungrier than I am."

"You have to eat." He motioned to her food with his

fork. "Tell me all about the other improvements you're going to do around here."

For the next hour, he listened to Raven talk about her plans for the resort. For the first five minutes, she picked at her food, but after she lost herself in the conversation, she finished everything on her plate, with the exception of a dry piece of toast she'd given to Blue.

"Gosh, I can't believe it's this late," she said when her phone chimed. "You must have to get to work yourself."

He smiled. "It's Saturday. I have weekends off. I thought I'd stick around here today. That is if you want me to."

"You'll be bored in five minutes," she warned.

He shrugged. "Blue and I can always take a walk." His dog's ears perked up and he had to add, "Later." Blue sat back down with a little whine.

The smile on Raven's face told him that she was feeling a little better.

As they stood up to head to her office, they both saw her aunt marching across the lobby, heading towards them.

He hadn't been prepared for the woman's first move. As if in slow motion, her hand rose and struck out. The sound of the slap across Raven's face echoed in the lobby area.

However, he was ready for her second move and easily blocked the next strike, pinning her arms to her side as she yelled and screamed profanities at Raven.

CHAPTER THIRTEEN

Raven's left cheek burned as she watched Cade hold back her aunt.

"You bitch," her aunt screamed. "You did this. It's all your fault. Everything was fine until you came back. You ruined everything." Roslyn was screaming.

"Blue. Sit," Cade said firmly.

"What's going on?" Cade's uncle rushed back to their side. His eyes traveled between the three of them and landed on Raven's red cheek, which she was still holding.

Raven hadn't realized the man had stuck around the resort. When her aunt quieted down, she heard a low growl emitting from the dog sitting directly on her feet, as if protecting her. The dog's eyes were glued to her aunt.

"Roslyn?" Sean turned to her aunt. "Is there a problem?"

"Yes." Her aunt jerked her hands free from Cade's hold, and she appeared calmer now. Cade released her and moved over to take hold of Blue's collar. Roslyn turned to Sean. "Is it true that you've placed my husband under arrest for murder?"

"We've taken your husband in for questioning," Sean said with a slight nod. "I'll be heading into the station now to question him myself."

"That girl"—her aunt pointed at Raven— "is responsible. You should be questioning her."

"I have," Sean said easily, "which is why I'm standing here right now."

"Why isn't she under arrest?" Roslyn crossed her arms over her chest and narrowed her eyes at Raven.

"Your husband"—Sean emphasized the word— "is not under arrest, yet. As I said, he's been brought in for questioning."

"Why haven't you brought her in?" She pointed at Raven again.

"Because she has answered all of our questions willingly. Your husband has refused to answer any questions, up to this point," Sean explained.

"He wouldn't have to answer any questions if she hadn't returned and screwed everything up. She's the one who lured that poor man to his death. She's the one who kicked my husband out of his home. She took everything, all of this"—she motioned around them— "away from him. It's all he's known, all he's worked on for the past ten years. Now he has nothing. Nothing!" she screamed.

Raven watched her aunt's face turn red again as she screamed.

Instantly, Cade moved to step between them again, to protect Raven once more.

Sean moved at the same time, taking Roslyn's arm and pulling her back a few steps.

"What do you say I drive you into town so you can see your husband?" he said easily. "That way you can rest assured that he's not under arrest. Just yet," he added again.

"Let go of me." Roslyn jerked her arm free. "She's the one who did this." She glared over at Raven. "She's destroyed everything."

Sean's hold on her never wavered as he started walking towards the front door. The whole time, her aunt continued to scream out accusations.

"Are you okay?" Cade asked her, releasing his hold on Blue and stepping closer to examine her face. His hand moved up and gently brushed her burning cheek.

"I'm fine," she said automatically.

"We should get some ice on it," he suggested.

"There's an ice machine by my office." She looked down at the dog. "You were going to protect me, weren't you?" She bent down and gave Blue a scratch and a hug. "You deserve a bigger treat than dry toast. I'll have the kitchen bring something up for him."

"He likes bacon," Cade said. He chuckled when his dog's ears perked up.

"Bacon it is then." She smiled when Blue licked her cheek.

She opened her office and waited with Blue while Cade disappeared to grab some ice for her cheek.

She hadn't expected her aunt's actions and words to sting so much, but by the time Cade returned with a clear bag of ice, tears were rolling down her cheeks again.

"I'm really never this emotional," she said as she wiped her face dry.

Cade moved around the desk and knelt in front of her, then gently placed the bag of ice over her burning cheek.

"You deserve to be, currently," he said softly.

His face was so close to hers that she had to blink in order for him to come into focus. Then she was mesmerized by the richness of his eyes. The worry she saw hidden there. Worry for her.

For a split second, she wondered why Cade didn't remind her of Reggie, but then her eyes moved down to his lips and the desire to feel them against her own overpowered all other thoughts.

Her breath hitched; her heart jumped in her chest as he moved closer.

Just then her office door burst open and Darby and Carrie rushed in. She glanced over as Cade leaned back and dropped his hand, holding the ice bag away from her face. Her friends were standing just inside her office, gawking at them.

"We heard..." Darby started. "What happened. Are you okay? Why didn't you call us?"

"How did you hear so quickly?" Raven asked, touching her now chilled cheek.

Her friends frowned at her.

"Didn't the murder happen last night?" Carrie asked.

Raven's mind cleared from the fog that had fallen over it due to Cade's closeness. Right. The murder. She'd found her father's close friend's body last night.

"Right." She nodded and stood up.

"You should have called us," Darby said again. She rushed over to hug her. "Are you okay?"

"Yes," she said as both of her friends hugged her.

"Why is your cheek bright red?" Carrie asked when she leaned back. Her eyes moved to Cade.

"Don't look at me," he said with a shake of his head. "You can thank her aunt for that. I was helping." He held up the ice bag.

"Boy, I know you'd never hurt our girl," Carrie said with

a head bobble. "You're too afraid of us coming for you." She motioned between her and Darby.

Cade smiled. "Damn straight." He handed the ice to Raven. "Now that your friends are here, I'm going to run some errands. Will you be okay?"

"Yes," she said, lifting the ice to her cheek. "Thank you for staying with me."

"Any time," he said, then he snapped his fingers. "Come on, Blue."

"Oh!" Darby knelt down and gave Blue some attention. "I've missed you, Blue. Bring him by the diner again soon. I've always got a juicy bone for him."

Cade smiled. "Will do." He nodded before leaving.

"Girl." Darby turned on her. "You'd better open a window, cuz it's steamy in here." Her friend waved her hand in front of her face, doing her best Carrie imperson-ation as Carrie laughed.

"You need some new jokes," Carrie said, sitting on the edge of Raven's desk. Her friend's smile fell away. "Tell us what happened."

For the next hour, she hung out in her office with her friends, filling them in on every detail about what had happened over the last twenty-four hours, ending with her aunt's actions.

"So, your aunt and uncle are both down at the police station right now?" Darby asked.

They'd ordered coffee and some blueberry muffins from the kitchen and sat in the old leather sofa and chairs that sat across from the desk. She remembered the furniture from when her father used the office and had been surprised it was still in fairly good condition.

"The sheriff made a point to mention that my uncle

wasn't under arrest. That he was just down there for questioning," Raven clarified.

"And he questioned you last night and this morning?" Carrie asked.

"Yes, well, I was the one who found Joe." She felt a shiver race through her and closed her eyes while she tried to control her emotions.

"That's it. You're staying over at my place tonight," Carrie said firmly. "Both of you are. We've needed a catch-up girls' night since all this happened. Safety in numbers and all."

"I..." Raven started but stopped when Carrie narrowed her eyes at her.

"Girl, you are not going to deny me. I..." She shook her head and grabbed Darby's hand. "We," she corrected, "are not going to let you stay in this massive place alone after someone's been murdered here."

"I'm hardly alone," Raven said.

"How many other guests are staying on your floor?" Darby asked.

"None," Raven answered, causing Darby's eyebrows to lift.

"How many are staying in the same building as you?" Darby asked.

Raven sighed heavily. "None."

"Then it's settled." Carrie glanced around. "Are you really going to work today? Or can we please play hooky and go shopping before girls' night?"

Raven thought about the pile of paperwork and decided that her mind just wasn't on it.

"Let's go shopping," she said to the joy of her friends.

Raven hadn't known she'd needed the day with her

friends until they were sitting at a restaurant in Redding overlooking the river and laughing while drinking a glass of wine.

"God, I needed this," she said with a sigh. The tears leaking out of her eyes now were happy tears. "A day with you two. I've missed the both of you."

"Well, you're the one who has been so busy since you returned," Darby pointed out.

"For good reason." Carrie nudged Darby. "Look at all you've had to take on. I mean, who would have thought that over the years your uncle and Morgan Roche would be stealing from you."

"Not really from me," she corrected. "From the resort. Most of the money taken was earmarked for hiring employees, general maintenance and repairs, those kinds of things. My uncle never wavered on depositing my allotted funds in my account. I think he knew that if he did, I'd find out about the other money he was taking."

"That makes sense." Darby nodded.

"I'll wager he never expected you to return," Carrie added.

"I hadn't planned on it," she admitted out loud.

"What made you change your mind?" Darby asked.

"My gran. The night before she passed, we had a talk." She took a sip of her wine and swallowed the pain of losing her grandmother. "She reminded me of my parents' sacrifice to turn the resort around. How much it meant to them and, she reminded me, how much it meant to me."

"I'm so sorry." Carrie reached across and took Raven's hand.

Raven nodded and smiled. "Once her estate was settled, I decided to come back and use my inheritance to fix the resort up once more." She frowned. "I hadn't expected to spend all my money. I had hoped to purchase a place of my own, but after seeing the state of things." She shook her head and finished off the last of her grilled shrimp salad. "I'm going to be lucky to get everything on my list done."

"It's that bad?" Darby asked.

Raven shrugged. "Some items will just have to wait until next year." She was determined to keep a positive attitude.

"So, you are for sure sticking around?" Carrie asked.

Raven tilted her head slightly and glanced out over the water. "Part of me misses the city life. But no." She shook her head. "There's nothing left for me in San Diego."

"You've got us here," Carrie added as she tipped her glass towards Raven.

"To the three amigas." Darby held up her glass.

After lunch, the three of them hit every store in town. Well, okay, not every store, but by the time they headed back to Cannon Falls, her feet felt like they had.

She wanted to tell her friends that she was okay for the night, that they could drop her off, but part of her still didn't want to be alone.

She was happily surprised when Cade texted her midday to ask her how things were going. She filled him in quickly on playing hooky and staying at Carrie's for the night.

He replied that it was a good idea and to have fun.

She'd wanted to ask him if he'd heard anything else from his uncle but didn't want to put a damper on her good mood.

Carrie parked in front of a small cottage home just inside town.

"Is this your place?" Raven asked eagerly.

"It is. I had it built with the insurance money. It's small, because the money was tight, but it's everything I need. Besides, I spend most of my time down at my office," she answered with a shrug.

"I love it. It's... perfect," Raven said, getting out of the car and grabbing her overnight bag and the bags of items she'd purchased. She shouldn't have spent the money, but she'd found a pair of boots and a couple of new tops she wanted.

"Dad and I are just there," Darby added, pointing across the street and down a few homes. "The blue one."

"Wow, I can't believe I didn't know where you guys lived." She felt her heart skip at the realization that she hadn't even thought about what had happened to her friends after the fire. She'd been so... lost. There hadn't been room for anything other than her own pain.

"It's okay." Darby walked up and wrapped her arms around her. "We all bounced back. Some of us just took a little longer."

Raven smiled down at her friend. "Did you get short-er?" she joked, earning a poke in the ribs from her friend.

"Does that joke ever get old?" Carrie chuckled as she unlocked her door. "Welcome to mi casa," she motioned with a flourish.

Raven stepped into the home and smiled. Carrie had always been an artist at heart. Even if she did spend most of her time with her nose stuck in a book.

The vibrant colors that filled the small space somehow made the nine-hundred-square-foot home feel bigger.

"I spent months scouring through small home designs before settling on this one."

"Settling?" Darby shook her head. "You designed this place yourself."

"You did?" Raven asked, setting her bags down just inside the door.

"Yeah," Carrie said with a smile. She took Raven's hand. "Let me show you around."

Raven had to admit, the place was so efficient, that she doubted she would feel like she was short of space if she lived there.

There were hidden cubbies and drawers everywhere, places to tuck away items and store them out of sight, keeping the main areas free from clutter.

As with the living area, Carrie's bright color choices flowed throughout the entire home, bringing cheer and happiness into each space.

"Oh, and the best part is..." Carrie walked over to a wall in what she'd described as her home office and flipped what Raven assumed was a light switch. Suddenly, the wall slowly lowered, revealing a full-sized bed. "The guestroom," Carrie added with a wave.

"Wow, how did you design all of this?" Raven asked.

"It was easy. I was tired of living in the small government trailer," Carrie added with a shrug.

Raven sat on the edge of the bed and felt her shoulders sink. "I'm so sorry."

"For?" Darby asked.

"Leaving you. Both of you. I should have... stayed in town. After." She looked between her friends.

Darby and Carrie sat on either side of her and wrapped their arms around her.

"We all lost someone we loved. You just got hit with a double whammy," Darby said softly. "Losing my mom was hard, but at least I had my dad to help me. You had no one." Darby hugged her.

"Not to mention losing Reggie. You two were perfect

for one another," Carrie said, wrapping her arms around the both of them.

Raven felt a twinge of pain when she heard Reggie's name. She must have tensed, because Carrie asked.

"What?" They both leaned back and looked at her.

"Reggie." She shook her head. "I found out, just before..." She closed her eyes. "That he'd cheated on me."

"What?" Darby gasped. "No way." She shook her head.

"No, it's true." Raven sighed. "And so ten years ago. It shouldn't matter..."

"But it does," Carrie added, pushing a strand of Raven's hair behind her ear. "We need more wine. Then you can tell us everything." She jumped up from the bed.

Half an hour later, the three of them sat around Carrie's kitchen table. A plate of brie, crackers, and some fruit sat in the middle, along with some assorted chocolates Carrie had pulled out and a bottle of red wine.

"So." Carrie motioned to her. "You know everyone's been dying to find out exactly what happen to you that day. How did you end up in the cave? Alone?"

Raven was thankful for the wine. Somehow, it, and knowing she was among friends, helped her get through her story.

"I don't really know. It was the morning of my birthday."

"Your seventeenth," Darby added in.

"Right. Later that night, we were supposed to have my party at the resort. Mom had spent so much time decorating and planning it. I was excited but acted like I wasn't. I couldn't show my parents that I wanted the party. I was way too cool for that. I remember going to Redding with her and picking out the perfect dress." She closed her eyes on the wave of pain, missing her mother. "Reggie had asked me to meet him at our spot at midnight so he could be the first one to tell me happy birthday."

"Aww, that was sweet of him," Carrie said.

"Yes." Raven nodded and smiled, remembering all the sweet times she'd had with Reggie on the hill that overlooked the town. He'd taken her there after their first date. He'd spread out a blanket and the two of them had watched the moon rise. It was the first place she'd made love. The place where she'd first admitted to him that she loved him. It was her favorite spot. Or had been. "He said he had a special surprise for me and wanted to give it to me alone. We agreed to meet just before midnight."

"You said you found out he cheated on you?" Darby asked.

"Right." She took another sip of her wine. "I ran into... Julia Garza. She used to work as a waitress here all through high school."

"I fired her a few days back." Darby rolled her eyes. "Long and different story. Let's just say that no one in town will hire her now. Not after the craziness she did." Darby waved her hand. "Another story for another time. What did Julia say?"

Raven really wished Darby would continue but decided she could get the rest of the story out of her friend later.

"Julia told me she knew, firsthand, that Reggie had cheated on me at Venessa's party the weekend before."

"The one you didn't go to?" Carrie asked.

"Yeah. I was in Redding with my mother, buying my birthday dress." She glanced down at her fingers and took a deep breath.

"And you believed her?" Carrie asked.

"She showed me the picture she'd taken on her phone," Raven answered.

"Of?" Darby asked.

"Reggie, kissing a girl." She shrugged.

"Who was it?" Carrie asked.

"I don't know. It was from behind; all I could see was it was Reggie and the girl had darker hair. It didn't matter, at that point. I knew it was true. So, I went up there to meet him, knowing I was going to break it off."

"Did you?" Darby asked.

"No, not really. I went there, met him, and he..." She closed her eyes and shook her head as the memory played over in her mind. She hadn't realized tears were once again rolling down her face.

"It's too hard," Darby said, wrapping an arm around her. "You don't have to tell us."

"No, it's okay. I think that once I do, somehow I'll be lighter." She smiled and hugged Darby back. She took a big gulp, finishing the glass of wine. "He had a picnic all laid out. A moonlight celebration. There was a single cupcake with a candle sitting in the middle of the blanket along with a bottle of champagne that he'd snuck out of his parents' wine fridge. It was so romantic, but all I could think of was him, kissing someone else." She took a deep breath as Carrie poured her more wine. "So, I confronted him." Closing her eyes, she replayed the next fateful moments in her head as she continued to tell her friends.

"Did you make out with someone else at Venessa's party last weekend?" she'd asked him, not even taking the cupcake he offered her.

"Where'd you hear that?" Reggie asked. The single candle lit up his face, along with the bright full-moon and the camping lamp that was sitting in the middle of the blanket.

"Does it matter? Did you?" she asked, crossing her arms over her chest. She'd worn shorts and a tank top, since

summer was in full swing, even though school wasn't set to end for another few days.

"I..." Reggie had frowned. "It's not what you think."

Reaching out, she took the cupcake and tossed it over his head before turning around and storming away. Reggie followed her for a little while, but then his voice dropped away. Then she heard his screams for her to run.

When she looked back, there was a wall of flames, and Reggie was nowhere to be found.

She ran, fumbling through the darkness, tripping over tree roots or rocks. Then she huddled in the dirt and gave in to the smoke. She didn't remember crawling or making her way into the cave. Nor did she remember when Sean Stone found her later. She spent her entire seventeenth birthday unconscious, lying on the floor of a cave, while her family and so many others in town burned up and died in their beds.

"It was all my fault," she said, burying her face into her hands.

"How?" Carrie asked her.

Raven wiped her eyes and blinked a few times, returning to the here and now.

"The cupcake. The candle." She sighed. "Don't you see... It started the fire. I started the fire. If I wouldn't have thrown it." She closed her eyes. "I killed everyone."

"Oh, sweetie." Both of her friends engulfed her in their arms.

"From what we understand, no one really knows how the fire started," Darby said. "I heard it was a discarded campfire."

"I heard it was lightning," Carrie added with a shrug.

"For all we know, it could have been aliens," Darby added dryly. "Fire kills. My mom's gone and so are your parents," she said to Raven. "But one thing is clear to at least us." She waved between Carrie and herself. "We don't blame you. We never have. We both know that you had nothing to do with their deaths."

"Thanks, but I know I did," Raven said with a sigh. "And that's all that has ever mattered."

CHAPTER FOURTEEN

I t took Cade a few days to finally get back up to check on Raven. He'd texted her and even called her, but he'd been too busy to make the trip out there.

The entire town was alight with a fresh wave of gossip. The murder was the hottest topic, besides Roslyn's little outburst.

So far, Cade was thankful that no one was pointing their fingers at Raven. Instead, Colin Brooks and even Morgan Roche were the main masterminds in these tales.

It wasn't until Tuesday afternoon that he and Blue finally drove out to the resort with plans to meet Raven for dinner. She claimed that she had a surprise for him and Blue.

He figured it was a dog treat or a toy, but when they parked, he noticed the string lights in the courtyard and Raven standing under them, her soft-pink dress almost glowing under the soft lights. Her red hair glowed like flames in the night. He felt his heart skip. Then he noticed she was standing next to a table.

"What's all this?" he asked as they approached her,

willing his heart to settle back down. She was even more beautiful than he remembered.

"First things first." She smiled and bent down to set a plate with an entire steak on it, cut into bite-sized chunks, in front of Blue.

"Hey, I hope you have one of those for me?" he said, jealous of his dog.

"I do." She chuckled. "Ours, I figured you'd want warm." She motioned to the table. "This is to say thank you. To you both." She glanced down at Blue, who was wolfing down his steak.

"For?" he asked, pulling out the chair for her to sit down.

"Staying with me the other night," she answered after he took the spot opposite her.

"It was nothing. Any friend—"

She held up her hand.

"I have ulterior motives," she said with a smile, leaning a little closer.

"Oh?" His eyes moved to her lips. She was wearing a pale pink lipstick that matched the dress she was wearing. She had diamonds in her ears that sparkled in the overhead lights every time she moved.

She nodded and leaned back. "This is a trial run." She turned away from him and nodded.

Suddenly, two waitstaff appeared from the darkness and handed them menus.

"Oh," he said a little less enthusiastic. She laughed.

"Hey, you get a free meal out of it. Not to mention the company of a... friend," she added, her eyes meeting his over the menu.

"Okay." He nodded in agreement. "I'm game." He

scanned the new menu and whistled. "You've added a few more fancy meals on this."

"We have," she agreed. "I've been working with an up-and-coming chef who aspires to run the kitchen here one day," she said with a smile.

"Oh? Well, let's see if he or she is any good."

"He," she added.

After placing their orders, Blue settled down at Raven's feet and instantly fell asleep.

"He's always like that after a big meal," Cade added with a chuckle.

"I received a call from your uncle today." She sipped the wine that she'd ordered. He'd stuck with a Coke, since he knew he'd be driving home later.

"Yeah? What did he have to say?"

"He claims that my uncle hired a lawyer and has refused to answer any questions. He also said that my aunt has moved out of the resort and is staying with him in a hotel in Redding." She played with her wine glass.

"You didn't know your aunt had moved out?"

"After the other day, I sent word through my cousin Cal to let Roslyn know she was no longer welcome here. Now it's just my cousin Liza who is still hanging around." Raven shrugged. "Something tells me she won't be attacking me anytime soon." She shook her head. "Cal assures me that the last thing Liza wants to do is stay at a second-rate hotel with their parents."

"Interesting. I find it fascinating that they continued to all live here over the years. They moved in after the fire, right?"

"Yes. They had a home on the edge of the burn area but ended up selling it after I left. I think they've grown accustomed to having people wait on them hand and foot."

"Are you planning on staying here or finding a place of your own in town?" He and so many others in town were curious about her intentions.

"I had wanted to look to purchase a place of my own, but now..." She shrugged. "Things have taken a turn with finances. I'll move over to the east building until the west is up to date. Then, when things are more stable, I'll look for my own place."

"You haven't moved to the east building yet?" He shook his head. "Can I stress the importance of doing so, again?" He leaned closer.

"Yes." She smiled. "I've been... busy. Besides, I was hoping to wait until David's crew had a chance to finish some of the rooms before moving over. They're due to start updating the fire system on the west side next month. Do you know, I have more construction men running around here than I do staff at the moment?" She shook her head and leaned back. "I'm not sure where David is getting them all from."

"That's a good thing. You still have a lot to do." He motioned towards the doors. "How's it going inside?"

"Good. They have the bar area done. I think... with everything that happened, David pulled all the men together to finish the job early. They've removed the plastic sheets and put up some temporary plywood walls instead." She shivered.

"That's good." He nodded.

"They've torn out the old flooring and are replacing it now. They should be done in a day or two. Then they'll install the new planters we'll use as separaters..." She stopped suddenly. "You didn't come out here to listen to me talk about the work." She waved her wine glass. "How is your work?"

He smiled. "Boring compared to what's going on around here."

"No, please." She motioned towards him. "I'd like to hear."

"Okay." He shrugged. "Let's see. First thing Monday morning, we received a call about Brett Dove setting a trash bin on fire."

"Brett?" She frowned. "Old man Dove?"

"The very same."

"He's still alive?"

He chuckled. "And setting his trash on fire at least twice a month. Since the big one, as everyone in town calls it, every time someone lights a cigarette, we get called." He watched a sadness creep into her eyes, so he moved on quickly. "Next, I went back to the firehouse, checked all the oxygen tanks, updated my reports, and played a practical joke on the two newbies." He shrugged. "It's sort of a rite of passage."

She smiled. "See, your job isn't boring," she said just as their food was delivered.

"This coming from the woman who's rebuilding an entire ski resort," he said once the waiter left.

"I'm not rebuilding it with my own hands." She waved her fork.

"How was your night with your friends?" he asked suddenly before taking a bite of his steak.

"Much needed." She took her own bite of steak.

"Okay, your new chef has my blessings," he said after he swallowed. The steak practically melted in his mouth, and the mixture of flavors caused his entire body to tingle with food delight. He couldn't remember tasting anything this good in the past few years.

Raven smiled. "I agree. My god, Tim made me

lunch today and it was the best salad I've eaten in weeks, so when he suggested he make me dinner..." She took another bite and closed her eyes on a low moan. He watched her intently, his mind switching away from hunger for the food to hunger for her. "I think I'm going to have to bump him up from waiter to chef."

"He has my vote." He tried to focus on the food instead of the sexy little moans emanating from Raven.

They ate in silence for a while, enjoying the cool evening of summer. In a few more weeks he knew they'd been in full drought as the summer heat dried up the California hills that surrounded the town.

For now, everything around them remained green, lush, and alive.

"I wish I knew more about how Joe died," Raven said after she pushed her plate away. "I can't stop thinking about it."

"My uncle is keeping it under tight wraps. I think he doesn't want it spreading around town." He took his last bite and then leaned back in the chair. "I thought you would know how he died."

"How, I mean, sure, I saw the aftermath." She shrugged and closed her eyes. "But *how*..." She shook her head. "I mean, I don't even know where they found..."—she took a deep breath— "the rest of him."

Cade frowned into his drink. He hadn't expected the conversation to take this dark turn, but she had probably been thinking about it since that night. The fact that he was one of the only people she could talk to about it had him leaning forward.

"More important is the question of who would or could have done such a thing?" she asked.

"Okay, so let's figure it out together. My uncle doesn't share work with me, but I have heard a few things."

She smiled slightly. "I was hoping you'd say that." She bent down and pulled a notepad from her purse. "My friends and I have made a list." She flipped the pages.

"Is this one of the reasons you asked me here tonight?" he teased. "To play cop."

Her eyes grew wide and her cheeks turned pink. She looked even more beautiful in the sparkling lights as she grew flustered.

"No," she said quickly and started putting the notepad away.

"I was joking," he said with a smile as he covered her hand with his. "I've been thinking a lot about who would do this and why also," he said, not willing to tell her the other questions that raced through his mind. "Let's go over your list. Who knows, it might help."

He was very curious to see what the friends had come up with. He'd heard rumors all throughout town about Joseph Ramsey. Everyone who had known the man claimed that he'd been a nice enough man.

So far, what Cade had heard about the man was just the basic facts. He'd never been married and had lived in town until his home and business had burned down along with all the rest. Then he had moved to Redding. That was it. He'd also learned from Raven that he'd been friends with her father back in the day.

"Well, the most important questions we had were..." She opened her notepad and scanned the pages. "Who did Joe have a meeting with? Why was he in that elevator? Who had something to gain from his death?" She glanced up at him. "Those are the biggest questions besides how he died. I mean, the technical aspects. I can't imagine that overpowering someone is easy, let alone…" She made a motion by swiping her finger over her throat.

"Right." He nodded. "Okay, as for the meeting part, I'm sure my uncle has figured that out. If he was any good at his job, Joe would have had records. Calendars." He shrugged. "Schedules."

"Right." Raven nodded. "I'd hoped to talk to Ruth Downing about it, but she rescheduled our meeting until next week."

"Joe's assistant?"

"Well, more like partner. The way Joe introduced her, it sounded more like Ruth was running the business and Joe was just helping out occasionally. He retired a few years back," Raven added.

"Right. Okay, let's assume we get the information on who he was meeting. As to why he was in that elevator… You said that night that you'd believed you'd shut it down. Was that due to maintenance?"

"Yes and no. It wasn't that the elevator was broken, though most of them on the property need some maintenance, which is scheduled." She held up her finger. "Now that I've hired back the maintenance company, they'll be here first thing Monday morning to start inspecting each elevator and doing repairs."

"Then why was it shut down?" he asked.

"Because of the construction. That elevator is the dining elevator."

He shook his head. "The…"

She smiled. "It's a quick access to the dining room. For guests heading down to dinner. It exits in the formal dining room. Instead of waiting for a main elevator, guests could take it instead."

"Right." He shrugged. "I guess that's a thing."

She chuckled. "It was when this place was built." She glanced around at the main buildings hovering over them. "The main building"—she motioned behind him— "was built in nineteen thirty-two. The time when men wore tuxes and women were draped in silk, furs, diamonds, and pearls as they made their way down to dinner." Her voice had turned dreamy, and her eyes became unfocused. "This place was one of the first luxurious ski resorts within driving distance of San Francisco. Of course, back then it would have taken guests a lot longer to drive up here from the city, which meant they stayed longer." She leaned her elbows on the table, and he watched her disappear into the daydream of the history of the place. "There was just the main building back then, and only two ski runs." She chuckled and her eyes turned to him. "You should have seen what they considered a ski lift back then." She shook her head. "I remember seeing pictures in my father's office." She seemed to snap out of the daydream. "Sorry, I'm getting off topic."

"Right." He smiled.

"Dinner elevators." She straightened. "Okay, so, I had it shut down a couple days before. I remember David mentioning that his guys had cut the power to it. They didn't want any guests or employees accidently walking in on the construction zone. Besides, we don't need it running, at least not until guests start arriving."

"Okay, so how did it get turned back on?" he asked.

She tapped the notebook. "Another question we have. I asked David, and he claims that he's asking his workers and will let me know when he finds out. He's shut it down again, at least until the maintenance crews come on Monday."

"Which leaves us with the question of who had something to gain from his death," he pointed out.

"Right." Raven frowned. "My uncle and Morgan Roche are top of that list." She glanced down at the notebook. "They had the most to gain from his death to keep Joe from finding out about the money they'd stolen."

"So you're saying they killed Joe to keep their embezzling from being exposed? From going to jail?"

"It's a theory."

"Hadn't you already exposed them?"

"To a point. I mean, Joe was looking into the accounts further. To build the case against them." She bit her bottom lip.

"I'm not buying that," he said after a moment. He leaned back and crossed his arms over his chest.

How many times had he believed Raven was guilty of all the horrors the townspeople had accused her of? How many years had he believed that she was guilty of not only the destruction of the entire town, but of basically murdering thirty people? Including her own parents.

He ran his eyes over her face and realized he'd been such a fool. He'd fallen into the trap of believing what was easy because of his pain and his anger. He'd wanted to blame her for his pain because she'd been absent. A faceless, guilty party at which he could direct all the pain that had been inflicted on him and others. If he had learned anything over the past few weeks since Raven had returned, it was that everything was not always as it seemed.

"Not everything is as cut-and-dried as it first seems." He leaned forward suddenly and locked eyes with her, then lifted her hand into his, lacing their fingers together. "Take you for example."

"Me?" Her voice was barely a whisper in the night air.

"Sure." He pulled her up to stand next to him, then nudged her closer until they were so close, the scent of her soft perfume mixed with that of the freshly planted rose bushes a few feet away. "If I believed everything that was said about you, then I wouldn't be here, with you, like this." His eyes ran down to her mouth. "Wanting to kiss you."

Her breath hitched and her lips curved up.

"Then I suppose we need to look at the possibility that my uncle and his mistress are innocent." She wrapped her arms around his shoulders.

"There should be music," he said suddenly. "And a dance floor." He started to sway with her as the sound of crickets filled the air.

"I'll add it to my list of improvements." She moved easily with him. "Where did you learn to dance?" she asked after a moment.

He smiled. "Are you kidding? I was raised by two women." He chuckled. "Both Reggie and I were taught the proper way to dance since the moment we could walk."

A slight frown curved her lips downward. "I... can't remember Reggie ever being this smooth."

He sighed as she rested her head on his shoulder. "He was just a kid," he said, his eyes going unfocused. "It's strange, but I can't really remember him sometimes. I'm thankful my gran had some photos."

She remained silent. "I wouldn't mind seeing them. There's a lot I've forgotten. I only have pictures of my parents that were left here at the resort," she said softly. He could hear the pain in her tone.

He brought their swaying to a stop and looked down at her. "I really want to kiss you," he said, his eyes searching hers.

She smiled up at him. "I'd like that."

The last time he'd kissed her, it was to distract her from

the horrors she'd just witnessed. This time, it was for purely selfish motives.

He couldn't remember ever feeling lips as soft or perfect against his own before. The way her body fit against his, it was kismet. A perfect fit.

When she tilted her head, giving him better access, he took more. Needed more. He no longer cared where they were, how many people could be watching, or how much time had gone by. All that mattered was breathing her in.

When he felt her tense, he refocused and then heard Blue's low growl. He knew too well that that sound meant that his dog was uneasy about someone approaching.

Glancing around, he scanned the darkness beyond the ring of stringed lights overhead.

"It's probably one of my staff," Raven said easily. "They're no doubt waiting to clear up this mess so they can go home." She sighed. "Thank you for coming tonight." She knelt down to pet Blue and comfort him. His dog settled down immediately and exposed his belly in a shameless attempt to get more attention. Raven chuckled and gave his dog everything he wanted, making him a very jealous man once more.

"We'd better head out." He snapped his finger for Blue, who immediately stood up, gave Raven a sloppy kiss, and moved to his side. "Thanks for the dinner." He glanced down to Blue. "Tell Raven thank you for the steak."

Raven laughed when Blue let out a few happy sounding barks.

A dark shadow watched the couple dance and flirt with one another from a few floors above them. Cast in darkness, filled with rage as the two lovers kissed.

Memories blinded, split off, and caused fury so deep, so pure, that the blackness consumed. Someone would pay for it later. Someone would be the unwitting victim and suffer as pure delight would replace the rage.

CHAPTER FIFTEEN

FIGURE OUT WHAT LIGHTS YOUR FIRE THEN
CHASE THE MATCH.

The following day, Raven had a meeting with Rachelle bright and early. She wanted to make sure the manager knew all about her plans to turn the courtyard into more space for fine dining options.

And she wanted to start the process of adding a dance area and speakers for music.

She liked Rachelle. It was strange, but the woman was the only person in the resort, other than Cemal and Tom, who was friendly towards her.

Raven assumed it was because the woman wasn't a fool and had known all along who the boss was.

Something told her that Rachelle had been biding her time until Colin and Roslyn sunk themselves too far down the hole before striking out and taking over everything herself.

When she'd finished telling Rachelle about her plans for the courtyard, she'd suggested adding live music, maybe even rolling out the grand piano and hiring an orchestra for bigger events.

"Something tells me," Raven started to say as she

poured more hot tea for Rachelle, "that if my aunt and uncle hadn't been in your way, this place would have been in a much better state when I returned." Raven smiled as she handed Rachelle a cup of hot tea.

The older woman chuckled. "Something tells me you're right." She took a sip.

Raven sat back down and took a drink of her own tea.

"Are there any local bands or orchestras that we can hire?" Raven asked.

"There might be." Rachelle frowned slightly and tilted her head. "I'll look into it." She set her mug down and pulled out her phone to take a note.

Since Raven had returned, Rachelle had been instrumental in helping Raven organize and plan future changes. There was no doubt in Raven's mind that her statement was true. If the woman hadn't been held back by her family, the resort would have flourished under the manager's guidance.

Raven only wished she could say the same for Liam Montford, whom her uncle had called his business manager. The man hadn't shown his face once in her office since she'd taken over. She knew it was only a matter of time, since she'd stopped paying his paychecks after determining that he'd managed her uncle instead of the business.

Since she'd let her uncle go, she no longer needed someone to manage him.

Then there was Eddie Mimms. Eddie's official title was Ski and Snow Resort Manager. Which meant that the man should have worked during the season only. However, according to her uncle's accounting, he was receiving a paycheck year-round.

When she'd had a brief meeting with the man, she'd found him proficient and confusing at the same time. He dressed professional, but she could tell that he was an outdoorsman through and through. She figured he'd dressed up for their meeting, which meant that he was serious about keeping his job.

Eddie was unclear about why the accounting showed that he'd received paychecks year-round. But the salary seemed to match that of what he claimed on his taxes, so he hadn't looked into it further.

Eddie oversaw all of the seasonal employees, such as the ski lift crew, the ski and snowboard instructors, and the employees in the rental facilities and guest shops.

It was a vital role, but it was only necessary when the snow started falling.

In her meeting with him, she mentioned opening the slopes in a few months for downhill summer sports. The man seemed eager and excited and even mentioned renting bikes or selling bike accessories.

Since he seemed capable and was excited to finally be given free rein, Raven allowed him to proceed with the new plans.

Which brought her back to Rachelle. The woman was easily one of her greatest alliances in town. When someone didn't want to work for the villainous Firestarter who was responsible for everyone's past pain, Rachelle stepped in and somehow convinced them that working for the resort only assured the town's full recovery.

It was how they'd gained more than half a dozen new employees already, including a few of Raven's old classmates.

"I heard last night's dinner was a huge success," Rachelle mentioned.

"It was." Raven smiled. "I plan to tell Tim later today that he's earned his position as sous chef. For now."

"That's wonderful. I know he's worked hard on moving

up. I can remember when he first came to us." Rachelle chuckled. "I caught him making grilled cheese sandwiches." She leaned forward slightly. "I still have dreams about them even though I'm lactose intolerant."

Raven smiled as her office phone rang. "Sorry, give me a moment."

"That's okay, I've got a million things to do." Rachelle stood and set her teacup down. "Thanks for the break."

Raven answered the phone as the woman stepped out of her office.

"Miss Brooks? This is Ruth Downing. Joseph Ramsey's business partner." The line was a little choppy, and Raven had to strain to hear the other woman.

"Yes, Mrs. Downing. I was hoping to have a moment to sit down with you," Raven said, pulling out her notepad.

"I'm so sorry I haven't been able to contact you before now. As you can imagine, Joe's death has got all of us in the office working in overdrive."

"I understand." Raven pressed the phone up against her ear to hear the woman.

"I've emailed you the information we talked about that day in your office. I know Joe wanted you to be able to start the process with the police."

"Thank you," Raven said, eagerly booting up her laptop.

"I hope that, even after Joe's passing, you'll consider keeping me on as your CPA. There's going to be some restructuring, but I plan on continuing with the business."

"I'd be happy to keep you on," Raven said. There wasn't another CPA she trusted within a hundred miles. If Joe had trusted Ruth Downing, that was good enough for her.

"Wonderful. If there's anything else you need, please feel free to contact me. I think we have you all set up on the new software," Ruth said.

"Yes, I'm getting the hang of it. Thank you." Raven opened her email and smiled when she noticed the email from Ruth. Then she frowned when she noticed the email below it. The subject line read, *"His blood is on your hands."*

The rest of Ruth's conversation fell away, and Raven made some quick excuse before hanging up.

With shaky fingers, she clicked on the email and read the rest of the message.

"You should have never returned. Joseph Ramsey's death is your fault. Just like all the others died because of you all those years ago."

The email address was a long string of numbers and symbols.

Leaning back, she took a couple of deep breaths before deleting the message and moving on to print out every ounce of proof Joe and Ruth had found on her uncle and Morgan Roche.

With a folder full of proof, she stepped outside her office door, determined to head down to the police station and file an official report.

She hadn't expected to see her aunt standing just outside her office door, her hand raised as if ready to knock.

"Oh." Raven almost fell over. "I didn't see you." She caught her breath and steadied herself.

Her aunt took a deep breath and then raised her chin slightly. "Raven, dear, I was wondering if you had a moment."

Raven glanced down at the folder and then back at her aunt. Her aunt's normally disheveled look was gone, replaced by a carefully tidy and professional appearance. The burgundy blouse looked new and expensive, as did the dark grey dress pants. Even the low heels she wore were suited for any boardroom. She had even tied her short messy blonde hair back in a modest bun.

Raven nodded and unlocked her office door before motioned for her aunt to step inside. Setting the folder down on her desk, she motioned for her aunt to sit. "Please." She waited for her aunt to sit then decided against sitting down herself and opted to stand at the corner of her desk instead. "What can I do for you?"

"I'm here to ask for your forgiveness," her aunt said, surprising her. Raven decided it would be better to remain quiet and let her aunt continue. "Colin has had a few days to come to terms with what has happened. We're willing to testify. Both of us."

Raven shook her head slightly. "I'm sorry, testify?"

"Yes," Roslyn said, scooting forward in the seat. "Your uncle and I realized after talking with the police what really happened. How we were both duped into believing it was within our legal rights, as guardians over this place, to withdraw extra funds for its care. We didn't know the legality of it all." Roslyn waved her hands around as if searching for the words. "We left that up to Morgan Roche, whom we hired to take care of all of that." She tilted her head and smiled slightly. "We're willing to testify that Miss Roche misguided us. She's the reason money was misplaced from the resort's accounts."

Raven sat on the edge of the desk and swallowed. "You're telling me..." She wanted to laugh but took a deep breath instead. "That Morgan Roche convinced you that it was okay to steal money?"

"We never stole," her aunt jumped in, sounding shocked. "We were informed we could withdraw funds and use them as we saw fit for the business."

"Right," Raven said slowly, "and do you have receipts for these... business transactions?"

Her aunt took a deep breath. "I'm sure I could find some... if you'll tell me how much we're talking about."

"Three million dollars." Raven crossed her arms over her chest.

"What?" Her aunt stood up. "That's a lie!"

It was strange watching her aunt go from a docile mouse to a roaring lioness in a heartbeat. Roslyn's pale skin turned a bright shade of purplish red, almost the color of a ripe beet.

Raven stood up and prepared to stand her ground.

"There has to be some sort of mistake," her aunt said after taking a few deep breaths. "I can assure you, the amount of money your uncle and I know about is nowhere near that."

"Numbers don't lie," she said, motioning to the folder.

Her aunt looked between her and the folder. "Give me a month."

"For?" Raven asked.

"To prove to you that we had nothing to do with the missing money," her aunt answered.

It was laughable. Really. Raven was positive that once she turned over the proof to the police, they'd get a warrant to gain access to her aunt and uncle's finances and find the corroboration.

"I'm sorry," she started to say, shaking her head.

Her aunt moved closer to her until she was a breath away. Her hand jerked up and gripped Raven's arm like a tight vice. Her longer fingernails dug into her skin, causing Raven to hiss with pain and try to jerk free.

"You'll give me a month. If you don't, I'll tell everyone

what you were really doing out there in the woods that night," her aunt hissed.

Raven's eyebrow shot up. "What was I really doing?" Forgotten was the pain in her arm as curiosity peaked.

"I know who you were meeting. I found the notes."

Raven was able to jerk free. "You're out of your mind." She moved to stand behind her desk, hoping to put some space between them.

"You think this is a joke? Meeting with a man twice your age? Is that the reason you killed him? Because he threatened to tell everyone about your... liaison?"

"What?" Raven gaped. "Joe? You think Joe and I..." Raven did laugh this time.

"I'll go to the police. I kept the notes hidden." Roslyn smiled. "They're proof enough that you started the fire to cover up your affair. That you killed him."

"You need to leave." Raven walked over to the office door and held it open. "You're just as crazy as I remember you being."

Her aunt glared at her as she passed by. "One month. Give us the decency of one month. If not for me, then for your uncle and cousins." When Raven wouldn't agree, she jerked around and left quickly.

She wanted to take a moment to compose herself but as she was walking out, she saw her cousin Liza storm across the lobby towards her.

Holding in a groan, she held the folder tight against her chest and waited as her cousin stopped directly in front of her.

"Don't do this," Liza hissed in a low tone.

"What?" Raven asked.

Her cousin glared at her, much like her mother had just done. "Word is going around that you have..."—she tapped the folder— "something you're taking to the police that will send my parents up the river."

Raven wanted to laugh at her cousin's analogy but instead braced herself for the next onslaught.

"I think it's terrible what you're doing," Liza said.

"Your mother just paid me a visit," she countered. "If she couldn't persuade me, then none of your threats can."

Liza swayed back slightly then shrugged. Her cousin's eyes ran over her. "You'd be surprised at the things I hear around here."

"Like?" Raven said with a sigh.

"Like rumors about you having a fight with your boyfriend the night the fire started." Liza crossed her arms over her chest.

"Is blackmail your family's go-to move?" Raven shook her head. "That's old news. You're ten years too late." She moved to walk around her.

"I also know who he cheated on you with and why," Liza said, causing Raven to stop walking. She wanted to fall for the bait, really, she did. But why Reggie cheated on a sixteen-year-old naive Raven no longer mattered to her.

Instead, she walked out the front door of the resort, climbed in her car, and set the folder on the seat next to her, even more determined than she had been before.

When she walked into the police station, she never expected to be as nervous as she was. Her palms were sweaty, and her voice even shook when she asked to talk to Sheriff Sean Stone.

She was taken to a small waiting room and had to sit on her hands to keep them from shaking as she waited for Cade's uncle to come into the room.

"Miss Brooks." Sean smiled at her as he walked into the

room. "I was going to be heading your way later today. This saves me a trip."

"Oh?" she asked, slightly worried about something new now.

"I received a very interesting email earlier today." Sean sat down across from her and pushed a piece of paper in front of her.

She looked down and reread the email she'd received and deleted herself earlier.

"You should have never returned. Joseph Ramsey's death is your fault. Just like all the others died because of you all those years ago."

"How did you... Where did you get this?" she asked, looking up at him.

"It was in my inbox when I arrived this morning." Sean leaned forward. "I take it you received a copy as well?"

"Yes, and I deleted it." She pushed the paper back towards him. "Do you know how many times over the years I've received messages like this?"

She watched Sean's eyes and could tell the moment he realized the truth of her words.

"Okay, if you're not here for this..." He set the paper aside.

It was her turn to push paper in front of him. "The proof you'll need to open an official investigation against my aunt and uncle along with Morgan Roche for embezzling." She held her breath as Sean looked through the paperwork.

When his eyes turned up to hers, she relaxed slightly. Cade's uncle looked so much like Cade, somehow it had a calming effect on her.

"You're willing to drag your family through the mud? You know the chance of recovering any of the money is slim," Sean said.

Raven raised her chin slightly. "It's not about the money. It's about morals."

His eyes ran over her for a moment. "Do you remember that I was the one who found you after the fire?"

She swallowed and nodded slowly. Most of her memories from that night and her seventeenth birthday were fuzzy, with the exception of that small detail.

"I never got to thank you," she said softly.

"When everyone else in town was spreading rumors, I remembered finding you, tucked into a small ball, covered in mud, soot, and ash. Seeing your tears, hearing your anguish when you found out what you'd lost." He watched her closely.

"You lost Reggie," she pointed out.

"We both did. Did you ever know that he was found less than a quarter of a mile away from the cave? My guess is, he was trying to make it there."

"No." She shook her head as tears rolled down her cheeks. "I never knew."

Sean sighed and shook his head. "This"—he motioned to the file— "might open a lot of old wounds in this town. Wounds that have started to heal."

"Are you trying to talk me out of doing what's right?" she asked, her back straightening.

"No," Sean said quickly. "I'm trying to see if you have what it takes to stand up. All the way up. Last time, you were so young. If you do this, you can't run and hide away for another ten years when things take a dark turn and the accusations start to fly."

She raised her chin again. "I'm not going anywhere."

After a moment, Sean nodded and smiled. "Good. Shall we begin?"

CHAPTER SIXTEEN

Cade watched Blue race around the yard, sniffing and peeing on practically every blade of grass. He turned when he heard a car drive up his driveway, then smiled when he noticed it was Raven.

He walked around to the side of his house where his driveway was and stood on his porch as she climbed out of her car. Instantly, he could tell something was bothering her.

How was it that he had changed his mind so much about the woman in such a short time? Only two months ago, he'd been angry, hurt, and bitter every time he'd heard her name. Now, when he thought of her, his body jumped to attention for completely different reasons.

"Evening," he said smoothly as she stopped at the base of the porch stairs, looking up at him.

"Evening," she said with a slight smile as she shaded the sun from her eyes.

"What brings you around?"

She glanced over when Blue raced around the house. When he noticed the mud on his paws, he tried to stop him from racing to her and jumping on her, but by the time he reached them, it was too late. Blue had left two perfectly muddy paw prints on her clean skirt.

Still, Raven was laughing and hugging the muddy dog as Blue rained kisses over her face.

"Blue," he scolded, "down."

"He's fine," Raven said, chuckling. "He's just what I needed right now." She glanced up at him. "I just got back from your uncle's office. I've officially filed a report about the embezzling."

"You did?" he asked as she stood up.

Cade snapped his fingers, sending Blue to the front porch.

"I did." Raven smiled.

"I guess that earned you a beer."

"I agree the occasion totally calls for one." She followed him into the house.

He grabbed two cold beers from the fridge, then motioned towards the back door. "Want to sit outside?"

"I'd like that." She took her beer from him.

"Sorry, I don't have any fancy cheese or finger foods."

She shrugged and replied. "I grabbed dinner at the diner before coming over here."

They sat out on the porch as Blue started racing around the yard once again.

"Does he ever get tired?" Raven asked with a chuckle after taking a sip of her beer.

He smiled. "I was thinking of getting him a friend. When he visits my uncle's house, he loves playing with his three-year-old golden retriever, Al."

"Al?" She chuckled.

"It's short for Al," he joked as he glanced over at her.

She laughed and then her smile slipped slightly.

"Your uncle thinks this is going to cause a stir around town." She glanced down at her beer.

"It probably will. After all, it's big news when the mayor stubs his toe," he joked, then he sighed. "Do you think you're up for it?" he asked, suddenly concerned.

She glanced over at him and her chin rose slightly. "I am." She took another sip.

"Rumors can be hard to outrun." He glanced off over the yard as he remembered hearing all of the rumors about Raven over the years.

"I tried to leave them behind, but in the end, they were right here waiting for me when I returned." She took another sip of her beer. "It's just a good thing these new rumors won't be about me."

"That won't stop people from bringing up your past."

"No, I suppose it won't." She rolled the beer bottle in her hands. "My aunt pretty much threatened to blackmail me today."

"Oh?" He shifted slightly to get a better look at her. "What's she got on you?" he asked lightly.

She chuckled, a rich smooth sound that had his body responding.

"Absolutely nothing." She smiled at him. "She thinks she has something, but at this point, she's grasping at straws."

"They're probably desperate to keep their secrets," he suggested.

"How did they get away with it? I mean, that much money?" She shook her head. "That's three hundred thousand a year extra, over their set income. In the city, I doubt anyone would notice, but out here..." She motioned with the beer bottle. "People notice if you've got extra money. It's not like they've flaunted it around town. I asked Cal, he claims there weren't any extravagant vacations. No big purchases such as houses, cars, or vacations." She shook her head. "Where did it all go?"

"Maybe they still have it?" he suggested.

She shook her head. "I doubt it." Then she titled her head. "Now, Morgan Roche. I've heard stories about her yearly trips to Paris. She certainly wears expensive clothes."

"Drives a new Porsche SUV too."

Raven's eyebrows shot up. "Maybe she is the first one the police should be looking at."

"If I know my uncle, he's planning on it."

"Still, my aunt and uncle aren't the kind to just sit back and watch someone take money. They knew about it. Had to have known." She reached down and scratched Blue's head when the dog sat by her feet.

It was strange, seeing her there, on his property with his dog, looking so relaxed. She looked like she belonged there.

"I guess we'll find out soon enough now that you've filed a police report." He set his beer down.

She set her almost empty beer bottle down next to his. "Well, I'd better..." She moved to get up but stopped. "Thanks."

"For?" he asked, watching her closely. There was so much he'd miscalculated about her. He was beginning to question everything, since his libido wanted to take over his mind where she was concerned.

"For listening." She ran her hands over her legs. "Darby's a good friend and all, but..." She shrugged. "She's just too busy at the diner to really listen."

He held in a slight wince. There was no way he wanted to be stuck in the friend zone. Not when his body reacted quickly every time that she stood close to him, and especially not when he thought of kissing her every single time she nibbled on her lips.

"Is that what we are?" he asked in a low tone. "Friends?"

Her eyes met his and she sucked her sexy full bottom lip between her teeth. His body reacted again, instantly.

She surprised him in the next moment when she stood up and moved over to straddle his hips. His hands instantly went to her waist.

"I think we're beyond just friendship." Her eyes ran over his face before she leaned in and kissed him.

"Raven," he warned, feeling his body instantly react to her closeness. The soft sexy scent of her skin and hair drove him absolutely crazy. His hands started to move over her as she continued to kiss him, forcing his dick to respond with each soft moan.

Her hands moved quickly over him, starting in his hair, heading down his neck, then pulling his jacket off his shoulders. All he could do was follow her lead, since he was so caught up in her demands.

Then she shifted over him, and he felt the rest of his control slip.

"Raven, don't start something you can't finish," he warned as she reached for his jeans. His hands covered hers as their eyes locked.

"I intend to finish," she purred next to his ear. "The question is..." She took his earlobe between her teeth and nibbled, causing his dick to jump against her. "Do you?"

For the next few moments, his body took over completely. He lifted her in his arms and somehow managed to push the back door open and get through it with her in his arms. All the while, Blue trailed behind him and snuck in before he kicked the door shut.

They landed on the sofa in a heap, their mouths never really leaving one another's as clothing was pulled, pushed, tugged, and, in the case of the sexy red pair of panties she'd been wearing, ripped off.

When he covered her pussy with his mouth, he knew there was no going back for him. Just feeling and watching how she reacted to his touch had him growing even harder. He enjoyed lapping at her while she tensed, moaned, and gripped at his hair. The sexy sounds she made encouraged him on.

He had only a brief moment to appreciate the view of her spread out on his sofa before he slid on a condom and pumped into her. The rest was a blur until he felt her legs wrap around his hips, holding him as she cried his name out.

Moments later, as he looked down at her red hair fanned out on his sofa cushion, her pink lips held between her teeth, and those damn sexy eyes glued to his, he followed her over the edge.

"I hadn't planned on doing that," she said, a few moments after he collapsed next to her.

"From where I'm lying, it looks like you knew exactly what you were doing," he managed to say, breathing in the scent of her hair and enjoying the way her soft naked body felt against him. "From how good you feel next to me, chances are, I'll know exactly what I'm doing right back to you... soon."

She chuckled as she turned slightly to look over at him. "Honestly, I did just come here to talk."

Reaching up, he brushed a strand of her fiery hair away from her face. "I'm thankful," he said honestly. He leaned over to kiss her. "I do have a bed." He rested his forehead against hers.

She smiled. "Oh?"

"If you want to stay?" he suggested as his hands circled over her ribs, slowly moving lower.

She narrowed her eyes slightly then sighed. "I should get back," she said, but when he slid a finger into her heat again, he watched her resolve fade away, replaced by desire.

He slid off the sofa, gathered her in his arms, and carried her towards the stairs. Her arms wrapped around his shoulders as she rested her head on his shoulder.

"I've never been carried upstairs before," she said with a slight sigh.

"I've never carried someone up these stairs before," he admitted just as he reached the top of the landing.

When he stepped into his bedroom, she lifted her head and glanced around.

"Nice," she said.

"I'll show you around... later." He leaned down and kissed her again. He wanted her again. Stopping at the foot of his bed, he figured this time, he'd go slow and enjoy as much of her as she'd give him.

He let the kiss continue as he slid her body down his. The friction from their naked bodies had him heating even further.

When she tried to pull him onto the bed, he took a step back.

"This time, I want to go slowly. Savor you." His eyes ran over her. He was thankful she wasn't the shy type who'd try to cover herself. Instead, she stood in front of him, confident, while she ran her eyes over him.

He knew that he spent enough time in the gym and doing drills for work that he shouldn't be ashamed of his physique.

He was too enamored by her soft lean body, those

perfect perky breasts, to think about himself, anyway. Reaching up, he brushed the back of his hand down her pale perfect skin and watched as her eyes slid closed on a soft moan.

"So perfect," he said when he brushed a finger over her nipples and they peaked. "So responsive." He smiled slightly when a soft moan escaped her lips. "Do you like that?" he asked, brushing his hand over her again. She nodded in response, her body swaying. He continued to trail his hands and fingers over her, working his way downward. His hands snaked over her ribs quickly and watched for all signs of arousal from her.

When he cupped her butt with one hand and her sex with the other, her eyes flashed open.

"Cade," she reached for him. The moment her fingers touched his chest, he knew that if she touched him anymore, he wouldn't be able to control himself.

"Let me." He took her hands and guided her to sit on the edge of the bed. "I want to taste you again," he said, kissing her. This time, he trailed down her body with his mouth until he settled between her thighs.

Feeling her respond to him was like icing on top of a very sexy cake. She twisted, moaned, and gripped him until he felt her convulse under him and tasted her sweet release on his tongue.

Only then did he slide up her lax body and enter her once more. Moving slowly at first, he watched as she built up once more, enjoying the way her eyes turned an even lighter shade of greyish blue.

Her long hair was laid out over his sheets, and her nails scraped his sides, urging him onward while her legs wrapped around his hips.

This time when he felt her convulse around him, he allowed himself to fall with her.

He woke sometime later when her breathing quickened. He could tell instantly that she was dreaming and debated waking her. Instead, he pulled her closer and soothed her by running his hands slowly over her shoulders and arms.

When she settled down, he kissed the top of her head and settled back down next to her.

Unfortunately, now that he was awake, his mind ran over the enigma he was holding in his arms.

Raven Brooks.

From what he'd heard about the woman his entire life, she was not only popular in school, but she'd also been not a little selfish. Then again, everyone he'd heard that tidbit from had also asserted that she'd been guilty of starting the fire all those years ago.

How many people in town had tried to persuade everyone else that she was guilty? Shortly after the fire, there had been a mob of people calling for her arrest.

His uncle hadn't been sheriff at the time, but he'd stuck his neck out for Raven. Cade knew that it was probably due to the fact that he'd been the one to find her that following morning.

Over the years, he'd tried to get more details from Sean about the circumstances that morning, but his uncle's story had remained vague.

How many people had been out searching with hope about the possibility of loved ones being found safe?

They'd been out there that morning looking for Reggie. Every step Cade had taken over the charred ground, he'd prayed that he'd find his brother alive.

With each step, however, he'd known the reality of the

situation. He'd found countless dead animals lying in the ash and soot.

Then he'd gotten the dreaded call from Sean. Of course, everyone had been excited about the girl who had lived. Out of the more than two dozen people who'd still been missing at that point, she'd been the only one to be found alive.

At first, every news station within a thousand miles had focused on Raven Brooks. How the courageous young now-orphaned seventeen-year-old had survived the horrors that had consumed everything she loved, including her boyfriend of almost a year, Reggie Stone, whom had been found less than a quarter of a mile away from the cave. He'd found out a few years later that the fire had started in the direct center between the two of them.

For years he'd believed that this fact held some significance. He'd wondered if something had happened, sending the two running in different directions, Raven to the safety of the cave while his brother had rushed off in the other direction.

His uncle painted a picture of his brother heading towards the cave. Towards the fire. But in his heart and his head, Cade questioned this.

He hadn't realized he'd remained awake for the rest of the night, pondering, until he noticed the sunlight streaking into his bedroom.

Thankfully, he had the day off from work. He patiently waited until Raven stirred before finally shutting out all the questions. When her body pushed gently against his, his mind went in the completely opposite direction and stopped working all together.

Letting his body take over, he slowly let his hands roam over her, waking her up more quickly.

"Morning," she moaned as he placed a kiss on her bare shoulder.

"Morning." He trailed his mouth down until he covered her breast with his lips.

Her hands pushed into his hair, holding him where she wanted him.

This time when he slid into her, he kept the slow pace, enjoying the feel of her morning softness.

"I hadn't planned on staying the night," she said when they lay together, their breathing leveling.

"I'm glad you did." He rolled them over. "Do you know how long it's been since I've showered with someone?" he asked, pulling her off the bed.

She chuckled as she followed him into the bathroom. She stopped just inside his bathroom door.

"My god, I thought your bedroom was huge," she said, looking around.

When he'd built the place, he'd designed the main bedroom and bathroom to be big enough that he wouldn't ever feel cramped.

"I like my space," he said with a shrug as he turned on the water in the shower.

She chuckled and walked over towards him. "Your shower is as big as my current bathroom."

He pulled her close. "I take it you've moved into the east building then?"

Her wince and look of guilt had him sighing.

"How about I take the day to help you move?" he suggested.

"I don't..." she started, but when he gave her a look, she nodded. "That would be helpful."

He pulled them into the shower and, for the next half hour, enjoyed showering with a sexy redhead.

CHAPTER SEVENTEEN

Raven couldn't believe she'd actually slept with Cade. Let alone spent the entire night wrapped in his arms. Then she remembered the shower they'd enjoyed together and smiled.

Cade and Blue were in Cade's truck, following her. He claimed he was on call that weekend and couldn't afford to be without his own vehicle.

She didn't mind. The drive back up to the resort gave her some time alone to think.

The fact that she'd only ever slept with two men, and they were brothers, hadn't even crossed her mind. Until she'd been alone.

As with before, she couldn't figure out why she never compared Cade to Reggie. It wasn't as if the brothers looked nothing alike. Sure, Cade looked more like his uncle and Reggie had taken after his mother, but still, there were enough similarities between them that it should have crossed her mind once while he'd been kissing her.

As she pulled into the long drive of the resort, she finally figured it out. Reggie had been a boy. At seventeen, he'd been the man of her dreams, but she'd been so young and naive herself.

She could remember Cade at that age. She'd never once thought of him as young or naive.

Just being with him, being around him, she knew that he was more man than she'd ever experienced before.

That was why Cade stood alone in her mind. Why, when he touched her, kissed her, her mind didn't revert to thoughts of Reggie.

The few times Reggie and she had had sex, they had fumbled together. Back then she'd found it to be romantic, had thought what was between them was love.

Maybe it had been love, of sorts. Young love.

Now, however, she had more knowledge. More years behind her and a hell of a lot more needs. Especially since they'd been building up for ten years.

Had Cade guessed that she was short on experience?

That thought had her face heating when he parked next to her car.

"This place sure looks a lot different than it did a month ago," he said as he helped Blue out of the truck.

Raven glanced around. Sure enough, the once-dead courtyard was now alive with colorful blooms and green grass, and there was the new paved area under the hanging string lights that would be utilized for romantic dinners under the stars.

The fresh coat of paint that had been applied to the balconies changed the entire look of the buildings. Instead of the dull dark brown, she'd lightened things up with a soft cream that matched the stonework on the lower levels. It made the buildings look newer and more modern.

"It's getting there," she agreed as she watched Blue race across the yard.

"You could always add a dog park," Cade suggested as he walked over to pick up Blue's mess with a small plastic bag he'd pulled out of his jacket.

Up until now, the resort had had a no-pet policy. But times were changing. She liked animals and didn't see any reason, outside of a few mishaps, that would stop her from letting guests bring their pets. For a small up-charge, that was.

"Good idea." She glanced around. "A gated area, over there?" she suggested, pointing to a corner. "It's out of the way of the ice rink in the winter and close enough to the doors for guests."

"You're going to start up the skate rink again?" Cade asked, depositing the trash into one of the outdoor bins.

"I am," she answered with a smile. "It is one of my favorite memories as a child."

Cade leaned closer to her. "I got my first kiss on that rink."

"Oh?" She locked her arm through his. "Who with?"

"Katie Plaskett." He sighed and looked a little wistful. "Then she went and broke my heart by pushing me down."

Raven laughed. "How old were you?"

He snapped his finger for Blue to follow them. "Ten," he answered as they walked in together.

She was laughing as they passed through the lobby and headed towards the elevators. When the doors started to shut behind them, a hand pushed in, stopping the doors from closing.

Her uncle stepped forward, blocking the doors from closing.

"Raven, do you have a moment?" Colin asked, avoiding Cade's eyes. Cade instantly stepped between them.

Placing a hand on Cade's shoulder, she stepped around him.

"I'm sorry, Uncle Colin. I've been told by the sheriff not to have any contact with you at this point," she said smoothly.

"So, it's true." Colin sighed and pushed the doors back again as they tried to shut on him. "You've gone to the police about this?"

"You knew I would," she said firmly and took another step forward. "You stole over three million dollars."

Raven watched her words sink in. Her uncle's face turned pale white before shooting to bright red as anger took over.

"You'll pay for this," he said in a low tone before stepping back and letting the doors shut.

She couldn't stop the shaking that ensued once they were alone in the elevator.

Cade's arms wrapped around her, holding her close as he whispered soothing words to her.

When the doors opened again on her floor, Cade pulled her out the doors. She walked as if in a daze with him down the hallway towards her rooms.

The moment she unlocked her room, she tensed and knew there was something wrong before she even turned on the light.

Cade was once again there, pulling her back, shielding her.

"What the..." He broke off when he turned on the light. Then he turned to her. "Don't touch anything. I'm calling my uncle."

She stood in the hallway, looking in at the destruction of her rooms, as he relayed the information to his uncle.

"He's on his way." Cade wrapped his arms around her again.

"Who would do this?" she asked, closing her eyes, locking the scene of destruction out.

"I hate to say it, but we did just have a run-in with your uncle," Cade supplied.

She nodded. "My aunt was here yesterday before I left to talk to your uncle."

He nudged her down the hallway a little and helped her sit down on the bench by the elevator doors.

"You okay?" he asked as he sat beside her.

She had taken a few deep breaths, which had helped her put things into perspective. All she had was clothes and her toiletry items. She'd gotten rid of everything else before heading back to Cannon Falls.

"It's just clothes," she said with a slight smile. "I can always buy more."

He chuckled. "If anything, it's a good excuse to." He took her hand in his as his smile slipped. "We'll figure out who did this."

She closed her eyes and shrugged. "Does it matter? Their point was made clearly."

"Want to back down already?"

Her eyes flew open. "Hell no."

His smile was back. "That's my girl." He hugged her.

Just then the elevator doors opened, and she tensed until she saw Sean step out, along with a female officer.

Raven stayed where she was while Sean and Cade walked through the destruction. The female officer, Karin Taper, sat with her and took her statement. The sandy blonde–haired woman looked vaguely familiar, and Raven realized she must have known her before she'd moved away.

Karin wrote down each of her responses in a small notebook.

When Sean and Cade stepped out again, Karin turned to her.

"If you'd like, I can help you gather some of your things?" she offered.

"Thank you, but at this point, I think I'll just go shopping." She smiled.

"Good idea." The older woman touched her hand. "Everyone in the station knows what you're going through. I just wanted to tell you that I went to high school with your parents. Your mom and I were friends. Not close, but..." She nodded. "Friends nonetheless. If you need anything..."

"Thank you," Raven said easily.

"I think we have what we need," Sean told her. "I've taken pictures, but something tells me it wouldn't do any good to take fingerprints. Hotel rooms can be complicated as a crime scene. I think we'd do better asking employees who was around and who knew where your rooms were."

She nodded in agreement and looked over to Cade. "My family... they all knew."

Sean sighed. "Yeah, they're top of my list." He glanced over at Cade. "Any chance I could convince you to move into a different room? Maybe keep it under wraps for a while? At least until the heat of the situation cools off some?"

"We were here to move her things to another room anyway. I've requested that all guests be housed in the other building until all the rooms and the fire system can be updated in this one."

"Good." Sean glanced over at Cade, then back at her. "Cade says that you were at his place after our meeting?"

"Yes," she answered, unembarrassed about her choice to

be with Cade. After all, if last night and this morning was a sign of how things could be, then she hoped to spend a lot more time with him. She knew people in town would find out sooner or later.

"Any chance you could be convinced to stay at his place for a while?" Sean asked.

Raven stilled as her eyes moved over to Cade, who just shrugged.

"I'd be open to it," he said quickly.

What would it be like to live with Cade? Every fiber of her being wanted it. Dreamed of it. But it was too soon, and she wasn't ready to give up that much of her freedom. Not that Cade was the kind of man who would consume her and control her. She doubted that completely.

No, it was more herself that she was afraid for. She'd never lived with someone. Hell, until last night, she'd never spend the night with a man before.

Sure, she'd enjoyed her time with him, but it had been only one night. She hoped it would lead to more nights, but living with him?

"No," she answered after a moment. "Sorry, I..." She shook her head. "I need to be here." She avoided Cade's eyes.

"Okay," Sean said quickly. "Then I'll leave you two to it. We're going to head down and talk to some of your staff."

She nodded and looked down at her hands as they shuffled into the elevator.

"Hey." Cade sat beside her and took her hands in his. "Don't feel weird about my uncle." He chuckled. "He was just trying to ensure your protection. I don't feel weird about you not wanting to move in with me." Her eyes moved up to his.

"It's not personal," she offered.

He chuckled. "How can it be? If you'd turned *me* down, that would have been one thing. But having my uncle ask you..." He shook his head. "He really was just trying to look out for you. He could have just as easily asked if you'd move in with my grandmother."

"I know," she said with a slight smile.

"Okay, so if you're determined to stick around here, let's see what we can do to ensure that this won't happen again." He squeezed her hand and she stood up with him.

Before they stepped into the destruction, Cade wrapped his arms around her once more.

"I'm so sorry someone did this to you. Just remember, this time it's not you on trial," he said softly.

Those words echoed in her mind. What had Cade meant by them? Was he trying to tell her that he'd believed at one point that she was guilty of setting the fire all those years ago?

She stepped into her rooms and held in a groan.

Every single piece of clothing and hotel furniture was destroyed. Her clothes and personal items lay in piles on the floor and the furniture, including the bedframe and night-stands, were broken into pieces and piled in the middle of the floor, as if ready to be set on fire.

"Who would do this?" she asked again. "I can't see my uncle or aunt..." She turned around and thought about their anger. About their words towards her in the past few days. If anything, she could see them lashing out at *her*, but doing this? She just couldn't see it. "I can't see them doing this."

Cade was silent for a moment.

"This does all seem a little... over the top." He frowned. "You know, when I broke it off with Julia, she cut up a sweatshirt I had left at her place and returned it to me in a shoe box."

"Your point?"

He motioned to the dress she'd worn out on their date. The material was, as he had just described, chopped up in little pieces and laid in a pile.

"Do you think this was her?" she asked.

"No. I'm saying, or rather asking, if you have someone in your past that might not like that you've moved on?"

She couldn't help but laughing as tears rolled down her cheeks at the loss of everything she had.

"What?" he asked, moving closer to her.

Taking a deep breath, she closed her eyes to compose herself.

"Cade, the last person I dated was your brother," she finally said.

She watched for his reaction. His smile surprised her.

"What?" she asked, frowning as he moved closer to her.

"Sorry." He sobered. "It's just... nice, I guess, knowing that I'm the one you chose to break your dry spell."

"Dry spell?" She held in a chuckle. "If you want to call me being afraid to put myself out there a dry spell."

He pulled her close and kissed her. "I've had a dry spell myself." He kissed her again. "One that I'm very happy is over."

The kiss had her knees shaking slightly and almost buckling. How could this man do this to her? Even while she stood in the middle of the mess of everything that used to be hers, he could easily take her mind off of the predicament.

Instead of focusing on the destruction, she was now dreaming of getting naked with Cade again.

Then he stepped back and took a deep breath.

"What do you say we get some trash bags and start

going through your things? Then we can spend the rest of the day shopping for what you need."

"I have a better idea." She smiled. "What do you say we go find another room for me to stay in." She ran her hands over his chest and met his eyes. "Then spend some time breaking the room in before heading out to shop? This mess can easily be cleaned up by the hotel staff. There's nothing here I want to keep." She waved her hands around the mess.

"Nothing?"

She glanced around and then shook her head. "No, nothing. Thankfully, I left my laptop locked downstairs in my office." She winced. "My office."

"Want to go check on it?"

"Yeah, I guess we'll need to do that when we're downstairs getting me another room," she relented.

"Are you sure there's nothing in here... worth salvaging?" he asked.

She took a moment to glance around once more, then walked into the bathroom. Seeing all of her toiletries destroyed and shoved into the bathtub and sink, she felt angry tears sting her eyes. Then she turned away and stormed out of the room with Cade on her heels.

"You okay?" he asked as they rode the elevator down to the lobby.

"No." She glanced up at him. "But once I find out who did that and why, I might be."

CHAPTER EIGHTEEN

Cade stood by while Raven talked with a few of her staff members after they had checked to make sure that her office hadn't been touched.

He agreed with his uncle on this matter. Whomever had broken into her rooms and destroyed everything she owned had done so because it had been easy.

After all, Raven was the only person staying in the massive building. There were a handful of guests, all of whom had been moved to the main building when construction began in the east and west buildings. Even her cousin, Liza, had been moved out of the rooms her family had occupied for years in the east building and was now in the main building as well.

He refrained from jumping in and asking her employees any questions since she was doing a good job of it.

More than a dozen employees came into her office one at a time. Raven calmly asked each of them if they knew anything about who had destroyed her rooms. Cade knew most of the people but was slightly surprised to see a few employees that she'd hired. A handful of them were some of the biggest gossipers about Raven's guilt. Including Heather Craft.

The woman looked a little taken aback when she'd spotted him in the office. He could remember all the times she'd spread gossip about Raven in town. At one point, shortly after Raven had returned to Cannon Falls, she'd tried to rally everyone against taking jobs at the resort, so he'd been surprised when he'd found out that she'd taken a bartender position.

Still, Raven had handled Heather like an expert.

"You'd make a mighty fine detective," he said when he and Raven were alone in her office again.

She was writing some questions and answers down in a notebook and glanced up at him.

She shrugged. "I like true crime and crime fiction television."

He smiled. "It happens to be one of my favorite genres to watch too." He leaned forward. "What's next, partner?"

She leaned back in the chair and closed her eyes. "Now, I suppose we let your uncle see what he can come up with."

He stood up, waking Blue, who was fast asleep on the sofa next to him.

"Everyone claims they saw your aunt leave yesterday right after you did." He leaned on the edge of her desk.

"Yeah." She turned towards him. "And no one saw her or anyone out of the ordinary head up the west building's elevator." She walked over to the window and looked out. He watched her in silence. After a moment, she turned back to him. "I need a few basic things in town, a new room to stay in, and then some food. Up for a trip into town?"

He thought about spending the rest of the day shopping

with her for clothes and toiletries. Normally, he would have searched for any excuse to bow out. But just thinking about her alone, exposed, in town, had him agreeing quickly.

After a quick stop to drop Blue off at home, they headed to the town's main street, where more than a dozen small shops kept the townspeople in the latest fashions and home supplies.

Growing up with his gran and his mother, he'd spent many hours trailing behind a woman while she looked for items. With experience, he'd learned how to answer any of what he called their trick questions.

"Do you like this color?"

"Would this color look good on me?"

"Do you think these shoes go with this outfit?"

He had a standard answer for every last one and had been fully prepared to supply Raven with his, 'opinions.'

But Raven was very focused, and he had a difficult time keeping up with her. She'd taken a shopping cart and had started quickly placing items into it. About the only thing she was checking was the sizes of the items.

He wanted to tell her to slow down, to try on a few items, but he had to admit, the things she was picking out were nice. Very nice.

He tried to keep his tongue in his mouth when he watched her toss a sexy red dress and matching panties and bra set into the cart.

Before he knew it, she was standing at the checkout paying for everything, and his mind was still stuck on imagining her in the little number.

"That's it?" he asked as he helped her cart the bags to her car.

"Hm?" she asked, glancing over her shoulder.

"That's how you shop? You didn't even try anything on," he practically whined. He really had hoped for a chance to see her trying on the dress.

She chuckled and shook her head. "I'm a pretty standard size. If something doesn't fit, it's not like I have to go far to exchange or return it."

She shut the trunk of her car and glanced around. "Besides, I'm starved." She motioned towards the diner. "Want to head over for a burger?"

"I'm impressed," he said, taking her hand and walking across the street with her.

"At how I shop?" she asked with a chuckle.

"My gran or mother would have spent hours purchasing as much as you just did." He leaned towards her and lowered his voice. "But don't tell them I said so."

She was laughing as they stepped inside. He watched her eyes move around the diner and noticed her smile slip. Glancing over, he realized why instantly when he spotted her aunt and uncle and cousin Liza sitting in the back booth. The three of them immediately spotted them, and he felt Raven tense beside him.

"Want to go someplace else?" he asked softly.

"No." She lifted her chin and walked over to sit at the bar area.

They hadn't even settled before Darby rushed out of the back room with a tray full of food. When Raven's friend spotted them, her smile grew, then her eyes darted to the back booth.

Darby rushed over to them, tray and all.

"Hey, they're done eating. I can give them a nudge if you want?" she said to Raven.

"No, it's fine. Sooner or later, we're going to bump into

each other," Raven said with a shrug. "It might as well be in public."

"Okay, I'll just deliver this and be back to take your orders," Darby added with a smile.

It was as if the moment they'd walked into the diner, everyone had stopped talking and was waiting for the show to start.

Raven leaned closer to him and whispered, "It's like they're all expecting something."

"I was thinking the same thing. Normally, this place isn't this quiet." He looked over the menu while trying to hide the fact that he was scanning the room.

"They're getting up," Raven said, tensing beside him.

He reached over and quickly took her hand under the table as her family approached them.

"You think this is over," her aunt said when they stopped directly behind them.

Raven swiveled the stool until she was eye to eye with her aunt. He followed a little more slowly, his eyes squarely on her aunt. Her uncle appeared to be smart enough to keep his distance.

"What?" Raven said smoothly.

"You know what you're doing to this family. To this town," her aunt continued. When the woman started to move forward, he held up a hand, easily keeping her a few feet away from Raven. The older woman's eyes narrowed at him before turning back to Raven. "The entire town knows who you are. What you are. I've exposed you." Her aunt's smile turned and twisted into something just short of evil.

Cade couldn't remember seeing anything like it before, short of on a character in a movie. He'd known Roslyn Brooks for most of his life. Never in all those years had he ever witnessed the woman as pissed as she was now.

"Just what do you think you've exposed? I hope it's not that silly affair story you tried to hit me with earlier?" Raven said smoothly. Then she leaned forward and lowered her tone. "Everyone who knew me back then knew how much I was in love with Reggie. As I said before, you have nothing on me."

He felt his own heart skip a beat at the look her aunt gave Raven. A look that assured him that whatever her aunt had, she was positive that she would win the fight. There wasn't any doubt that Roslyn had something. The only question was whether it was actually something true about Raven.

He tended to side with Raven, since they'd talked about it earlier. He had believed her story. Still did. Especially seeing the pure crazy look now in her aunt's eyes.

"We'll let the town decide." Roslyn leaned closer. "Just as they decided your guilt long ago."

With this, Raven's aunt turned on her heels and stormed out of the diner. Her husband and daughter followed suit without so much as a word.

"That was fun," Darby said loudly, gaining a chuckle from everyone still in the diner. "Now, who wants free water?" she asked, holding up a pitcher of water.

"Are you okay?" Cade asked Raven as they spun back around.

"I'm fine," Raven said calmly.

He ran his eyes over her and, the strange thing was, he could tell she *was* fine.

"You are," he agreed with a smile. "How about a burger and some fries?"

She smiled. "I was thinking I'd finish it off with a slice of chocolate cream pie."

"Now that's a plan I can get behind." He squeezed her hand.

When Darby stopped to get their orders, Raven quickly told her what had happened to her that day.

Less than five minutes later, Carrie showed up and Darby took a break from work. The four of them moved to a booth, and Raven filled both of them in while they ate.

They didn't pay any attention to the looks or the gossip surrounding them for the rest of the night in the diner. Oh, he knew that she understood it was going on behind her back, but he could see the strength she felt when surrounded by her friends.

Only once did he notice something bothering her. After they had paid and he was walking her back to her car, she tensed as two men walked by them and said her name loudly.

He eased her mind by reaching over and taking her hand in his again and felt her instantly relax.

"You okay?" he asked when they stopped by her car.

She took a deep breath before answering. "Yeah, I'm okay."

"If you need—"

She stopped him by leaning against his chest.

"Cade, I'll be fine. I knew that coming back here was going to be rough. I had a feeling I'd have to deal with my family. My grandmother had prepared me for her son's... shenanigans."

He enjoyed the feeling of her body against his and wondered if he should push his luck and invite her back to his place again. Then she glanced down at her phone and sighed.

"I'd better go. I have an early morning meeting with the

kitchen staff." She leaned up on her toes and placed a soft kiss on his lips. "Thanks for... last night and for today."

His hands ran slowly up her sides as he kissed her again. "Call me if you need any help putting your new things away." He smiled, remembering the sexy items she'd purchased. "Especially that little red number."

She chuckled. "I bought that with our next date in mind."

"Friday," he blurted out, causing her to laugh.

"Saturday?" she countered.

"I'll pick you up at six."

"Make it six thirty." She kissed him again. "Good night."

"Night." He watched her drive away before climbing into his own truck and heading home.

When he got there, he sat out on the back porch and waited while Blue enjoyed the dying sunlight as night fell around them.

He had to admit, he felt the emptiness of his home for the rest of the night. Even Blue's company couldn't break him out of his loneliness.

What he wanted was someone to spend the rest of his nights with. Someone to talk to. Someone to hold.

Lying in his bed alone, his mind kept playing over how different tonight was than last night. Finally, he gave up trying to sleep and pulled out his cell phone and sent her a text message.

"Did you get settled in your new room okay?"

He was happy to see an almost immediate response.

"Yes, I'm in room four-eighty-two. It's smaller than the last room, but it will do until the west building is up to date."

He was still reading her response when another text from her came in.

"Thanks again for being there for me today. I don't think I could have handled that alone."

"Something tells me you could have handled it just fine. But I'm happy I could help," he texted back. Then he smiled. "So, what are you wearing?"

She sent him a little emoji that looked a lot like her with a bunny suit on, which had him laughing.

"Sexy," he replied.

"It keeps me warm." Then she added, "I'm saving the red number for Saturday night."

"Looking forward to it." He realized he really was anxious to see her again. To be with her again. And not just for sex, even though it was really great sex.

How long had it been since he'd felt excited to just spend time with someone? With Julia, he couldn't even remember wanting to spend time with her. In his mind, that relationship had been purely sexual. She'd been the one to drag him around for dates.

"I'd better get to sleep. I have an early meeting," she texted.

"Good night," he replied.

"Night."

He shut off his phone and sat it in on the charger. Suddenly, he felt tired and lay back in the bed. Blue was snoring at his feet, and he was just drifting off when Blue jerked his head up and started growling, then barking.

His dog normally didn't turn on his security dog mode at night. During the day, Blue would bark at squirrels or racoons, but at night...

Cade climbed out of bed and followed Blue to the glass door that led to a small balcony that sat off his bedroom. He glanced out and was reaching for the light switch when a dark figure darted across his side lawn.

"Shush." He nudged Blue slightly and twisted to get a better view of the figure, who had disappeared behind his garage.

Rushing to the bathroom, he looked out the window and watched, but when he didn't see anything, he headed to the guest room and looked out that window. Blue had lost interest and had climbed back up in the bed. Since he was up, Cade grabbed a flashlight, put on his mud boots and jacket, and headed out to see if he could figure out who was sneaking around.

He flipped on all the flood lights. The moment he stepped outside, Blue was on his heels, looking excited to be going out in the middle of the night.

He made two rounds around his place and couldn't find anything out of place. He didn't spot so much as a single footprint.

Maybe he'd dreamed it? Either way, when he finally climbed back in bed, he was totally exhausted and fell asleep immediately.

The following morning, when he and Blue climbed into the truck to head to work, he realized what had happened.

The piece of paper on his windshield hadn't registered with him at first. He'd had to climb back out and gather the note. The words were slanted and had obviously been written by a very drunk person, but he continued reading.

"Tell the stupid bitch to get out of my business. The slut actually thinks she can take over! This is my town. I'll do whatever it takes to get her out of my way."

He felt his anger grow.

·   ·   ·

He decided to swing by his uncle's office before heading into work.

"I found this on my windshield this morning." He tossed the note down on his uncle's desk. "Saw someone sneaking around my yard last night around one," he added as he sat down.

Sean opened the note and frowned down as he read the threats.

"Stupid son of a..." Sean shook his head and then glanced up at him. "I'll swing by and have a talk with Colin."

Cade glanced down at the note and felt his anger rise again over the threats Raven's uncle had aimed, not at him, but at his niece if Cade didn't back away from her.

"So, you and Raven?" Sean said, changing the subject.

"Yeah." He ran a hand through his hair. "What of it?"

Sean held up his hands as if in defense. "Hey, don't aim that anger at me. I'm all for it. Her parents were my friends. Her uncle and aunt"—he tapped the note from Colin— "not so much."

Cade relaxed slightly. "How can two people be so..."

"Selfish?" Sean finished for him.

"I was going to say stupid, but they both apply. I mean, the man practically signed his name to a death threat." Cade waved his hand, motioning towards the note.

"Which is why I'm going to head over there and have a nice chat with him right now." Sean stood up.

"You're heading to Redding?" Cade stood as well.

Sean's eyebrows shot up. "Redding?"

"Isn't that where they're staying?"

"No, Colin and Roslyn rented the old Ellington place just outside of town," Sean answered.

"You mean, they're staying only a mile from the resort?" Cade felt his entire body shake with anger.

"Yup." Sean nodded. "They moved in yesterday." Sean stopped him from storming out by placing a hand on his arm. "Son, let me deal with them. You head on into work. I've got this."

Cade wanted to argue, but he knew better and instead headed to work.

CHAPTER NINETEEN

LIFE, LIKE A FIRE, BEGINS IN SMOKE AND ENDS IN
ASHES. ~ ARABIAN PROVERB

R aven stayed too busy during the week to really think about anything other than work.

David had hired a special certified crew from Redding to start replacing the fire system in the west building. His workers moved up and started on all the guest rooms.

There were five massive dumpsters delivered to the back entrance of the building. In just two days, most of them were filled to the top with the old carpet they had pulled out of the rooms.

She couldn't wait to see what the rooms would look like with the fresh paint and flooring. They had received a massive shipment earlier that week with all the new bedding, furniture, and room accessories. The huge boxes were all sitting just inside the loading dock, along with the rest of the modern furniture that would fill the lobby and other public areas.

Some had been immediately unpackaged and put into place. She had happily helped with the work and enjoyed seeing the new furniture in the lobby.

Already, the resort was looking classier and more

modern, and she could feel the excitement from the employees. She couldn't wait to start having guests walk through the doors.

She was looking forward to it as much as she was looking forward to her date with Cade on Saturday night.

So much had changed since she'd returned home. There was so much she hadn't planned for. Cade being at the top of that list.

Even though her aunt and uncle were huge problems, she remembered that they had always been the black sheep of the family.

Her grandmother had told her stories of how Colin had been growing up. There was one thing that had been obvious from the moment she'd returned: Colin hadn't changed.

She had been thankful when she'd heard a rumor that her uncle and aunt had moved all the way to Redding. Then Cade had mentioned that they'd moved back into town the morning after the break-in.

After that, she was fairly sure it had been her aunt who had broken into her rooms. She couldn't see her uncle trashing the place out, but her aunt? Totally.

She doubted that her cousin knew about it. It wasn't in Liza's DNA to trash anything. Other than human souls. Besides, Liza never did anything if there was a possibility that she might break a fingernail.

In one of their calls one day during lunch, Cade had mentioned to her about the note he'd found on his windshield.

He hadn't told her what it had said, only that it had directly threatened her. He'd asked her to be on a lockdown of sorts.

Whenever she left the resort, Cade wanted her to text

him and let him know where she was going. Not that she had any place to be. Other than a few errands or quick runs into town to get more personal items, her entire life centered around the resort.

Not that she was complaining. At least for now. Once the doors opened, she was hoping to have some sort of normalcy.

Such as more time to go on dates with Cade. Maybe a few trips into the city? Or someplace tropical?

Either way, until the resort was back under control, she was staying put. She hadn't expected to love the work or to fall back in love with the resort itself.

Every time she turned a corner, memories of her childhood played in her head. The nostalgia was so strong, and she wished she had more pictures of her childhood. Her grandmother had given her a handful of pictures, which she kept on her phone. The originals were tucked away in a safe back in San Diego, along with her great-grandmother's pearl necklace and earrings and the deed to the resort itself. It had legally been changed over to Raven's name shortly after her parents' deaths.

The bar area restoration had succeeded in bringing people in each night. Normally, Raven didn't enjoy the bar scene, but she spent Thursday night sitting in the bar area, her eyes scanning the room and the guests as she tried to figure out what improvements would enhance the place even further.

After the first busy night, the staff hinted at the need for another beer fridge behind the bar. The next morning, she'd ordered one, along with more custom printed coasters with funny little sayings or games on the backside. They had been a huge hit. She even thought about starting a trivia game night once a week to drag in more of the locals.

Word had gotten out around town about the resort's amazing new chef, Tim, and a steady flood of locals streamed into the newly opened dining area in the lobby and bar. The main dining hall was still being worked on and would be shut down for at least two more weeks.

She'd found an antique chandelier at an online auction that was perfect for the center of the dining hall. The old chandelier was beyond repair and too outdated for Raven's tastes. The plan was to place the grand piano directly underneath it, in the center of the room, with the tables in a circle around it and the massive two-story stone fireplace, which was being converted to gas.

The chandelier was being delivered early next week, which meant that the rest of the dining hall had to be ready by then.

David's original crew were working quickly on getting everything ready. Each day when she walked through, she was even more impressed with how well his team worked.

Rachelle kept proving to her just how invaluable she was to the resort. She always lifted the morale of the employees. Just before her weekly meeting with Rachelle early Friday morning, Raven made a quick determination to give the woman a raise.

She clearly deserved it. Besides, Raven knew that she had been seriously underpaid over the years while her aunt and uncle had been grossly overpaid.

"Morning," Rachelle said, knocking on Raven's open office door. "Coffee and muffins?" She held up a mug and a plate of muffins.

"Yes." Raven motioned her inside. "I didn't get a chance to head down to the kitchen and eat anything yet."

"I figured as much." Rachelle sat down and handed Raven the coffee as she set the plate of muffins down on the desk. "So, I've heard from the bar crew that the new fridge was set up before shift last night. It should be helpful for the crowd that we're expecting tonight."

Raven sipped the coffee and watched Rachelle open a notepad and skim through the pages.

"First order of business..." Rachelle started.

"I'm giving you a raise," Raven broke in.

Rachelle's eyebrows shot up. "You... are?"

Raven smiled. "You deserve it."

"Of course, I do." Rachelle laughed. "I just never expected to get one. I've worked here for so long and this will be the first."

"Seriously?" Raven was shocked. She'd known she was underpaid, but surely, she'd at least gotten one raise in the last eight years.

Rachelle shrugged. "The work was my only reward, until now." She smiled. "Do I get a fancy new title as well?" she joked.

Raven laughed. "What is your official title now?"

"Hotel Manager." Rachelle rolled her eyes. "Not bad, but it doesn't really encompass everything I do."

Raven thought about it and nodded. "How does Resort Director sound?" Raven asked.

"Fancy," Rachelle said with a smile. "I'll take it."

"Good. Now what do you say we get this meeting started." She flipped open her own notebook and got to work.

Even though she hadn't seen Cade all week long, they had been texting or calling one another multiple times each day and each night.

Darby and Carrie were meeting her in the lobby later for dinner for girls' night, which was becoming a weekly thing with the friends. She'd convinced them to have dinner at the resort and hang in her rooms since she hadn't wanted a repeat of last week.

She knew from the gossip going around town that her aunt and uncle had been questioned about the break-in, but just like Joseph's murder, it appeared that the police weren't sure about who had done it. At least not yet.

The gossip about Joseph's death hadn't died down yet. Speculations were floating around town and rumors had her at the top of the guilty list. At least she shared the number-one spot with her uncle. It wasn't the first time she'd been guilty without proof in the eyes of the townspeople.

Since she'd been avoiding going into town all week, she hadn't run into her aunt or uncle now that they were back in town.

Liza, on the other hand, was still living in a room in the main building where Raven had her own room. She'd moved twice already, trying to stay out of the way of the construction. She didn't mind it since she currently only had a suitcase worth of clothes. She'd gone into town one day and had purchased a few more outfits for work along with some more casual clothes. Still, they all easily fit into the small hotel closet.

After meeting her friends in the bar, the three of them settled down at a table near the back of the area.

There were four employees working in the bar area tonight, and Raven had wanted to keep an eye on two of the newer ones to make sure they could handle a busy night. Not that she didn't trust Rachelle's judgment in the matter. But Raven knew one of them personally.

It wasn't as if Heather was going around causing problems. Rachelle had let Raven know that, since she'd been hired, she'd convinced a bunch of the locals who still held grudges against Raven to start frequenting the resort bar.

Raven was fairly sure it was for her own selfish reasons, since she needed the tips.

The new uniform for the employees was classy and sleek, but somehow, on Heather, it looked downright slutty. Raven had watched the woman flirt as she worked the room, and Raven realized that the outfit she'd changed into after work was far from sexy.

She'd picked a pencil skirt and a cream-colored blouse with a matching pair of boots that she'd found at the local shoe store in town. She knew that her friends would expect her to wear something better than work slacks and this was the best she had currently. Besides the sexy red dress, which she was saving for tomorrow night.

Her friends were both dressed in what Raven would describe as club attire, making her feel even more ordinary.

Darby was dressed in a little hot-pink number with heeled boots. Her blonde hair had been curled, and she was easily wearing twice her normal makeup.

Carrie had on a slinky black dress that hugged her curves and showcased her long curly hair.

When she'd noticed what her friends were wearing, she'd instantly wished that she could have made it into the city to get something a little sexier.

"You seemed preoccupied," Carrie said after their drinks had arrived. "Did something else happen?" she asked with a slight gasp.

"Your aunt and uncle? Did they do something more?" Darby jumped in.

"No." Raven shook her head and then took a sip of her wine. "No, I haven't seen or heard from them since I saw them in the diner."

"Good." Darby leaned back. "They haven't been back since."

"What's on your mind then?" Carrie asked.

"I have a date tomorrow night with Cade," she answered.

"Oh." Darby smiled. "I knew there was something between the two of you."

Carrie rolled her eyes. "Duh-doy. Everyone in town knows that Raven spent the night at Cade's last week. That's how someone broke into her rooms and..." Her friend stopped talking and reached over and laid her hand over hers. "Sorry."

"It's okay. I'm over it. I hated my wardrobe anyway." She tried to make light of the situation. Over the past few days, she'd been consoled so many times about her ruined things that she was almost numb to it. After all, it wasn't the first time in life she'd lost everything dear to her. This time it had just been clothes. Last time it had been so much more.

"When we head up to your room, we'll help you pick out something sexy for your date," Carrie said, holding up her wine glass.

"I have a little red dress Cade's been looking forward to seeing me in," she replied with a smile.

"Go, girl," Darby said, holding up her wine glass.

"Let's forget men and enjoy girl time." Carrie held her glass up.

The three friends clicked their glasses together and drank.

Less than five minutes later, Andre Walker strolled into the bar with a few of his friends.

"Oh my god," Darby sighed as she watched the men settle at the bar. "He's just so... damn hot."

Raven watched her friend's eyes go dreamy as she looked at the group.

"Which one?" Carrie asked. The tone of jealousy in her friend's voice had her eyes moving over towards her.

Carrie's eyes were glued to Andre. Was there something between the two?

"Tony Ellis, of course," Darby clarified, sounding a little shocked and offended. "Not Andre." Darby rolled her eyes.

"What is going on between you two?" Raven asked.

Darby leaned closer; her eyes glued to Carrie's. "Everyone in town knows that Andre and Carrie..."

Raven's eyebrows jumped. "You two?"

"No," Carrie denied it quickly. She took a sip of her wine as her eyes moved away from the group of men.

"No as in... not any more or no as in... never?" Raven asked with a smile.

"No as in... no." Carrie's tone turned sad. "Everyone in town knows Andre's father is very anti..."

"He's the biggest racist in town," Darby jumped in.

"Doesn't his family own the large ranch outside of town?" Raven asked, trying to remember more about the man. She knew that he'd gone to school with them and was a year or two older than they were. But outside of that, she was drawing a blank.

"And the local hardware store," Darby added. "Benjamin Walker purchased up most of the businesses in town after the fire. The grocery store, hardware store, and even the gas stations. He bought them all for pennies after the fire and has made so much money. Not that they needed it. They were loaded to begin with."

"What does Andre do?" Raven tried to remember something about the guy. He was extremely good-looking, almost a little too good-looking for her tastes. She leaned towards the more manly, outdoorsy alpha-male type.

"He's studying in the city to become an actor, and works

as a volunteer fireman. So do the rest of the gang with him," Carrie supplied.

"Including Tony," Darby added with a wishful sigh.

"God. Why don't you head over there and ask the man for a drink already?" Carrie nudged Darby's shoulder.

"Me?" She shook her head and looked a little scared.

"Ugh." Carrie jumped up from the chair and headed towards the bar. Darby watched with a shocked and scared look on her face.

"Relax. You know she wouldn't do anything to embarrass you," Raven said, touching Darby's arm. "You have it bad for this guy?"

"Tony has come into the diner every day for the past year." Darby's eyes turned towards hers. "Every single day. He's sweet, sexy, and..." She turned back to the scene at the bar. "One of the nicest men I know."

"And slow," Raven added with a chuckle. "If he hasn't asked you out once in the past year."

"Yeah." Darby sighed, then stiffened when Carrie motioned towards their table. The fact that she was talking to Andre and not Tony had assured Raven that her friend wasn't embarrassing Darby.

Suddenly, the entire crew of men started heading towards their table. Raven wondered where Cade was since it appeared as if girls' night had now changed directions.

The three friends were joined by Andre, Tony, and a guy by the name of Kevin. She remembered seeing both Tony and Kevin helping Cade out before. Kevin was shorter than she was by at least half a foot, and as thick as her uncle. He wasn't bad looking, but he was a few years younger than she was.

The moment Kevin sat next to her and gave her a look

of interest, she jumped up and made a quick excuse about needing to make a phone call.

Stepping into the quiet lobby, she punched Cade's number. He answered on the second ring.

"Hey, I was just thinking of you," he said smoothly.

"What are you doing right now?" she jumped in.

"Blue and I are sitting on the back porch," he answered. "Why?"

"Come save me from a very awkward predicament. My girls' night has now turned into an impromptu triple date."

"What?" She could hear the frown in his tone.

"Just come to the bar. I'll explain later. Save me from Kevin," she begged.

"Kevin?"

"We're at the bar at the resort. I'll see you in ten." She hung up when her friends called her back over to the table.

The next ten minutes were the longest in her entire life. She swore that she could even hear the tick of the second hand on her digital Apple watch.

She kept having to scoot her chair farther away from Kevin when he talked to her. Darby and Tony were huddled together, flirting, and Carrie and Andre seemed to be in a heated conversation. Which had left Kevin's attention solely on her.

Without coming right out and saying she wasn't interested, she sat in the corner and sipped her wine while her friends downed their second and third drinks. They'd switched from wine to shots and beers after the men had arrived. She'd stuck to the wine.

When Cade finally strolled in, she realized just why she was so drawn to him. The man oozed sex appeal in everything he did. Even walking into a bar.

"Hey," he said, stopping directly behind Kevin's chair, "you're in my seat."

Kevin glanced up and then between his friends, who all nodded. Then he slid over to the empty chair with a slight frown.

"Hi," Cade said to her with a smile. "You look nice tonight." He took her hand in his and then waved for a waitress.

"Thanks," she said, trying not to fidget. She was still feeling seriously inferior to the rest of the crowd that had gathered in the bar.

Heather walked over and, after taking Cade's and the rest of the table's orders, she disappeared.

"So," Cade said, leaning a little closer to her. "Girls' night turned into something more?"

She rolled her eyes and lowered her voice. "Apparently, Carrie and Andre,"

Cade chuckled. "Old news."

She shook her head. "To some. Well, Darby and Tony..." Cade's eyebrows shot up as his eyes moved to the pair, who were laughing about something on Darby's phone.

"That one's news to me," Cade offered.

"Yeah, when your guys showed up..."

"My guys?" Cade asked.

Raven shrugged. "Apparently you own anyone who works at the fire station."

Cade smiled. "Does that make all of these people your workers?" He motioned to Heather, who was walking towards them with a full tray of drinks.

"Something like that."

For the next two hours, the six of them laughed and enjoyed their time together. Kevin had made some excuse a few moments after Cade had showed up and left. Raven felt a little bad, but then Cade hinted that he had a live-in girl-friend, and Raven stopped feeling bad for the man, who'd obviously been on the prowl.

Almost four hours after her friends had walked into the bar, the three of them stepped into the elevator together. Andre and Tony were getting rides home from Cade, who had nursed a single beer since arriving. She wanted to kiss Cade good night, but since he was practically holding up Tony, she settled for telling him that she'd see him tomorrow night.

She had to admit, she was thankful that they had decided to stay in her rooms for the night instead of trying to drive back into town. After three glasses of wine, she could barely hit the correct floor number button in the elevator. Even then, she was giggling so hard at something Darby had said that she had to hold onto the railing to stop herself from sliding to the floor.

"I can't believe Tony finally asked me out," Darby said with a sigh as she rested her head back against the mirrored wall of the elevator.

"Finally," Carrie snorted. "I heard you dropping hints all night."

"He's just shy," Darby supplied.

"I didn't think he was really interested in you at first, but the way that boy looks at you..." Raven tapped her heart.

"Like Cade looks at you," Darby added.

"Girl, the way Cade looks at Raven is nothing like how Tony looks at you. Not yet anyway." The elevator stopped. "Cade looks like he wants to devour Raven. Tony looks like a lost little puppy willing to follow Darby around anywhere."

The friends were laughing as they stepped out of the elevator.

When Darby gasped and cried out, at first Raven didn't understand why. Then she followed her friend's gaze and felt her stomach lurch. Rachelle lay just outside the elevators, her pale skin a dark ashy grey, her glassy eyes staring up at the ceiling, unseeing.

The desire for blood had to be quenched.

Even if, this time, no blood had literally been spilt. There were, after all, other ways to feed the flames. Watching the ash color flood over the normally soft-pink complexion was even more rewarding than they had assumed.

"More," the monster deep inside growled. Now that it was awakened, it was a daily battle to quench the thirst.

Tempering the desire to put something in the proverbial town's well hadn't been easy. Still, knowing that, once again, their staging would shock the one person they hated the most fulfilled those desires.

Giddiness overcame upon thinking of the three friends finding their prize. Yes, they would have to do this again. Soon.

CHAPTER TWENTY

FOUL WATER WILL QUENCH FIRE ~ ENGLISH
PROVERB

Less than five minutes after stepping inside his house, his phone chimed. Seeing his uncle's number on his screen, he frowned and began to worry.

"Hey, what's up?" he answered.

"Hey, better head back up to the resort. Something tells me that your girl is going to need your support right now," Sean said.

"What's wrong?" He turned back towards the door and grabbed his coat. He decided this time to take Blue with him.

"She and her friends found Rachelle Braun's body," Sean answered.

Blue followed Cade outside and jumped into the truck when he opened the door for him.

"What happened?" Cade asked, starting the engine.

"We're not sure yet. The coroner will have to do an autopsy. Raven and her friends seem really shaken up though."

He thought about how the three women had headed towards the elevators happy, laughing, and extremely drunk. Then he thought of Raven finding another dead body in her resort.

He knew she'd take it hard, especially since she'd grown close to Rachelle, but also because the entire town was still talking about the first murder. If it turned out that Rachelle hadn't died of natural causes, this could be seriously detrimental to the grand reopening that Raven had planned.

"I'm a few minutes out," he told Sean before hanging up.

When he stepped inside the lobby doors, he noticed Raven, Darby, and Carrie all huddled together under a large blanket.

Blue got to Raven before he did, and he watched from a few steps away as she bent down and wrapped her arms around his dog's neck.

"Hey," he said, running his eyes over the friends' faces. "You guys okay?"

"No," Darby sniffled.

"I don't think I'll ever be okay again," Carrie said. "That's the first dead body I've ever seen."

"I was with my dad when we found my mom." Darby closed her eyes. "That was hard but this..." Then Darby gasped. "Oh, I just remembered you found your accountant." Her voice lowered. "Without a head." She laid a hand on Raven's shoulder. "Sorry," Darby sighed, "still a little drunk."

Raven's face was buried in Blue's fur, but he heard her sniffle.

"Hey." He knelt beside his dog. Raven mumbled something incoherent. "What was that?" he asked softly.

Raven lifted her face, and her eyes were red and puffy from crying.

"I'd just given her a raise," she said as tears rolled down her cheeks.

"Oh, honey." He pulled her into his arms. "I'm so sorry."

Just then his uncle walked over to them.

"We're taking Miss Braun out the side doors," he informed them. "We won't know anything further for a few days, but the coroner believes Rachelle's death wasn't due to natural causes."

Raven covered her mouth and closed her eyes.

Two murders under one roof. Cade was desperate at this point to get Raven out from under that roof. But she was stubborn, and he figured he would have to maneuver her so she thought it was her idea. So, he was shocked at her next words.

"Can I stay at your place?" she asked, her eyes searching his.

It took him a moment since he was still trying to figure out how to get her to agree to the move. When her words registered, he nodded quickly.

"Can we stay there tonight too? I don't think any of us want to be left alone," Darby asked, running her hands through Blue's soft fur. "And I don't want to wake my dad up. He took the morning shift for me."

"Sure." He touched Darby's shoulder.

"I'll need to meet with you in the morning and ask you all a few questions," Sean said.

"You know where they'll be," Cade said, pulling Raven up to her feet. "Do you need anything?" he asked her.

She glanced towards the elevators. "No."

"Our bags are in your room," Darby said.

"I can have one of my men bring them down?" Sean suggested.

"Thank you." Carrie stood up. "They're just inside the door." She turned to Raven, who reached into her small purse and handed Sean her room key.

"Do you want anything?" Sean asked.

Raven's eyes moved to Cade's. He remembered the last time she'd spent the night at his place. They'd slept in the nude, holding one another all night long. However, knowing that her friends would be there, most likely in the guest room just down the hallway, he nudged her slightly.

"I can go up…" Raven started.

"No," he broke in. "Whatever she needs, I'm sure I have something she can wear for tonight."

"Thanks," Raven agreed.

"Come on. Let's go home." He wrapped his arms around her just as Blue happily barked at one of his favorite words.

They rode in his truck in silence, the only sound other than the engine was Blue snoring as he lay across Darby's lap.

"We should talk about it," Carrie said suddenly.

"I don't think I can," Darby replied.

"I know I had a few glasses of wine earlier, but I'm totally sober now," Raven said with a slight sigh.

"I could totally go for some chocolate," Darby said as they approached the general store.

"I can run inside and get you ladies something," he offered, even though it was past one in the morning.

"Cookies," Carrie suggested.

"Brownies," Darby added in.

"With double fudge ice cream," Raven suggested.

He pulled over and parked, then turned around. "Anything else while I'm in there?"

"Wine," Carrie said with a slight sigh. "If I had a little

buzz again, maybe I could get a few moments of sleep tonight."

"Any preference?" he asked.

He took their orders and tried to quickly grab everything they'd requested. By the time he walked out of the store with a bag of sweets and three bottles of wine, the ladies were talking. He hated interrupting their conversation, since he knew it was probably the best therapy for them.

As he figured, they stopped talking the moment he got settled in the truck.

He was surprised when they continued talking when he pulled out of the parking lot. Raven was telling her friends how much Rachelle had meant to her and the business.

"I doubt I'll be able to find anyone else like her," she said with a sniffle. "We were beginning to really be close friends."

"I'm so sorry," Carrie said as he pulled into his driveway.

"I'm so thankful you guys were here with me this time," Raven said, touching her friend's hand.

The friends climbed out of the truck, and they all held onto one another for a moment.

"I've been wondering what this place looked like on the inside," Darby said as they stepped inside.

"Take a look around," he suggested, shifting the bags of groceries. "I'll put this stuff in the kitchen."

"I'll show them around. We can put their bags up in the guest room," Raven offered.

He guessed that the friends needed a few moments alone. He could hear them talking quietly as they moved about his house. Blue was on their heels as if it were a game.

After putting the ice cream in the freezer, he pulled out

a few glasses for the wine and then took out a beer for himself. He'd only had one earlier and figured if he was going to play host for the remainder of the evening, he might as well have a drink.

When the three friends came back downstairs, he'd started a fire. Even though it was dead summer, the night had turned chilly. He had set out a bowl of crackers, some cheese, and some grapes he had as well as the junk food they'd requested. He figured they'd want some more healthy food, since for the past few hours, they'd only been drinking.

"I don't think I could fall asleep for days. Every time I blink, I see Rachelle," Darby said, sitting on the sofa and grabbing a handful of chips.

"For some reason, I'm starving," Carrie added, grabbing some grapes.

"It's called survivor's syndrome," Darby added with a shrug. "After losing Mom in the fire, Dad and I went to counseling. You'd think by now I'd be able to handle death," she added through a mouthful of food.

"I doubt seeing death ever gets easy. Even for those who deal with it every day," Raven said softly. She had chosen the chair closest to the fireplace and reached around to pull the throw blanket over herself.

"Does anyone need anything else? I have an early morning and am going to head up," he said.

"No. Thanks for letting us crash here," Darby said.

"Thanks," Carrie added, reaching for some more grapes.

"Help yourself to whatever." He motioned towards the kitchen as his eyes landed on Raven. "Are you okay?"

"Yes," she said with a weak smile. "Thank you."

Nodding, he glanced down at his dog, who was curled

up next to Darby. "You can keep him," he said with a smile. "Advanced warning. He farts at night."

The three friends smiled, then chuckled after Blue let out a loud fart while remaining dead asleep.

He thought it would take him a while to fall asleep, but the moment his head hit the pillows, he was out.

It had been years since he'd had the dream, so when it started, it was as if it was the first time.

It was ten years ago. The charred ground was still smoking and there were still small flames crackling through some of the larger downed trees.

He was running, his eyes scanning the black ground, looking for Reggie. He had to be there somewhere. His burned-out car had been found parked just off the road less than half a mile from there.

Cade knew that the once-beautiful hillside had been a popular hiking spot, one that his little brother had always loved.

If his car was nearby, that meant Reggie was somewhere close.

He continued to call out his brother's name until his voice grew hoarse. He coughed from all the smoke that had settled over the blackened land.

Instead of the true memory of him returning home empty-handed that day, in his dream, he came to a small clearing. There, kneeling over his brother's charred remains, sat Raven. Her red hair floated wildly in the wind. Her crystal blue eyes pierced his as she laughed over Reggie's body.

He woke with a start, swiping his hands over his face, and instantly realized he wasn't alone in the bed.

"Are you okay?" Raven asked, shifting to sit up.

"Yeah." He held her down and wrapped his arms

around her, burying his face into the red hair he'd just dreamed about, knowing that what he'd dreamed hadn't been real. "Bad dream."

She sighed and laid her head against his shoulder.

"Did your friends get settled?" he asked.

"They fell asleep about an hour ago. I thought it would be okay to sneak in here," she said against his bare chest.

He felt his body instantly react to her closeness. He ran his hand over her bare shoulder.

"Yeah," he said, nudging her chin up until he could lay his lips over hers. "I'd understand if you don't want—"

She stopped him by laying her lips over his.

"Cade, I need you," she said softly.

It was all the encouragement he needed. He slid her tank top over her head, exposing her perfect breasts. Rolling slightly, he pinned her under him and bent his head down to lap at her milky skin.

Her fingers dug into his hair, holding, nudging him on while he explored, tasted, and enjoyed running his mouth and his hands over her.

In the darkness, with horrors echoing in both of their minds, they found one another. Clung together. The slow pace was needed by both of them at this time.

This wasn't fast-paced, crazed, survivor's syndrome sex. This was something beyond anything he'd ever experienced. Something deeper than he wanted to explore at the current moment. Instead, he focused on how wonderful her naked body felt against his. How perfect he fit inside her, around her. How her legs wrapped around his hips, holding him close to her heat.

"Cade, I can't," she said, biting her bottom lip.

He knew she was trying to keep quiet, since her friends were just down the hallway.

Leaning in, he placed his mouth over hers and swallowed her soft cries as he continued to pound into her until he felt her convulse around him. With his own release, he buried his face into her soft hair and moaned her name.

"That was the absolute best distraction from a bad dream that I've ever had," he said once he'd shifted slightly so he wasn't pinning her to the mattress with his weight.

She giggled softly as she ran her fingertips over his lower back.

"I needed this. I needed my friends earlier, but then I needed you," she said with a slight sigh.

"Distractions." He glanced over at her.

She was quiet for a moment. "I don't know how I'm going to do it without Rachelle. She's been carrying so much weight around the resort."

"You know, my mother might be able to help you out. At least until you find someone else to take Rachelle's place."

"Your mother?" Raven leaned up and frowned down at him.

"She did work at the resort with your parents," he reminded her.

Raven's frown grew. "I'd forgotten."

He smiled. "She was directly under your parents for years."

"She's hired," Raven said and laid back down. "If she wants the job."

"What do you say we invite her over here for breakfast? I guarantee Sean will be here at sunup anyway with donuts and coffee. I'll text her in the morning. But for now..." He pulled her close again. "Sleep."

"Yeah." She rested her head on his shoulder. "Thank you. For everything."

Just as Cade had expected, his uncle walked in with a box of donuts and coffee shortly after sunup. Cade had texted his mother the moment he'd woken up with his alarm.

He had a few meetings that morning but guessed that he was needed here more, so he called Tony and asked him to fill in for him until he could make it into work.

After hanging out with the man last night, Cade was pretty sure the guy was going to move up in the job quickly. Not only was he smart, but he was easily one of the hardest workers he'd ever trained.

By the time his mother walked into the house, all the ladies were showered and sitting at the kitchen table, nibbling on the donuts and sipping freshly made coffee.

Darby and Carrie had changed out of their dresses into casual clothes, while Raven sat at his kitchen table in a pair of his rolled-up sweats and a sweatshirt, her long red hair still wet from the shower he wished he could have shared with her.

"I'm so sorry about Rachelle," his mother said, walking over and placing a hand on Raven's shoulder.

"Thank you," Raven replied softly.

"How are you three holding up?" his mother asked, sitting next to Sean and reaching for a donut.

"It helped staying here last night," Darby said.

"I think we needed each other," Carrie added.

"I know last night was tough on you three, but I'm still going to need to ask you some questions," Sean broke in.

"Oh, Sean, do you have to right now?" his mother asked.

A look passed between his uncle and his mother, one he'd seen plenty of times before.

"If it was up to me," Sean finally said with a shrug. "Rachelle's family deserves answers."

"Ask your questions," Raven broke in.

Cade reached over and took her hand at the same time Darby took Raven's other hand. Then Darby took Carrie's hand, as well.

"Okay." His mother nodded. "How about I make something better than sugar to eat?" she suggested as she stood up.

She disappeared into his kitchen, Blue on her heels, no doubt hoping that she'd drop something on the floor. Sean pulled out his notepad and flipped through it.

"I've pretty much narrowed the timeline down. The three of you left the bar at twelve-twenty, shortly after the bar closed. You said your goodbyes to Cade"—his uncle nodded towards him— "Tony and Andre, whom Cade drove home." His uncle flipped the page. "I called Cade at five after one, which means he'd probably just made it in the door."

"I still had my coat on," Cade supplied.

His uncle nodded. "The three of you found Rachelle at twelve-twenty-two and called 9-1-1 at that time."

"I called," Darby said softly. "I was the first one to notice Rachelle."

His uncle wrote something down in the notepad.

Sean ran his eyes over the four of them. "Did any of you notice anyone else leave the bar while you were there?"

"Just the employees leaving shortly after midnight," Raven answered.

"On shift last night was..." His uncle flipped a couple pages and listed off the seven employees for the bar area and the kitchen staff.

"I'd have to check my schedule, but it sounds about right." Raven nodded.

"Do you know of any employees who had issues with Miss Braun?" Sean asked.

"No." Raven shook her head. "Rachelle was well liked. She could be tough on employees who goofed off, but for the most part, everyone liked her. It was one of the reasons I'd just given her a raise and a promotion."

Sean's eyebrows rose. "How long ago was that?"

"Hours." Raven shut her eyes. "Hours before she was..." She shook her head. "Earlier that morning." She pulled out her phone and gave Sean the exact time. "During our Friday morning meeting, I had officially made her Resort Director."

"Was this common knowledge?" Sean asked, not taking his eyes from the notepad.

"No. I mean, I'm not sure who Rachelle told, but it wasn't something I spread around. Honestly, it was a spur of the moment kind of thing. Rachelle had been doing so well around here. She saved my butt a few times since I was being pulled in so many directions due to all the construction. I figured I'd better show her my appreciation before someone else snatched her away."

"Was she looking for another job?" Sean asked.

"No, I don't think so." Raven shook her head.

"Miss Braun was hired by your aunt. Do you happen to know when?" Sean asked.

"I'd have to look at her employee record," Raven answered.

"Do you know anything about the relationship between Miss Braun and your family?" Sean asked.

"I know that my aunt and uncle used Rachelle and didn't fully appreciate her."

"Have you given any other employees raises?" Sean asked.

"Some," she said after she thought about it.

"Have you fired any?" Sean asked.

Raven's eyes moved to his before she answered. "A few. You don't think that someone..." Then she shifted and her eyes grew wide. "Is this your way of saying that Rachelle was murdered?"

CHAPTER TWENTY-ONE

IF YOU CAN'T HANDLE HER FIRE, LET SOMEONE
ELSE ENJOY THE FLAMES.

Raven began to feel light-headed until Darby squeezed her hand. Then she gulped in a deep breath of air and waited for Sean to answer her question.

"At this point, I can't confirm anything. I'm just covering my bases," he said smoothly.

"Do you think it was an employee at the resort?" Carrie asked.

"I'm not saying that." Sean glanced towards Carrie. "I'm also checking into Miss Braun's personal life." Sean flipped a few more pages in his notebook before looking up at her. "Do you happen to know if Miss Braun was seeing anyone? Personally?"

Raven shook her head. She felt bad that she hadn't gotten to know Rachelle a little better. The woman had been almost twenty years older than her. The age gap, along with the fact that she had been the woman's boss, had forced Raven to keep their relationship from growing too personal.

Still, she could have asked the woman a few personal questions.

"Hey." Cade squeezed her hand. "Are you okay?"

"Yeah." She nodded and swallowed the guilt that was building in her gut. Guilt so much like she had felt all those years ago after the fire.

"How about we break for some breakfast?" Cade's mother stepped into the room and set a plate of eggs down on the table. "Sean, why don't you come grab some plates for everyone."

"Fiona, I'm working," Sean started, but upon Cade's mother's look, he sighed and stood up, shutting his notebook.

"Mom has Uncle Sean wrapped around her little finger," Cade whispered.

"Dah doy." Darby giggled. "They've been dating for years."

"Dating?" Cade almost yelped the word.

"Oh, snap." Darby gasped as her eyes moved to the kitchen. "Was it a secret?"

"Dating?" Cade said again as his eyes moved to where his uncle was helping his mother get a stack of plates down from the cupboard. "Dating."

"Are you okay?" Raven asked, squeezing his hand.

"Yeah, I guess..." He shook his head. "I guess part of me knew, but it's just..."

"Here we are now." Fiona walked in and set a stack of dishes on the table while Sean set down a large a bowl of hash browns and a plate of toast.

During breakfast, Raven could see that Cade was watching his mother and his uncle like a hawk.

Each time his uncle's hand brushed his mother's, Cade got a strange look on his face. Raven wanted to soothe him, to assure him that everything was okay.

While the six of them ate, Sean continued to ask them questions. None as difficult as before, but questions about who else was in the bar that night.

Between the four of them that had been there the night before, they were able to compile a list of almost everyone there.

Raven was more relaxed with the idea that the culprit was a guest who had been in the resort last night rather than one of her employees. Still, she agreed to Sean interviewing each of the employees that had been working last night.

Which meant she needed to return to the resort. She'd known she had to go back—after all, the place was her life now—but part of her had hoped that she could remain there, with Cade and Blue.

Once the dishes were cleared away, Darcy and Carrie got rides home from Sean. Darcy was excited and claimed she'd always wanted to ride in a cop car but groaned when Sean informed her that he was in his personal car that morning.

Cade asked why he hadn't driven his patrol car. Instead of answering, Sean had glanced over at Fiona and shrugged.

"I haven't been to the office yet," Sean had answered.

The moment his uncle left, Cade turned on his mother.

"Is there something between you and Uncle Sean?" he asked his mother.

Raven held in a smile when Fiona's coffee mug almost slipped from her fingers.

"What?" she asked, looking a little shocked.

"You heard me," Cade said slowly.

"Cade," Raven started, but she stopped when Cade gave her a look.

"Are you and Sean seeing one another?" he asked again.

"Cade." Fiona sighed. "We decided to keep what's between us quiet. For many reasons."

"I'll take that as a yes," Cade said, then surprised Raven and Fiona by smiling. "You know I love you both." He sighed. "But damn it, you've made me lose a bet."

"A... bet?" his mother asked.

"Yeah, I bet Andre a few years back that it would take Uncle Sean fifteen years after Reggie's death to finally ask you out. He bet me it would take less than ten." He smiled. "I guess I lost a hundred bucks."

"You..." His mother smiled. "You aren't mad?"

Cade stood up and walked over to his mother, then wrapped his arms around her. "How can I be mad when I see how happy you've become?" He kissed the top of her head. "Besides, everyone knew it was only a matter of time. The two of you have been crazy for one another for years. God knows Sean worships the ground you walk on."

"It's been two years," Fiona said softly. "Two years since we first..."

Cade held up his hand. "I don't want to know anything more about it. Other than he makes you happy."

"He does." Fiona smiled. "He does."

"Good, then it's settled." Cade straightened. "Now, Raven has a proposition for you." Cade glanced down at her. "I'm going to go let Blue out." He turned and left with Blue tagging behind him.

Raven took a deep breath as Fiona turned to her. "A proposition?"

Taking a sip of her now cold coffee, she worked up the nerve. She liked Cade's mother, she always had. Even when she'd been dating Reggie. Now, however, there was a lot more at stake. Especially since she was starting to have real feelings for Cade. Feelings she'd never experienced with Reggie or anyone else.

"Don't think me..."—she shook her head— "dark. But I really relied on Rachelle around the resort. Honestly, she was the only employee I could really rely on. Cade reminded me that you used to work under my parents."

"I did." Fiona smiled. "When they passed and your uncle and aunt took over, I stepped down." Her eyes grew sad. "After losing Reggie, I..." She shook her head. "I spent a few years living under my mother's roof, since I lost my own home in the fire. It took me a few years to get back on my own feet. By then, your uncle had run the resort... well, you know the rest." She stopped talking.

"I understand." She smiled. "If you're amenable, I'd like to ask you to fill Rachelle's position. It could be temporary or..."

Fiona laid her hand over her own. "Raven, I'd be happy to help you out. To be honest, I've been bored lately and looking for something new to fill my time."

"Seriously?" Raven asked then felt guilty when Fiona nodded. "I know it's not the best circumstances. The resort is still in need of leadership. Some of the employees are still struggling with me being in charge."

"Honey, at this point, it can only help to have someone like me around," Fiona said.

"How so?" Raven asked.

"Everyone in town knows that I don't listen to gossip. After all these years of hearing rumors about Sean and I." She leaned closer. "Make no mistake, I was true to my husband until the day he died. Cade is his father's son, who happens to strike a remarkable resemblance to his uncle."

Raven smiled. "I look like my grandmother. I saw

pictures of her when she was young." She remembered seeing the black and white image of her grandmother and freaking out at how much she looked like her. "I used to believe I was adopted." She chuckled.

Fiona smiled. "Remember, I was close friends with your parents. I held Rosemary's baby shower for you."

"Then it's settled." Raven smiled. "We won't pay any attention to rumors."

"Agreed." Fiona held out her hand and Raven shook it. "So, when do you want me to start?"

"Today, if possible," Raven said after a moment. "Sean has requested interviews with employees, and I'm going to need to do damage control. One murder was bad enough, but two." She closed her eyes.

"We'll get through this," Fiona said in a soothing tone.

Just hearing those words from someone who Raven understood had her back made her feel instantly better.

Since Cade had to head into work, Raven rode with Fiona back to the resort. After a quick dash upstairs to change into some of her own clothes—avoiding the elevator and using the stairs—she met with Fiona in her office to go over all of Rachelle's duties.

Raven was happily surprised to see how quickly Fiona picked everything up.

"It's as if I never left," Fiona said a few hours later. "Except for the new computer systems." She rolled her eyes.

"You'll pick up on it soon enough," Raven promised her.

"I've asked Cemal to request all employees gather for a meeting at noon in the bar area. I plan on explaining Rachelle's death and letting them know you'll be filling in for her," Raven said, glancing down at her watch. It was less than an hour until noon. "If you want, I'll show you to your office and you can get settled until then?"

"Thank you." Fiona stood up and then surprised Raven by pulling her into a hug. "I meant to do this earlier. I'm really sorry for your loss. After this morning, after understanding how you felt about Rachelle, I'm terribly sorry about your loss."

"Thank you." Raven's eyes stung as she held onto Cade's mother.

After showing Fiona to Rachelle's small office just down the hallway from her own, Raven headed downstairs to the kitchens. She wanted, no needed, another cup of coffee.

She hadn't planned on overhearing the latest gossip as she stood in the hallway.

The double doors to the kitchen area were always closed but today, they stood wide open. She was about to close them when she heard her name. Normally, she would have turned around and left, since she hated listening to gossip about herself. She knew what others had been saying over the years. But something made her stop and listen this time.

"It was Raven," a woman was saying. "I heard that she was close to firing Rachelle because she was jealous that employees listened to Rachelle instead of her. After all, we all know that she's the one who started the fire all those years ago."

"Those are just rumors," a man said in reply.

"Rumors with some truth. The cause of the fire was never really found out. Besides, she's probably the one who killed that accountant in the elevator. I'd heard that he was blackmailing her."

"Blackmailing?" the male voice asked. "What for?"

"She'd been sleeping around. From what I hear, she was

keeping the company of some important person in town and the accountant had proof," the woman said. "I mean, she's been back here for less than three months and is already in Cade Stone's bed."

Hearing Cade's name shook her out of the stupor.

Without really thinking it over, she stepped into the kitchen. Seeing the male dishwasher leaning against the counter with the maid practically in his lap, Raven felt her temper surface.

"Out." She pointed to the door. The couple immediately jumped apart upon being discovered. "Out," she said again.

When the female started to leave, Raven stopped her.

"No, I don't think I've made myself clear. You're fired." She turned her eyes to the young boy who had worked in the kitchen for less than a few weeks. "You too." She motioned. "Both of you. Collect your things and your last check on your way out."

The pair looked dumbstruck for a moment, then the girl grabbed the boy's hand and pulled him out of the kitchen.

If Raven had been in her right mind, she would have thought to ask her where she'd heard the rumors. Instead, she leaned against the counter and took several deep breaths until she felt her heart return to its normal beat.

By then, she was too upset to even think about coffee and turned around and headed back upstairs. Besides, it was less than ten minutes before her scheduled meeting with all the employees.

For the next few minutes, she ran over what she wanted to say to everyone. Two minutes before noon, Fiona knocked on her door.

"Ready?" Fiona asked. She waved her inside the office.

"Help." She motioned to her notes. "What in the hell am I going to say?"

Fiona ran her eyes over Raven's notes and then sat down. "This is a good start."

"It sucks." She rolled her eyes. "I come off sounding weak and shallow. Honestly, before Rachelle's even buried, I hired her replacement."

"Because business has to go on. You're just looking out for your investment and also thinking about your employees. It wouldn't do to let them worry. It's key to let them know you have their backs and that they have security in leadership. Don't let your doubts weigh you down. You've got this."

"I do," she said after a moment, feeling a little steadier.

"Ready to do this?" Fiona stood up and handed her the notepad.

"Yes." She took the notepad and set it down.

"Don't you need that?" Fiona asked.

"No. I've got this." She felt her entire body start to shake.

It was just like debate class in high school. Every single time she stood in front of two or more people and had to talk, she freaked. Her knees shook, her voice shook, her heart raced, and her palms grew sweaty. Like they were currently doing.

Wiping her hands on her slacks, she took a deep breath and followed Fiona out of her office and down the hallway into the bar area, where every single one of her employees was waiting on her.

She was thankful to see Sean and officer Karin Taper waiting in the lobby area.

"I thought you'd need backup," Sean said as he glanced towards Fiona, who nodded and mouthed, "Thanks."

When the four of them stepped into the bar area, the low chatter stopped, and the entire place grew quiet.

"Thank you," she said, hating the mellow tone of her voice. Her entire body was vibrating with nerves and yet her voice sounded soothing and was laced with security, betraying her emotions. "As many of you may have already heard, Rachelle Braun passed away late last night." Several employees gasped while a few others started crying softly. "Rachelle is going to be missed, and I know this is hard on all of us. I've scheduled a grief counselor to be available for anyone who needs it." She glanced around the room and noticed more dry eyes than wet ones.

She knew that Rachelle was liked by most, but Raven understood that most employees hated their bosses, no matter what. Especially in the hospitality world.

Just then Sean shifted and got her attention.

"Sheriff Stone has requested to meet with each of you at some point this week," she said, causing several people to groan. Holding up her hands she continued, "I know that all of us want to get to the bottom of what happened with one of our own." The groans stopped. "I'll expect everyone to carve out some time to meet with the sheriff."

"Thank you in advance for your cooperation," Sean said, stepping forward.

"Was Rachelle murdered?" someone shouted.

Sean glanced at her, and she motioned for him to take over.

"At this point, we're looking into every possibility. Until we find out, I'm just doing my job," Sean said smoothly.

He stepped back and everyone turned to her again. "Many of you know Fiona Stone." She glanced over at Cade's mother. "Fiona used to work with my parents before Rachelle was hired and has agreed to come back to lend us a hand during this challenging time." She stepped back. "Fiona, would you like to say something?"

Cade's mother stepped forward. "Thank you. I know it's been a tough time, but I hope that I can ease any of your concerns about the work and what is expected of you around here." Fiona was a pro. As Raven listened to her talk and ease the employee's minds, she wondered what it would take for her to be that confident.

When Fiona stopped talking, Raven stepped forward again.

"Is it true you fired Max and Kim today?" someone asked.

Raven didn't see who it was that asked, but when several employees chimed in with other questions, she felt her face flush.

"Does that mean more of us are going to be fired?"

"Why did they get fired?"

While other questions were thrown at her, she felt her pulse spike. Thankfully, Fiona stepped forward and laid a hand on her shoulder.

"Any employment questions can be directed at me. If you'd like to know why Max and Kim were let go, I'd be happy to meet with you. For now, the answer to the other questions is no. At this point, I don't plan on letting anyone else go. Just as long as you show up to work on time, maintain a professional attitude, and stick to your jobs." Fiona smiled warmly. "Now, I'm sure Miss Brooks is ready to turn us all loose and let us get back to work."

"Yes." Raven stepped forward. "Thank you all for making time this morning. You are released to head back to work." She turned to leave but stopped when Sean motioned her over.

"Do you have a moment?" the sheriff asked her.

"Sure, we can head back to my office." She led him down the hallway.

Sitting behind her desk, she started to feel a little more like herself. That fell apart with Sean's next words.

"We just heard back from the coroner's office. It appears that Rachelle Braun was poisoned."

CHAPTER TWENTY-TWO

There was a lot that Cade liked about his hometown. And then there was a lot he didn't like. Today, he'd found out just how vicious some people in town could be. It had been less than a week since word had officially gotten out that Rachelle had been murdered.

Since then, Raven had made it a habit to stay at his place each night. He figured it was because she was scared to be alone. Whatever the reason, he was happy to have her in his bed each night.

Today, he was at Jay's Groceries certifying their fire extinguishers when he overheard a young woman, whom he vaguely remembered seeing in town before, talking about Raven.

"Can you believe the bitch fired me? Everyone knows it's because she was jealous of me. I mean, there's only so much this town can take of that woman. Am I right?" she asked. The woman she was talking with nodded and looked bored. "We all know she started that fire years ago."

"What were you? Ten?" the other woman asked.

The first woman looked shocked and annoyed. "Does it

really matter? I suffered just the same." She sounded annoyed. Then her eyes moved around, and he could tell instantly that she'd spotted him. "Speaking of suffering." Her tone changed. "I hear she's torturing everyone who works at the resort because she's crazy. My cousin who lives in San Diego heard that she spent almost ten years in therapy because of guilt from murdering more than thirty people all those years ago. Including her boyfriend, whom it's widely known that she cheated on." The girl giggled as her eyes narrowed at him. "With multiple people. Something tells me Raven Brooks is a bigger slut than Heather Craft."

Just then the sound of a shattering glass bottle echoed throughout the store, a deep voice cried out as in pain and someone immediately said over the loudspeaker. "Clean up on aisle ten."

The two women glanced in his direction and giggled as they continued down the aisleway. He'd steamed about it the entire time he was working at the store. What was he saying? He was angry about it for the rest of the night. That was until Raven distracted him by rubbing her naked body up against his own.

"You seemed distracted tonight," she said once they were lying in each other's arms, their bodies cooling off.

"Me?" He tried to shake the statement off.

"During dinner, you were very quiet." She leaned up and looked down at him. "Is something wrong?"

He thought about keeping what he overheard from her and then figured she'd handled a lot worse over the years and told her everything.

To his happy surprise, she shrugged and dismissed the conversation.

"It was probably Kim. I fired her earlier this week when

I overheard her and Max, a dishwasher I fired as well, gossiping about me in the kitchen." She shrugged. "I'm the boss. I can hire and fire anyone I want," she added with a smile.

"Remind me never to work for you." He chuckled. "Or piss you off." He kissed her. "How's my mom doing, by the way?"

"She's really saving my butt." She relaxed back down against his chest. "She's wonderful with the employees. Did you know she has a type A personality? She has everything more organized than Rachelle or I ever did." She shook her head. "Have you heard anything new from your uncle?"

"Other than the fact that he's been dating my mother for a few years now?" Cade said a little sarcastically.

"About the murders," Raven clarified softly.

"No," he replied after a low sigh that rumbled his chest. For the past few days, he and everyone else in town had been living under the cloud of knowing that there was a murderer walking among them.

Someone they knew, talked to, walked by, or trusted had killed someone. Possibly even two somebodies, if he listened to rumors that were going around town.

Sean believed that the murders were unrelated. Joseph Ramsey had been lured to his death, attacked, and hit over the head with a sharp object that was yet to be determined or found. After he was dead, he'd been half-stuffed into a broken elevator. The moment Raven had hit the button to send the car to the main floor, he'd been sheared in two. Rachelle Braun, on the other hand, had been poisoned with common pesticides in her evening tea. What she'd been doing on the top floor was still a mystery. The woman lived alone in a small rental. Joseph's death was described by his uncle as a crime of passion because of the apparent last-minute antics, while Rachelle's had been more carefully planned out. Where had the pesticides come from? It wasn't as if they were just lying around.

To Cade, the murders were related in only one major area. They'd both happened under Raven's roof. He couldn't shake the dread that whoever was behind both murders was out to frame Raven. Either that or they were out to destroy her by taking away the one last thread holding her to this town—the resort.

By causing controversy surrounding the place, they could kick up enough rumors and gossip to keep the rooms empty after the grand reopening. Then again, he could remember staying at a few choice hotels in New Orleans that boasted several murders and even claimed to be haunted.

Besides, this idea was just comical. What was the assailant going to do? Murder enough people to cause guests to fear for their lives? Surely his uncle was a good enough cop to catch the killer before too long.

He realized Raven had fallen asleep on him when he heard her soft level breathing. Shifting slightly, he reached over and flipped off the lamp by the bed. He noticed a new message flash on her screen. He didn't want to wake her but happened to catch sight of the image that popped up.

Frowning at her uncle's face, he took up her phone and swiped the image he'd sent her.

The photo was grainy and old, like an old print that had been digitized, but he could clearly make out Joseph Ramsey's face. The man was much younger in the picture than the last time Cade had seen him before his death. Squinting, he realized that Joseph was naked from the waist down. His back was slightly turned towards the camera, and he looked over his shoulder. There appeared to be a woman kneeling in front of him. He couldn't make out the face of the woman, but he guessed instantly what she was doing to the guy. It was obvious now that Joseph had just been caught literally with his pants down.

Cade stilled when he noticed the flash of bright red hair.

If this image had been taken when he thought it was, Raven would have been far too young. Sixteen or seventeen at the most. Joseph was easily in his fifties, since the man had been sixty-two when he'd died.

Sitting up quickly, he dislodged Raven from his side.

"Cade?" she asked sleepily. "What's wrong?"

"What is this?" he asked, holding her phone out towards her.

Raven blinked a few times and then rubbed her eyes before taking her phone from his hands. Her frown was instant as she squinted at the image. The moment the scene registered in her mind, she dropped her phone.

"Why on earth would my uncle send me this?" she gasped.

"You tell me," he said, trying to hold back his anger. "Is that you?"

She turned to him, her eyes going wide. "Seriously?" she said after a moment.

"It's hard to tell, but you'd be, what? Sixteen? Seventeen?" he asked. She didn't say anything, so he continued. "What was Joseph Ramsey? Fifty?"

Without a word, she tossed the covers off her and jumped out of the bed. She quickly pulled on the clothes that he'd peeled from her less than an hour earlier.

He waited until she was fully dressed before climbing out of the bed to block her from the doorway.

"Talk to me," he demanded in a low tone.

"Go to hell," she threw back at him. She tried to get past him by placing her hands on his shoulders and pushing. He didn't budge and she grew more agitated. Her eyes, which had moments ago been sleepy, sexy, and sated, now shot metaphorical daggers at him as she glared at him.

"Raven," he started, only to have her push his shoulders again.

"Let me go." She practically screamed it.

"Not until we get to the bottom of this." He reached out and took her shoulders in his hands to hold her steady.

"You want to get to the bottom of this?" She pulled out her cell phone from her pocket. "So do I." She pulled up the image again. "Why on earth would you think that this is me?"

He glanced at it again, this time with the help of the bedroom light Raven had turned on. Somehow, he could see more clearly.

"The red hair." He motioned to the screen. "I thought..." He groaned. "God, I'm so stupid." He reached for her, but she sidestepped away from him.

"Why do men always jump to that conclusion? Why are women more guilty than men?" She almost hissed the question.

"Raven, I was—" When her eyebrows arched up, he stopped and took a deep breath. "Stupid," he finished.

"Yah think?" She crossed her arms over her chest. "Apparently my uncle and aunt believe it's me in that picture as well." She paced towards the door, her shoulders hunched.

He walked over and wrapped his arms around her, feeling her tense at first and then relax against his chest.

"I was half asleep," he defended. "I know it's no excuse, but... I wasn't fully thinking."

"I never cheated on Reggie. He was my first." She turned in his arms and looked up at him. "You were my second."

He felt his heart skip and then jump in his chest as he bent his head and kissed her.

"Forgive me?" he asked when he pulled back.

"I'll think about it." She smiled up at him.

In one quick move, he hoisted her up into his arms and carried her back to the bed and then tossed her down on the mattress playfully. "The good thing about me is, I never make the same mistake twice." He kissed her.

This time when he pulled her clothes from her body, there was a sense of urgency, of need, that hadn't been there before. As if he needed to prove to her just how much this meant to him. How much she meant to him.

As if she felt the urgency along with him, she pulled and tugged at her own clothes, trying to remove them as quickly as she could.

Finally, when she was naked again, she ran her body slowly over his, her skin vibrating under his touch. When he entered her, he shook with the want and need. His body took over, knowing the moves, as easy as breathing. He knew what he had to do to please them both. Knew just how to fill her entire being with his own. There was too much riding on it not to experience every ounce of pleasure. Every iota of ecstasy.

This time when he emptied into her, he told her just what he felt for her and was thankful when she didn't stiffen upon hearing his words. It was his turn to fall asleep after, holding her in his arms, tight against his chest, listening to her sporadic breathing, slow and shallow along with his own.

When he woke, his bed was empty and for a moment,

only a few seconds, he wondered if he'd exposed too much. If he'd lost her.

Then he heard Blue barking, and Raven's laughter coming from the backyard, and relaxed. He pulled on his pants and glanced out the window. He smiled down at Raven trying to get a stick from Blue's mouth, who was playfully tugging on it.

He knew that she had to be at work soon and, since he had the day off, he planned to probe his uncle to see if he'd found out anything else, after his normal Sunday morning brunch.

He'd hoped that Raven would be able to join him, but since Rachelle's death, Raven had been working overtime, along with his mother. Which meant that his Sunday morning brunch was just going to be him and his gran.

Still, he planned on spending as much time as he could with Raven before she had to head to work. When he stepped out on the back patio, Raven was sitting on a chair, sipping a cup of coffee, with Blue fast asleep at her feet. He'd poured himself his own cup before heading outside.

"Morning," he said, sitting beside her.

"Morning." She glanced over at him. "I didn't want to wake you. I know you have brunch with your grandmother later."

"I wanted to spend some time with you before you head to work." He took her hand in his. "I hope we could have some time to talk."

"About last night?" she asked, her eyes running over him.

"Yeah." He nodded as he looked down at their joined hands. The more he thought about it, the more he realized she had remained quiet after his declaration of love. Did that mean she'd been freaked out? Was she feeling the same way?

How the hell had he gotten here so quickly, anyway? Especially after spending years believing she was the reason he'd lost Reggie. It had only taken one look at her to know that she was innocent.

Whatever people had said about her over the years, there, in her eyes, was all the proof he needed of her sincerity and innocence.

"I don't know if I'm ready for..." Raven shook her head. "Cade, the only time I've ever had a relationship... Things didn't work out well."

"I get it," he said with a sigh. "Losing my brother was..." She made a soft little sound that had him stopping and looking over at him. "What?" he asked after seeing the strange look she was giving him.

"I... Reggie..." She closed her eyes. "That night. I found out that he..."

His heart sank. Cade understood what Raven was getting at. It was written clearly on her face.

"He cheated?"

She nodded slightly. "I found out earlier that day."

He rolled that information around in his head. Reggie had never really been a player. Still, he knew his brother had been... eager and young.

"I'm sorry," he said. "For whatever happened between the two of you in those final days."

She shook her head. "Everyone I've loved seems to disappear."

"I'm not going anywhere." He pulled her into his arms.

"Not by choice. My aunt and uncle will use everything they can against me." She pulled back slightly to look up at him. "Like the picture last night."

He held in a groan. Hadn't he easily fallen for one of their tricks? What more were they going to throw at them? He understood that she feared he'd react like he had last night at whatever else they tossed their way.

"If I promise not to fall for their games again, do you think we can finish this discussion over dinner?" he asked. Blue woke up and looked up at them.

Raven smiled. "I'd enjoy that. I should get done with work around six."

He thought about how he could make the night special for her. It was the least he could do after blurting out his feelings for her.

She leaned in and kissed him, then stood up. "I'd better head in. See you tonight."

He sat there for a few moments, sipping his coffee while Blue lay at his feet.

After stopping off to get some fresh cut flowers for his grandmother, and having another bundle delivered to the resort with another apology for Raven, he pulled into the driveway and parked behind his uncle's patrol car.

He'd sent a text to him asking for a few moments of his time today. He hadn't planned on him joining them for brunch but figured that it would free up his time so he and Blue could possibly go on a hike later.

"Morning," he called out as he walked into his grandmother's home. The old place was a classic stone Queen Anne Victorian home that had been built in the late eighteen hundreds. It was one of the first buildings in Cannon Falls and one of the only that had survived the fire.

All the old hardwood floors squeaked, even after he'd spent half of his summer a few years back sanding and restaining all of it. Most of the doors in the place had had to be sanded down and repainted so they didn't stick.

His grandmother had spent a fortune a few years back to have all the electricity and plumbing updated. The rest of the house his grandmother had cared for herself. Fresh paint, beautiful rugs, curtains, and furnishings. The home always looked pristine and cozy.

"Back here," his grandmother called out.

When he walked into the kitchen, Janice Williams was sitting at the table sipping a cup of coffee from a bright blue coffee cup that he'd given her a few years back for Grandparent's Day. Sean was sitting across from her, dressed in his uniform.

"Morning," he said, walking over to place a kiss on his grandmother's head. He set the flowers down in front of her.

"Oh, how lovely." She took up the bundle and lifted them to her face.

Cade noticed how her hands shook slightly with age. She'd damaged one of her knuckles gardening a few years back and now it was stuck at a permanent bend, locking her wedding ring on her finger forever.

The fact that she'd never removed it after his grandfather had died more than twenty years earlier was a testament to her love for the man.

"Morning," he said to his uncle. He still didn't know how he felt about Sean and his mother being together. It was strange being around them together, now that they knew that he knew about them.

"Morning." Sean nodded.

"I'll just put these in a vase and get the quiche out of the oven." His grandmother stood up and moved into the kitchen.

"What's the word?" Cade asked, sitting down across from his uncle.

Sean's eyes moved past his shoulders to make sure his grandmother was out of earshot.

"Word on the street has Raven in the number-one spot as suspect," Sean said in a low tone.

"That's bull—" He stopped himself and glanced over his shoulder to make sure his grandmother hadn't heard him.

"Yeah." Sean nodded. "I agree. Her aunt and uncle are top of my list. The crazy thing is there's a serious lack of evidence. No fingerprints on the teacup or tray. No witnesses saw her in the kitchen that evening."

"She lives at the resort?" he asked. He'd wanted to ask Raven but had refrained from bringing up anything about the murders with her. He figured she'd dealt with them enough already.

"She did. She was single, no immediate family in the state. She has a brother in New York." Sean glanced over his shoulder again. "Colin and Roslyn have become very outspoken about their niece in the past few days, telling anyone who will listen about her troubled past. Even going as far as claiming Raven had an affair with Ramsey back when she was sixteen and he was in his fifties."

Cade thought of the image Raven's uncle had sent her and felt his temper begin to boil.

He quickly told his uncle about Colin sending the grainy image to Raven last night.

"Do you think you could get me a copy of it for evidence?" Sean asked.

"Yeah, I'll have Raven send it over to you." He narrowed his eyes. "It's not Raven," he warned. "You can clearly see that if you look closely enough."

"Right." Sean nodded. "The question is, why do her aunt and uncle believe it is?"

"It's the red hair," he admitted. "I suppose they assume she was the only young redhead in town."

"Back then?" Sean looked like he was thinking about it. "I doubt it. There are four other females with hair as red as Raven's in town now." He shrugged.

"None of them naturally red-haired though. Raven takes after Ellen. She's the spitting image of her grandmother." His grandmother interrupted as she set a large platter down on the table.

All talk of the murders and of Raven or her family's part in them stopped when his grandmother sat down. Instead, the men let her go on about how she and Ellen had been best friends growing up. How they'd married within months of each other and then had gone their separate ways.

Both Sean and Cade knew better than to discuss anything close to business at the table when there was food present.

After brunch, however, he and his uncle stepped out into his grandmother's garden and finished the conversation.

Sean informed him that he was bringing in a forensic specialist from the city to help go over all the evidence.

"It's hard to admit, but I'm way over my head with these murders." Sean sat on the bench they had built together a few years back. "In the past eight years, since I took the job, the closest we had to a murder was when someone ran over the Hawthorn's prized sheep."

Cade sighed. "The murder of Snowflake." He shook his head.

Sean chuckled. "Finding a teenager who'd snuck out and taken a joyride on a four-wheeler and hit a sheep was a lot easier than finding a murderer who would hit a man over the head, killing him, and then rig it so an elevator would snap his head right off. Or one that would know how much poison and what kind to put in a woman's tea so that she wouldn't taste it and spit it back out too quickly."

"Are those the official causes of death?" he asked.

Sean looked at him. "Yes and no. The elevator is a little trickier than that." He sighed. "Damned if I know how someone bypassed all the security measures on the old thing. The best we can tell is that, at some point, the power to the elevator had stopped. Ramsey was locked inside and had pried open the doors. He was in the process of climbing out of the cabin when someone hit him over the head with something heavy, which was the official cause of death. Then the elevator's power came back on, and when Raven hit the button..." Sean made a motion with his hands, simulating doors sliding shut. Cade winced when he realized that if the doors hadn't done the trick, the elevator cabin going between floors would have finished the job. "Ramsey had been dead at that point for almost an hour," Sean added. "Or so the coroner claims."

"Don't most elevators have security measures in place to stop the doors from closing and the cabin from moving if something is in the door?" he asked.

"Yup, which is why I said it gets tricky." He sighed.

They grew silent for a moment, then Cade glanced over at his uncle.

"So, you and my mom?"

Sean tensed.

"Where's that going?" He let the question hang in the air.

CHAPTER TWENTY-THREE

Spending her day off working wasn't the worst thing that had happened to her lately, so Raven figured she might as well go through the day with a smile on her face.

It helped that she got to enjoy the fabulous lunch Tim had made specifically for her. He was trying out a few new menu options, and she didn't mind that he was using her as a guinea pig.

After stuffing herself with delicious fresh veggie lasagna and homemade garlic bread, she balanced a plate with a large slice of French silk pie with fresh cream on top in one hand and a cup of coffee in the other. Her laptop was tucked under her arm as she made her way back to her office.

She was halfway down the hallway to her office when Cemal came rushing out of the bathroom and bumped into her.

Thankfully, she managed to save her laptop and the pie, but her coffee mug toppled over and spilled down the front of her shirt and slacks.

"I'm so sorry," Cemal began as she wiped frantically at Raven's blouse.

"Cemal, it's okay." Raven stopped her. "At least you didn't get my pie," she joked.

"Or your laptop." Cemal sighed. "Your shirt is probably stained though."

"It's fine. I have another one in my office I can change into." She shifted her laptop to her other arm. "Are you in a hurry?" she asked, when Cemal glanced down the hallway.

"No, yes," she corrected quickly. Then she sighed and her shoulders slumped. "It's just... That man makes me nervous."

Raven's eyebrows shot up with concern. "Which man?"

"Tom," Cemal answered, looking over her shoulder again. Tom? Tommy? The bellboy? He wasn't a man. Wasn't he still in school? So far Raven had seen nothing but professionalism from the kid, after her first encounter with him. He'd not only appeared to appreciate his uniform, but since her aunt's departure, the kid had blossomed in his job. Actually, Raven was thinking of moving him up to head bellboy.

Raven took a step closer to Cemal. "Has he done something to..." Cemal's head jerked around and Raven watched horror then humor cross the girl's face.

"No, nothing like that. It's just..." She sighed. "Gosh, he's just so..."—Raven noticed the attraction in the girl's eyes before she even finished the sentence— "dreamy."

Smiling, Raven started towards her office again. "Well, the two of you work together. It's going to be hard to avoid him for long."

"I know, it's just... I sort of embarrassed myself this morning." Cemal followed her into her office where Raven set her laptop and the piece of pie down. She opened her bottom desk drawer and pulled out the bag containing another shirt she could change into.

"What happened?" Raven asked.

"I..." Cemal closed her eyes and took a deep breath. "I dropped a very important receipt behind the copy machine, and he helped me move the heavy thing so I could get it."

"That doesn't seem so bad," Raven replied.

"I had tried to move the copier myself and... well, I was stuck when he found me like that," Cemal said.

"Stuck?"

"I thought that if I could wedge myself between it and the wall I could... push. But instead, I got stuck. When he walked in and found me..." She glanced down at herself. "My skirt was... higher."

Raven glanced down at the simple black pencil skirt Cemal was wearing now. It came to just above the girl's knees.

"Higher?" Raven tried to hold in a chuckle. She knew that Cemal was more modest than most of her other employees. She figured it was the girl's age.

Cemal's eyes moved back to hers before she nodded slowly.

"What did Tommy..." she shook her head. "What did Tom do?"

Cemal's caramel skin turned a deep shade of red. "He looked at me and froze in place. I had to ask him twice before he finally moved to help me." She looked back down at her hands. "It was so embarrassing."

Raven smiled and walked over to the girl to set her hand on her shoulder. "Cemal, take it from me, Tom wasn't... He was..." She didn't quite understand how to explain that the boy was probably turned on by what he'd seen. Taking a deep breath, Raven shook her head. "If you ask me, I think Tom likes you."

"He does?" Cemal's head jerked up. "How do you know?"

The conversation confirmed to Raven that Cemal hadn't had much experience with dating. Not that she was an expert at it herself.

"Why don't you ask him yourself?" she suggested.

"Oh, I couldn't do that." Cemal shook her head.

"Okay," she said after a moment of thinking, "you don't necessarily have to verbally ask him. There are trivial things men do when they are interested in a woman." She sat on the edge of her desk and, for the next few minutes, enlightened the girl on everything she knew about flirting.

She would have loved to stick around and watch the two young people progress, but after changing her shirt, she sat at her desk and ran over the multi-page spreadsheet containing every single dime she'd spent on fixing up the resort to date.

By the time the sugar from the pie had worn off, she had a better handle on her finances. Or lack thereof. Personally, she was broke. Since returning to the resort, she had yet to take a paycheck for herself. She'd not only sunk every dime she'd saved over the years into the place, but her inheritance from her grandmother was earmarked to finish up all the other repairs and changes.

By the time the place was done, she would have only a few hundred dollars left. Which meant there wasn't a lot of room for errors or extras.

Her aunt and uncle's high salaries easily paid for the extra workers Rachelle had hired.

Fiona had filled Rachelle's position and had immediately suggested lowering the pay to a standard rate. Raven couldn't with a clear conscious pay a woman less for the same amount of work.

She supposed it was Fiona's way of trying to help, but the fact was, the woman was making a big difference. Raven knew her worth would really be obvious when they finally opened the doors again for guests.

She'd worried at first that working with Cade's mother would be odd. But so far, she'd only had a pleasant experience. Over the last week, she'd had several lunches with Fiona and had enjoyed the woman's company immensely.

When a knock sounded at her door, she glanced up and waved Gloria, her new head of housekeeping, into her office.

"Afternoon, Miss Brooks." The woman stood in her dark grey uniform just inside her doorway.

"Gloria, what can I do for you?" she asked, closing the screen with all her numbers on it. Not that the woman could see her computer screen, or that it really mattered, but Raven wanted to get in the practice of keeping things like that to herself. Why let the employees worry when they didn't have to?

"I was hoping to have a talk with you. Several of my employees are worried about some rumors going around," Gloria started.

Raven waved the woman to the chair across from her desk.

"Rumors?" Raven asked after the woman sat down.

"About Mr. and Mrs. Brooks," Gloria answered as she rung her hands together.

"My aunt and uncle no longer—"

"No, I'm sorry, I'm not talking about them," Gloria interrupted.

Raven frowned. "My parents?" She shook her head. "They've been dead for over ten years."

"Yes, but before then, the rumors say they were members of..." The woman crossed herself quickly. "Members of a group that openly hated people like me, and over half your staff."

It took Raven a few moments to understand what the woman was talking about. Then it dawned on her.

"Are you saying that my parents were racists?" she asked, trying to keep a calm tone.

Gloria nodded. "Some of the staff have been around for a long time. I was only a housekeeper when your parents ran this place."

Raven laid her hands on the desk and took several deep breaths. "What do you remember of my parents?"

Gloria met her eyes. "Your parents were good people. Which is why I'm coming to you now. I don't like what I'm hearing from my staff. I didn't want this to get back to you, but figured..."

Raven relaxed and finished for her. "That it would be better coming from you."

Gloria nodded. "You have been so wonderful to all of us. Regardless of... who we are or how we live." She waved her hand in the air. "When you made Tim sous chef..." Gloria smiled. "That boy deserves his own kitchen, and even though your uncle was trying to fire him after your uncle found out about his personal life, you stepped in and promoted him."

"Tim is easily one of the best chefs I have ever had the pleasure of knowing," she replied, making Gloria's smile grow.

"I've done what I could to stop the rumors among my employees, but my reach only goes so far." Gloria stood up suddenly.

"Thank you." Raven stood as well. "Do you happen to know where the rumors started?"

Gloria frowned. "I'm afraid I do. Thankfully, you have already fired the girl," Gloria answered.

"Kim?" she guessed. Gloria nodded. "Thank you for bringing this to my attention."

After Gloria left her office, Raven sat at her desk and tried to think of her next move. If employees were gossiping about her dead parents, it really didn't bother her. Or so she tried to tell herself.

But the longer she sat there staring at her dark computer screen, the more irritated she grew.

She glanced down at her watch and decided that a short walk would help her clear her mind. She changed out of her low dress heels and pulled on her tennis shoes, then locked up her office and headed outside.

It was the peak of the summer. The flowers in the court-yard were still in bloom and the grass that had been planted a few weeks back was now green and plush.

If she hadn't known better, she would have guessed that the grounds had always looked this good.

Taking the pathway that would lead her to the base of the ski runs, she tried to figure out why it bothered her so much what people thought of her parents. They had always been good to her. Sure, there had been plenty of fights. But the quibbles they'd had had been the standard parents-versus-teenage-angst variety—being grounded due to bad grades or for not completing her chores.

Looking back at her life with her parents, she could only really remember the good or the happy times.

She hadn't realized she'd reached the base of the slopes

until she heard a dog barking, which shook her out of her haze.

Glancing around, she somehow expected to see Blue rushing towards her. Instead, a pure white husky with piercing blue eyes jogged over to her, it's tail wagging and its tongue dangling from its mouth.

"Hi." She bent down and gave the dog some attention. "Who do you belong to?"

"Skid?" a man's voice called out. "Leave the boss lady alone." Raven glanced up to see Eddie Mimms walking towards her, a smile on his face.

"Hey," she said, standing up and shielding her eyes from the sun. "Is this your dog?"

"Yeah, we were just out for a walk. You?" he said, as Skid wandered off slowly.

"Yes." She glanced up at the hill. During the summer months, the hillside looked less intimidating. Sure, it was an almost straight upwards climb, but it was something anyone in decent healthy shape could enjoy. Raven knew full well that, after first snow, the hillside she was looking at was one of the scariest and hardest runs at Cannon Falls.

"It looks so harmless," Eddie said, getting her attention.

She chuckled. "I was thinking the same thing."

"Does it remind you of anyone?" he asked.

She glanced over at him, and he chuckled. "When you returned, a lot of us around here thought you'd last a week." He shook his head and they started walking down the pathway towards the lifts. "Then you stood up to your family and fired them." He whistled slightly. "Which took as much guts as it took brains." He stopped at the base of the lifts and laid a hand on the large metal base. The chairs were off the lifts, currently getting repairs or being replaced, leaving long poles hanging from the thick wires above.

"Then you started putting money back into this place." He tapped the metal, sending an echoing sound vibrating from the base. "Smartest move yet."

"Thank you," she said easily, and he chuckled.

"Whatever has you out here, looking worried, it shouldn't matter. You've proven yourself in the three months you've been back here."

"Gosh, has it only been three months?" she said, jokingly.

He smiled back. "Three more and this place will be covered in snow and full of tourists. I can almost guarantee it."

"I'm excited to see what you come up with for next summer's outdoor ventures around here. Will you be sticking around until the season starts?" she asked, tilting her head slightly. After several meetings with him, she believed that he could be a big asset to the summer ventures they were adding. He was very excited about the prospect of having downhill racing year-round.

"Nope." He smiled. "Skid and I are heading up to spend a few days in Montana after this. We just came back here to send Rachelle off." The man's smile faltered.

"Were the two of you close?" she asked.

"You could say that," he answered with a sigh. "I should have asked her to marry me a few years back."

"I'm so sorry." Raven felt her heart slide to the bottom of her stomach. How had she not known Eddie and Rachelle had been a thing? Did Sean know?

"No one else knew." He broke into her thoughts. "Rachelle feared that if your aunt and uncle found out, they'd find some way to use it against us."

"They really are assholes," she admitted, and he smiled.

"Skid and I were up in Montana when we got the

news." He glanced over to where his dog was peeing on a tree. The man's eyes filled with sadness. "Who would do such a thing? Rachelle was always so good to her employees. Kind to everyone she knew." He shook his head.

"I'm sure the police will find out who killed them," she said softly.

He glanced over at her. "So, you think the murders are connected?"

She sighed. "I'm not sure, but there has only been one murder in Cannon Falls in the last thirty years. Now we have two murders within a month of each other and under the same roof." She shrugged. "It stands to reason."

"Right." He nodded slowly. "We're having a little thing for Rachelle tonight in the center square. There will be live music and barbeque. You're welcome to join," he offered.

She had heard a few employees talking about it but had figured that she hadn't been invited because she was the boss. Rachelle had requested to be cremated and hadn't wanted a fuss to be made over her. Or so the woman's lawyer had stated.

"I'd like that," she agreed, already thinking of sending Cade a text about their change in plans.

"And since everyone in town knows you and Cade Stone are an item"—he smiled— "he's welcome too."

"Thanks." She glanced down at her watch. "I'd better get back."

"See you tonight," Eddie called after her.

When she sat down behind her desk again, she realized she no longer cared what gossip was going around about her parents. Anyone who knew them, knew her, understood what the truth was. All others could go to hell.

She sent Cade a text message about the event, and he agreed to meet her there after work. When she was done working, she headed up to her room, once again avoiding the area just outside the elevators, to change.

After showering, drying her hair, and adding just a touch of makeup, she pulled on a simple black dress and low matching heels.

When Raven parked in the small parking lot near the center of town, a quick moment of anxiety hit her. This was the first time she'd be around so many townspeople. She could see more than a hundred of them gathering in the grassy park near a pristine white gazebo that marked the exact middle of Cannon Falls.

At this point, everyone in town knew she was back and no doubt knew everything about her—that she was fixing the resort up and that she'd fired her aunt and uncle. Most everyone even knew that she and Cade were seeing one another and that she spent most of her nights at his place now.

So why was she so nervous?

A knock on her car window made her jump and her hand went to her heart.

"Sorry," Cade replied with a smile just outside her window.

God, he was so good-looking. He'd changed into a black button-up short-sleeved shirt and black jeans. Part of her wished he had a black Stetson to put on, completing the look. She knew it was too much to ask for. Not that there wasn't a hint of cowboy in him. He'd been raised in the country, but to her knowledge, he'd never ridden a horse or roped a cow.

Still, every time she caught sight of him in his full fire gear, she salivated enough that she had a difficult time getting any work done.

"Are you coming out of there?" he asked, and she realized she was still sitting in her car fantasizing about him.

She grabbed her purse and cell phone and climbed out of her car. Cade reached in and took her hand, helping her out.

"Everything okay?" he asked her, his eyes running over her face, her shoulders, her hair.

"Yes." She tried to smile and hide the immense force of desire pulsating from her body.

Cade didn't seem to notice and led her towards the growing crowd. She could feel eyes on her as they passed people. Still, Cade didn't stop until they were near the front of the crowd.

A band had set up in the gazebo and was already playing soft music while everyone arrived.

Less than five minutes later, Eddie got up in front of everyone and held up his hands to get everyone's attention.

"I want to thank everyone for coming out tonight to celebrate the life of Rachelle Braun. Only a handful of people knew that Rachelle and I go far back." Eddie's eyes landed on hers and then quickly moved away. Raven heard a few whispers behind her, but then Eddie continued talking, telling the mourners a few personal details about the woman he'd loved but had been too afraid to commit to. Raven glanced sideways at Cade and remembered him saying those three special words she had yet to respond to.

Since he'd spoken them to her, she'd avoided the talk about what it meant to them, what it meant to her, other than the short conversation they'd had.

What if something happened to either of them? Would she regret not telling him how she felt about him? Would he know? Did he know already?

As she listened to Eddie finish talking and welcome others to speak on Rachelle's behalf, she thought about her own life. Her own procrastinations. How she had avoided returning to Cannon Falls for over ten years, trying to keep the hurt, the pain, and the guilt hidden from everyone else.

She'd put herself in that bubble and had convinced herself that what she had with Cade was just attraction. Just sex. But the truth was, he'd snuck in behind her carefully guarded walls. Somehow, he'd convinced her that life wouldn't be as great without him in her life.

The fact was, she was in love and wasn't sure what the hell came next.

Time to make the bitch pay. Twisted fates. Ropes tangled like webs.

You think this is fun? You think you can get away with saying whatever you want? Doing whatever you want?

Someone has to pay tonight. Someone needs to die. It might as well be you.

CHAPTER TWENTY-FOUR

FOUL WATER WILL QUENCH FIRE ~ ENGLISH
PROVERB

Standing next to Raven in the middle of the town square, surrounded by everyone he knew, a sense of pride fell over him. Here he was with the woman he loved, in the town he fought every day to keep alive.

He couldn't think of a better place to be. When the band kicked on and he remembered why everyone was gathered there, he realized it could have been for a better reason.

He hadn't known Rachelle all that well. Each time he'd inspected the resort before Raven had returned, he'd dealt with Colin. Glancing around, he wondered if her aunt and uncle were present tonight.

As the sun sank lower behind the hills, candles were lit along with the town's string lights and the spotlights that lit up the gazebo.

If it wasn't for the murder of a woman, the scene could be described as very romantic.

He held onto Raven's hand with one hand and a candle someone had given them in his other while a bead of sweat rolled down his back.

As fire marshal, he wanted to warn everyone about extinguishing their candles properly, but he knew that the town square was doused every morning with sprinklers, so the grass wasn't dry.

Besides, when he'd been informed a few days earlier of the event, he'd scheduled his guys to be there with the fire truck parked in plain sight, just in case.

Shortly after nine, the band stopped playing and the mayor got up and spoke for a few moments and then told everyone the event was over due to the town's noise ordinance. The crowd started to leave.

"You okay?" he asked Raven as they walked back to her car, making their way through the crowd. She'd been quiet since the moment he'd helped her out of her car.

"Yes, I was just..." Suddenly, she jerked forward. Since the pathway was dark and there were a lot of people around him, he hadn't seen what had happened. He didn't know if she'd been pushed, or someone had bumped into her by accident.

"Watch it," he called out and turned to help Raven.

"Bitch," someone hissed, and this time he saw a young blonde woman lift her hands and shove Raven backwards. Thankfully, he was there to catch her. Immediately, he put his body between hers and the other woman.

"Kim," Raven said calmly.

"You think you have it all figured out, don't you?" Kim said, pushing her shorter and smaller frame towards them. She was trying to duck around him and get to Raven.

"It looks like you're drunk," Raven replied, holding onto his arm to steady herself as Kim swung her arms frantically around, trying to hit Raven.

"Who do you think you are?" Kim spat. "You think you're hot shit and can come into town and fire everyone?"

"It's within my rights as owner," Raven said calmly.

He took a slap on the shoulder when Kim tried to get to Raven and another one on the opposite arm as the younger woman tried to maneuver around him.

"Cade, I can handle..." Raven started to say.

"Is there a problem here?" Sean stepped towards them.

Kim spun around and, after one look at his uncle in full uniform, she bolted down the street, laughing hysterically. Cade shrugged his shoulders at his uncle, who turned around and headed towards a group of loud people.

"That was fun," Raven said dryly.

"That's easy for you to say. You're not the one with the bruises." Cade rubbed at his shoulder.

"Oh." Raven wrapped her arms around him. "Did the little girl hurt your big..."—her hands wrapped around his biceps— "hard"—she leaned closer to him— "muscles?" She squeezed his arm, and he completely forgot about Kim or the slight sting to his skin.

"Let's go home," he said, taking her arm and practically dragging her to his car.

"What about my car?" she asked with a giggle.

"We'll get it tomorrow." He opened his car door for her.

Before she could respond, he nudged her inside, ran around, and had the engine roaring. His place was only five minutes outside of town, but thanks to the crowd of people leaving at the same time, it was close to fifteen minutes before they finally pulled into his driveway.

He had yet to cool down and still wanted her just as badly as he had in the town square.

"Raven," he said, opening her car door for her.

"No, don't." She placed a hand over his lips. "Let's talk later." She took his hand in his and pulled him towards the house. "After."

He wasn't stupid. You didn't have to tell him something twice. Especially when it came to the possibility of having really great sex with the woman he'd grown to love.

The moment they stepped through the door to his place, she plastered her body against his.

He'd enjoyed the view of her in the little black dress she'd worn that evening. Even though it was extremely modest, he liked the look of her in it. Liked the soft sexy scent that surrounded her everywhere she went. The feeling of her skin against his own when he pulled the dress off of her.

He could no longer hold back his feelings, nor did he want to. With each article of clothing that he removed of hers, he took his time exploring her, savoring her, consuming her.

Somehow, they moved away from the front door and ended up in the kitchen, where he hoisted her naked body onto the bar top and stepped between her thighs. Their lips never left one another as he slowly entered her with her legs wrapped around his hips.

"Tell me," she asked softly as she sucked his earlobe in between her teeth.

In the middle of the haze of lust, he somehow understood what she was asking.

"I love you." The words burst from him as if she controlled every aspect of his physical being.

"I love you too," she said just as he felt her tighten around him, forcing him to lose himself completely in her.

When he regained himself, he hoisted her up in his arms and carried her upstairs to the bedroom. There, they lay in each other's arms, talking in hushed tones until he felt her drift off to sleep.

It seemed like he'd just fallen asleep himself when the doorbell rang and Blue barked, jolting him awake.

"What?" Raven pushed her hair out of her face and looked around as if she'd forgotten where she was.

"I've got this." He pulled on a pair of sweats and headed downstairs. As he walked by, he grabbed his cell phone, which he'd left in his jeans pocket when he'd tossed them on his living room floor earlier.

Seeing the more than dozen texts and calls from his uncle, he knew automatically who was waking him up at three in the morning.

"Hey." He answered the door and stood back as Sean walked in.

"Tell me Raven is here with you," Sean said, stepping in and glancing around. His uncle's eyes locked onto the sexy black dress she'd been wearing earlier, now draped over a barstool, and he relaxed.

"What's up?" he asked, glancing towards the stairs.

"Didn't you read my texts?" Sean asked.

"No, I left my phone downstairs," Cade answered.

"Along with the rest of your clothes." Sean pushed aside one of Raven's heels, which was sitting in the middle of the entryway. "Kim McKinney was murdered."

"What?" Cade hadn't meant to shout. His eyes jerked up to the top of the stairs where Raven was standing in a pair of his sweat shorts and a T-shirt, a hand on the railing.

He rushed to the base of the stairs. "You could have stayed in bed," he said, rushing up to her.

"I..." She shook her head. "Kim is dead?"

"Tell me the two of you were here, doing what I think you were doing, from the moment you left the event tonight," Sean said, sounding a little weary.

"We were," Cade responded as Raven sat down on the

sofa.

"Good." Sean started to leave.

"How?" Raven asked. "Where?"

His uncle stopped and sighed. "How, I'm going to find out. Where... the gazebo." He shook his head.

"What? In the middle of town?" Cade asked.

"Yup, right under all those sparkly pretty lights." Sean shook his head. "I had hoped..." He stopped suddenly. "Never mind."

"You don't know how she died?" Raven asked as she wrapped the throw blanket over her body.

"She was tied up, strung up. Like an animal. We're not sure if she really died from suffocation or something else at this point."

"How horrible." Raven shook her head. Then she gasped. "You think... Because of what... Oh my god." It hit her at the same time it hit him. "You think I had something to do with it?"

His uncle was there, checking to see if Raven had an alibi. Because everyone in town had witnessed the fight between the two women, he knew that most people in town would assume the same thing his uncle had. That Raven had killed Kim.

"No." Sean held up his hands. "I never thought it. I'm only here to assure you have a tight alibi. That's all." Sean moved over and sat across from Raven. "I never believed you could hurt Kim, or Rachelle and Joseph. Never," he clarified.

Raven nodded slowly. "Thank you."

"Now, I have to head back out. But I need your promise that the two of you will stay put." He glanced over at Cade.

"We have the day off tomorrow," he assured his uncle. "We were going to take a hike."

"For now, I think it's best if you stick somewhere I can keep an eye on you." Sean turned to Raven. "I don't really think someone is out for you, but it appears that they really want to make this all about you."

"You think someone is setting her up for the murders?" Cade asked, moving to sit beside Raven.

His uncle shrugged. "It's a working theory."

"We'll stick around here tomorrow then," Cade responded.

"Thanks." Sean stood up. "Sorry to wake the both of you."

"Who found Kim?" Raven asked as his uncle started to leave.

Sean stopped, glanced back, and sighed as his eyes locked with Cade's. "Your mother did."

The moment his front door shut, Cade fumbled his cell phone out of his sweat pockets and dialed his mother's number.

"Mom?" he said when she answered quickly. "Are you okay?"

"I am," his mother reassured him. She sounded tired and weary.

"Want to come over? I think we're up." He glanced over at Raven, who nodded.

"I'm fine, I'm just..." He heard her sigh. "I'll bring something to eat."

"I'll make coffee," he added before hanging up.

"How does she sound?" Raven asked.

"Shaken," he admitted. "For as long as it took me to get past Reggie's death, it took her twice as long." He leaned in and hugged her, then kissed her on the top of the head before getting up to start a pot of coffee.

By the time his mother arrived, Raven had changed into

a pair of her yoga pants and an oversized sweater. She'd braided her hair and had helped him pick up their discarded clothing.

His mother had stopped off at the town's bakery and had a large box of freshly baked donuts, scones, and muffins.

His grandmother showed up just after sunrise with some fresh fruit and homemade biscuits and gravy. Sean came back just before noon with takeout Chinese food for everyone.

The day was filled with food, his family, and more questions than answers.

"The coroner has confirmed Kim's cause of death was asphyxiation. He has the death down at around ten."

"Less than an hour after everyone left last night," Raven said.

"What were you doing there so late?" Cade asked his mother. He'd assumed that she'd found Kim shortly after everyone had left.

"I was..." Her eyes moved to Sean.

"She was leaving my place," Sean said with a sigh.

Cade's eyes narrowed. "You didn't let her walk home alone." It was a statement.

"No," Sean said clearly.

"So the two of you found Kim?" Raven asked.

"Yes," Sean said, looking at Cade.

"Why hide..." Raven started, then she chuckled. "I think Cade knows by now that you two—"

"It's fine," Cade broke in. "You don't have to hide things like this from me."

"It's just..." Sean looked a little uncomfortable.

"Son, our love life is none of your business," Fiona broke in. "If Sean wants to keep certain details from you, he can." She stood up to clear the dishes.

A look passed between Cade and his uncle, then Cade held out his hand. "If you promise to keep some details to yourself, I'll promise not to hit you."

Sean laughed and shook Cade's hand. "If you think you can hit me, by all means, try."

Cade smiled. "You're just an old man. Slow." He narrowed his eyes and tightened his grip on his uncle's hand. It was an old game between them.

The truth was, Cade was happy for them. It was obvious there was something between the two of them. He'd often wondered why his mother had started being happier in the past few years. He assumed it was thanks to his uncle.

"Old?" Sean laughed and tightened his grip, and Cade had to hold back a wince as pain shot up his arm. "I can still take you down."

"Is that a challenge?" Cade asked playfully.

"Boys." His mother stepped back into the room. "As entertaining as it is to see the two of you argue, I'm just not in the mood today," she said dryly.

When she sat back down, he realized just how tired she looked. He dropped his uncle's hand and reached over and took his mother's hand.

"Why don't you head upstairs and lie down in the guest room?" he suggested.

She smiled at him. "I think I'll head home."

Sean stood up. "I'll take you."

Her eyes narrowed at him. "I can drive myself."

Sean glanced over to him for help. He knew that his uncle was thinking the same thing he was. Neither of them wanted her to be alone at the moment.

"I'll be fine." His mother laid a hand on both of their shoulders.

"Of course you will. I raised a strong independent

woman." His grandmother stood up suddenly. "As you head that way, you can drop me off at home." She winked at Cade.

His uncle left shortly after his mother and grandmother did.

The moment Cade and Raven were alone, he pulled her onto the sofa and wrapped his arms around her.

"What do you say to spending the rest of the day on the sofa, watching movies?" he said, holding onto her.

"That sounds amazing." She sighed as she put her feet up on the sofa. Blue jumped up and, after spending almost a minute trying to get comfortable, finally settled at their feet with a slightly annoyed groan.

"I think he's upset I took his spot," Raven said.

He chuckled. "Yeah, he's spoiled and normally lays up here with me."

He turned on the television and flipped through several channels before finally settling on a Clint Eastwood movie that was just starting. When he'd been changing channels, she'd mentioned how Eastwood was one of her favorite actors and the movie was one of her favorites.

A few minutes after the movie started, she turned to look up at him.

"Who do you think wanted to kill Kim?" she asked a few moments later.

He glanced down at her. She was leaning with her back towards his chest. His arms were wrapped around her. He couldn't see her face, but he'd known that her mind wasn't on the movie.

"I've been asking that same question." He sighed and turned the volume down. "Not just Kim, but Rachelle and Joseph too. I agree with my uncle that whoever is doing this is trying to frame you."

"But why?" She shook her head. "It's not like I have many enemies." She was silent for a moment. "I mean, sure, some people in town still believe I started the fire, but I can't imagine any of them murdering three people to... what? Pay me back in the hope that I'll be implicated?" She shook her head. "I just don't see it."

"Right," he agreed. "Okay, so then that theory is out. So... what? Coincidence that the three people murdered worked for you?"

"I do run the largest business in town."

"True. But if it's just coincidence, then what do Kim, Rachelle, and Joseph have in common besides working at the resort?"

"Well, Rachelle and Joseph knew my aunt and uncle. Joseph lost his job when they took over the resort." She shifted so she could look at him. "Rachelle worked under them for years. Who knows what bad blood they had between them?"

"And Kim?" he asked.

She frowned. "Rachelle had hired Kim a week after I kicked my aunt and uncle out."

He sighed heavily. "So, no link?"

She shrugged. "Maybe it's totally random? I mean, it could be a drifter?" She motioned to the movie they were watching. "The killer in here has zero connections to the people he murdered."

He glanced at the screen and, after thinking about the plot, nodded in agreement.

"Are there any drifters in Cannon Falls?" he asked, more to himself than to her.

"Even though the resort is technically shut down, we still have a few rooms rented out," she supplied.

"You do?" he asked with a frown. "Does my uncle know?"

"Yes."

"How many rooms?" .

"Six. The Garrisons, who have been renting the same room for three weeks every summer for the past twenty years. They're in their late seventies. I doubt either of them are strong enough to... well, you know." She shifted again as Blue started sneaking up towards them. Raven's hands ran over his soft fur, and he doubted she realized his dog had maneuvered her to get belly rubs. "Then there's a single woman." She narrowed her eyes. "I forget her name. Stephanie or Stacy." She shook her head. "She's in town writing a book. I'm told she orders all her meals and never really leaves her room. There are two families that know each another. They spend most of their days hiking and biking through the countryside. A single businessman who just came into town a few nights ago and..." She frowned. "I'm not sure who the last person is. I only saw the name, Pat Parsons." She leaned her head back.

"How many were in town when Joseph was killed?" he asked.

"Just the Garrisons. The rest came later."

"Okay, so if we exclude all of them..." He thought for a minute. "Who in town had motive or gained something from all three deaths?"

"That's a question your uncle will hopefully find an answer to." She shifted back to lean against his chest. "I'm suddenly very tired."

"We did only have a few hours of sleep." He pulled her closer to him, feeling a little overwhelmed and tired himself.

Her turned the sound for the movie back on and, less than fifteen minutes later, they both fell asleep.

CHAPTER TWENTY-FIVE

Word about Kim's murder changed the entire town. It was strange. When Joseph had been found with his head missing and Rachelle had been poisoned, people in town hadn't really blinked an eye. But hearing about Kim strung up in the middle of the town square somehow shocked everyone to the core.

Everyone in town was finally taking the murderer seriously, something Raven had done from the moment the elevator doors had slid open and she'd found Joseph.

Since that first night, she had only been able to get a few hours of sleep here and there. Now that she was staying at Cade's most nights, she realized she was able to get more uninterrupted sleep.

She didn't know if it was thanks to the extra physical activities or if it was because she felt safe with Cade's arms wrapped around her in slumber.

Whatever the reason, the few nights that she returned to her hotel room alone were restless ones. There had been a few nightmares, like she'd had after the fire. Dreams that woke her or kept her up until late at night, worrying.

Because of them, she'd moved a few things to Cade's place and spent more and more nights with him. It was only a few changes of clothes, some makeup, and shoes. Nothing major. But enough that she was self-conscious about keeping her things tidy at his place.

It wasn't as if he was a total neat freak. She'd lived with one of those before. Her mother had been your typical type A personality. Everything had its place and if it wasn't in its place, someone was bound to hear about it. Usually, her and her dad.

Still, Cade's place was always clean and organized, which made her want to be better than she'd been. Ever since her things had been destroyed, she'd only had a handful of things to keep track of. Now, at least half of her stuff was over at his place.

Which, of course, instigated another round of gossip in town. Thankfully, accusations about her murdering Kim had been cut down quickly thanks to Sean and Cade, who adamantly told anyone who would listen that Raven was with Cade all night.

Most people had witnessed her leaving that night with Cade, anyway. Still, it didn't stop the rumors that she'd killed Joseph because he was an ex-lover of hers from her high school days.

Rumors of the grainy image that her uncle had sent her was circulating around town and, somehow, even the image was floating around.

Of course, her friends could immediately tell the girl in the image wasn't her. Darby even brought one of her old yearbooks to the diner to prove to everyone that Raven's hair had been shorter than the girls in the photo back then.

Her friends were sticking by her side wholly, which made her feel happy and guilty at the same time. Her friends shouldn't have to put their reputations on the line. Then again, no one in town should be accusing her of murder when the police had completely cleared her.

Still, she'd lived in a little town long enough to know how they worked.

As days turned into weeks, she stayed focused on the repairs around the resort to keep her mind from the murders.

Unlike the first two, there had been some DNA evidence left behind with Kim's death. What appeared to be blood was found on the rope that had been tied around the woman's neck, as if whoever had strung her up had cut their hands doing so.

Cade's uncle was convinced that this murder had nothing to do with the first two, since Kim's ex-boyfriend had been released on parole in Redding for drug charges two days prior to her death.

They were having the DNA checked against his, but since they were a small town and it wasn't a high-profile murder case, it was going to take two weeks to get the results back.

Still, the ex-boyfriend was dragged into the police station and questioned. Since she was friends with Sean, she knew firsthand that the man claimed to have been in Redding at the time of the murder. Sean had confirmed with one of the man's friends that he really had been in Redding that evening, but he was still waiting to hear back from the girl the guy claimed to have spent the night with.

As far as the resort went, the work in the dining room was finally going to be finished by the end of that weekend. Raven was so excited to see the finished product that she kept sneaking peeks at the place once all the workers left.

Since they hadn't put up the walls of plastic, she wasn't as nervous as she'd been shortly after Joseph's murder.

Still, every time she stepped out of the elevator on her floor, she saw Rachelle's crumpled body lying on the rug.

When a knock sounded at her door, she glanced up and waved Fiona into the room. Cade's mother was a true asset to the resort and to Raven's mental stability.

"I just wanted to let you know that I am heading out," Fiona said with a smile. "Sean has the evening off, and we're heading into the city for dinner."

"Oh? Hot date." Raven smiled back at the woman.

Fiona's smile slipped slightly. "The man's been trying to figure out how to propose to me for months."

"Really?" Raven jumped up from her seat. "How exciting."

Fiona laughed. "I hate to revel in his anxiousness. But the fact is, I love seeing him like this. The man is always so sure of himself." She shook her head. "It's nice to see him sweat."

"Does Cade know?" Raven asked.

"No." Fiona's smile slipped again. "I hadn't planned on telling him until... later."

"I'm sure he's going to be thrilled." Raven hugged the woman.

"Sean and I... we go way back. To be honest, if Henry hadn't died, I think Sean would have left Cannon Falls long ago." She glanced towards the window. "Fall is just around the corner." She shook her head. "How did time go by so fast? One day Henry and I were welcoming Cade and Reggie into our lives, then I lost Henry and a few years later, Reggie." The sadness in Fiona's eyes showed a distant fondness instead of full sorrow. "Sean was instrumental in helping me get out of the funk after losing my men." She smiled again. "We've been seeing one another for two years this week."

"Two years?" Raven shook her head slightly. "That long?"

"Yes." Fiona laughed. "I think that half the fun in the relationship was keeping it from everyone."

Raven could understand what the woman meant. There'd been a little hint of excitement when she and Cade had started seeing one another.

"Well, I'd better hurry up and leave if I want to be ready in time," Fiona said, looking at her watch.

"Have a wonderful time," Raven said.

"I will. See you on Monday." Fiona turned and left.

Raven turned back to her desk. Fiona had been right about time passing. Somehow Raven had blinked, and summer was almost gone already.

The sky was dark and grey, and she knew that in less than two months, there would be enough snow on the hills to delight skiers and snowboarders alike.

There was still so much to do, so Raven sat down behind her computer to get back to work.

The new advertising from the marketing firm she'd hired had done its job. They had sent a professional photographer to take shots of the lobby and bar areas and some of the finished rooms. The dining room would have to be photographed later and added to the next round of ads.

The marketing firm had paid for key spots in some of the best travel magazines in the city. Already, they were flooded with room bookings.

With only two and a half months to go to the official reopening, they had the entire west building to finish besides the dining room.

All the ski lifts had been updated and officially certified

safe by the company that had installed them years ago. The ski resort still needed fresh carpet to be installed along with all new ski and snow rentals.

She had been shocked to see the state of the rentals her uncle and aunt had allowed to represent their business. She had to admit that seeing all of the new equipment being unpackaged and on display excited her beyond anything.

She'd realized that she hadn't been on the slopes since before her seventeenth birthday. She wasn't an expert at skiing, but she did really enjoy fresh powder.

If the resort had been open all summer long, she liked to think that people would have enjoyed all the improvements she'd made. Now, the grounds flourished with bright flowers, neatly trimmed bushes and shrubs, cleared cleaned pathways to stroll on, and the occasional park bench for sitting and enjoying the view.

She'd utilized those benches herself already. Most days, she would eat her lunch outside and enjoy the heat of the day.

After running through the to-do lists and updating items, she realized that the only way they would be completely ready for the grand reopening was if she had David and his men concentrate on the upper floors of the west building first. She figured she could shut down a few floors while they continued updating the rooms on the lower floors.

The upper floors were the bigger money makers anyway since they had some of the best views of the hills and ski slopes.

She hadn't expected to work overtime that evening, but when her phone buzzed, she realized it was an hour later than she normally left.

She saw Cade's face flash on her screen and smiled as she answered his call.

"Working late?" Just his voice caused her body to fill with desire.

"Yes, I suppose I got caught up," she admitted as she stretched her neck and shoulders.

"How about I meet you up there and we have dinner?" Cade suggested.

She really wanted to finish the work she was doing before she left. If he drove up here, she would have just the right amount of time to do so.

"Sounds perfect."

By the time Cade's knock sounded on her office door, she had finished with the latest budget and was extremely anxious to open the doors again. It was coming down to ten thousand dollars. She knew that would seem like a lot to many, but to her, running a multi-million-dollar-a-year-business, ten thousand dollars was pennies.

"Everything okay?" Cade asked, coming in for a hug.

"Yes," she lied. Cade pulled back and looked into her eyes.

"You're worried."

"I am," she admitted with a sigh. "I was just working on the budget."

He nodded as his hands ran up and down her arms. "Is there anything I can help with?"

She shook her head and felt her heart swell at his offer. "Not unless you have a tens of thousands of dollars lying around."

He chuckled as he patted his wallet. "Not especially."

"I didn't think so." She sighed. "We'll make do."

"You'll get through this. Soon enough, the doors will be

open, and people will be flooding in to spend their money. Just wait and see."

"I know, it's just... I know," she agreed. "Dinner," she reminded him. "I skipped lunch."

He frowned as a worried look flooded his eyes. "Again?"

After locking up her office, they strolled down the hallway hand in hand. Instead of walking into the bar area, he tugged on her hand and pulled her towards the plywood wall separating the dining area from the lobby.

"Cade, it's not ready yet," she said, remembering the last time she'd snuck behind the walls to get a look.

"Dave called me earlier today." He motioned as he opened the door.

She stepped in and her breath sucked in with the surprise of seeing the work was completed. Then she noticed a single round table sitting in the middle of the room. The crisp white tablecloth, fine china, and lit candles added to the beauty of the room, as did the massive chandelier she'd purchased.

The wood slat boards that had replaced the old ceiling not only were classy but warmed up the entire room. She couldn't get over how new the large wood beams looked after some sanding and fresh stain.

"This all looks..." She felt her eyes sting as a memory of standing in this very spot with her parents over ten years ago surfaced.

"Mom, I don't want a big party for my birthday," she'd complained with the fervor of a seventeen-year-old girl. She *might have even stomped her foot at one point.*

"Honey, every seventeen-year-old girl deserves a party," her mother had said eagerly. *"Besides, I've thrown you a birthday party every year of your life."* Her mother's tone

dropped as it always did when the discussion was over. "And I have no intention of stopping now."

All Raven had wanted that year was to be left alone. Maybe a quiet night with Reggie and her friends. She'd attended a few of her friend's birthday parties earlier that year and, to be honest, didn't care to host one herself.

The last party she and her friends had gone to had been a complete disaster. Heather's parents were some of the richest in town, and they had gone all out for her seventeenth birthday party last month.

That hadn't stopped Heather from complaining all the way through it or her friends from making fun of her for weeks after, all because her mother had decorated everything in pink, as if Heather were still a little girl instead of a seventeen-year-old.

"Dad, talk to Mom." She'd rushed over to her father, who had been directing some waitstaff.

"About what sweetie?" Her father barely spared her a glance.

"My party," she'd whined.

"Don't worry, your mom says she has everything under control."

"That's the thing. I don't want a party," she'd reiterated.

"Honey, I'm working." Her father had waved her away. "Go talk to your mother."

"I did. Daddy." At this point she was positive that she had stomped her foot.

"Raven." He'd finally looked at her. "Go. Now." The tone of his voice had assured her that he was done playing around. So, she'd left.

That was one of the last memories she had of her parents.

"Hey." Cade pulled her into his arms. "What's wrong?"

Shaking her head, she took a deep breath. "It's nothing.

I was just remembering my parents. They would have loved all this." She motioned around them.

"They'd be proud of you," he told her. "Now, I called ahead and had Tim make us something special." He dropped his arms from around her and walked over to pull out a chair for her.

"I'm underdressed." She motioned to her grey slacks and black blouse.

He smiled. "You look perfect." He leaned in and kissed her before she sat down.

As if by magic, two of her waitstaff appeared out of thin air and poured them each a glass of water and then wine.

"I heard my uncle took my mother into Redding for dinner tonight," Cade said right as she took a sip of her wine, "I hope he wasn't planning anything... special."

She couldn't help it; he'd spoken right as she'd taken a sip of wine. For the next minute, she coughed and choked on air while Cade gently slapped her on the back.

"You okay?" he asked when she could finally breathe.

"You did that on purpose," she accused him. His guilty grin was the only reply she needed. "How did you know?" she asked.

"My uncle has been acting strange for a while now." He took his own sip of wine.

"And what? You figured he was going to propose to your mother because of it?" she asked.

It was his turn to choke on the wine. Now it was her turn to slap his back until he could breathe.

"Jesus, who said anything about proposing? I was thinking they were..." He shook his head and took a deep breath.

"What?" she asked as she sat back down.

"Moving in together," he admitted with a slight shrug.

CHAPTER TWENTY-SIX

A BURNT CHILD DREADS THE FIRE ~ ENGLISH
PROVERB

For the rest of the dinner, he tried to get his mind off of his mother and uncle getting hitched.

Tim had outdone himself this time with the meal of beef Wellington, fresh honey-glazed carrots, and new potatoes. He'd always enjoyed the guy's meals, but this time, he was seriously thinking about ordering seconds.

Raven leaned across the table and lowered her voice.

"Do you think it would reflect badly on me if I ordered this meal every day for the rest of my life?" she asked.

He chuckled. "God, I was thinking the same thing. How fat would we get if we ate dinner here every night?"

"Okay, so we're in agreement. This"—she motioned to her empty plate— "goes on the menu."

"For sure." He nodded. "I can't wait to see what's for dessert."

The Baileys and coffee cheesecake was some of the best he'd ever had. Not that he was a big cheesecake fan. His mother tried each year to get him excited about her fresh blueberry cheesecake, but he just couldn't get behind it as a dessert. He rather enjoyed anything with chocolate instead, which this cheesecake had plenty of.

"If my mother made this kind of cheesecake"—he pointed with his fork— "I would have been a much heavier kid."

"My mother used to make this caramel almond toffee each Christmas that I couldn't get enough of."

It had been one of her favorite desserts, and her mother made it just for her. She hadn't thought of that dessert or of her mother in that way for so long that tears streamed from her eyes immediately.

Cade reached across the tale and took her hand in his.

"I'm just emotional." She waved her free hand and then quickly picked up her wine glass and downed the rest of the dark liquid. She knew she was being overly emotional but didn't care. The lack of sleep mixed with hormones was wreaking havoc on her system. Besides, she figured she deserved to be a little emotional every now and then. At least once a month anyway.

Cade had showed only kindness and understanding when she'd told him that she'd wanted to stay at the resort for the last few nights.

She'd never really been around men during... well, except her father. She didn't plan on starting with Cade. She knew from past experience that she could be... well... emotionally challenging.

The one thing she was sure of was that she didn't want anything to get between her and Cade. Least of all her period.

"You're allowed to be," Cade responded. "After all, look at all that you've accomplished." He waved his hand around the room, his eyes following the movement. "I can only imagine how wonderful it feels to see something you've worked so hard on turn out this... wonderful."

She smiled. For a moment, she'd believed he was going to treat her like some emotional woman. Even though rationally she knew she sometimes was, that didn't mean she didn't want to be treated as such. He hadn't done so before, and she didn't want him to now.

"It did turn out rather grand, didn't it?" She beamed as she looked around. "We can have guests dining in here this weekend." The smile slipped. "If the tables weren't set to arrive on Monday." She groaned.

"Don't rush it," he said, getting her attention. "For now, we get to enjoy all this ourselves." He held up his glass of wine. Somehow, during her complaining, her wine glass had been refilled.

Lifting it, she smiled. "Remind me to give the waitstaff a raise." She tapped her glass against his.

"I was thinking the same thing." He sipped his wine.

They sat in the gorgeous room for at least another hour, chatting about all the improvements. She hadn't realized she'd had the equivalent of an entire bottle of wine until she went to stand up. The entire room tilted and, thankfully, Cade was there to catch her.

"Easy." He chuckled. "I'll walk you up to your room." He wrapped his arms around her.

"No, I want to go home," she said, leaning her head against his shoulder.

"Actually, I was thinking of crashing here. My grandmother has Blue for the night." He wiggled his eyebrows.

"That would be great. I can't sleep without you," she admitted drunkenly, her arms thrown over his shoulders while he walked them into the elevator. "I can't even ride in these without thinking about Rachelle," she blurted out.

She knew her speech was slurred. That she was wobbling on her feet. But at this point, she didn't care. When the elevator doors shut, she plastered her body against his.

"God, I love these," she said, running her hands over his arms, his chest. "I love the way you feel against me." She trailed her mouth down his neck. He'd shaved for their dinner tonight, and she couldn't get over how smooth his face and neck were. She wanted to run her tongue all over his face, taste every inch of him with her lips.

"Raven." His tone was a warning.

"You taste so good," she moaned as she started working on the buttons on his shirt. When the elevator doors slid open, she no longer thought of Rachelle. The only thing in her mind was getting Cade naked and in her room.

She fumbled with the credit card key several times before Cade took it from her hands and easily opened the door.

"I'm not used to the new system," she mumbled as she tossed her shoes off her feet and reached for him.

"Raven." He took her hands and held her at bay. "You're drunk."

She laughed. "And horny." She jerked his shirt open, sending buttons scattering around the room.

He laughed, a burst of it echoing in the smaller room.

"Raven." He laughed again when she pushed him onto the bed.

Her eyes ran over him. The worn black jeans he wore. The tanned, toned skin of his arms and chest. His messy hair from her fingers. The look he was giving her. All of it together had her wanting him even more than before.

In one quick move, she tossed off her shirt and slacks,

leaving her in only a pair of black cotton panties and a matching bra.

"I like those." Cade ran his eyes over her. Then they locked with her own. "I like you."

She hesitated for a moment and in that split second, she came crashing down to reality. She wanted to be with him but couldn't. She didn't know how to tell him. What to say to him?

Then Cade stood up, took her hand, and pulled her into the bathroom.

"Let me. There's a lot we can do. If you trust me," he said softly as he ran his mouth over her jawline.

She melted. At that moment, she would have gladly given anything, let him try anything.

He reached in and turned on the shower and smiled as he turned back towards her, his eyes running over her.

"Give me a moment." She held up her hand and stepped into the private bathroom area.

When she came out again, he was standing, gloriously naked, under the spray of water.

She stepped in behind him and ran her hands over his back, across his shoulders, down his back. Then she reached around to his front and gripped him.

His breath hitched and then he moaned as she started running her hands up and down his length.

He turned around and nudged her against the tile wall and covered her mouth with his.

"I've missed you. Missed this." He ran his hands over her, sliding down her wet body. Then he cupped her and glided a finger into her heat.

She arched into him, moaned his name as he pleased her. She'd never imagined it would feel this good. That it could feel this good even while the cramps tightened her gut. When he thrust into her, she was consumed with pleasure. Obsessed by his every movement.

She'd never felt more alive than she felt now, here with him.

She told him that while he moved inside her. When she felt her powerful release vibrate her entire body, she dug her nails into his shoulders and cried out his name.

She felt him start to run his shampooed hands across her body, massaging his fingers throughout her hair, and groaned with pleasure.

She leaned against the tile and let him pleasure her in a different way. After he turned off the water, she allowed him to wrap a towel around her.

When they climbed into bed, she was wearing her cotton pajamas, her long hair braided back away from her face. Cade wore his boxer briefs and spooned her like he had missed her.

She slept like the dead, enjoying a full eight hours of deep sleep, catching up on the sleep she'd missed over the past few nights.

When she woke, Cade was there, smiling down at her.

"Morning," he said, shifting above her.

"Morning." She smiled.

"I thought that since we both had the day off that we'd take a hike. We can pick Blue up from my grandmother's and head out to enjoy some of this nice weather," he suggested.

"I'd like that." It had been so long since she'd gone up into the hills that surrounded the resort. She desperately wanted to see the view from the top of the ski runs but hadn't dared to go up there alone.

"If possible, I'd like to head up the hill." She motioned

towards the window. "It's been ages since I've seen the view from above."

"We can pack a picnic lunch," he replied. "How about after we order room service, I head into town, grab Blue and my hiking boots, and pack us a lunch? Then I can meet you back here."

"Sounds like a plan. God, I love living in a hotel," she admitted.

Since she was feeling particularly pleased, she ordered strawberry French toast with extra whipped cream on top. Cade had one of his usual breakfasts, steel cut oatmeal with fruit and a cup of coffee.

"I'll eat healthy later," she joked with a grin.

"You don't hear me saying a word." He smiled over his food. "My mother taught me one of the most important lessons ever—once a month, you don't complain about what a woman eats or wears." He leaned forward and grinned. "No matter what."

She couldn't help it. She laughed. "Smart woman." She nodded. "Even smarter man for heeding her advice."

After Cade left, she showered and changed into some hiking clothes. She decided to head down to her office until Cade returned.

She was surprised to see her aunt in the hallway just outside her office door. Temper surfaced quickly. This was the first time she'd seen Roslyn in the resort since she'd threatened her last time.

She pulled out her cell phone to call security, only to have her uncle yank the phone out of her hands.

"I think it's about time we sat down and had a talk." Her uncle took her arm and pulled her towards her office. She thought of screaming, but then her uncle warned. "Don't."

"You changed the locks," Roslyn complained as she held out her hand for the keys.

"Go to hell." Raven narrowed her eyes at her aunt.

"Soon enough," her aunt replied with a smile. "But not before we get what we're due."

"You're not due anything."

Her uncle's hold on her arm tightened, and she cried out slightly at the pain.

"Don't you think we'd be more comfortable having this conversation inside?" he asked.

She pulled her keys from her pocket, if only to make him loosen his grip.

Colin shoved her inside, and Roslyn shut the door behind her and locked it.

"Now, isn't this cozy?" Colin asked. He walked around the desk and sat in her chair.

She wanted to bark at him to get out of her seat, but stood there, rubbing her wrist where he'd twisted it instead.

Roslyn walked over to the file cabinet and tried to open a drawer.

"You locked this too?" Her aunt turned to her. "What's the matter? Don't trust anyone else?"

"No," she said, holding her chin up in defiance. "What do you want?"

"Where is the policy?" her uncle said calmly.

"Policy?" she asked, having no clue what he was talking about.

Her uncle's greyish eyebrows shot up. "The insurance policy?" he answered, as if she knew what he was talking about.

"If you're talking about the policy with you and Roche as beneficiaries' if this place goes up, I cancelled it," she answered easily.

Roslyn's eyes moved to Colin's. "What?"

"She's lying. The policy is in our names."

"No." Raven shook her head and crossed her arms over her chest. "It wasn't." She took her keys and unlocked the bottom drawer on the file cabinet. She handed the piece of paper to her aunt and stood back to watch the repercussions of her uncle's deceit.

After five minutes of listening to them argue, she interrupted them.

"As fun and as entertaining as this is, I have a date." She tried to look bored and glanced down at her watch.

"Enough of this deceit. Where are the real papers? The ones with our names on it?" Colin shouted.

"There is no such thing," she said clearly. "Whatever policies you signed up for are gone. I have one policy on this place." She motioned around them. "And if this place is destroyed, you get nothing."

"Not this place," her uncle spat back just as the office door was flung open.

"Are we late?" Cade asked, stepping inside, his uncle in tow. "We thought we'd stop in since Cemal was kind enough to inform us that there was a surprise party going on in here."

Raven had never been so thankful to see Sean before. Then Blue came trotting in and jumped up on her, demanding attention.

Cade walked over to her, and she saw his eyes darken when he noticed the redness of her arm where her uncle had grabbed her. She grabbed his arm and stopped him from turning on her uncle.

"Don't. He's not worth it," she warned in a soft tone.

"He hurt you," Cade replied.

"Is that true?" Sean asked, his eyes going to the redness of her wrist.

"I didn't do anything," Colin spat out. "Whatever she says, she's a liar. Besides, if you touch that girl, she turns red." He pointed a finger in her direction.

She glanced down at her wrist and realized it was now a dark purple. "Yeah," she motioned, not wanting to deal with her uncle any longer, "he did this."

Over the next half an hour, her uncle was cuffed and hauled away by one of the other officers while Sean took her official statement. All the while, Roslyn screamed, cursed, and at one point, tried to kick Sean. Sean placed cuffs on her as well.

Shortly after they both were hauled away, Cade, turned to her.

"Are you still up for a hike?" he asked her.

"Even more so now. I have all this…"—she motioned to her chest— "pent up."

He smiled and then the two of them and Blue stepped outside and headed up the pathway to the top of the ski runs.

It had been too long since she'd been outside in nature, spending her day breathing fresh crisp mountain air.

Halfway up the hillside, she was breathless, her thighs were burning, and she had a stitch in her side. The anger she'd felt towards her family was still burning inside her, but now it was more a slow burn than a raging forest fire. She pushed on with Blue in the lead and Cade directly behind her.

"I'm not slowing you down, am I?" she asked a little winded.

He chuckled. "It's okay. I'm enjoying the view."

Since she was completely breathless, she didn't talk again until they reached the summit.

The view was simply breathtaking. Or maybe it was the climb that had taken her breath away? Either way, she stood for a few moments, just taking it all in.

The three massive buildings were like dark shadows on the beautiful countryside. If they weren't her entire world, she would have thought that they should have never been there in the first place. In a way, they marred the nature surrounding them, darkened the natural beauty.

Then she remembered all the wonderful times she'd had within those walls. How so many in town counted on the income from the resort. How they relied on her.

"It's stunning, isn't it?" Cade asked, wrapping his arms around her.

"It looks so small from up here."

He chuckled. "I haven't been up here in years." He glanced all around. "I'd forgotten you can see the town from here. It's strange, I never really think about the mountain being almost between the resort and town."

"Me neither." She turned in a compete circle and then her eyes landed on the hillside where they'd found her. Where she'd hidden in a cave and waited out the fire. Where she'd met Reggie that fateful night.

The last place she'd been happy. Genuinely happy. Carefree. Unhindered by guilt. Sorrow. Loss.

The once-charred hillside was now completely covered in short, green, lush trees, the last remnants of the damage caused ten years ago long gone.

"How about some lunch?" Cade asked, breaking into her thoughts.

Tearing her eyes from the park, she turned towards Cade and nodded.

"Are you okay?" Cade asked her.

"Yes," she smiled, remembering everything she had now. How she'd spent a wonderful night wrapped in Cade's arms.

Focusing on the good instead of the bad caused her heart to swell and lift.

She moved over and sat back to watch Cade pull out a perfect summer picnic. She knew there were a few more weeks before this hillside was covered in fresh snow and flooded with vacationers. The earliest she could remember getting snow was the first day of October back when she was ten.

"Maybe next summer we can get up here more often," Cade said, handing her a bottled water.

"I'd like that. With everything going on this year, it's been difficult for me to just breathe."

"You really have done an amazing job." He glanced down the hillside towards the resort. "I'm sure you're going to be packed to the rafters soon enough."

"They've finished installing the new system in the west building." She smiled. "I just got word after you left."

"That's good news," Cade responded.

"You may have to come in for another inspection," she suggested. "I rather liked working with you. Seeing you in that sexy uniform."

He laughed. "So do I. Like working with you. Every-thing you wear is sexy," he added, causing her to smile.

Sitting on the hillside eating lunch with Cade was easily one of the best days she'd had in years. She'd never laughed or flirted as much as she did with him on the top of the mountain, overlooking everything she'd worked hard for.

"So, what happens now?" she asked him once the sand-wiches, cheese, and fruit he'd packed were all gone.

"Dessert?" he asked, pulling out a bag of cookies.

She laughed. "I mean with my uncle and aunt."

"Oh." He sighed and handed her a couple of cookies. "Now they'll have to post bail. Hopefully, they have learned a lesson to leave you alone."

"They wanted some sort of policy." She remembered her uncle's words right before Cade and Sean walked in. "I thought they were talking about the insurance policy on the resort that my uncle had taken out. The moment I found out about it, I called the company and cancelled it. Since he technically wasn't owner, it hadn't been that hard."

"Seriously? He took a policy out on the place?" Cade asked.

"Yeah, with him and Morgan Roche as beneficiaries."

"Seriously?" Cade asked again. "How stupid could the man be?"

"My aunt wasn't too pleased to find out about that," she said with a smile. "I think that was the last nail in the coffin of their marriage."

"You would think. Something tells me those two idiots love to be miserable together." Cade shook his head, and he ate his cookie.

"So, I'm not sure what policy they were talking about. They kept insisting that there was a different one," she said.

"What kind of policy?"

"I'm not sure." She shook her head. "But something tells me I need to call and ask around."

"I can help if you need," Cade offered.

"Thanks." She relaxed back as he wrapped his arms around her. "This was almost a perfect day," she said with a sigh.

"Almost," he agreed. "We still have to get down the hillside."

She laughed. "I have a thought about that." She glanced over at him. "I've arranged to get a ride."

"A ride?" he asked, his eyebrows rising slightly.

"I needed to test out the lifts now that they're fully functional. They even have these new baskets for pets to get up and down the mountain. We're going to use them next summer, when we open the hiking and bike paths."

He bent his head down and kissed her. "Have I mentioned how much I love you today?"

She smiled and held onto him and kissed him back.

Waves and waves of anger washed over them. It was getting harder to separate reality from fiction. There were moments the red haze overcame them, and they disappeared into the smoke and haze that surrounded them.

The only moments of true coherence were when they killed. The hunger. The desire to make others suffer was so great that sinking into the darkness no longer affected them as much as it had before.

Why had they waited so long? Now that they had a taste of it, there was no stopping it.

CHAPTER TWENTY-SEVEN

It took a few days for Cade to come to terms with the fact that his mother and his uncle were going to be married. To his and Raven's surprise, they decided to host the wedding the week before the grand reopening at the resort.

Since his mother was officially in charge of coordinating and scheduling the events, it wasn't that hard. She decided that her wedding would be the perfect event to use as a soft opening as a prequel for the official reopening event.

Raven seemed excited about it. She thought that it would make for a great dry run for her employees.

Either way, he had a little over a month to prepare for his mother and uncle's marriage. So far, he hadn't had a chance to talk to his uncle alone.

By the time he got around to stopping by his uncle's office, he'd come to liking the idea. Partially because of Raven's influence and partially because he noticed how happy his mother really was.

"Hey." He knocked on Sean's door.

His uncle looked up and waved him inside while he pulled off a pair of reading glasses.

"This is a happy surprise," Sean said as he leaned back. "What can I help you with today?"

"I meant to stop by earlier. After the incident with Raven's aunt and uncle."

"They posted bail within an hour." Sean shrugged. "They're both due in court next week. Most likely they'll be charged a fine and have community service. Raven has filed a restraining order against both of them."

"Yeah." He nodded. "She wanted me to ask you to look into whether her aunt and uncle have some sort of policy out on the resort. She thinks there's something legal you can do to help her find out the truth."

"Policy?" Sean asked.

Cade shrugged. "It's what they were in her office asking her about that day."

"I can't officially request a subpoena on their finances unless I have cause," Sean admitted.

"I figured as much." Cade sighed.

Sean narrowed his eyes. "I do have a friend that can look into it though."

Cade smiled. "Thanks." He moved to get up but stopped and sat back down. "So, you and my mom..."

"I thought we worked through this already?" Sean said with a chuckle.

"That was before you decided to put a ring on it," Cade tried to joke.

Sean nodded. "I should have talked to you before..."

"You didn't have to," Cade admitted.

"Respect for you and for my brother would have dictated it," Sean said, setting his hands on the desk. "You know that I love her."

"That's obvious," Cade admitted. "I think the entire town knows it now."

Sean smiled. "We don't have any real problem, do we?"

"No, it's just taken me a while to get used to the idea of having a dad again."

Sean's face changed. "I have no intention of taking the place of Henry. You know that, right?"

"No more than I had any intention of taking Reggie's place with Raven," he agreed. "Love happens."

Sean nodded and looked a little more relaxed. "Love happens."

"Okay, now that that's over." Cade made a move to stand again.

"There is one more topic of business we need to discuss." Sean stood with him. "I need a best man, and I was sure hoping you'd fill the vacancy."

Cade smiled and held out his hand for Sean's. "I'd be honored."

After leaving his uncle's office, he headed to the diner to grab a sandwich with the guys. His workdays weren't too demanding, except for a few days a month when they trained in the tower.

The tower was a large, state-of-the-art steel building that quite literally was lit on fire. Once a month for three to four days, they filled the tower with fire and smoke, all in the name of training. At this point, since he'd gone through the drill so often, there was a hint of fun to the task.

Not that he'd let on to the newbies, since they were all sweating bullets whenever he called for drill days.

Today was the calm before the storm. He'd already given a twenty-four-hour warning that drills started first thing in the morning. Today, his men were calm, relaxed, and enjoying themselves. Tomorrow, they'd be sweating and training as if their lives depended on it. Which they did.

"Hey, chief." Tony waved him over to the table where all his men were gathered.

"Hey." He grabbed the empty chair and sat next to Tony and Andre. The two men seemed to always be glued to each other's sides. He knew they were best friends and had grown close now that Tony was officially dating Darby, and Andre and Carrie were... well, that was more complicated. Andre happily told everyone that they were dating, while Carrie adamantly denied it.

Raven's opinion on the couple was that Carrie was trying to save Andre from his father's wrath. After all, when the only black woman in town dated the man whose father was the biggest racist, things tended to get ugly.

As far as Cade could tell, word about the relationship hadn't reached Andre's father yet. At least that was the working theory since Andre's old man had yet to have one of his famous public drunken scenes. Even though he was one of the wealthiest men in town, the man liked to drink. A lot.

"Ready for tomorrow?" he asked Andre.

"As ready as I ever am." Andre gave a weak smile.

"This will be your fifth time?" he asked.

"Seventh," Andre corrected.

"Wow, seven? I guess time does fly." Cade shook his head. The fact was, Cade had lost count of the times he'd hauled his butt through the burning building himself. Within the first year, he'd run the course more than a dozen times. "Are you nervous?"

"Naw, I lost my nerves after the second time," Andre told him, then his eyes moved beyond Cade. Without glancing over, he knew instantly that Carrie had walked into the building.

"You sure look nervous now," Cade leaned in and whispered, smiling.

"Why won't she agree to date me?" Andre ran his hands through his hair.

"It could be because she's afraid of your old man," Kevin broke in. "He does own half the town."

"Naw," Andre replied, his eyes following Carrie as she sat on a barstool near the front. Her eyes landed on the group and locked with Andre for a split second.

From where Cade sat, there was no denying the fact that Carrie was extremely interested.

"Maybe it's nerves?" someone else threw in.

"Shut up," Andre hissed. "My love life is none of your business."

That statement set off the entire table. Carrie's name was said loudly several times just so it was totally obvious to everyone in the diner that they were talking about Andre and Carrie.

Finally, Darby walked over to the table and glared down at him.

"Can't you control your men?" Darby narrowed her eyes as she spoke.

"Me?" He pointed to his chest. "I don't..." Darby's eyes got even narrower. He sighed and turned to the table. "Enough," he said in a steady voice. To his surprise, everyone stopped talking. "Place your orders and leave the teasing to teenage girls."

"Thanks." Darby patted his shoulder as she started making her rounds to collect orders.

Somehow the talk at the table turned to the murders. Each of his team had speculations about who the murderer was and theories as to why people in Cannon Falls were dying.

The craziest of the theories was that Kim was Rachelle and Joseph's love child. Why they had all been murdered wasn't discussed.

The only theory that caught his attention was that Kim had been killed because she had overheard Raven's aunt and uncle discussing stealing money from Raven and murdering Rachelle and Joseph.

At least some of the townspeople were on Raven's side.

After leaving the diner, he had a few more rounds to make. One was his monthly call to old man Dove's residence. The man was at it again, trying to burn his trash in a pile by the edge of the road.

Cade made it there before the fire truck this time and easily put the fire out with the extinguisher in his trunk.

When the crew on shift showed up, they riled him and claimed that with him around, there wasn't any reason for them to be on duty.

After his last stop for the day, he headed to the store to pick up a bottle of wine and something to make for dinner. Raven was heading to his place once she was done with work.

He grabbed a couple of steaks and some fresh salad fixings and was heading towards the wine aisle when he spotted Julia walking towards him. She was pushing a cart full of items, including several bottles of wine.

"Well, if it isn't Cade Stone," Julia said with a slight purr, almost abandoning her cart to stop directly in front of him. "Where have you been hiding yourself?" she said, running a finger down his arm.

"Not hiding and not interested," he said clearly as he sidestepped her. She moved and blocked him easily. Since he wasn't a monster, he didn't push her aside but stood there letting her block his way.

"Julia, I'm pretty busy," he warned.

"Oh, you've got time for me." She pushed his basket to the side and tried to step closer to him.

In this area, he could defy her without being a jerk. He took a giant step backwards and moved his basket back between them.

"I'm involved," he clarified. "You know that."

"Oh, I hear people talking in town." Julia waved her hand. "It's just talk."

"Not this time," he clarified. "I'm with Raven."

"That bitch?" Julia shook her head as if she were disappointed in him. "Everyone in town knows what she did all those years ago."

"You're pushing it."

"Well, well, isn't this a cozy scene," he heard someone say from a few feet way.

Shit. He rolled his eyes. That's all he needed. Another crazed woman to put on a show.

Heather Craft strolled towards them, a smile plastered on her face.

He took another giant step away from Julia when he realized just how close they were standing.

This time when he tried to pass Julia, she let him go to face off with Heather.

Since he was done with the drama, he grabbed the first bottle of wine he knew the label of and left. He happened to hear a few choice words as the two women squared off in the wine aisle—slut, whore, cheater. As he thought about their tones, he realized that the women weren't fighting. They were gossiping. He didn't know what worried him more. That they were friends or that they had decided to pool their evil powers together to face off against one common enemy. An enemy which just happened to be the woman he was in love with.

When Raven walked in the front door a few hours later, he had the entire dinner laid out on the table.

The moment she walked over to wrap her arms around him, he could see the weariness in her eyes.

"Problems?" he asked while holding onto her.

"We lost a stove today." She leaned against the counter and took the wine glass he offered her.

"Lost it? Did it grow legs and run away?"

She smiled. "No, it died a slow and horrible death. Or so Tim has told me. He's been complaining about it since he took over in the kitchen."

"So, you'll find a new one." He shrugged.

"A restaurant grade stove costs close to five thousand dollars," she replied with a slight groan.

"And you have how much left in your budget for items like that?"

She winced. "Three thousand dollars."

It was his turn to wince. He picked up his wine glass and held it up to hers. "I have a few thousand in savings that I'm not doing anything with at the moment. You're welcome to it."

She stopped, frozen in place. "I will not take money from you."

"Call it a loan." He smiled. "I know you're good for it."

"No." She shook her head. "Cade, I... can't. I won't be in debt."

"You won't be." He wrapped his arms around her after taking her glass from her and setting it down. "There is no debt. You need a new stove. You get a new stove, and I get to help the woman I love."

He felt her shaking her head.

"Don't make me call my mother," he warned with a chuckle. "Or bring out the big guns and call my grandmother."

She laughed and the sound of it warmed him and confirmed that he'd won this round.

That night as they fell asleep holding one another, Raven whispered. "Thank you for the loan. I'll pay you back as soon as the doors open."

He smiled and held onto her. The truth was, he didn't care if she ever paid him back.

There was no doubt in his mind that she was good for it. Just looking at the changes around the resort, he could imagine the place being packed full of skiers and guests the moment the first snowflake drifted to the ground.

The next morning, he woke before sunrise when his alarm went off.

"Training day," he said when Raven groaned. "Go back to sleep." He kissed her and rolled out of bed to get ready.

When he walked into the fire station, the morning mist still hovering over the ground, most of his men were already there, eager and ready to start the day.

Most early morning shifts started with donuts, coffee, and gossip. Today was different. Oh, there was still coffee and donuts, but instead of gossip, the conversation was filled with stories of past training events.

Everyone nervously sat around waiting for the training to begin. The moment the last crew member showed up, he called his team to attention. After a brief but thorough security briefing, everyone suited up and headed out.

The morning mist was long gone and the sun was just breaking over the hillside, heating everything up.

The five-story steel building sat on the edge of the fire

house property. Just carting your own gear out to the tower wore out most of the youngest recruits.

Today, even he was breaking a sweat when they reached the building. At the end of the first drill, he was swimming in sweat, even though he hadn't entered the tower himself yet.

The heat emanating from the building was enough to melt even the strongest of wills. He watched his crew closely, making sure each person who went inside came out and clocking the time that it took them to run through the course.

By lunchtime, they'd only made it through four crewmembers. His standard practice was to deal with the newbies first while the more experienced crewmembers looked on and helped.

Sitting in the field eating a cold sandwich and downing a soda with the rest of them, he realized just how much his life had changed in the past few months. He was on a totally different path than he had been before Raven had returned. Even though he still had the same home, the same career, his future was different.

The way he looked at life had changed. Before Raven, he'd been so sure of what he believed in. Somewhere in the back of his mind, he'd assumed she had something to do with the fire. With Reggie's death.

Why had he allowed so many others to influence him? He listened to the people around him chatting and talking about the town and the people in it, alert for any talk about Raven or the murders.

It was as if the entire town was holding its breath. Waiting for something more to happen or for someone to confess. Like that was ever going to happen.

Whenever he spoke to his uncle about the murders, he

grew frustrated. He knew Sean was doing his best to find out who was responsible, but he couldn't help but think that, if they were in the city, if they had the resources of a larger community, that they would have answers by now.

"You heard about Roslyn and Colin?" someone said, gaining his attention. Looking around, he realized it was Kevin speaking.

"What, are they finally getting a divorce?" someone asked.

"Did they confess to the murders?" someone else added.

"Heard they were leaving town," Kevin replied.

He scanned the group of men around him. There were two women on his crew, but they were sitting in the other group huddled together under a large tree.

"Leaving?" he asked.

"Fleeing is more like it," Tony said. "Having gotten away with murder, they've decided to leave town."

"So, you believe they're responsible for all three deaths?" Kevin asked.

"Don't you? Doesn't everyone? They're the ones who stood to lose the most," Tony replied.

It was the theory he thought was strongest as well. Who would have to gain from the deaths? Each time he and Raven asked themselves that question, they were the obvious answer. Her aunt and uncle were top of everyone's list, including his uncle's.

But his uncle claimed that as long as there wasn't any proof, there wasn't anything that he could do.

Cade understood this to be the case. After all, he wasn't a fool. If they arrested her aunt and uncle and had zero proof, they'd just be allowed to go.

"Any idea where they're moving to?" Cade asked, figuring he'd talk to his uncle the moment he could.

"Rumor is they're headed to Redding," Kevin said with a shrug.

"I say good riddance," Tony added in. "They've been making problems for Darby down at the diner ever since Raven kicked them out of the resort. Causing scenes and making people feel uncomfortable."

"Scenes?" Cade asked.

"Sure. They got in a huge fight the other night with Cal. Darby claims that Cal finally came out of the closet and informed them that he and Tim were getting married," Tony added.

"Cal's a good guy. He didn't deserve the humiliation his father put him through the other night. The entire town is rallying behind Cal and Tim," Andre broke in.

If anyone in town knew what being an outsider was like, or rather, being with an outsider, Andre was near the top of the list. Having a racist father and dating the only black woman in town obviously put a large bullseye on him. Gossip about Andre and Carrie ran like wildflowers through town. Not as much as the murders, but more than any other gossip did.

He'd known about Cal and Tim being together and being engaged, thanks to Raven. He liked both men. Actually, Cal was one of the only members of Raven's family that he did like.

"We missed the show," Barry, one of the guys who had been on his crew for more than five years, said. "What happened?"

"Apparently Colin and Roslyn showed up when Cal and Tim were out on a date. Instead of trying to hide it, Cal stood up and finally told his parents. I thought Colin was going to blow his top," Tony told them. "When Darby over-heard what was going on, she marched over there and kicked Colin and Roslyn out of the diner. She even told them they're banned for life."

"Good for her," Andre said.

He'd have to make sure he let Darby know how proud he was of her the next time he saw her. He'd known the little woman had spunk; he just hadn't known how much.

They'd wasted enough of the day gossiping. He got everyone's attention and went back to work. With the exception of one twisted ankle, day one of the training went off without a hitch.

He hobbled into the house just before sunset and grabbed an ice pack. Without showering or changing, he fell onto the sofa, propped his left foot up with the ice pack on his ankle, and immediately fell asleep.

"What happened?" Raven asked, waking him up a few hours later.

Blue had climbed into his lap at one point but now scurried off to welcome Raven home.

He shifted to sit up, and the now-thawed ice pack fell to the floor.

"Twisted my ankle," he answered, moving to get up.

"No, stay there." Raven rushed to his side and took his ankle into her hands to examine it.

"You've got some bruising." She touched the swollen spot gently and he winced. "Hurt?"

"Only when you poke it."

She leaned closer to him, her eyes running over his face, his clothes.

"You're filthy and you stink."

He smiled. "I didn't have the energy to climb the stairs and shower."

"What if I help you?" she offered, standing up.

It took the rest of his energy to pull himself up the stairs and stand by while she removed his soiled uniform. He sat on his shower bench and let the hot water wash away the day's sweat.

"You have to do this again tomorrow?" she asked from outside the glass doors.

"Two more days." He laid his head back. "But today was the only day I had to make it through the tower."

"Why did you go through it? Aren't you the boss?" she asked.

"Doesn't mean I'm less responsible for ensuring that I'm up for the task. Every man, and woman, has to prove themselves capable."

"Okay, so you've made it through," she said, sounding more relaxed.

He didn't want to tell her that he'd barely made it through. And that he'd basically gotten the worst grade of the day since he'd come out the other side with a twisted ankle. Oh, it wouldn't stop him from doing his job, but it did mean that he had some more training to do.

Hell, the young kids fresh from high school had kicked his ass today.

"Will you be okay in there? I can head down and make us some dinner?" Raven offered.

"Just as long as you don't judge me for eating it in here," he replied.

"I'll bring it up." She disappeared down the stairs.

Closing his eyes, he relaxed back and let the hot water relax every inch of his body.

He must have fallen asleep sitting up with the hot water flowing over him. When Raven came in, he jolted awake.

"Are you still doing okay in there?" she asked, and he could hear her moving around the bathroom.

"Yeah, I'm coming out." He reached up and shut off the

water. "It's a good thing I have a tankless water heater," he joked as she wrapped a towel around his hips. "Endless hot water."

"I figured you'd want to eat in the bedroom instead of the shower." She helped him into a pair of his sweat shorts and a T-shirt.

He sat propped up in bed and ate the grilled chicken salad, tomato soup, and grilled cheese sandwiches Raven had made for him.

He had to admit, it felt wonderful knowing there was someone there to look out for him. As a man, he would ever admit that he needed it, but it was nice all the same.

Immediately after finishing the meal, he fell fast asleep again, this time in his own bed and with his arms wrapped around Raven. The next morning, he dragged himself to work after taking a couple of ibuprofen to reduce the swelling in his ankle.

He watched more than a dozen people on his crew repeat the same drills he'd done the afternoon before.

He knew every turn, every stair, every step of the tower by heart. Still, in the dark, surrounded by smoke and heat, his mind and the fear wanted to take over all his rational thoughts.

This was what all the training was for. To train each and every member on his team to not allow fear to win. The best way out of a situation was with rationality and thought.

When he'd first joined the crew, it had taken him almost two years before he was able to go through the drills and not see his brother's face in the smoke. To not wonder what Reggie had been thinking when the dark cloud of smoke or the wall of flames had surrounded him, consumed him. Killed him.

Still, sometimes after he went through the drills, nightmares of the same thoughts surfaced, keeping him up at night.

Now, however, his training usually kicked in and took over, allowing him to see clearly, to feel his way out of situations where his eyes, his ears, and his surroundings were against him.

Maybe that skill was what had allowed him to see Raven clearly? To see past all the hate that had been spread in the town over the years.

Whatever the reason, he was thankful she was there with him now.

For the next two days, life was a haze. He'd always looked forward to training days, but this time they seemed to drag on and, more importantly, they were kicking his butt.

Each night Raven was there to pick up the pieces and fill his evenings with normalcy. She brought burgers home from the diner the next night. The night after it was lasagna from the dining hall at the resort.

He couldn't admit it to her, at least not yet, but he wanted her to make it official and move in with him. He understood she wanted to keep her room at the resort, if for no other reason than to have a place to stay when she worked late so she wouldn't have to make the drive to his place.

He knew that when the snow started falling, the fifteen-minute drive could easily turn into double that time. It was smart for her to keep some of her things there.

Hell, after the third day of training, he even wished he had a cot in his office at the station. There were beds upstairs in the fire house for crew members who worked night shifts. He remembered sleeping up there himself when he was a rookie.

Now that training was over, he was looking forward to the weekend and having some real peace and quiet. He'd initially planned for them to go on another hike, but since his ankle was still giving him problems, he decided on a long drive to the beach instead. It had been a few months since he'd taken Blue to play in the surf.

He hadn't been there with Raven yet and was looking forward to getting out of town with her, even if it was only for a day.

Now he just needed to make it through the next two workdays and the chore he dreaded the most—telling everyone their drill rankings, which would in turn dictate each of the crew's available shifts.

He knew that getting the best shift schedule was motivation enough for some to excel in the training. Thankfully, since he was fire marshal, his hours were locked in on standard workday hours with the occasional on-call schedule when needed.

Since there was still a lot of construction going on up at the resort, Raven's hours wavered. Some days she was there before sunup and there past midnight, while others she had normal nine-to-five hours.

After her aunt and uncle's last visit, she'd agreed to call or text him when she was going to be late.

The more he thought about what she meant to him, the more he realized that he didn't want it to end. The hard part was convincing Raven that he was worth taking a chance on.

CHAPTER TWENTY-EIGHT

FIRE HAS NO BROTHER ~ NIGERIAN PROVERB

If Raven had to admit anything about her and Cade's relationship, it would be that it felt good to have someone to come home to each night. Something and someone to look forward to seeing. To spending time with.

How long had it been that she'd had that in her life? Too long. Even when she'd lived with her grandmother, she'd come home to an empty house most evenings after school. Her grandmother had been very involved in her church and had been out most nights.

Walking into Cade's home each evening filled her with thoughts of happy-ever-after. She could own up to the fact that, at one point not too long ago, those same thoughts would have scared her.

But that was before Cade had confessed his love for her and she had done so in return.

Somehow, putting her emotions on the line had opened her up to the possibility of more. She'd enjoyed taking care of him during his training. It was obvious how much the task took out of him.

The last couple months when he'd trained, she had

slept in her room at the resort, even though she'd started staying at his place each night.

It was strange—she could only gauge time passing based on how many times he'd gone through the drills.

The first time she hadn't been at his place because she'd had to work extra hours. The second time, she'd needed to change rooms.

Now that most of the top rooms in the west building were done, she was debating changing rooms again or just asking Cade if she could move in full time with him. She doubted that he'd mind, since on the nights she hinted at staying at the resort he would talk her into driving to his place instead.

Now that training was over, he'd suggested they take a drive to the beach that weekend instead of the hike they had planned. She knew his ankle was still giving him problems and had tried to convince him to go in and see a doctor about it. Each time she brought it up, he shrugged the suggestion off and reminded her that he'd been pre-med and knew what a sprained ankle looked like.

Part of her was thankful that he had the training he did. He was the first person she'd called when one of the kitchen staff had sliced off the tip of her finger. Cade had already been on his way up there and had made it there faster than the ambulance could have gotten there. He'd been so much help because the girl, Rebecca, a teenager whom Fiona had hired in the kitchens in the evenings, had gone into shock.

After seeing two dead bodies in the past couple months, she'd been able to keep her cool during that ordeal.

She couldn't believe that in less than two weeks the resort would host its first event, even if it was unofficial. Hosting Cade's mother and uncle's wedding was going to be the perfect start, not only for her but for everyone who worked at the resort.

Raven understood that Fiona had spent a lot of her time after work planning and organizing to make her second wedding perfect.

She'd even sat in on a few of Fiona's meetings to make sure that her staff were in line. Okay, so she was curious herself about the event and what Fiona was planning for her big day.

The official ceremony would be held in the courtyard with the mountains as a natural backdrop. By then, the fall colors would have flooded the trees, turning the green hills into an explosion of color. Those shades would also be brought into the dining hall with flowers and decorations, transforming it into a glorious new world. She couldn't wait to see how it all looked.

She'd had David and his team start work on the new ballroom she'd devised. In the base of the west building there had been a number of large storage rooms on the main floor. She'd gotten the idea to turn them into one large ballroom after having a discussion with Darby about hosting prom at the resort. They had decided that the dining hall would be cool, but what they really needed was a ballroom so that guests could still enjoy dinner without having to deal with a bunch of teenagers.

The ballroom would be great for indoor weddings or parties, so she'd had David add the demolition of the storage areas to his first phase.

Less than an hour before she planned on clocking out and heading home—and doing a little mental dance at the thought that home equaled Cade and Blue—Cemal knocked on her office door.

"Come in." She waved the woman in.

"I hate to bother you so close to quitting time," Cemal said, glancing down at her watch.

"It's okay." She closed her screen down. "What can I help you with?"

"It's about a new rumor." Cemal sat down when Raven motioned to the chair.

Raven sighed. "What is it this time?"

She was thankful that she'd made a friend in Cemal at the start. The girl kept her ears open and often came back to Raven with any stories she'd heard.

"This one is a little different." Cemal leaned forward. "This one is about you directly. I overheard a few of the waitstaff talking about you as if they'd known you in school. Before you left. Before the fire."

"We have a few on staff who I went to school with. Let them talk." She relaxed slightly. "It is a small town, and the potential employee pool is pretty shallow." She smiled and turned back to her computer.

"Yes, well, these rumors involve you sleeping with Mr. Ramsey and..."—Cemal took a deep breath— "your uncle."

"What?" Raven laughed. "Seriously?"

Cemal nodded as she wrung her hands together.

"Who..." Raven started then held up her hands. "Never mind. We agreed that you'd relay the rumors to me, not snitch on who you'd heard them from."

She knew the girl didn't feel comfortable tattling on her fellow co-workers.

Raven leaned back in her office chair and had a thought. Pulling out her cell phone, she sent a text to Cade, asking him to meet her there for dinner.

The dining hall was officially open to the public. Most times it was filled with locals and employees. Still, she was happily surprised at how many people showed up each day for meals. She credited Tim and the new kitchen staff for most of the excitement. But she knew that a lot of locals were dying to see what she'd done with the place or just needed a different choice other than the diner. Something a little fancier. More upscale.

Previously, if they'd wanted to experience that, they would have had to drive all the way into Redding.

Besides, it was where two people in town had been murdered. Some people in town found that totally fascinating.

Cade replied to her text almost immediately, saying that he'd see her there at six. That gave her two more hours to come up with an official plan.

When she couldn't think of a way to stop the gossip about her, she figured a way to add fuel to the fire instead. Maybe stir things up with some obvious lies?

She even made lists of some of the best ones. Still, she didn't know how any of them could stop the current rumors flying around the resort. Giving up, she tossed the list into the trash and started pacing her office.

"Problems?" Fiona asked, knocking on her door.

"How do you stop a rumor?" she asked, falling into her chair.

Fiona frowned. "Rumors usually die by themselves once the truth is revealed."

"What if there isn't any way to reveal the truth?" she asked, feeling slightly defeated. "When there's a lack of proof or those involved are dead?"

"This is in regard to the new rumor about you?" Fiona asked.

"I know it shouldn't bother me at this point, but it just..." She shook her head.

"Irks you?" Fiona finished for her.

"Yes," she said with a slight chuckle at Fiona's choice of words. "In high school, it used to drive me crazy. Then, after the fire..." She shrugged. "Years of counseling and my grandmother taught me to put aside those things that I couldn't control."

"So why is this rumor any different?" Fiona asked.

Raven thought about it before answering. "Because, at some point, it needs to stop. I can't let my aunt and uncle win."

"You think this new rumor was started by them?" Fiona asked.

"Obviously." Raven leaned back in her chair.

"What would your uncle have to gain from spreading such disgusting lies? And including himself in them?" Fiona asked.

In the past hour and half, she had thought of a million ways to stop the rumors, but not once had she wondered why they'd been started in the first place.

"I can see by your silence that you haven't thought that one through yet," Fiona said with a slight nod. "Okay, so let's start figuring out why he'd start the rumor."

By the time Cade walked in, she and Fiona had a list of possibilities, revenge being at the very top.

"This is a surprise." Cade walked over and kissed the top of his mother's head. "I would have thought that you'd already be home."

"Sean and I have decided to join the two of you for dinner," his mother said cheerfully.

"Another wonderful surprise." Cade walked over to place a kiss on Raven's lips. "Ready for some food? I'm starving."

"Yes." She took one more look at the list she and Fiona

had made and then shut down her computer. She stood and wrapped her arms around Cade. "How is your ankle?"

"What's wrong with your ankle?" his mother broke in.

"Nothing now," Cade responded. "I sprained it a few days back." He shrugged and stood back as both women stepped out of the office.

Raven took the arm Cade offered, and his mother took his other arm, and they made their way to the dining hall. Sean was just walking in the front doors when they stepped into the lobby area.

"I like what you've done to the place," Sean said after he placed a kiss on Fiona's cheek.

Raven noticed that Cade only stiffened and then winced slightly upon seeing his mother's and uncle's physical affection.

"This is fun," Sean said as they stood just outside the dining hall. "We should do this more often."

"Yes," Cade said at the same time as Raven.

The moment the four of them stepped into the new and improved dining hall, Raven pulled Cade to a stop just so she could admire the view.

Here it was, Thursday night, and the dining hall was half full. The bar area was standing room only.

"Can you imagine what it's going to be like after we open the doors for real?" Raven said, trying not to sound so excited.

The truth was, if things continued to go this well, she'd be able to complete the next list of repairs and upgrades around the place, including adding a gift shop, a larger swimming pool with slides for summer guests, and even one more ski lift or two.

"I can see that you're plotting world domination again,"

Cade whispered in her ear. "Or at least what other updates you can do around the place once you have the cash."

She smiled and turned into him. It was strange and nice to know that he could pick up on her moods so well. She wrapped her arms around his shoulders and gave him a quick kiss.

"I'll stop plotting, as you put it." She took his hand as they were seated at a table near the wall of glass overlooking the mountains.

She knew that she got the executive treatment, since she was the boss, but still, from any seat in the dining area the view was pretty much the same—a stunning wall of absolute mountainside beauty, no matter the season or the weather.

Currently, the sun was setting, lighting up the hillside with bright shades of orange and red, making it appear as if the entire hillside was on fire. It would have taken Raven's breath away if she were alone and not having her first official dinner with her boyfriend's parents.

"How are the wedding plans coming along?" she asked Fiona after they'd ordered their food and their drinks had been delivered.

While Cade and Sean broke into a conversation about work, Fiona filled her in. She couldn't remember being this comfortable around his family before. Actually, if memory served her right, when she and Reggie had been dating, she'd had dinner at Fiona's house, the one that had burned down. She'd been so silly back then. So naive. So... utterly young. So nervous.

When Cade's hand found hers under the table, she smiled and felt a wave of warmth flood her. It had been so different with Reggie.

As she laughed and enjoyed dinner, her thoughts kept

returning to the rumors spreading around. Revenge couldn't be the only reason her uncle had it out for her.

Sure, she'd taken away everything he had. His home, his job, his life, and his reputation, but he'd gotten away with millions. How much money did one man really need? Where had it all gone?

It wasn't as if they'd been hobnobbing around town. Actually, the word was that they were staying at a friend's place in Redding now. Completely broke.

Liza was sticking it out in the room upstairs. She'd even gotten a part-time job at one of the boutiques in town to help pay for the room.

Liam Montford had shown up on Raven's radar a month after she'd fired her uncle. The man had actually put the resort down on his resume as a reference at a casino in Vegas that he was trying to get the manager's position at.

Morgan Roche was lying low. The woman had pretty much disappeared shortly after she'd been brought in for questioning about Rachelle's murder.

"You're quiet," Cade said with a squeeze of her hand.

"Just thinking about Morgan Roche. I haven't seen her around town for a while," she answered.

"She's in Paris," Sean broke in.

"You let her leave town?" Cade almost barked the question out.

"She was cleared of all three murders," Sean replied.

"What about the case against her about the money?" Raven asked.

"She's got a very good lawyer." Sean sighed. "He claims that since she has dual citizenship, she is required to go back to France every six months. They worked something out with the judge."

"Didn't she just return from Paris?" Fiona asked.

Sean nodded. "Yeah, like I said, she had a really good lawyer. Apparently, her family has a lot of money."

"Enough money that my three million looks like change?" Raven asked.

"Her father is not only an ambassador, but one of the wealthiest men in the country due to his business dealings," Sean answered.

"Then why the hell—" Cade stopped when his mother gave him a look. "Excuse me. Why the heck does she live in Cannon Falls and own a business and work as a CPA?"

"Daddy issues," Sean suggested dryly with a shrug.

"I hear my aunt and uncle are in Redding again?" Raven asked.

"Yeah." Sean nodded. "I'm having the local PD keep an eye on them. I'd be happy if they never returned to Cannon Falls."

"You and a lot of people," Fiona said softly. "Sorry." She winced and looked at her.

"Don't be. I'm one of those people," she admitted.

"There are a lot of new rumors going around town," Sean said, causing Raven's entire body to stiffen.

This time it was Fiona who reached across the table to take her hand. "They're just rumors," she said clearly to Sean.

"Right." Sean nodded. "I never give any clout to anything I hear in the diner." He smiled across the table at her.

"We made a list of reasons why Colin would start spreading this new one," Raven admitted.

"You think it was your uncle who started it?" Sean asked.

"Who else?" Raven asked.

There was a moment of silence before Sean answered.

"The murderer," he finally said.

A silence fell over the table, and Raven felt a shiver race up her spine.

"I'm going to find whoever is stalking this town," Sean promised. "Whoever has everyone looking over their shoulders in fear."

Just hearing the words made Raven's heart leap. She wasn't alone in her fears. As much as she wanted to succumb to them, she had to endure, to rise above and show the world that she was stronger than them.

"Rumors don't matter," she told the table and herself. "But if someone is starting them, couldn't we use that to lead us back to the beginning?"

Sean's eyebrows shot up. "Hunt a killer by finding the source of the rumors?"

She nodded slowly. "If you believe the person starting them is the killer."

Sean surprised her by smiling. "Damn. Why the hell..." When Fiona gave him a look, he cleared his throat, much like Cade had done moments ago. "Why the heck didn't I think of that?"

"I blame all the detective shows I watched as a child."

After this, they ordered dessert and the conversation turned away from the murders and back towards the wedding.

As they were walking out and passing the bar area, Raven stopped for a moment to appreciate just how packed the place was.

"This has turned into quite the hot spot," Fiona said.

"Yes, it has," Raven agreed with a smile as Cade's arms wrapped around her.

"So, have you two made it official? Are you living together?" Sean asked.

"Sean." Fiona slapped him on the shoulder.

"What?" Sean acted hurt. "Everyone in town wants to know. I mean, if you're the kind of person who listens to rumors..."

Raven smiled as Cade laughed.

"No, we haven't made it official. Actually, I was going to ask Raven this weekend, on our trip to the beach"—he turned towards her and winked— "if she'd move in with me full time."

"Of course, I will." She hugged him and laughed when he spun her around in the air.

It was time. There was no more holding back the fire. The spark had started and now the fire was raging on. But as with before, this time there were no carefully laid plans. With each kill, they grew more relaxed, stronger, more desperate for the thrill.

CHAPTER TWENTY-NINE

Cade counted the hours until he could clock off work on Friday. He hadn't looked forward to a weekend this much in a long time.

Normally, Raven worked on Saturdays, but she'd planned to take the entire weekend off just so she could be with him.

He didn't want to let her in on the secret, but he'd booked a room at a little B and B in Fairhaven starting tonight. He'd planned on springing the surprise on her when he stopped by the resort and picked her up. Since she still had clothes at the resort, he figured it wouldn't take her long to get some clothes together for the two-night stay.

The B and B sat directly on the beach and allowed dogs, so they didn't have to leave Blue behind.

He knew that Raven had been working hard since returning to Cannon Falls, and this would be her first full weekend off since she'd come home.

He hadn't had a weekend off in so long that he couldn't remember when it had been. And he'd never taken a weekend with the woman he loved.

"Hey, boss." Andre walked into his small office. He had less than an hour to go before he could clock out.

"Hey." He motioned to the chair across from him. Maybe Andre could help fill the time. "What's up?"

"I heard you were planning on asking Raven the big question this weekend?" Andre said with a smile as he wiggled his eyebrows.

"What?" Cade shook his head.

"Marriage." Andre laughed. "I heard you got her a ring and all."

Cade frowned as his heart leapt at the thought. "Who told you that?"

Andre shrugged. "I heard it around."

Cade leaned forward and lowered his voice. "Who told you that?"

He didn't know why it mattered. After all, it wasn't the type of rumor that the murderer would spread around. Was it?

Not that he hadn't thought about it. But after only dating four months now, he knew it was far too early. Besides, she was so preoccupied with the resort, he didn't want to detour her from her goals. Not yet at any rate.

What if they'd been right all along? Whoever had murdered Joseph, Rachelle, and Kim had done so to get to Raven. What if the person was obsessed with her? Wouldn't they know everything about her? Were they spreading the rumors to get inside her head?

Why this new one? Sure, she seemed excited to move in with him, but marriage? If the rumor caught her off guard, what would she do? Freak? Pull away from him? Dump him? Maybe the reaction would play right into the murderer's hand.

"I overheard someone at the bar last night." Andre answered with a shrug. "Does it matter?"

"It might." He felt his entire body tense.

"Um, I'm not sure. I guess it was one of the bartenders. I'd had a few drinks and well." He shrugged. "Sorry, most of the night is a blur."

Without waiting for more information, Cade stood up and stormed towards the door.

"I'm clocking out early," he said, turning to Andre. "Lock up, will you?"

He didn't even stop by the house to pick Blue up as he'd planned. Instead, he headed out to the resort as he called Raven's cell phone.

When she didn't answer, he knew without a doubt that something was wrong. He could almost feel it in his bones. Like he had when Reggie...

He stopped that thought from metastasizing and pushed the gas pedal down farther.

When he rushed through the front doors of the resort, he noticed his uncle in the lobby area, talking to two of his men, and frowned.

"Where's Raven?" he barked out.

Sean turned and frowned at him. "How did you..."

"I've been trying to call her. She's not answering." He held up his phone, not wanting to explain about the feeling and Andre's conversation.

"Your mother said she stepped outside for a walk during lunch and hasn't returned. No one noticed until about half an hour ago. We were just going to head out and start looking for her ourselves."

Cade's heart sank. "She likes to walk towards the lifts for lunch," he said, remembering a conversation they'd had a few weeks back.

"Right. Want to take that route?" Sean asked, and Cade took off at a sprint. "Call if you find out anything," his uncle called after him.

He was totally breathless when he reached the park bench that she'd mentioned. He called out her name and tried her cell phone again.

"Damn it," he said loudly enough that the sound echoed.

His eyes scanned every blade of grass, looking for any sign that she'd come this way hours earlier.

When his phone rang, he jumped at the loud sound and fumbled to answer the call from his uncle.

"She never picked up her lunch," Sean said quickly.

"What?" he asked.

"We checked in the kitchen. She called down an order for lunch, but never picked it up. Which means..."

Cade turned to look at the massive buildings in the distance. "She's still inside." He started running back. His ankle throbbed and burned as he rushed up the back stairs.

He didn't even know where to begin looking. Where could she be? Who had her?

The bar.

Andre's words echoed in his head. He'd heard the gossip at the bar.

Taking the stairs from the back of the building two at a time, he rushed to the front area and stopped when he noticed a handful of people sitting around the bar top enjoying lunch or drinks.

It was Friday afternoon, and he knew that soon the place would be packed.

Had Raven come this way? He asked a few people he knew, who all shook their heads in response.

Then his eyes caught his own in the new mirror that

hung behind the bar, and he remembered the extra space that had been changed back there. Only employees would know about the space.

He pushed past the crowd to check the space, only to come up short when he bumped solidly into Heather. She was straightening her bartender's apron and hair and looked pleased to see him.

"Cade Stone. To what do I owe this pleasure?" she purred.

"Have you seen Raven?" he asked, his eyes scanning the small dark space.

"Why do you want her when I'm right here?" Heather wrapped her arms around his shoulders.

He moved to push her aside, but then stilled when a memory of how Heather looked back in high school flashed in his mind. It was as if he was seeing her for the first time. His hands froze on her wrists as he looked at her. Really looked at her.

She was vaguely the same build as Raven. A little shorter and a few pounds lighter. But back when they'd been seventeen... They'd been almost the same. At one point, she'd started dying her hair different colors. He couldn't remember it ever being red, but then again, he'd been away at college. Anything was possible. Right?

He remembered the rumor Raven had told him about Reggie and Heather hooking up just before the fire. Another rumor that had made the rounds and broken Raven's heart.

"Did you used to have red hair in school?" he asked as he felt his heart start to race.

The moment he spoke, the version of Heather that had been standing in front of him—the crisp bartender's outfit, the pleasant smile, the feminine sexuality—all of it changed.

Even the way she held herself... shifted. She someone became more masculine. Stronger.

"Very good." Even her voice had changed, to a lower pitch, almost a baritone. "I believe you're the first that has followed my trail of clues." She laughed a sickening sound so low he shivered.

"Why?" He started to put his hands in his jacket pocket for his phone but stopped when Heather pulled a gun from the black bartender's apron that she wore and pointed it at his chest.

"Look who wants to play?" She motioned towards the narrow set of stairs that sat directly behind a stack of boxes. "Come join the fun below."

"Tell me Raven's alive," he warned without moving.

Her eyebrows rose slightly. "Why don't you come see for yourself." She chuckled and waved the gun.

"If you shoot me, everyone will hear it," he said, still not moving.

"We'll simply tell them you attacked us." She turned her head slightly, and he noticed a dark bruise on her cheek. He hoped that Raven was the one who had given the mark to her.

Then her words hit him.

"We?" he asked, feeling his stomach roll. If it was just Heather, there might be a chance he could overpower her. But if there were two...

"She likes to go into hiding." Heather's face twisted slightly. "So, I take over and do what needs to be done."

What was she talking about? She? Heather? Then he stilled and realized he was no longer talking to Heather. Whoever it was standing in front of him wasn't the sexy brunette that always flirted with him. Instead, it was the murderer pointing the gun at his chest. The gun waved towards the stairs. "Down the stairs or you won't see the bitch again."

"I'm not going anywhere with you," he reiterated, still trying to understand it all.

"Fine by us." Heather shrugged. "But if you want to see that bitch alive"—she glanced down at her watch and smiled — "you have about five minutes left before she suffocates."

Cade jerked towards her, but she held up the gun and then motioned with it towards the stairs.

"Tut, tut, do you honestly think you could search this entire place in that short of time?"

He turned and walked fast, taking the stairs quickly, ignoring the pain in his ankle as he went.

"Where?" he barked out. When she motioned with the gun towards a door, he pushed through it quickly. He couldn't remember being in this part of the resort before. It looked old, untouched by all the changes and upgrades. Which meant chances were good that no one had been down here in a while.

There were shelves and shelves of bottled wine and unopened bottles of hard liquor and soda machine syrups. The entire room was no bigger than his closet.

"Where is she?" he growled out.

Heather smiled. "Aren't you going to ask us why?"

"Why?" He continued to scan the room in search of Raven.

"Why we killed old Joe, snooping Rachelle, and gossip Kim." She laughed, the deep sound reverberating in the small space. "Not to mention the worst party throwers on the face of the planet, controlling Steve and his dumb wife, stupid, gullible Amy." He lost what she was saying. Who were Steve and Amy? Then he stilled when he heard the next name. "As well as the boy who wouldn't give us the time of day, until I roofied him at a party." Another laugh. "Cheating Reggie." Her smile grew. "That was a fun night. Until he threatened to tell on us." Cade's eyes grew at the knowledge that his brother had basically been raped by this girl more than ten years ago. "That's right. Now you're catching up." Heather's eyes practically glowed with mischief, and he could see more of the madness within. Could tell for sure that this was no longer the woman he'd seen around town. The girl he remembered from school. This was something darker. Something full of evil. Full of hate.

"You. You're the one who set the fire?" he asked.

"Ding, ding, ding." She laughed as the gun wavered. "I was stuck. The bitch somehow locked me away until she needed me again, when the original bitch returned and brought old Joe back into town. Delivered him right into our hands."

For the first time since running into her, he watched as worry flashed in her eyes. As if Heather, the real Heather, was trying to break free.

"She thought she'd gotten rid of our past. That he'd walked away. Then he came back and threatened to expose our little high school enterprise."

"Enterprise?" he asked.

She laughed. "Since our parents wouldn't pay for all the things we liked, we had to make money somehow. So, I was born." He remembered the grainy image of the redhead and Colin causing him to recoil at the memory. "I kept her safe and did what had to be done. I always have and always will."

"You... and Colin, as well as Joseph?" he asked.

"Just a few of our clients that kept her in the style she

liked. In what she deserved." She shrugged. Cade thought about the other people she'd murdered.

"Why the fire?" he asked.

"You were long gone by then, but they had the audacity to throw us the worst party ever. People were talking about it, making fun of her. Gossiping." Her voice rose to an almost scream and he got a glimpse into her ugliness.

"So, you set the fire?" He shook his head. "That doesn't add up."

"She hated it. Hated them all. Everyone needed to burn." A slow smile twisted her lips. "Here's a little tidbit that no one else knows. Both of her parents were already dead when the house burned up." She laughed again. "I knew all about Raven and Reggie's plans to meet at midnight for her birthday. Of course, her parents, being the perfect people they were, would have the perfect party once again for Raven. So, we followed the two lovers out there, held in our rage and laughs as they quarreled over poor ol' Reggie's infidelities. It was too perfect when Raven threw the candle down. We finally had a way out of this hellhole. A way to get rid of everyone we hated. Everyone who had betrayed us. Controlled us. Used us."

He wanted to glance at his watch. Surely more than five minutes had passed by now. Was Raven still alive? Had Heather just been lying about the time?

"We never expected the bitch to live," Heather said with a sigh. "But even that worked out to my benefit. There was someone to blame. Misdirection. Until she returned."

"Where is Raven?" he asked forcefully.

"Don't you want to hear about ol' Joe?" She tilted her head slightly. "He was easy. We'd planned it out for a while. A little flirting with the repairmen working on the elevators.

He showed me how to turn the power to the elevator on and wait for ol' Joe to step in, then off they went, halfway up. We hadn't expected it to be so perfect." She waved the gun. "A knock over the head was easy enough with this when he was trying to climb out of the stuck thing. Then, after turning the power back on and disabling the security controls on the outdated elevator"—she laughed and swiped her finger across her throat— "the doors did the rest. All I had to do was hit the button." She shrugged and laughed again. "It was perfect seeing his blood all over Raven. We enjoyed watching her slip and slide and fall into it. Very funny."

He felt his anger grow and understood that there wasn't anything he could do to stop her from telling him everything.

"Do you want to hear all about Rachelle?" she asked cheerfully. "You see, Rachelle and our mother had been besties." She rolled her eyes as she crossed her arm over her chest, propping up her gun arm as if she were tired of holding the thing pointed at his chest. "She suspected about us. Somehow, she knew. Then she found the Polaroids we'd kept and well... intuitively knew it was us. She confronted us, accused us of killing old Joe and of needing counseling because of the photos." Heather's laugh turned higher. "She thought we'd been raped by ol'' Joe. Then she started to demand that we go get help." She laughed, the gun shaking with her movement. "Like there is any help for us. So..." She smiled. "We took some of the pesticides they keep stored in the supply room across the hallway and asked her to meet us for some tea to discuss it. After I slipped a little into her cup, that is. Simple as that."

He bit back the desire to call her sick. "Where is Raven?" he asked in a calm voice instead.

Heather glanced down at her watch and smiled. "We

still have two minutes on our break." She shifted her eyes back to him. "Now, where were we? Oh right, Kimmy, Kim, Kimber." She chuckled. "That bitch didn't know how to keep her mouth shut. We're the only one in town who can spread lies." She drew out the S sound. "And she had no right gossiping about us in the grocery store to everyone."

"So, you killed her?" he asked.

"Oh, it was easy. The girl was high as a kite that night, thanks to a few pills we'd sold her earlier in the week. Besides, she was a small little thing. Not very heavy." She shrugged. "Our only regret was that we couldn't stage her death in this grand ol' place."

"Where is Raven?" He took a step towards Heather.

She sighed, one of those I'm-so-annoyed-and-bored kind of sounds as she motioned with the gun.

"What are you going to do? Shoot me?" He shook his head.

"Did you know that this room is not only airtight but soundproof?" She smiled and lifted the gun again, this time pointing it at his head.

He felt the air leave his lungs as his heart raced.

It was true, Cade thought. Moments before death, your life really did flash before your eyes.

Raven felt groggy and cold. So cold. Her teeth chattered and her body shook uncontrollably.

She moved to sit up and bumped her head, which sent ice particles raining down on her head.

"What..." She coughed when frigid air filled her lungs. Reaching out, she scraped the ice over her head, her nails, sending more ice particles falling over her already frozen body. Her knuckles split as she punched at the icy roof, and the knees on her slacks split open when she used them to kick against her prison.

Her throat burned as she screamed to be released.

Once the sheer panic of being locked in an icy coffin dissipated slightly, her brain kicked into gear.

It was obvious she was in an old freezer. The kind she used to get ice cream out of in the kitchens at the resort when she was younger. They used to have those small orange sherbet cups that she loved. The kind that had their own wooden spoons.

Then she realized she was most likely still at the resort and wondered vaguely if this was the very same freezer.

If it were... she held her breath as she searched for the release handle her mother had forced her father to install in the freezer for fear that their eight-year-old daughter would accidently get locked inside, just like the little boy they'd seen on a special news report who had suffocated inside his parents' freezer in their garage.

There was several years of ice buildup to claw through, and it seemed to take hours, but when she felt the cold metal of the bright red handle her father had installed all those years ago, warmth seeped into her body.

Older model freezer lids wouldn't lock, but this kind had a small button you could push on the outside to lock it. The handle overrode the lock and latch, allowing the lid to pop open freely.

Even though her parents had died more than ten years ago, they were still here. Protecting her. Saving her life.

The moment the lid popped open, she took a deep gulp of warm air, relishing the heat that seeped into her body. Still, her entire body shook as she used her frozen limbs to climb out of the box.

As she scanned her surroundings, she realized instantly where she was. The one room she hadn't had a chance to really survey yet. It was a small storage area that was tucked behind the wine and liquor supply room.

The moment she could feel her limbs again, she crawled towards the doorway. Seeing a light under it, she leaned against it and took several deep breaths as she tried to remember how she'd gotten there.

When the answer rushed in and hit her over the head, she gasped. Heather.

At the moment she thought the name, she heard the woman speaking. Fear leapt into her and she frantically looked around for someplace to hide or for a weapon.

Then she remembered the gun Heather had used to get her to follow her down into the storage area.

At first, she'd been convinced to head down there when Heather had called her to the bar area, claiming that someone had broken in and stolen some wine and had broken a bunch of other bottles.

When they'd arrived downstairs, Heather had pulled out the gun.

She couldn't remember getting into the freezer, but now that her body was warming up, she could feel a dull ache in the back of her head. Heather had most likely hit her and then put her into the freezer herself.

Leaning her head against the door, she listened again. It was definitely Heather talking.

When she heard Cade's voice, she almost cried out. But then his words sunk in.

"What are you going to do? Shoot me?" he asked.

Images of Heather holding Cade at gunpoint flashed in her eyes. She needed to do something. And quick.

Then she felt her cell phone vibrate in her pocket. It

was as if the device had just connected with the internet now that it was out of the metal box.

Pulling it out with shaky fingers, she sent a text to Sean with frozen fingers, quickly telling him where they were.

Still, she doubted the man would get there in time. From the sound of things in the next room, she had seconds. Not minutes.

She would not let this woman take the man she loved from her. Not again.

Seeing her grandmother's heavy sterling silver tea set sitting on a shelf over the freezer, the tray her mother used to make her shine every holiday season, she got a very stupid idea.

She opened the door, and her eyes raced around the room and connected with Heather. With all her remaining energy, she threw the silver tea kettle at Heather's head and jumped in front of Cade's body and the end of the gun.

The shot rang out, almost deafening in such a small space. She felt the sting of it, the heat of it. Then Cade's arms were around her, holding her, guiding her as the room filled with shouting voices instead of more shots.

"Shit," she gasped. "That stings." Then everything went dark.

When she opened her eyes next, Cade was there, looking down at her.

"You little fool," he said, but since there was a smile on his face, she figured her stupid plan had worked.

"My grandmother's silver platter?" she asked. "Did it survive?"

He chuckled. "I'm afraid it gave it's life for yours." He motioned to the floor. Sure enough, there was a very large dent in the tarnished old thing. "You've been watching too much *Dirty Harry*."

"Wrong movie," she said, sitting up slightly and wincing when her ribs ached.

Since her blouse was untucked, she assumed that Cade had looked at where she'd been shot. Well, where the bullet had dented in the heavy tray at least.

Since she didn't see any blood, she figured she'd walk away with some bruising, maybe a broken rib, since she was having a difficult time breathing. Her body was still too cold to tell much, but she figured she'd feel everything later. For now, she was just going to enjoy being alive.

"No." Cade smiled and helped her sit up. "I'm pretty sure that's *Dirty Harry*."

She held in a laugh and hugged her sides. "The Man with No Name," she corrected. "*A Fist Full of Dollars*." She shook her head. "I'm not sure I can move in with you now," she said through heavy panting breaths.

His eyes sobered and he swallowed. "I know this is probably the worst timing ever and the last thing I want to do is scare you..."

"Nothing will scare me after this." She motioned to where his uncle was hauling Heather away.

"I'm counting on that." He brushed his lips against hers and wrapped his arms around her gently, as if he was just trying to hold her upright and not hurt her. "Marry me."

She smiled. "Why would I want to marry a man who doesn't know his Clint Eastwood movies?"

He chuckled. "You can teach me," he offered. "I'm a quick learner."

She felt her body heat even further or maybe it was the fact that someone had thrown a blanket over her shoulders? Or that Cade's body was pressed tightly against her own? Whatever the reason, she knew the answer instantly when she looked into his eyes.

"Of course I'll marry you," she said, wrapping her still-frozen arms around his neck and no longer feeling the pain. Any pain. All she could feel now was him. The love she felt for him. The burn of a new fire in her life. One that she welcomed with open arms.

EPILOGUE

WHAT YOU LOSE IN THE FIRE, YOU WILL FIND
AMONGST THE ASHES. YOU WILL FIND AMONGST
THE ASHES. ~ FRENCH PROVERB

"Of course, there would be snow on my wedding day." Fiona stood looking out the window at the beautiful countryside. The ground was a crisp white, covered in a fresh layer of snow.

"Don't worry." Raven moved to stand next to her. "I had the employees move all of the chairs and the archway into the ballroom."

"We have a ballroom?" Fiona glanced over at her.

Raven laughed. "It was a secret." She shrugged. "It's not officially open yet, but the crew finished it up last night. The paint might still be a little wet, so don't lean against any walls."

Fiona smiled. "Where have you been hiding an entire ballroom?"

Raven smiled. "Main floor, west building. It's all set up for your special day. I thought we might need a backup plan for big events. You know, in case the weather didn't hold up. Besides, now we can host prom and other school dances in there."

"You think of everything." Fiona turned and wrapped her arms around her.

It felt wonderful, so much so that tears stung Raven's eyes. She no longer felt the twinge from her broken ribs that had healed up nicely, or so Cade had claimed.

"You know," Fiona said softly, leaning back to look into her eyes, "once you and Cade marry, I'll finally get that daughter I've always wanted."

How long had Raven gone without a parent? How many times had she wished, dreamed, that hers could come back?

Their love had saved her. Their forethought and concern were the only reason she was still alive. Cade too. That and the fact that her grandmother's cherished prized possessions had ended up forgotten in a room, buried over time. Raven felt more loved than she had in years. Her entire family had looked out for her.

Cade was even having the old tea set repaired for her. A specialist in Delaware was banging out the large dent where the bullet had stopped and making the piece look new. He claimed it would be the perfect wedding present. She told him if he wanted it to be perfect, he should have left the large dent in it.

"Maybe for our wedding, it will be warm. I'm thinking of a small ceremony at the top of the hillside."

"Oh, that would be wonderful," Fiona said with a smile. "I'm just sorry your parents won't be here for it."

"They will be." She smiled. "Along with the ones who are still here that matter."

"Your uncle and aunt are officially divorced," Fiona asked.

"Liza mentioned it." Raven nodded. "Colin will be spending some time behind bars now that his gambling debts have become clear since we found proof just where the money went. Not to mention the life insurance he'd put on me. He'd hoped the killer would get me next, and they could cash out."

"Who does that? Who gambles away three million dollars?" Fiona shook her head. "Then lies about it?"

"The same type of person who murders three people," Raven said.

"Heather's a sick individual." Fiona shook her head. "Split personalities are tricky. Sean says it will be hard to convict. She'll most likely spend the rest of her life locked in a psych ward."

"Good. It's where she belongs."

A knock on the door had Fiona jumping. "If that's Sean, tell him he can't see me."

Raven walked over to the door, fully prepared to tell the groom he would have to wait half an hour more. She came up short when she noticed Cade standing on the other side of the door. The man filled out a tux like he belonged in it.

Cade took her hand and pulled her outside into the hallway.

His eyes ran over the soft blue dress she was wearing. "You look sexy as hell. Are you sure we can't skip this shindig?"

She laughed. "It's your mother's and uncle's wedding."

He shrugged and pulled her into his arms. "So?"

She laughed even more. "And you're the best man."

He smiled. "Then give me a kiss to last me until we can go home."

Leaning up on her toes, she wrapped her arms around him and kissed him like he was the man of her dreams. Because he was. That and so much more.

Remember, if you've enjoyed this book, please leave a review where you downloaded it. Thanks

ALSO BY JILL SANDERS

The Pride Series

Finding Pride

Discovering Pride

Returning Pride

Lasting Pride

Serving Pride

Red Hot Christmas

My Sweet Valentine

Return To Me

Rescue Me

A Pride Christmas

The Secret Series

Secret Seduction

Secret Pleasure

Secret Guardian

Secret Passions

Secret Identity

Secret Sauce

The West Series

Loving Lauren

Taming Alex

Holding Haley

Missy's Moment

Breaking Travis

Roping Ryan

Wild Bride

Corey's Catch

Tessa's Turn

Saving Trace

The Grayton Series

Last Resort

Someday Beach

Rip Current

In Too Deep

Swept Away

High Tide

Lucky Series

Unlucky In Love

Sweet Resolve

Best of Luck

A Little Luck

Christmas Wish

Silver Cove Series

Silver Lining

French Kiss

Happy Accident

Hidden Charm

A Silver Cove Christmas

Sweet Surrender

Second Chances

Entangled Series – Paranormal Romance

The Awakening

The Beckoning

The Ascension

The Presence

The Calling

The Chosen

Haven, Montana Series

Closer to You

Never Let Go

Holding On

Coming Home

The Hard Way

Pride Oregon Series

A Dash of Love

My Kind of Love

Season of Love

Tis the Season

Dare to Love

Where I Belong

Because of Love

A Thing Called Love

First Comes Love

Someone to Love

Wildflowers Series

Summer Nights

Summer Heat

Summer Secrets

Summer Fling

Summer's End

Summer's Wish

Distracted Series

Wake Me

Tame Me

Stand Alone Books

Twisted Rock

Hope Harbor

Raven Falls

For a complete list of books:

http://JillSanders.com

ABOUT THE AUTHOR

Jill Sanders is a New York Times, USA Today, and international bestselling author of Sweet Contemporary Romance, Romantic Suspense, Western Romance, and Paranormal Romance novels. With over 70 books in eleven series, translations into several different languages, and audiobooks there's plenty to choose from. Look for Jill's bestselling stories wherever romance books are sold or visit her at jillsanders.com

Jill comes from a large family with six siblings, including an identical twin. She was raised in the Pacific Northwest and later relocated to Colorado for college and a successful IT career before discovering her talent for writing sweet and sexy page-turners. After Colorado, she decided to move south, living in Texas and now making her home along the Emerald Coast of Florida. You will find that the settings of several of her series are inspired by her time spent living in these areas. She has two sons and off-set the testosterone in her house by adopting three furry little ladies that provide her company while she's locked in her writing cave. She enjoys heading to *the beach, hiking, swimming, wine-tasting, and pickleball with her husband, and of course writing. If you have read any of her books, you may also notice that there is a love of food, especially sweets! She has been blamed for a few added pounds by her assistant, editor, and fans... donuts or pie anyone?*

Join Jill's Newsletter and get book and sales updates monthly. https://jillsanders.com/newsletter.html

facebook.com/JillSandersBooks

twitter.com/JillMSanders

amazon.com/Jill-Sanders/e/B009M2NFD6?tag=jillm-com-20

bookbub.com/authors/jill-sanders

instagram.com/jillsandersauthor

www.ingramcontent.com/pod-product-compliance
Lightning Source LLC
Chambersburg PA
CBHW051156190726
48288CB00006B/1683